R0201265287

W9-BGS-098

A Single Spark

Books by Judith Miller

The Carousel Painter
The Chapel Car Bride
The Lady of Tarpon Springs
A Perfect Silhouette
A Single Spark

FREEDOM'S PATH

First Dawn
Morning Sky
Daylight Comes

BELLS OF LOWELL*

Daughter of the Loom
A Fragile Design
These Tangled Threads

LIGHTS OF LOWELL*

A Tapestry of Hope
A Love Woven True
The Pattern of Her Heart

POSTCARDS FROM PULLMAN

In the Company of Secrets
Whispers Along the Rails
An Uncertain Dream

THE BROADMOOR LEGACY*

A Daughter's Inheritance
An Unexpected Love
A Surrendered Heart

BRIDAL VEIL ISLAND*

To Have and To Hold
To Love and Cherish
To Honor and Trust

DAUGHTERS OF AMANA

Somewhere to Belong
More Than Words
A Bond Never Broken

HOME TO AMANA

A Hidden Truth
A Simple Change
A Shining Light

REFINED BY LOVE

The Brickmaker's Bride
The Potter's Lady
The Artisan's Wife

www.judithmccoymiller.com

*with Tracie Peterson

A Single Spark

JUDITH MILLER

BETHANYHOUSE
a division of Baker Publishing Group
Minneapolis, Minnesota

© 2020 by Judith Miller

Published by Bethany House Publishers
11400 Hampshire Avenue South
Bloomington, Minnesota 55438
www.bethanyhouse.com

Bethany House Publishers is a division of
Baker Publishing Group, Grand Rapids, Michigan

Printed in the United States of America

Library of Congress Cataloging-in-Publication Data
Names: Miller, Judith, author.
Title: A single spark / Judith Miller.
Description: Minneapolis, Minnesota : Bethany House Publishers, [2020]
Identifiers: LCCN 2019055370 | ISBN 9780764235290 (trade paperback) | ISBN
    9780764236310 (cloth) | ISBN 9781493425174 (ebook)
Subjects: GSAFD: War stories.
Classification: LCC PS3613.C3858 S57 2020 | DDC 813/.6—dc23
LC record available at https://lccn.loc.gov/2019055370

Scripture quotations are from the King James Version of the Bible.

This is a work of historical fiction; the appearances of certain historical figures are therefore inevitable. All other characters, however, are products of the author's imagination, and any resemblance to actual persons, living or dead, is coincidental.

Cover design by Kirk DouPonce, DogEared Design

Author is represented by Books & Such Literary Agency.

20 21 22 23 24 25 26   7 6 5 4 3 2 1

For Lori Baney Mattingly,
who is always quick to encourage with
her loving heart and joyful spirit.

WAR, AT THE BEST, IS TERRIBLE,
AND THIS WAR OF OURS,
IN ITS MAGNITUDE AND IN ITS DURATION,
IS ONE OF THE MOST TERRIBLE.

—ABRAHAM LINCOLN

ONE

Washington Arsenal, Washington, D.C.
August 1862

Clara McBride carefully counted ten cartridges before dividing them into a double stack of five. Her lips moved as she silently alternated the position of each bullet. *Up, down, up, down, up, down.* Bright sunshine poured through the high, narrow windows and zigzagged across the room, the warmth enveloping her like a thick, cozy quilt. *Up, down, up, down.* Both her lips and fingers slowed, the heat and repetition finally lulling her eyes to half-mast.

"Miss McBride!"

Clara jerked to attention. A cartridge slipped to the floor, and gunpowder spilled at her feet. Looking up, she met the harsh gaze of Mr. Grant, the packing room supervisor. A deep frown creased his jowly face as he signaled to one of the young boys near the door. "You've lost your ability to concentrate since leaving the packing room, Miss McBride."

Clara's cheeks burned as she picked up the cartridge. She didn't look up, but she could feel the other girls gawping. Those who had been subjected to the same embarrassment would feel pity. Others would revel in the rebuke. The combination of reactions was the same in every section of the Washington Arsenal, where one worker's misstep could provide a higher-paying position for another. Her own ascension from the packing room had been due to such circumstances.

She mumbled an apology and continued stacking, counting, and packing while wishing she could return to the cylinder room. This was the second time in the past month she'd been required to assist in the packing room, for once trained, the girls would apply for positions in other sections of the laboratory. Rooms where the work wasn't quite as monotonous, and the supervisor didn't enjoy berating employees.

"Mr. Grant, a word with you, please."

The workers glanced over their shoulders toward Lieutenant Brady, who stood in the doorway. When the lieutenant stepped into the packing room, Clara spied Dottie Wilson leaning against the doorjamb. Except for her darting eyes, the young woman remained as still as a statue—until she spotted Clara. In that moment Dottie's shoulders straightened, and her eyes narrowed in a dark glare.

Clara flinched, her thoughts racing as she attempted to think of any way she might have wronged Dottie. Anything that would have been serious enough to bring the lieutenant into the packing room during the middle of the day. Clara chanced a quick look at Mr. Grant and the lieutenant. Mr. Grant's face was the pinkish-purple shade Clara had observed during a few of the supervisor's angry moments in the past. Whatever had happened, there was little doubt it concerned Mr. Grant, Dottie—and Clara.

"Miss McBride, please vacate your position."

Clara stood and waited until the workers to her right stood and sidestepped their way to the end of the bench. She squeezed around them and moved to Lieutenant Brady's side.

Mr. Grant gestured to Dottie. "Take her seat, Miss Wilson. I do hope you're more wide awake than Miss McBride. She created quite a mess for us this morning."

Dottie smirked at the supervisor's remark, but the lieutenant turned on his heel at the comment. "If that is truly what happened, Mr. Grant, you should be thanking me for taking her out of the packing room. Why did you argue to keep her here?" Without waiting for a response, the lieutenant escorted Clara from the room.

Clara quickened her step to keep pace with the lieutenant's long stride. Before they arrived at the door of the cylinder room, he stopped and turned to her. "We have a new employee, a Miss Hodson." He hesitated. "I don't recall her full name, but you can inquire after I make introductions. I want you to train her. While she has no experience, since her recent move to Washington, she's been eager to secure work here at the Arsenal."

"I enjoy training the new girls, so I'll do my best." Clara's lips curved in a fleeting smile. "May I ask why Dottie—Miss Wilson—was angry with me?"

"She didn't want to replace you in the packing room and said she could train Miss Hodson." The lieutenant hiked a shoulder. "That didn't prove to be true. Her anger is misdirected. I'll speak to her."

Clara shook her head. "No, please don't. I'm sure she'll be fine once she returns to the cylinder room. There are few who enjoy the packing room."

"Or Mr. Grant?" He arched a brow.

A soft chuckle escaped Clara's lips. "That too."

Clara captured a loose strand of chestnut-brown hair and tucked it behind her ear as she followed the lieutenant to the other side of the room. Miss Hodson sat in the lieutenant's chair and jumped to her feet as they approached. When the young woman fluttered her eyelashes at the lieutenant, Clara suppressed a gasp and gave him a sideways glance. Did he think the new employee's behavior charming or unseemly? Or had he even noticed? He'd been at the Arsenal for only a month now and appeared to be more interested in production than charm, although his good looks were often a topic of discussion among the girls who worked in the laboratory. In truth, the young lieutenant frequented Clara's dreams quite often—a fact that both disturbed and delighted her.

"Miss Hodson, I'd like you to meet Miss Clara McBride. She's one of the very best employees in the cylinder room. She is well qualified to train new employees in the packing room, filling room, cap cylinder room, and the cylinder room. If you heed her advice, you'll learn quickly."

"I'll do my very best to please you, Lieutenant." She leaned in as she lifted her head and batted her lashes.

The lieutenant took a backward step. "It's Miss McBride you need to please. If she finds your work suitable, it will satisfy me." He looked at Clara. "You can begin your training, but I'd like to speak to you before you depart this evening."

Clara nodded. No doubt he wanted an explanation about the happenings in the packing room. After his generous comments about her abilities, it would be difficult to tell him she'd nearly fallen asleep at her worktable.

She pushed the thought from her mind and turned to Miss Hodson. "Even though you've received some training from Miss Wilson, let's start at the very beginning." She glanced toward one of the long tables. "Do you prefer I address you as Miss Hodson?"

The young woman shook her head. "No, please call me Beatrice. And you?"

"Clara. Last names seem far too formal when we're sitting next to each other all day making bullets to help win the war." Clara gestured toward the hard wooden benches on one side of the table. She leaned close to Beatrice's ear. "Our hooped skirts and crinolines make it difficult, but we need as many women as possible working on each side of the bench, so push in as far as possible."

Beatrice wrinkled her nose. "It's uncomfortable sitting so close, and there's no way off the bench without making the others get up. When I had to move, I discovered it irritated some of the ladies. You'd think they would be understanding when someone needs the necessary."

"You'll soon discover most of them to be very kind and helpful." Clara smiled and walked to one end of the table.

"This is the beginning of the process. The women at this side of the room roll paper cylinders that will become cartridges once they're filled with gunpowder. There are exacting instructions that must be followed when making the cylinders." Clara pointed to a young lady holding a wooden dowel with a point at one end. "That piece of wood is called a former, and it's the same width as a finished cartridge."

Beatrice frowned. "Is this what I'm going to be doing? Dottie had me trying to fill those things with gunpowder in the filling room, but she said I would likely work in the cap cylinder room."

Clara frowned. "The lieutenant wouldn't assign you to the cap cylinder room."

Beatrice tipped her head to the side. "And why is that?"

"The cap cylinder room requires workers with very small hands."

Beatrice spread her fingers. "Did he tell you my hands are large?" Her brow creased as she extended her arms. "Place your hands beneath mine." When Clara didn't immediately move, Beatrice reached forward and grasped her arm. "Come on—let's see who has the larger hands." Rather than have Beatrice disturb the other women, Clara complied. Beatrice inhaled a long breath. "There, you see. My hands are no larger than yours."

Clara sighed and nodded. Had she known Beatrice was going to be so prickly about hand size, she never would have mentioned the matter. "Perhaps Dottie knew there were several openings in the cap cylinder room and she assumed you'd be assigned there."

"So, the lieutenant didn't say I have big hands?"

Clara took a moment before she responded. How had this conversation taken such a silly turn? "The lieutenant didn't mention your hands at all. I was merely attempting to explain why you wouldn't be assigned to the cap cylinder room. The girls who work there are usually younger than us and have tiny hands. I can take you through and show you what they do later in the day. If I offended you in any way, please know it wasn't my intention."

Beatrice beamed. "Thank you for your honesty—and your apology."

Clara offered a weak smile, thankful the matter had been set aright. "I believe you'll soon discover that I'm honest with others and I hope they'll be the same. When I'm wrong, which is more often than I care to admit, I'm quick to apologize." Clara nodded toward stacks of precut paper on the table. "If you come closer, you can see how the women place one piece of paper against the former and roll it into a cylinder." They watched for a moment before she nudged Beatrice and pointed across the table. "Watch her. Once the paper is wrapped around the former, the pointed end is tied with a string. That's called choking. Now she places a minié ball at the tied end and wraps a second piece of paper around and chokes it with string."

They stood for a moment and watched the woman fly through the process. As soon as she'd tied off the second choking string, she removed the former and placed the cylinder in a box.

"This looks more difficult than filling the cylinders with gunpowder," Beatrice said.

"Once you've worked here a few days, you'll be as quick as these ladies."

"Would you ask the lieutenant if I can work in the filling room with you—at least for now? Since Dottie's gone and he was having her train me to work beside her, there must be a position. We've just moved here, and I don't know a soul. It would mean so much to me if I could work near you."

Clara wasn't one to make special requests, yet she found it impossible to resist Beatrice's pleading look and woeful tone. Some of the women didn't hesitate to ask for special favors—a request to leave early or take an extended noonday break for one reason or another. Such requests were usually denied, though occasionally a supervisor would be generous. Perhaps the lieutenant would agree, since this request wouldn't require any time away from the laboratory.

"Please? Will you at least try?" Beatrice grasped Clara's hand and squeezed.

"I suppose it won't hurt to ask. You stay here."

Beatrice gave Clara's hand another squeeze and nodded toward the lieutenant. "He's quite good-looking, don't you think?"

Clara tugged her hand loose. She didn't want to admit that she thought he was the most handsome man she'd ever seen. If she did, she'd never gain the courage to approach him. Instead, she whispered, "It doesn't matter what he looks like. What matters is your assignment."

The grin vanished from Beatrice's lips. "Yes, of course."

The walk to the filling section had never seemed so far. Lieutenant Brady remained at a desk not far from the tables in the filling section. Clara stepped to the side of his desk and waited.

When he looked up, his lips curved in a smile. "Done training Miss Hodson so soon?"

Clara cleared her throat. "I've described the work in the cylinder section, although she hasn't yet attempted to make a cylinder. I thought perhaps she could work beside me in the filling room rather than in the cylinder section. If you approve, that is. I think she's quite capable of—"

He held up his hand. "I trust your judgment, Miss Mc-Bride. We have openings in all sections of the laboratory, so wherever you think she would prove most useful. She appeared to be having difficulty earlier, but if you think she's capable, I'll leave it to you."

"I believe she's overcome some of her earlier nervousness and will do fine."

"You work alongside her, and if she has difficulty, we'll move her elsewhere." That said, he gave a slight nod and returned to his paper work.

As they were approaching the bench, Clara unbuttoned the cuffs of her dress and rolled up her sleeves to just below the elbow. She touched a finger to Beatrice's cuff. "You'll want to keep your dress as clean as possible—unless you own many more dresses than most of us. Gunpowder is fine as flour and black as coal. It will leave ugly stains. And loose gunpowder is dangerous. You don't want to collect any of it in your sleeves. We receive lots of reminders from the supervisors about the need to be careful."

Beatrice inhaled a deep breath and swiped at one sleeve of her dress and then the other. "I noticed the other ladies, but Dottie didn't tell me I should roll my sleeves. Do you think I'm safe?" Beatrice slapped at her sleeves and shook her arms.

"I think you'll be just fine. All of the necessary materials for this next step will be on the tables. You saw the ladies in the cylinder room place a minié ball in the outer cylinder. We'll now add the gunpowder. You must be careful handling the gunpowder and remain alert." As Clara issued the warning, a remembrance of her earlier boredom in the packing room flashed through her mind. A reminder she needed to heed her own advice.

Beatrice gestured to the empty space on one of the benches. "Do we sit here?"

Clara nodded, and the two of them pushed down their hoops and squeezed onto the narrow bench. "The gunpowder is premeasured, so you'll need one of these funnels." Clara picked up a cylinder, inserted the tip of the metal funnel, and poured gunpowder inside. "Once it's filled, you gently tap the cylinder so the gunpowder settles. Next, you flatten the empty end of the paper and the cylinder is closed in a three-fold process. Watch." Clara flattened the end of the cylinder and nimbly made the proper fold. "Make certain each step is done exactly as I've shown you." Clara picked up a funnel and handed it to Beatrice. "Go ahead. I'll watch to make certain you understood my directions."

"Dottie didn't let me use one of the funnels when I was here earlier. She said she didn't have another one, so I should just cup my hand around the end of the cylinder. That's why I had trouble." Beatrice leaned close. "I don't think Dottie wanted me to succeed. She saw the lieutenant looking at me, and I think she was jealous."

"I don't believe Dottie wants anyone to fail. We need every worker we can get. Winning the war is important to everyone who works here, and our soldiers need these cartridges. As for the lieutenant, I doubt there was any jealousy involved. Dottie already has a beau."

Clara watched as Beatrice filled the paper tube with gunpowder, then folded the end and placed it in a wooden box.

"How did I do?" Beatrice straightened her shoulders and smiled like a child who'd presented a perfect paper to her teacher.

"That was flawless. You'll need another ninety-nine to fill that box. When it's full, push it toward the end of the table. Once the lady at the end completes her box, she'll take the other boxes to the cap cylinder room, where the tubes of percussion caps will be placed in each box before they go to the packing room. When she returns, she'll go to the other end of the bench and we'll all move down. That way we all receive a few minutes to straighten our backs and stretch a bit."

A frown creased Beatrice's face. "My back already hurts from sitting on this bench. We should have chairs, don't you think?"

Before Clara could respond, one of the circulating inspectors stopped behind them. He gestured to the cartridge box. "Less talking and more work, ladies."

Clara waited until he'd moved to the next table. "We're not supposed to talk while we work."

Beatrice glared at the inspector. "I don't think I'm going to take any pleasure in being around him. The lieutenant is more to my liking."

Clara glanced toward the lieutenant, whose desk was situated near the center of the room. She'd thought the very same thing the first time she laid eyes on him. Unfortunately, other than praising her work, he'd come calling only in her dreams. Maybe Beatrice was more to his liking. Silly as it was, the thought bothered her. Never had she cared if a man wanted to court her.

Yet Beatrice's interest in the lieutenant gnawed at Clara for the remainder of the day.

Two

*T*he moment the final bell announced the end of the workday, the women pushed away from the table. After sidestepping along the benches, they retrieved their belongings from the pegs on the far wall and hurried toward the door—all but Clara. After retrieving her bonnet and cape, she waited a moment before looking toward the lieutenant. He appeared engrossed in his paper work. Did he recall he'd said he wanted to speak to her before she departed?

She had taken only a few hesitant steps toward him when he looked up and motioned her forward. He nodded to a chair alongside his desk. "Sit down, Miss McBride."

Once seated, Clara folded her hands around a worn hand-kerchief. When he smiled, her heart thudded against her chest. "You wanted to speak to me?"

"I did. I mean, I do." His voice cracked. "I wanted to tell you that I'm going to be leaving my post here at the Arsenal and—"

"Oh, I'm sorry to hear that, Lieutenant. Are you being assigned to the front?" She tightened the grip on the hand-kerchief. She didn't want to imagine him leading troops into battle.

His smile faded, and he shook his head. "No. Reassignment to the infantry isn't in my future." He straightened his shoulders. "I'm being sent to the Allegheny Arsenal. You know of it?"

She nodded. "It's near Pittsburgh—in Lawrenceville. Isn't that correct?"

"Yes. I'll be leaving in the morning."

An odd sense of loss washed over her. She hadn't even had a chance to get to know the lieutenant. Still, she had hoped to gain an opportunity to do so in the future. Truth be told, her brief interactions with him had been the brightest spots in her days. She fastened her attention on her hands. "I'm sorry to hear that." She looked at the floor.

"I wasn't pleased, either. However, it's only a temporary assignment."

She snapped to attention and met his eyes. "So you'll be returning to Washington?"

"Yes. I'm being sent to the Allegheny Arsenal to observe the techniques used in their laboratory. The colonel received a report that the Allegheny Arsenal has a higher production than any of the other laboratories. He wants me to see if they are using any techniques that will help us increase production here."

"I see. Thank you for telling me." She understood why he was leaving, and she was thankful he'd confided in her, but she couldn't withhold her opinion. "I understand it's a matter of pride to be the most productive arsenal. Even so, I hope the colonel will remain mindful of the hazards within the workrooms."

"Safety is always our first priority, Miss McBride. But if there is an improved method we can use to supply munitions to our men at the front, we want to do so."

"Of course. I completely agree." She hesitated when he didn't immediately respond. Though she didn't want to leave his company, sitting there in silence would prove awkward. "If that's all . . ." She started to push up from the chair.

He grinned. "No, not exactly." He inhaled a deep breath. "We don't know each other well, but before I received this new assignment, I had hoped we would become better acquainted. Unfortunately, time and tide wait for no man, and I now regret my procrastination."

She wanted to tell him that she, too, regretted he hadn't spoken to her sooner. "And why did you delay, if I may ask?"

"I thought it likely you had a beau, so I couldn't gather the courage to inquire." He bowed his head. "I've never been bold when it comes to matters of the heart. However, I did attempt a bit of investigation." He sighed. "It proved unsuccessful."

Her mouth fell open. "What type of investigation?"

"I asked several of the ladies who work in the laboratory, yet I received conflicting answers. A few told me you were spoken for, while others said you didn't have a beau. I wasn't certain who to believe, so rather than asking you, I continued to procrastinate." He glanced down at his hands. "Now I find myself departing for Pittsburgh. It would set my mind at ease to learn the truth."

"I am neither betrothed nor do I have a beau." Heat rose in her cheeks. Had he been thinking of her as much as she'd been dreaming of him? The very thought set her heart racing. "I do hope that answers any questions you may have regarding my personal circumstances."

The corners of his mouth lifted in a smile. "It does—and it pleases me, as well. I'm only sorry I'm leaving." He leaned forward, resting his arms on the desk. "If you have no objection, I would like to write to you while I'm away. Of course, I'm willing to seek your father's permission."

Momentary pain shadowed her eyes. "I would be pleased to correspond with you during your absence, and I'm sure my father would give his permission, if he were alive."

The lieutenant's forehead creased into tiny folds. "The war?"

She nodded. "Yes. Bull Run."

He winced. "I'm sorry. I know how difficult that must be. Do you have other family here in Washington?"

Clara nodded. "Yes. I live with my mother."

He arched a brow. "No brothers or sisters?"

"One brother. Ezekiel. He enlisted along with my father. As far as we know, he's still alive, although we haven't heard from him in months. We hold out hope and keep him in our prayers."

"As you should. I hope you will hear from him soon." Whispers near the doorway captured his attention, and he looked up just as Beatrice Hodson jumped away from the door. "I think your friend is eager to go home. I probably shouldn't keep you much longer." He leaned back. "Shall I ask your mother if she has any objection to our corresponding?"

Clara shook her head. "No need. I'll speak with her. Besides, you'll have little time before you leave." She nodded toward his pen. "You might want to make note of my address—unless you discovered it in your earlier investigation."

He chuckled, shook his head, and picked up the pen. After carefully writing her address on a slip of paper, he folded it and tucked it into his pocket. "While I would enjoy a longer visit with you, I'm sure you need to get home. I don't want your mother to worry over your whereabouts."

He walked alongside her as they crossed the room. When they reached the door, she turned toward him. "I wish you safe travels, Lieutenant, and I look forward to your letters—and your return." Her heart hammered a new beat. Even if she had wanted it to quit, it would have been impossible. And right now she had no desire to end this moment of joy.

Clara had barely descended the steps of the laboratory porch when Beatrice grasped her arm. "I peeked inside and saw you and the lieutenant talking. He appeared very serious. Is he going to move me back to the cylinder room? Was he angry you asked to have me work beside you? Is that why he asked you to remain after work?"

Her worried tone surprised Clara and she stopped short. "No. He made no mention of changing your position. In truth, we didn't speak of you, so there's no cause for concern."

Beatrice released her hold on Clara's arm and offered a smile. "I'm sorry, Clara. I sometimes forget proper manners. I shouldn't have grabbed your arm. I didn't mean any disrespect, but I was frightened the lieutenant was angry with you because you'd made a request on my behalf. I'd never forgive myself if that happened."

"No need for an apology. Your concern was obvious." Clara smiled and started toward the entrance gate. "We best be on our way."

Beatrice hurried alongside Clara. "Please slow down. I have someone I want you to meet." When Clara didn't immediately stop, Beatrice shouted, "It's my brother. I'd like you to meet him."

The words brought Clara to a halt, and she turned on her heel. "Brother? You didn't tell me you had a brother who worked here." This girl was full of surprises.

Tugging the hand of a young dark-haired man, Beatrice rushed to her side. "I didn't tell you because we didn't have much time to visit at lunch break."

Clara arched a brow. There had been ample time for Beatrice to mention her brother during their lunch break, and yet she'd said nothing. Perhaps she hadn't wanted to discuss her brother in front of the other ladies who had joined them.

"Sometimes Beatrice would like to forget she has a brother." The young man's comment drew Clara from her thoughts, and she looked his way. "I'm Jeremiah Hodson, Beatrice's older brother. And you are?"

Beatrice jabbed him with her elbow. "This is my new friend, Clara McBride. We work side by side in the laboratory. She's teaching me the proper way to make cartridges to kill the enemy."

"Good for you, Miss McBride. Anyone who can teach my sister has my admiration."

Clara chuckled. The two didn't resemble each other in the least, yet they seemed to share the same camaraderie and joking spirit she'd always relished with her own brother. "Beatrice has proved a capable student, and unless she moves to another room in the laboratory, I believe I've taught her all she needs to know."

"Well, I'm impressed, Sister. I doubt my supervisor would have given me such a good report on my first day at work." He gave Beatrice a quick pat on the shoulder.

The three of them continued along the walkway toward the entrance of the Arsenal. "How long have you worked here, Mr. Hodson?"

"Please—call me Jeremiah. Mr. Hodson is too formal for one of Bea's friends." He shoved his hands in his trouser pockets. "I've been working here a week. The two of us arrived ten days ago, but I suppose my sister told you that."

"No. We enjoyed our lunch with a group of other ladies, so she didn't have time to tell me much about herself—or you," she said and grinned. "How do you like the Arsenal?"

"I like the Arsenal just fine. If it weren't for those stacked-up cannonballs near the entrance, you'd think this place was an enormous park. It's so big." He waved his arm in a sweeping motion. "And all these trees and green grass. When I first stepped through the gates, I thought the place quite wonderful." He gestured with his thumb toward the work area. "But as soon as you get a glimpse of all the buildings, you know you're not in any park. The great number took my breath away—must be forty or more." He blew out a breath. "I haven't yet discovered what they do in all those buildings, but one of the fellas told me there's everything from living quarters for the officers and enlisted men to a bakery, storehouses, stables, as well as carpentry and paint shops. Fact is, he didn't even know what work was done in all of them."

"Nor do I, and I've been employed at the Arsenal laboratory for almost a year. When I began work, I was always told to report to the laboratory and remain within my assigned work area. I knew there was a forge and stables. One of the men who lives in our boardinghouse works at the blacksmith shop." Clara pointed to the large brick building near the entrance. "Did anyone tell you that impressive brick building was once a federal penitentiary?"

"Truly?" Beatrice's voice rippled with excitement. "Do you know the names of any criminals who were imprisoned there?"

Clara shook her head. "No. I've never inquired." As they

passed the stacked cannonballs near the exit of the Arsenal, Clara glanced at Beatrice. "Do you two live nearby?"

Jeremiah leaned around his sister's shoulder. "We've got rooms on South M Street. Do you know where that is?"

Clara nodded. "Yes. My mother and I live in a boarding-house on South O Street. M Street is two blocks north of us."

Beatrice clapped her hands. "That's perfect. We can meet you each morning and walk together."

Clara didn't want to appear unfriendly, but most mornings there were crowds of workers making their way toward the Arsenal. The same was true in the evenings, but because she'd been detained by the lieutenant, tonight was differ-ent. Most of the workers were far ahead of them or already home. She didn't want to be rude, but committing to wait for them each morning could mean she'd be late to work. And tardiness was frowned upon at the laboratory.

"I usually turn south onto 4 ½ Street at five-thirty each morning. If I spot you in the crowd, we can walk together. If not, I'll see you when you arrive." She flashed a smile. "We can eat breakfast and lunch together if you'd like."

Beatrice bobbed her head. "That would be perfect. You won't mind if my brother joins us, would you?"

Clara glanced at Jeremiah. "I suppose he can join us if his supervisor doesn't object, but break times vary among the various workers in the Arsenal. You never did tell me where you're working."

Jeremiah shrugged. "I work in freight and shipping right now, but I don't think my supervisor knows where I am half the time. The fella who hired me said I was gonna be trained to handle the work in different areas. He said once I learned things, they'd move me around to wherever I was needed." He grinned. "I think he was pleased to get someone like me who had worked at a lot of different jobs in the past."

His cavalier attitude surprised Clara. Most new employees worried about pleasing their supervisors, but Jeremiah seemed to have little concern. "He may be watching more closely than you think. I'd be careful to follow the rules if you want to keep your job."

He circled around behind the two of them and came alongside Clara. He tipped his head close. "You wouldn't tell on me, would you, Clara?" He was so close, she was assailed by his tobacco-laced breath. Unnerved by his boldness, she took a slight sideways step.

Beatrice slapped his arm. "You need to mind your manners, Jeremiah. Acting a fool with me is one thing, but no one else wants to put up with your nonsense. Apologize to Clara."

He gave Clara a sideways glance. "I'm sorry, Clara. I didn't mean any harm. Sometimes my behavior is a little brazen. At least that's what Beatrice tells me. I hope there's no hard feelings between you and me—or you and Beatrice. She'll be holding a grudge for months if she loses your friendship over me."

Clara didn't look in his direction, yet she did nod and mumble her acceptance. She hoped he understood she didn't want him to treat her in the same mocking manner as his sister. She also didn't want Beatrice to scold him any further, at least not in her presence.

Hoping to ease the uncomfortable silence and tension among them, Clara turned to Beatrice. "Did you have difficulty finding a place to live when you arrived? One of the girls told me she had a terrible time locating a place she could afford."

Beatrice shifted her lunch pail to her other hand. "While I had hoped we would find something a little closer to the Arsenal, it seems the houses were more ramshackle and decrepit as we searched farther south." She inhaled a sharp breath. "But I'm sure your boardinghouse is quite nice, Clara. I hope you didn't think I was saying all the houses farther south are horrid. I need to think before I speak."

Clara shook her head. "No need to worry about your comment. Except for the Arsenal, this entire portion of town is nothing but shacks and run-down tenements for the working class. Wages may be lower at the other Union arsenals, but it costs considerably more to live in Washington. It's sad there aren't better accommodations when we are forced to pay such outrageous rent."

"Now, that's a fact." Jeremiah yanked his cap from his head and tucked it into his rear pocket. "Never knew so many fleas and roaches existed until we moved here."

Clara wrinkled her nose and nodded. "The pests aren't just in our area of the city. They're everywhere."

"Are you talking about the two-legged ones like me, or the fleas and roaches?" Jeremiah arched his brows.

"Don't start in again, Jeremiah. You're proving the two-legged ones are more difficult to control." Beatrice shot him a warning glare.

"I'm sure there are plenty of two-legged ones, but I meant the other vermin. There's no sanitation anywhere in Washington." Clara wanted Beatrice to know Jeremiah's comment hadn't offended her. She longed to discover a neutral topic, one that wouldn't increase the discord between brother and sister. "Where did your family live before moving to Washington?"

He glanced at Beatrice. "I'm surprised my sister hasn't

already given you the details of our life. Talking is her favorite pastime."

A frown creased Clara's forehead. Her efforts to ease the tension weren't going to be successful. It seemed Jeremiah was determined to annoy his sister.

Beatrice smiled and looped her hand through Clara's arm. "It's fine, Clara. I'm accustomed to my brother's prickly comments. He thinks that's why God created brothers—to annoy their sisters."

"That's right." Jeremiah nudged his sister's arm and grinned. "You have any brothers or sisters, Clara?"

"One brother. He enlisted along with my father. I'm not sure where he is right now. We haven't heard from him. My father died at Bull Run."

Beatrice patted Clara's hand and murmured her condolences. "This war can't end soon enough for any of us."

Clara didn't want to discuss the war, missing men, or death. Such talk merely deepened her own sorrow, and many times she'd heard talk of the war escalate into bitter arguments. Discussing painful issues with friends or family was one thing, but Beatrice and Jeremiah weren't family and she didn't consider them friends. Perhaps one day she would—but not yet.

"I may have asked before, but what brought you to Washington and where do you call home?"

"You did. But thanks to Jeremiah, our conversation got waylaid." Beatrice grinned. "We're from a farming area in Maryland near the Washington border. The only town nearby is so small no one has ever heard of it. We had a little farm, and then when Pa died of cholera, we discovered he owed more on it than it was worth, so we packed our few belongings and here we are."

"Our ma died of the cholera a few months before Pa." Jeremiah kicked a pebble with the toe of his worn leather work boot. "This hasn't been the best time for the two of us, but we're settled now and we both got work, so things are getting better, even with the war going on. Isn't that right, Bea?"

Beatrice nodded. "When Pa died, I made Jeremiah promise he wouldn't enlist. I couldn't bear to lose anyone else." She swiped at her eyes and looked away. "Thankfully, he didn't pass the military physical. While it was a relief to me, Jeremiah wanted to appeal the Army surgeon's disqualification notice, but I finally convinced him it was more important to remain with me. Besides, our work contributes to the war effort—just in a different way. Right, Jeremiah?"

Jeremiah grunted. Though he didn't appear convinced, Clara could understand Beatrice's position. Being left without any family was one of Clara's greatest fears, and the war was tearing families apart at every turn. In truth, she would have been pleased to have had her brother and father rejected by the Army. Not that she'd want them suffering any sort of ailment, but Jeremiah appeared as healthy as her brother and father when they'd enlisted. Yet she understood some ailments weren't apparent. While she'd like to know more about Jeremiah's affliction, she would never inquire—it simply wouldn't be proper.

"This is where I leave you." Clara slowed her step at the intersection of 4 ½ and O Streets. "I'll see you at the Arsenal tomorrow."

Jeremiah waved toward the intersection. "Not at the Arsenal. You'll see us right here. We'll be waiting for you."

Clara smiled and gave a nod before turning down O Street. She'd gone only a short distance when she glanced over her shoulder. Beatrice and her brother were quite a pair. At first, she'd thought Jeremiah a bit annoying, but it seemed he considered his behavior no more than innocent teasing. And they exhibited a strong familial bond. Clara liked that. Nothing was more important than God and family.

THREE

Joseph Brady grimaced and squared his shoulders. Hiding his limp was proving more difficult than usual this evening. Before his foot had completely healed, and against the doctor's orders, he'd fashioned a block of wood, lodged it in the toe of his boot, and forced his foot inside. At first the pain had been excruciating, but he'd learned to ignore the discomfort and hide his limp—at least most of the time. A change in the weather always caused him problems.

Thunder rumbled overhead as Joseph lifted his foot to rest it on the small footstool hidden beneath his desk. He wasn't ashamed of his deformity, but he didn't want sympathy. Even more, he didn't want to be treated differently. The Army had classified him unfit for battlefield service after his surgery and assigned him to this desk job at the Arsenal. At first, he'd told himself it was better than being mustered out, but nowadays his life more closely resembled that of a civilian than a soldier. Even though he took orders from the colonel and lived in the Arsenal's military barracks, his duties were much the same as the civilian supervisors. His uniform set him apart from the civilians, but little else distinguished

31

Joseph as a graduate of West Point who had once led men into battle. While it was true that producing munitions was important to the war effort, it would never fulfill his desire to fight once again for the Union.

He sighed, reached across the desk, and dipped his pen into the inkpot. Keeping records had become a tedious part of each day, but if he was to depart in the morning, he needed to finish. A flash of lightning streaked across the sky as he entered the final daily production numbers for his section. He blotted the entries and leaned back. As he pushed up from his chair, a gust of wind caught the door and slammed it closed. Joseph dropped back in his chair at the crashing sound. Once his heartbeat slowed, he silently chastised himself, stood, and crossed the room. *Will this jarring reaction to loud noises never end?*

Pulling the brim of his black felt Hardee hat low on his forehead, he descended the steps and made his way to the barracks. Dark clouds hung on the horizon, and the sound of rolling thunder followed him inside. Moments later, a slanting rain cascaded against the rows of windows that bordered both sides of the building. Joseph sat on the edge of his bed and massaged his lower leg. He longed to pull off his boot and permit his foot the freedom that would relieve some of the pain, but first he needed to pack.

He wouldn't be at the Allegheny Arsenal long—two weeks at most—at least that was what his orders had suggested. Due to the war creating travel interruptions, traveling to and from Pittsburgh would fill most of his time away from the nation's capital. He'd balked when he received the order from Colonel Furman, yet his arguments had fallen upon deaf ears. The colonel cared little that Joseph had been at the Arsenal for only a month and declared him the best candidate for the assignment. Joseph's pride wouldn't permit him to use his injured foot as an excuse. Painful or not, he'd have to make the journey and do his best to discover any useful methods that might increase productivity at the Washington Arsenal.

After packing and eating supper in the dining hall, Joseph reviewed his itinerary and returned to the barracks. He longed to remove his boots and go to bed. He needed to be rested before starting his journey. Regardless of the storm, he hoped he'd sleep well tonight. While he was in the hospital, one of the chaplains had suggested Joseph might rid himself of his frequent nightmares if he read a chapter from the Bible and prayed before retiring. The practice hadn't been foolproof, but it had helped. And it had restored a modicum of the faith he'd embraced in his earlier years.

He reached into his traveling case, retrieved his Bible, and opened to the Psalms. Joseph often found encouragement and comfort in the Psalms, especially those penned by David. Perhaps it was because David had been a warrior who had found strength in the Lord when facing difficult circumstances. As nightfall darkened the room, he slid the Bible back into his case, sunk into the thin mattress, and began to silently pray.

As the darkness deepened to an inky black, Joseph's dreams were interrupted by the boom of cannons and the clang of flashing bayonets. Hundreds of gray-uniformed men appeared and crested a hill, their cry for blood filling the heavens as they charged toward his company of ragtag soldiers. Captain Melrose shouted an order to advance, but instead of moving forward, the soldiers drew together and formed a giant orb of blue. A cannon thundered and struck its prey. Body parts hovered above him while droplets of blood dripped on him. Bloodcurdling screams pierced his ears.

Someone was shouting his name and yanking on his shoulders. "Lieutenant! Lieutenant! Come on, wake up! You're having some sort of nightmare."

Joseph awakened with a start. His heart pounded, and his limbs quaked beneath the sheet. The corporal in charge of the barracks stood over Joseph, his eyes wide with fright.

When Joseph sat up, the young soldier took a backward step. "Sorry, Lieutenant, but your cries were even louder than the storm. Some of the other men complained you were keeping them awake."

Joseph forced a deep breath and swallowed hard. "I'm sorry." He pointed his thumb over his shoulder toward the window. "I think that storm became a part of my dream." He paused, marshaling his memories. A drop of water fell on his head, and he recalled the dripping blood from his dream. "And I think there may be a leak in the roof."

The corporal looked up as another droplet fell. "Right you are, Lieutenant. Let's move your cot over a bit so you don't get soaked. I'll report the leak, and once the rain stops, I'm sure someone will get up there and patch the hole."

Joseph swung his legs off the side of the cot, edged to the end of the bed, and grabbed his right boot. He didn't miss the corporal's fleeting look of alarm as Joseph tugged on his sock and shoved his foot into the boot. He'd done his best to hide the affliction since arriving at the Arsenal. Discussing his injury created either sympathy or fear. He disliked the display of both, especially from his fellow soldiers.

He pushed up from the bed. "That will do for now. You can go on with your duties, Corporal. I can move the cot without help."

Joseph leaned down and grasped the edge of the bed. His booted foot clomped an irregular beat with the slapping sound of his bare foot as he pushed the cot across the narrow plank floor. When Joseph turned, the corporal hadn't moved. His eyes remained fixed on Joseph's booted foot.

With his head still bowed, he gestured. "Is that . . . did you . . . the battle where that happened . . . is that what caused your nightmare?"

Joseph grunted, sat on the bed, and pulled off his boot. "Get some sleep, Corporal. That's what I intend to do." He'd spoken with authority, and the young soldier quickly followed his order. Joseph lay back in his bed and covered himself with the sheet. The storm outside had abated, but the one raging inside him would likely continue for the remainder of the night.

The sun hadn't yet peeked from beneath the horizon, but the rain had stopped sometime during the night. For that, Clara was thankful. Walking to work in a spring or summer rainstorm wasn't for the faint of heart. The muddy, garbage-laden streets would bring messy boots and skirt hems trimmed with muck into the Arsenal this morning. With the arrival of each storm, Clara hoped the stench of the area streets would be miraculously cleansed, though she was once again disappointed. There seemed to be nothing that could purify the disgusting odors of Washington during the heat of summer—not even a soaking rain.

With a determined step, Clara approached the intersection of 4 ½ and South O Streets. If Beatrice and her brother were waiting, she'd walk with them. Otherwise, she didn't intend to break her stride. When a quick look about didn't reveal the couple, she melded into the crowd of workers and continued onward. Long ago she'd given up the practice of accompanying friends to work. After being tardy on two occasions due to such attempts, she'd decided it was more practical to walk alone.

The front porch of the laboratory was only a few feet away when Clara heard pounding feet and a woman shouting her name. She turned and caught sight of Jeremiah running toward the freight yard and Beatrice rushing toward the laboratory. With her bonnet askew and lunch pail swinging pell-mell, Beatrice hurdled up the porch steps. Clara held her breath and prayed the girl wouldn't knock her to the ground.

Beatrice held Clara's arm while she gasped for breath. When she'd finally recovered, she pulled a handkerchief from her pocket and wiped perspiration from her forehead. "I thought we were going to walk together."

"I hope you didn't wait for me. I'm certain I told you that if I saw you in the passing crowd, we would walk together." Clara continued toward the door. "We'd better hurry or we'll be late."

The two of them followed the other women into the laboratory, placed their lunch pails and bonnets along the wall, filed into their respective positions, and edged onto the long, narrow bench. A young man arrived at their table with supplies and placed them on the table. Clara picked up a dowel and paper.

Beatrice glanced about, then nudged Clara with her elbow. "I wonder why Lieutenant Brady isn't at his desk."

"He's gone." Clara was careful to keep her voice low.

Beatrice blew a long sigh and grinned. "I can see he's gone." She turned her gaze toward the door. "Perhaps he had to meet with the colonel before coming to the laboratory. His desk looks so sad without him."

Clara stifled a laugh. Beatrice certainly seemed the dramatic sort, especially to Clara, who had never entertained such histrionic thoughts. To her, a desk was a desk, either occupied or unoccupied. She'd never viewed a piece of furniture as an object that exhibited physical attributes. As she removed the former from the cylinder, she turned her attention toward the lieutenant's desk. *Perhaps it does look sad without him.*

After removing a handkerchief from her pocket, Beatrice pretended to blot her upper lip. "Do you know where he is?" The ruse to hide her whispers had failed.

In two long strides, the supervisor appeared at their side and rapped his knuckles on the table. "Ladies! That is enough! The day has barely begun and we are off to a poor start. I shouldn't need to remind you that visiting is prohibited. Focus! Your attention must be on your work. If you ladies continue this behavior, I'll be forced to discipline the entire group." After pinning them with a deep frown, he turned and strode toward a table on the other side of the room.

Once his back was turned, a woman seated across the table glared at them and mouthed the words *be quiet.* She pressed her index finger to her pursed lips.

Beatrice might not understand the supervisor's warning, but Clara did—and so did the other women sitting at their table. The supervisors had learned they could more easily enforce the rules if they threatened to discipline the entire group. Those who weren't at fault then sided with the supervisors. Losing an hour of pay or having a reduction in hourly wage was something none of them could afford.

When the bell rang announcing the midmorning recess for breakfast, the women filed out with their bonnets and pails. Beatrice grabbed Clara's hand. "Let's go over there under a tree."

Instead of cooling the air, the previous night's rain had left them with another layer of clamminess that made it difficult to breathe. While walking to an area where they could be alone, Clara considered how many of Bea's questions she wanted to answer. Clara surmised Bea had more than a passing interest in the lieutenant, since she'd earlier commented on his good looks and now was eager to know his whereabouts. By the time they sat down, Clara was certain she'd divulge the lieutenant's whereabouts but unsure if she should say anything more. Would it be more considerate to divulge their plan to write each other during his absence so Bea could set her sights on another fellow, or should she withhold the arrangement she'd made with the lieutenant?

The thoughts zigzagged through her mind as they continued walking to a grassy spot. Beatrice pointed to an oak tree with a vast crown and a trunk so immense it looked to be one of God's original creations.

After dropping her lunch pail, Beatrice glanced over her shoulder. "This looks like the best place. The others are sitting closer to the laboratory. We'll have more privacy over here." She sat down and molded her back against the tree before removing a thick slice of bread and hunk of cheese from her bucket. "Oh no. This is Jeremiah's pail. He's not going to be happy with me." She chuckled. "And he's going to be very hungry by the end of the workday. My pail has only one small piece of bread and an apple."

"Such a small amount for the entire day?" Clara was certain she couldn't manage to work all day with so little food. "Were you going to eat the bread at morning break and the apple for dinner break?"

Beatrice shrugged. "It wouldn't have mattered, but now I'll have my choice of cheese, buttered bread, a jelly sandwich, or an apple." She looked toward the rear of the complex, where her brother worked. "Unless Jeremiah comes searching for me."

Clara followed Beatrice's gaze toward the outbuildings. There was no sign of Jeremiah. Perhaps his supervisor was keeping a better eye on Jeremiah than he thought.

"So, do you know why the lieutenant is absent?" Beatrice bit into the wedge of cheese before breaking a small piece of bread from a thick slice.

"He's gone to the Allegheny Arsenal in Lawrenceville. It's near Pittsburgh. In Pennsylvania."

Beatrice jutted her chin. "I know where Pittsburgh is located, Clara. I'm not totally lacking in education."

Clara's mouth fell open. "My response was meant only to clarify the lieutenant's location. I apologize if I've offended you."

"I'm sorry. Looks as though I've gone and done it again— spoken without thinking and let my quick tongue get me in trouble. Please forgive me." Beatrice blotted her forehead. "I'd like to blame my quick response on this unbearable humidity, but that's not the case. I'm so accustomed to snapping at Jeremiah that I forget and do it with others." She finger-pressed the folds of her skirt and inhaled a breath. "Did the lieutenant tell you when you visited with him last evening?"

"Yes, he told me he was leaving and—"

"I wish you would have told me as soon as you left the laboratory. I would have gone back and bid him farewell. I do wish he was going to be here. There aren't many men as handsome as the lieutenant around here. At least not that I've seen."

Clara chuckled. "Well, you've been here only a short time.

I think you'll discover there are more men working here than you think."

Beatrice shrugged. "Perhaps. But I doubt there are many as attractive as the lieutenant."

Beatrice's comment confirmed what Clara had guessed. Bea was smitten with the lieutenant. But so was Clara. Should she tell Beatrice the lieutenant hadn't been permanently reassigned—that he'd be returning to the Washington Arsenal once he'd completed his duty and that she and the lieutenant planned to exchange correspondence during his absence? If she withheld the information, would Beatrice be angry if she later discovered Clara had been writing to him and known of his return?

Before she arrived at a decision, Jeremiah appeared in the distance. He was waving his lunch pail overhead, and his shouts were loud enough to wake the dead.

Beatrice frowned and pointed toward her brother. "I fear he's found us."

Clara tucked the remains of her breakfast in the pail and stood. "It's near time for us to return. We might as well meet him halfway, don't you think?"

"I suppose. Perhaps he'll cease shouting if he sees we're walking in his direction." She held the lunch pail aloft and swung it back and forth like a lantern signaling a lost ship.

Jeremiah came to a panting stop in front of them long before they'd walked halfway. "You have my . . ."

Beatrice extended the lunch pail that hung from her fingers. "I know. I ate all but the apple."

Jeremiah's eyes widened as he reached for the pail. "You better not have." He tugged on the lid and glared at her. "You ate the cheese."

Beatrice laughed and nodded. "You should be thankful

that's all I ate. Maybe you'll grab your own lunch pail tomorrow." The warning bell rang, and she shrugged her narrow shoulders. "Sorry, but you'll have to eat alone, dear Brother." She grinned and looped arms with Clara. "Come on, Clara. We'd better get back to the laboratory."

Today's exchange between brother and sister bore a different tone. It appeared that food was more important to Jeremiah than the familial bond Clara had first observed. She glanced back over her shoulder at Jeremiah. What an odd combination Jeremiah and Beatrice were. She'd seen siblings argue as children, but it seemed these two hadn't yet outgrown such tendencies. As they entered the lab, Clara considered her new friend.

Friend? After only two days, did she truly count Beatrice her friend? Perhaps that term was an overstatement. Still, Clara remembered her first days in the laboratory when she'd hoped someone would help her. She couldn't help but feel compassion for Beatrice. After all, it was never easy to be the "new girl." So far, she'd merely tried to make Beatrice feel comfortable in her new surroundings.

They'd exchanged pleasantries but little else. She wasn't sure she could call Beatrice a friend just yet, but Clara hadn't had a close friend since Nellie moved away a year ago, and Clara had to admit she missed the bond of friendship she and Nellie had shared. Of course, Nellie and Bea were nothing alike. Nellie had been timid and quiet, and Bea was the opposite. Still, Bea appeared to have a good heart and seemed to want a friend as much as Clara did.

Four

Both the block of wood in his right boot and the rainy weather had become Joseph's enemies during his journey. After arriving in Lawrenceville, he limped to the front of the train station and hailed a carriage.

The driver tipped his hat. "Where to, soldier?"

"Allegheny Arsenal. I need to go to its headquarters. Do you know where it's located?"

The old man nodded. "I'll get ya there in no time."

Joseph tossed his two canvas bags onto the seat. His foot twisted as he stepped up into the cab. With a grimace, he dropped onto the seat. He longed for a good night's rest and a chance to remove the boot from his aching foot. Yet that would have to wait.

His orders had been clear: Report to Colonel Simon, the officer in charge of the Allegheny Arsenal, immediately upon arrival. Unless otherwise instructed, the colonel would remain Joseph's commanding officer until his departure. His orders had signaled the significance of this assignment, and Joseph didn't intend to fail.

Despite his injured foot and limited knowledge of laboratory procedures, he was determined to carry out his mission with the same precision and resolve he'd summoned when he first charged into battle with a company of soldiers. Back then, General McDowell had placed Joseph in command of a small force before ordering them to cross Bull Run at Blackburn's Ford and test the Confederate defenses. The general had counted that brief skirmish a victory.

Certain victory was in the offing; General McDowell had ordered two divisions to attack the Confederates at Matthews Hill. When Confederate forces were driven back, additional Union troops crossed Bull Run. But that afternoon, Confederate reinforcements had arrived by train and soon broke the Union line. Under counterattack by the Confederates, the Union troops had retreated to the safety of Washington.

Joseph, along with the other wounded, had been admitted to the hospital tents at Camp Carver. After his release from the hospital, Joseph had inquired regarding the losses suffered by the Union. The numbers were still uncertain, but there had been over a thousand wounded, over a thousand missing or captured, and over four hundred dead. One of those men had been Clara McBride's father.

When she'd disclosed that her father had died at Bull Run, Joseph hadn't divulged that he'd fought there. Even though a year had passed, hearing the bloody details of those tragic battles wouldn't heal those left behind, any more than talking about it would help him now.

The soldiers' relatives he'd encountered always wanted to hear details of the battle. At first, he'd told a few, but now he refused. He'd watched the terror and pain illuminate their glassy eyes as he recounted the horrors of war. Rather than mending hearts, his words had only deepened the wounds for the surviving relatives, and also for himself. His nightmares had increased with each telling. He didn't want those ugly pictures to haunt Clara or her mother. His chest tightened, and he forced himself to draw in deep, steady breaths. He needed a clear head when he reported to the Arsenal commander.

The carriage wheels rumbled an irregular cadence as they traversed the brick streets through Lawrenceville. Joseph was thankful for the few moments of silence when they finally stopped in front of the Arsenal. A soldier standing guard near the fortress-like entrance approached and leaned forward to look inside the cab. Noting Joseph's uniform, he saluted. "Please state your business, Lieutenant."

Joseph reached into his breast pocket, retrieved a copy of his orders, and handed it to the private. After reading the orders, he returned them to Joseph, gave a nod, and signaled to the driver. "Headquarters Building is straight ahead. The one with the clock tower. You can't miss it."

"Thanks. I don't need directions. I'm out here at least once a week," the driver called out. As if to prove his response, the cab rolled forward with a jolt.

Joseph leaned forward and attempted to massage his foot through the heavy leather boot. He wanted to make a good impression upon meeting the colonel. During his rehabilitation, he'd learned to manage a regular stride but only for a short distance. He didn't want to limp—a matter of pride that he hadn't yet managed to overcome.

He stepped down from the cab, flipped a coin to the driver, and waited until he was certain his foot wouldn't give out on him before removing his bags. Lifting a bag in each hand, he walked up the steps and into the Headquarters Building and approached a private sitting at the front desk.

Joseph offered the young man a smile. "Good afternoon, Private." After placing his bags on the floor beside him, he reached into his pocket. "I have orders to report to Colonel Simon."

The private glanced at Joseph's paper work and gave him a nod. "I'll tell the colonel you're here." He gestured to a couple of wooden chairs. "You can have a seat over there."

The interior of the building was as impressive as its massive brick exterior. Winding staircases were strategically located at each end of the structure. A young private was hard at work shining walnut banisters that gracefully curved up the far staircase. Another soldier was sweeping dust from the wooden floor, and one was perched on a tall ladder washing windows.

None of the young soldiers appeared particularly pleased with their assigned tasks, but Joseph could understand. They'd likely envisioned marching off to war to save the Union. At the thought, he looked down at his foot. He wanted to tell them they should be thankful for their safe assignment, yet they wouldn't believe him. No doubt their thinking was just what his had been when he'd marched into battle. He had believed that someone else might die or be injured, but not him—at least not until it happened.

"Lieutenant Brady. I've been expecting you." Joseph pushed to his feet and saluted the approaching colonel. The colonel offered a quick salute in return before gesturing to the private. "Place the lieutenant's bags at your desk until we're through."

The private rushed forward, grabbed Joseph's bags, and quickly returned to his desk. Joseph offered his thanks before following the colonel down the long hallway. His stomach lurched as they headed toward the staircase, for it was almost impossible to hide his injury while climbing steps. Though he'd worked diligently to climb steps as he had before, it remained impossible. He couldn't properly maintain his balance when he attempted to use his right leg and foot. When they continued past the flight of steps, Joseph blew a sigh of relief.

The colonel slowed his pace and entered a door on the right. He continued through what appeared to be a reception area for his guests and entered a well-appointed office. The windows allowed a clear view of the Arsenal's parade ground. He rounded his desk and sat down in a Windsor chair that was padded with black leather cushions.

"Have a seat, Lieutenant." He tapped his index finger on Joseph's orders. "Let's discuss how best to complete your assignment."

Joseph was eager to hear the colonel's thoughts, though he would have preferred a good night's sleep before the meeting. He chose the straight-back wooden chair without any padding. Discomfort should help keep him attentive. At least that was his hope, since concentration would be key during this briefing. Otherwise, he wouldn't retain much of what the colonel had to say.

He folded Joseph's orders and extended the paper to him. "I don't need these any longer, but you may need them while you're here. However, I will make certain you have proper identification papers that will permit you entrance to most of the facilities here at the Arsenal."

"Thank you."

"If you'd like, I can assign one of the soldiers to give you a tour of the entire facility tomorrow. Then I'd suggest you devote at least half a day in each of our laboratory rooms. You may want to observe our shipping and freight departments, as well. Were there any other particular units you feel might be helpful?" He leaned back and traced his fingers along several pipes hanging in a dark mahogany rack before finally choosing one. He looked up after carefully filling the bowl with tobacco.

"I believe what you've outlined will be most helpful. Once I've toured the entire facility, I'll have a better idea if there are other units I'd like to observe more closely."

"Of course. Just advise your escort and he'll see to the arrangements." The colonel inhaled quick, puffing breaths until the tobacco glowed a soft orange. He blew a puff of smoke into the air. "I hope your visit will prove useful. We want to make certain our men have all the ammunition they need to win this war. When we hire new workers, we take time to explain that they are important to the Union's success." His bushy eyebrows dipped low as he took a draw on his pipe. "We now hire only women and girls in the cartridge rooms. Once the men joined the Army, we began hiring teenage boys to make the cartridges. We thought since their hands were smaller and more agile, they would be a good fit for the jobs."

Joseph shifted in his chair. "But they weren't?"

"After six months, we fired every one of them. They were hard to manage and liked to fool around too much. Boys will be boys, but a freight supervisor discovered matches packed with cartridge bundles, and an overseer in the cylinder rooms found unlit matches in rooms where gunpowder was stored. After several of the boys were seen smoking around boxes of cartridges, we had to take swift action. Their carelessness could have caused a disaster."

The idea surprised Joseph. There were several boys who worked at the Washington Arsenal. While none worked in the laboratories, he knew there were a few in shipping and freight. "So you don't employ any boys?"

"We still have a few who technically work for the laboratories, but they have specific duties such as sweeping up the gunpowder from the porches and roads. They aren't permitted in the cartridge rooms."

Joseph nodded, although he still didn't understand. If they feared the boys would cause explosions or fires, why would they let the youngsters sweep gunpowder? Granted, an explosion in a laboratory would be far worse, but if the boys weren't trustworthy, they shouldn't be working at the Arsenal in any capacity.

"You must remember that it's difficult to fill all the positions in such a large arsenal. We want to protect our employees, but we can't eliminate every boy from the workforce."

Joseph frowned. It was as if the colonel had read his thoughts.

The colonel grinned. "Your expression told me what you were thinking, Lieutenant."

"If that's the case, I had better not try my hand at reconnaissance."

The colonel tapped his pipe on the piece of cork that centered a large brass ashtray. "Not unless you become much better at hiding your thoughts." At the sound of a knock, the colonel looked toward the door. "Come in."

The private who manned the reception desk stood in the doorway. "Sergeant Taft has arrived, sir. He said you sent for him."

"Yes. Send him in." The colonel returned his attention to Joseph. "Sergeant Taft has been at the Allegheny Arsenal for five years. He's a good man, knowledgeable about all areas of the Arsenal. I'm going to assign him as your escort during your visit. Of course, you may call on me at any time if you have questions the sergeant is unable to answer."

Before Joseph could respond, Sergeant Taft stepped into the office. Joseph pushed to his feet, and Colonel Simon made the formal introductions. Once certain Sergeant Taft understood his orders, the colonel dismissed the men.

The sergeant walked alongside Joseph to the reception desk, where Joseph retrieved his bags. "The colonel arranged a private room for you in the officers' quarters. We can go there first and you can rest for the remainder of the day, or we can begin our tour of the facilities, whichever you prefer."

"Thank you, Sergeant. I believe I'd prefer to wait until tomorrow to begin. I want to be fully alert when I view the work and methods being utilized here."

The sergeant nodded and strode toward the doors at the south end of the hall. Joseph did his best to keep pace, but the constant stabbing pain in his foot wouldn't permit him to quicken his step. The sergeant didn't appear to notice Joseph's lagging.

When they neared the exit, Sergeant Taft glanced over his shoulder and came to an abrupt stop. His eyes shone with surprise and then something more. Pity perhaps? "I'm sorry, Lieutenant." He nodded toward Joseph's leg. "Muscle cramp?"

Joseph shook his head. "No, I have a problem with my foot. Once I elevate my leg, it will be fine."

The sergeant held his gaze. "Battle injury?"

"Bull Run."

The sergeant's eyes widened. "You were at Bull Run? I've never met anyone who fought at Bull Run. I keep requesting a transfer, but it hasn't happened." His lips drooped into a frown. "I joined before the war started, and I thought sure they'd transfer me to another company, one that was going to fight the war. It didn't happen, however. I made two requests for transfer, and both were ignored." He arched his brows. "Any suggestions?"

Joseph sighed. "Yes. Don't request another transfer. War is ugly. Stay here at the Arsenal and fulfill your duty. What you're doing for the war effort is as important as shouldering a rifle and marching toward the enemy. You won't suffer nightmares or carry battle scars. And most especially, your family won't receive a death notice."

"That's true enough, but I think the soldiers assigned to the Arsenal are viewed as cowards."

"Truly? Has somebody called you a coward?"

"No, but I see the hatred in their eyes—particularly the mothers of sons who have been sent to the front."

Joseph smiled. "I think what you're sensing is envy rather than loathing, Sergeant. No doubt they wish their sons were serving at the Arsenal. They likely resent the fact that you have been able to remain here—and you can't blame them. But most folks understand that soldiers have no say regarding their duty assignments."

The sergeant appeared unconvinced, though he didn't comment further as they made their way. He nodded toward a two-story brick building. "That's the officers' quarters where you'll be staying. Your room is on the first floor." He stopped when they were at the entrance. "I'll meet you in front of the mess hall tomorrow morning at six o'clock. There will be a soldier inside who will direct you to your room."

"Thank you, Sergeant." Joseph saluted the young man, turned, and climbed the three front steps leading into the building. The door opened before he could reach for the handle. He was greeted with a sharp salute from a young private. He smiled, returned the salute, and removed his Hardee hat. "Good afternoon. I'm Lieutenant Brady."

The private nodded. "Right this way, sir."

The moment the private exited his room, Joseph dropped to sit on the side of the bed. The thin mattress collapsed with a groan. It seemed the mattresses in the Pennsylvania barracks would prove no more comfortable than those in Washington. Yet even without a comfortable bed, he would sleep well once the ache in his right foot had eased a bit.

Fortunately, there would be time to escape from his boots for a few hours. With a hefty yank, he pulled off his left boot, but he was more careful when he reached for the right one. After wriggling his foot from the confines of the leather, he removed his grizzled cotton sock.

Reaching inside the boot, he pulled free the block of wood. He had taken great care to bandage his foot and surround the block with lamb's wool, but without additional padding he wouldn't be able to tolerate the pain tomorrow. However, more padding in the boot would make for an even tighter fit.

He glanced down at the deformity, then immediately averted his gaze from the misshapen appendage. Most days he was thankful the battlefield surgeon had been able to save his foot and large toe, but today the ugliness and pain outweighed his gratefulness. Encasing the end of his foot in one hand, he massaged the throbbing scar with his fingers. His touch was enough to reveal that both his foot and ankle had swelled. If he elevated his leg for the next few hours, perhaps the swelling would diminish. If so, he'd join the officers for dinner. Otherwise, he'd remain in his quarters and forgo the evening meal. At the thought, his stomach growled a loud protest.

FIVE

uring the final days of August, the heat and humidity at the Washington Arsenal proved even more intolerable than earlier in the month, and the weather was taking its toll on everyone. Day after day, the sun beat down on the town with an unrelenting intensity. On most nights, sleep proved to be an effort in futility. Each night the bedding turned damp with perspiration, and the mosquitoes attacked with a vengeance. And each morning Clara's legs and arms displayed more of the red, itchy welts.

The stifling conditions inside the laboratory made the daylight hours even more difficult to bear. Major Rourke had been assigned to temporarily fill the lieutenant's position as supervisor in the cylinder room. He immediately made it clear he was unhappy with the transfer. Like most of the officers at the Arsenal, he wanted to lead troops into battle. Instead, he'd been recruiting young men to train and serve. Now he'd been relegated to the laboratory to supervise a group of hoop-skirted women—a job far beneath his military qualifications, or so he told them in his daily tirades.

He entered the laboratory and marched to his desk while

the women took their places at the worktables. He watched the clock across the room, and when it had reached exactly six o'clock, he shouted, "Begin work!"

Only seconds had passed when he pushed away from his desk, stomped across the room, and stopped at the end of the table. "There are three workers missing! Where are they?" His booming voice echoed in the silent room.

When there was no response, he tapped the shoulder of the nearest woman, who merely shrugged and shook her head. He continued up and down both sides of the table. When he received no response, his anger mounted. Workers were expected to notify their supervisor if they would be absent. On the few occasions when Clara had been too ill to report, her mother had delivered word of her illness. Others sent word through a co-worker or friend, but today no one had appeared to offer an excuse for the absent women.

After verbally venting his anger, the red-faced major stomped across the room, retrieved his walking stick, and whacked it on the edge of his desk. He struck the desk with such force, the wood cracked. The broken stick and the snickers of several workers heightened his rage.

He turned on his heel and pointed the broken stick at the table of women. "You think this is amusing? Well, let us see if you find it amusing when I tell you that I shall divide the work of the missing women among the rest of you. I expect the same production numbers as we had yesterday." His snarling voice reminded Clara of a mad dog.

Without warning, Beatrice jumped to her feet. Her hoop pressed against the table and sent the back of her dress flying upward. Hoping to help Beatrice avoid humiliation, Clara tugged on the hem of the dress.

However, Beatrice didn't appear concerned that her rising

hemline was now revealing her drawers. Instead, she cupped one hand to her mouth. "You, sir, are a bully, and if you continue with your ridiculous punishment, we shall all leave, and then what will you do?"

"Beatrice! Sit down before you get us all fired." Clara managed to keep her voice low yet urgent. "Please!"

Beatrice glanced over her shoulder, but rather than sitting down, she continued to glare at the major. Clara inhaled a long breath and held it until she thought she might explode.

The major gave a slight nod and returned to his desk. He didn't say whether he'd relented on his decision, but he didn't assign the extra work. When they exited the building for their breakfast break, the ladies were hailing Beatrice a hero and praising her bravery.

While Beatrice basked in the adulation, Clara crossed the grassy slope and sat down under one of the large elms. Beatrice's lips curved in a wide smile as she approached Clara. "That was the most fun I've had since moving to Washington. I sure put the major in his place. He won't try that again."

Clara rubbed the back of her neck. She didn't want to disagree with Beatrice, but she wasn't sure the confrontation was over. She'd heard stories about Major Rourke and how he treated his men. She doubted he was going to let a woman embarrass him without retribution, but she hoped she was wrong. She didn't want Beatrice to lose her job, and she did admire the way she'd spoken up—even if it was foolhardy. On the other hand, Beatrice shouldn't have threatened a walkout. If the major had called her bluff, Clara didn't think most of those workers would have followed her in a strike. No matter the conditions, they needed the money to support their families.

"I felt you tugging on my skirt." Beatrice chuckled. "Were

my drawers showing?" She dropped onto the grass alongside Clara.

"Only a little." Clara smiled. "There was no one standing behind us, so you ran no risk of ruining your good reputation."

Beatrice had barely settled when she suddenly jumped to her feet. She waved with wild abandon before cupping her hands to her mouth and shouting, "Over here, Jeremiah! Hurry!"

Jeremiah raced toward them and then dropped onto the grass. Panting for air, he leaned against the base of a broad tree trunk. Perspiration traced rivulets from his forehead down the sides of his bright red cheeks. He swiped his forearm across his forehead before frowning at his sister. "What's wrong? The way you were hollering, I thought you were in some kind of danger." He inhaled a gulp of air.

Beatrice sat down beside him. "I didn't mean to frighten you, but I was so excited about what happened this morning. I was afraid we'd have to go back inside before I could tell you my news."

His eyebrows lifted high. "You got an increase in wages?"

Clara glanced at her friend and waited. If Jeremiah equated good news with an increase in wages, he was going to be sorely disappointed.

"No, even better." While her brother searched the contents of his lunch pail, Beatrice recounted her earlier threats of rebellion.

Jeremiah's eyes widened and turned dark. "What's wrong with you, Bea? Can't you keep your mouth shut just once?"

Beatrice drew back as he spewed the words at her. "I thought you'd be proud that I stood up for myself and all the other women."

He yanked a shiny red apple from his pail, angled his arm, and threw the fruit with frightening force. The apple thunked and splatted against the trunk of a nearby tree. Clara gasped, but it was Beatrice who grabbed his lunch pail. "You think tossing that apple changes anything? If so, I can give this lunch pail a good swing and you can go hungry."

He lunged forward and grabbed the pail from her. "Challenging the major was a mistake, Bea. You may think you won that battle, but ask any of the soldiers he commands. For that matter, you can talk to some of the fellas down in the freight yard and they'll tell you the same thing. The major *never* loses a battle, especially when someone tries to make a fool of him. And that's exactly what you did, Bea."

Bea squared her shoulders and tipped her nose in the air. "Maybe so, but I could be the first woman who's ever had the courage to confront him. I doubt he'll treat me or the other ladies the same way he treats his soldiers or your friends who work in freight and shipping." Her attempt to appear brave fell short. The warble in her voice and the fear that shone in her eyes said it all.

Clara watched the unfolding disagreement and longed to be anywhere but on this grassy hillside. Why did Bea think she needed to continue defending herself?

Jeremiah didn't appear to notice that his words had already placed a chink in Bea's armor. "I shouldn't have to remind you that we need these jobs, Bea. How will we support ourselves if you get fired?" He lowered his voice and spoke from between clenched teeth. "Don't even think about leading the women in a walkout. Do you understand me?" Jeremiah pushed to his feet and stood over her. "You go back into the laboratory and apologize to Major Rourke."

"W-w-what? You don't mean that, Jeremiah."

His nostrils flared, and he clenched his hands into tight fists. "I do mean it—every word. And don't go and speak to him privately. Stand up just as you did earlier and apologize so that all the ladies can hear you."

"I-I can't do that, Jeremiah. What will they think of me?"

"Keeping your job is what is important. How we gonna live if we don't have jobs? We need our wages. What those women think of you doesn't matter." When Clara reached for the lid to her lunch pail, the movement captured his attention and his features softened a modicum. "Except for Clara. We care what she thinks."

Clara forced as much of a smile as she could muster. What had happened to the lighthearted, bantering brother and sister she'd met only weeks ago? She wanted to help make things better between these two. Their financial well-being was obviously more precarious than she'd imagined. "If it would lessen your concerns, Jeremiah, I have a contact who works at the Treasury Department as a copyist. They frequently have openings. If Beatrice should lose her position here, I'm certain my acquaintance would put in a word for Beatrice."

"Thank you, Clara, but I have faith in my sister. I'm sure she'll be able to convince Major Rourke she's sorry." He turned to his sister. "Am I right, Bea?" Beatrice offered a faint nod. "That's my girl." He grasped his sister by the shoulders and kissed her cheek. "I'm going back to the freight yard. You two have a good rest of the day." He picked up his lunch pail, waved, and then sauntered down the hill as though the three of them had just enjoyed a relaxing visit.

Clara broke the silence as the two of them walked toward the laboratory. "The disagreement between you and your brother surprised me. In the past he's seemed rather carefree, and you were the one who was quick to anger. Your positions were quite the opposite today. Does Jeremiah's temper ever frighten you?"

"No." Beatrice shook her head as if to emphasize the response. "He seldom gets upset with me. After hearing what he had to say, I understand that my actions were improper. I let a sense of injustice get the best of me."

Clara looped arms with Beatrice. "Not one of us would disagree that the major's decision was completely unfair."

"Yet all of you had the good sense to remain silent." Her lips curved in a tight smile. "I'm not sure I'm going to be able to go in there and eat crow." She tipped her head closer. "If I apologize, I'll disappoint the other ladies. You saw how they lauded me when we came outside for breakfast."

"I did, but you can't be ruled by the opinion of others. The punishment Major Rourke planned to mete out was outrageous, but working here requires us to obey our superiors. And so does the Bible. I doubt anyone will criticize God's Word."

Beatrice tugged on Clara's arm as they neared the door. "Maybe I'll try speaking to the major privately first. If he doesn't accept my apology, I can do what Jeremiah suggested."

Clara arched her brows. "Suggested? It sounded more like an order to me, but the choice is yours."

When they entered the laboratory, the major wasn't present. Beatrice shrugged. "I suppose I'll have to raise my hand and ask to speak to him when he arrives."

They had been at work for several minutes when Major Rourke returned. As soon as he'd taken his position at the end of the long table, Beatrice raised her hand.

The major gave a slight shake of his head. "I see you have

something you'd like to say, Miss Hodson, but before you speak, I have an announcement. I have spoken to Colonel Furman and explained the difficulties in meeting our quota. I also informed him that I had hoped to resolve the situation by increasing cartridge quotas. However, the colonel stated that such an increase might lead to shoddy work, and none of us wants imperfect munitions shipped to our soldiers." A malicious gleam shone in his eyes as he looked at them.

Clara inhaled a sharp breath. This wasn't going to go well for any of them. Of that, she was certain.

"The colonel and I are aware that all of you ladies wish to maintain your positions and, no matter the cost, you want to help our soldiers win the war. Since we must increase your personal quotas until the other workers return to their duties, each of you will remain at work an additional hour each afternoon. In doing so, we will all meet our goals."

A young woman at the far end of the table raised her hand. "How many days will we be required to work the extra hour, sir? And will it be at the same rate of pay?"

"Oh, I'm sorry. I failed to say that you won't receive additional pay for the extra hour of work. You may consider it your contribution to the war effort. As for how many days or weeks or months this will continue, I can't be sure. That will depend upon those ladies who have failed to appear for work. If you dislike the extra hour of work, perhaps you can encourage your fellow workers to return to their duties."

A smug smile played on his lips. When Beatrice stirred, Clara immediately gripped her arm and whispered, "Don't. You'll only make it worse."

The major turned and pierced Beatrice with a look of triumph. "I almost forgot. You raised your hand earlier. Was there something you wanted to say?"

Clara held her breath and prayed Beatrice would either remain silent or offer a humble apology for her earlier outburst.

"No, sir, you've said everything that needs to be said. However, I do thank you for the additional opportunity to serve our soldiers."

Clara stifled a groan. It seemed as if Beatrice needed to have the final word—but so did the major.

The major's brows dipped low. "Since you have a deep sense of patriotism, Miss Hodson, you may continue to work the extra hour for the remainder of your employment at the Arsenal."

She dipped her head and smiled. "Thank you for the privilege, Major."

This time Clara didn't stifle her groan.

When the bell rang for the noonday meal, the ladies rushed from the room, but they didn't gather around to cheer Beatrice's efforts. Instead, several of them approached with condemnation shining in their eyes.

Melissa Reynolds planted her hands on her hips and glared at Beatrice. "I have four young'uns at home. How am I supposed to work here another hour and get supper on the table? Look what you and your big mouth caused." She reached toward another lady and pulled her forward. "Go ahead, Nancy, tell her what this is gonna do to you."

The other woman didn't appear as eager to speak, but Melissa urged her on. "Like Melissa said, we got little ones at home to feed and care for. An extra hour a day without pay is gonna be hard on us. I know you was trying to do right by us when you first . . ." A sharp elbow to her ribs momentarily silenced her. "That hurt." She rubbed her side as Melissa pulled her away.

As several other women approached Beatrice, voicing their anger, Clara stepped in front of her. "Listen to me! Your actions are unfair." She scanned the group. "Only hours ago you declared Beatrice courageous and cheered her on, yet now you've made her a villain and are eager to attack. Although her efforts didn't have the desired effect, her intentions were good. We might not all agree with her methods, but we need to stand together."

A couple of the ladies did thank her for trying to help, and Beatrice mumbled her appreciation for their support. Then she shrugged and said, "I think the only thing that's going to help is if we convince the other ladies to return."

Clara sighed. "And maybe we can get things straightened out when Lieutenant Brady returns."

Clara and Beatrice walked to their usual spot and opened their lunch pails. In the distance, Clara spotted Jeremiah. "Your brother's heading our way."

Beatrice looked up and nodded. "You don't have to stay if you don't want to. I'm sure he's going to be mad as a wet hen when I tell him I didn't apologize."

"Maybe not. The major didn't give you a chance when you first tried." Clara withdrew a piece of bread slathered in jam from her pail. "Besides, even if you had apologized, the major had already talked to the colonel and made his decision. I'll speak up if Jeremiah doesn't believe you."

"Thanks, Clara. You're a true friend." She lifted her apple in salute. "Just remember, if you ever need a favor, I'll be there for you, too."

Six

oseph jolted awake and gasped for air. The night-mare had ended, but the gruesome memories of Bull Run lingered and ripped through him like a jagged knife. *Where am I?* He glanced around the room searching for something familiar—something to anchor him in the midst of his fear. Moonlight spilled through the open window and cast shadows on the plaster walls and stark furnishings. Then he remembered. *The Allegheny Arsenal.* He was in Pennsylvania. Lifting a corner of the clammy bedsheet, Joseph mopped the perspiration from his face.

Turning sideways in the bed, he lowered his feet to the floor and stared at his deformed foot. Until the night before his departure for Lawrenceville, he'd thought the nighttime terrors were over, that he'd succeeded in wiping the horrors of Bull Run from his mind. But he'd been proven wrong again. Tonight's terror had been as merciless as what he'd experienced during his first nights in the field hospital.

Soon after being released from the hospital, he'd learned to withstand the frequent pain and crippling effects of the surgeon's saw, but he couldn't control the ghoulish night-mares that still occasionally interrupted his sleep. Had his travel and lack of sleep caused their return? Or perhaps it was his fear of failure. What if he was unable to discover a method to improve production of the cartridges? Since he couldn't return and fight with his men, he wanted to serve the Union in any way he could. He needed to be a part of the effort, to contribute and be of some value.

Without sleep, he'd be no good to himself come morning. Though fully awake, he lay down and closed his eyes. Pleasant thoughts might lull him into a peaceful sleep. He pictured Clara McBride sitting beside his desk the day before he departed. She was certainly a pleasant thought. There was something unique about Clara. Clearly she was attractive, and yet it wasn't her overall appearance that had captured his attention. Not to say that her creamy complexion, the sparkle in her hazel eyes, or the perfect curve of her bow-shaped lips hadn't attracted him. They certainly had. But there was more to Clara McBride than her lovely appearance.

Despite life's hardships, she possessed a gentle spirit and a kindness that many had lost since the outbreak of the war. Not that he could blame anyone for losing heart. Life was difficult nowadays. He knew how tough it was to maintain a positive spirit. While he'd possessed a bleak outlook when he was assigned to the Washington Arsenal, his outlook had since changed. Accepting the idea that he was doing all he could for the war effort had helped, but meeting Clara had given him a more personal reason to change his attitude.

As a warm breeze drifted through the open window, he wondered if Clara was asleep or if she was lying in bed thinking of him at this very moment. He smiled at the thought. Tomorrow he should write and tell her of his eagerness to return to Washington—and her. He wasn't particularly good with words, but he longed to tell her how often she'd occupied his thoughts since he'd departed.

His thoughts were of Clara as he once again surrendered to slumber. Though he couldn't be certain how long he'd slept, it must have been several hours, for he awakened to a soldier calling cadence. He sat up and stared out the window. A ragtag group of men were skip-hopping down the parade field in a zigzagging formation. Before being dismissed for the day, they'd be required to maintain a straight line and keep in step, a feat that would likely prove exhausting and do little to preserve their lives when they charged into battle. Nowadays recruits received very little training. There wasn't time for anything more. Far too soon they'd be reassigned and sent to the front lines. Sadly, most of them appeared either too young or too old to be going off to war.

As Joseph lathered his face and scraped a straight razor along his jaw, leather soles continued to buffet the hardened dirt outside his window. After donning his uniform, he examined his foot and adjusted the padding before pulling on his right boot. A booming voice startled Joseph, and he stepped to the window. A sergeant was hurling insults at one of the young recruits. The boy lowered his head until his chin rested on his chest. His shoulders slumped as he melted into a puddle of defeat. Joseph clenched his hands into tight fists. Humiliation would never win the respect or loyalty of soldiers. The sergeant should know that.

He retrieved his hat, left his room, and walked down the hallway until he reached the door leading onto the parade field. He likely shouldn't interfere, yet his conscience wouldn't let him ignore what he'd seen. He stepped onto the parade field and silently watched the men attempting to follow orders. There was little doubt the sergeant was unhappy with their performance. The scowl on his face said it all.

When he spotted Joseph, he arched his brows. "Halt! At

ease," he shouted. Several men ran into each other, and many appeared unaware of exactly what they should do. The sergeant approached Joseph and saluted. Joseph returned the salute and nodded toward the recruits, who were mingling and chatting.

The sergeant followed Joseph's eyes and sighed. "They think 'at ease' means they're free to do whatever they'd like. This group is more difficult than most."

"They can sense your frustration, Sergeant. I know training recruits is tiresome, but it can also be very rewarding. Their success in battle depends upon the training they receive. You don't have much time to prepare them, so it's important to gain their trust and respect. I'm guessing that young soldier you insulted is more focused on his embarrassment than upon how to properly shoulder his weapon. Try using a bit of praise. I think you'll achieve greater success."

The sergeant's lip curled in disgust. "Do you? Well, I respectfully disagree, sir."

"Then consider this, Sergeant. I could have walked onto this parade field and upbraided you in front of these men. I could have shouted that you are the most inept drill instructor I've ever encountered and that you don't possess enough skill to train a starving dog to eat." Anger burned in the sergeant's eyes, but Joseph wasn't deterred. "Would such behavior cause you to improve?" Joseph shook his head. "I think not. Instead, you'd be watching those around you and weighing their reactions. You'd worry they would think less of you and feel you weren't able to train them properly. The same holds true for that boy over there. He needs comrades among these men. They need to believe in each other when they charge into battle, and you're the one who can give them the training and courage they need." Joseph smiled at the sergeant and rested a hand on his shoulder. "If you treat them with dignity and respect, you'll be amazed at how hard they will work for you."

The sergeant didn't appear totally convinced. "If you'll excuse me, I'll return to the men. As you can see, they're no longer in formation."

Joseph nodded. There was so much more he could say to the sergeant, but if he was going to be on time for breakfast, he couldn't linger. He retraced his steps from the evening before and spotted Sergeant Taft waiting outside the officers' mess.

He saluted and gestured toward the entrance. "I'll meet you back here in half an hour. The enlisted mess is through the door on the other side."

Joseph waited until the sergeant had departed before climbing the few steps and entering the mess hall. He wasn't surprised to find most of the tables empty. The officers would have already reported for duty. He filled his plate, crossed the room, and sat down at one of the long wooden tables. When he'd finished his meal, he returned outdoors. The heat inside the mess hall had proved stifling, though the temperature was steadily climbing outside, as well. Sitting on the steps would likely be frowned upon, so he crossed what had once been a grassy area and leaned against the trunk of a towering oak tree. The few remaining blades of grass had turned brown from lack of water, although the absence of rain hadn't lessened the humidity. The unbearable weather had seemingly followed him from Washington.

He was preparing a mental list of questions for the sergeant when the young man approached. "I'm sorry, Lieutenant, I didn't think you'd be ready so soon."

"No problem, Sergeant. I was attempting to find a cool

spot to wait while I gathered my thoughts, but I fear there isn't such a place."

"I doubt there's any place in all of Pittsburgh where you could enjoy a cool breeze." Sergeant Taft gestured toward the far side of the Arsenal. "The laboratory, storehouses, and freight yard are this way. The laboratory opens at six o'clock. I thought there would be less confusion if we began your tour after work commenced."

Dust plumed with each footfall and dulled their boots to the shade of freshly dug potatoes. As they circled past the parade field, Joseph sighed. No doubt the drill sergeant would have the new recruits shining their boots until well after nightfall, but he needed to cease worrying over the recruits and turn his attention to work within the laboratory.

"How many workers are currently employed in the lab?"

"There are one hundred and eighty-six civilians. One hundred and fifty-six of those are girls and women. The remainder are young boys and men. The women attend to their work and follow orders without question. They don't participate in tomfoolery and remain silent while working—at least most of the time." He grinned. "Are most of the employees at the Washington Arsenal women?"

Joseph nodded. "Yes. We have a fine group of ladies who put forth their best effort each day, but I'm eager to observe the processes being used in your workrooms."

As they neared the complex, the sergeant gestured to his left. "Butler Street is off to our north. The laboratory compound is made up of four buildings. The buildings are divided into specific workrooms and an office." He waved Joseph forward. "We have a total of six rooms where cartridges are made—all employ the same methods." He pushed down on the door latch and entered the first workroom.

Only a few ladies looked up when they entered the room. The others remained focused upon their work. The room wasn't much different from those at the Washington Arsenal.

Joseph watched as the workers rolled and placed cylinders in a wooden box. As soon as the box was full, a boy who'd been standing close to the wall rushed forward, picked up the box, and hurried out of the room.

Joseph arched his brows. "Is he taking the boxes to the filling room?"

The sergeant nodded. "His job is to watch these two tables. As soon as a box is full, he takes it to the filling room."

"So the ladies never move from their benches while they're working?"

"No." The sergeant frowned. "Unless there's an absolute need for them to do so, of course. Still, any movement by the ladies slows the process."

There was certainly something to be said about their process of saving time. It speeded the progression with the women continuing their duties while a boy moved the boxes to the filling room. On the other hand, the ladies at the Washington Arsenal would likely protest such a change. No doubt they looked forward to arriving at the end of the bench and having a few minutes' respite.

The two of them exited the room, stepped off the porch, and turned in an easterly direction. They walked past the building directly across from the cylinder room and on toward the next low-slung brick structure. As they stepped onto the porch, the cautionary words of a supervisor drifted on a humid breeze. "Careful with your funnels, ladies. I'm observing too much spillage this morning." The older man was pointing to the floor when they entered. Before acknowledging them, he signaled to a boy. "Get this powder swept up."

The supervisor waved them inside the filling room. Their visit was brief, however, since the procedures were no different from those used in Washington. After thanking the supervisor for his time, Joseph followed the sergeant outside as a wagon pulled alongside the porch. The driver jumped down, lifted a barrel of gunpowder onto the porch, and positioned it near the doorway to the filling room. On several occasions Joseph had noticed the barrels of gunpowder positioned outside the workrooms at the Washington Arsenal. He thought the practice dangerous, but his concerns had been dismissed. Seemingly, this procedure was utilized in all the arsenals—not that he now considered it wise, but he had hoped to discover another method while here. One that would reinforce his argument against the practice.

The shipping and packing rooms were near the large storage buildings close to the river. The same was true at the Washington Arsenal, where Greenleaf Point afforded them ease in shipping and receiving goods. The rapid delivery of ammunition to Union soldiers was a high priority, so he hoped to discover more efficient methods surrounding packing and distribution. Such a thing would be looked upon with favor by his superiors.

Sergeant Taft kept a steady pace as they continued toward the packing rooms. "We increased our working hours to twelve hours a day. I expected to hear complaints, but it seems news of the advancing Confederate Army struck fear in the hearts of the workers. We've had no complaints since extending our work hours."

"Our hours have been increased to twelve hours, as well. Much is expected of all our citizens."

"You've certainly given a great deal, Lieutenant." His gaze settled on Joseph's right boot.

"Many have given a great deal more." Joseph offered a wan smile. He didn't want to discuss his injury and was thankful they'd arrived at the packing rooms before the sergeant could say more.

Several women glanced in their direction as the sergeant escorted him into one of the packing rooms. Inside, the boxes of cartridges awaited the final steps before being sent to the battlefield. Ladies sat at tables, where ten cartridges were removed and placed in two alternating stacks of five. One stack was positioned with the bullet pointing up, the other positioned with the bullet down. A cylinder containing twelve percussion caps was included with the bundle of ten cartridges. Other workers labeled the bundles with the name of the Arsenal, the date, and the caliber of the cartridges before snugly packing them inside wooden crates.

The sergeant beckoned to the supervisor. "How many rounds of ammunition in each of the boxes?"

The thin, balding man stepped to the sergeant's side. "One thousand rounds. We can fit one hundred bundles in each box. There needs to be a snug fit so they aren't jostled around during shipment. We screw them shut here and then each box is painted with a waterproof material. Can't have our ammunition getting wet." The supervisor gestured toward the crates. "Most days we receive and pack one hundred twenty-eight thousand cartridges."

Joseph inhaled a sharp breath. If the Washington Arsenal was going to match numbers with Allegheny, he'd need to discover significant differences in their systems of production. Thus far he hadn't observed any substantial variances that would help. What was he going to do?

SEVEN

September 17, 1862

Before Joseph had an opportunity to visit the shipping and freight divisions yesterday, Sergeant Taft had been called to an emergency meeting. However, he'd offered to meet Joseph at ten o'clock this morning near the warehouses that edged the river. Joseph would have more than enough time to have breakfast and review his notes before meeting with the sergeant.

When Joseph entered the mess hall, Colonel Simon signaled to him. "Join me for breakfast, Lieutenant. I'll brief you on the latest happenings, since some of it has affected Washington."

Joseph's stomach clenched. *Clara.* Had General Lee turned his troops toward Washington? If so, had General McClellan been able to protect the city and its inhabitants? His heart pounded as he considered the tragic possibilities. He couldn't fathom the thought of Confederate troops seizing the capital. Even more, he couldn't imagine returning to Washington and discovering Clara had been injured or . . . He shook his head. *No!* He wouldn't let his mind go to such a dark place.

He'd posted a letter to her only a half hour ago. Clara had to be fine—she simply had to.

Joseph startled when the colonel cleared his throat. "Sit down, Lieutenant." Using his foot, the colonel pushed a chair away from the table, then waved to a private on the other side of the room.

The young man rushed across the room. "Yes, Colonel?"

"Bring the lieutenant coffee and fill a plate for him."

The private hurried away to do the colonel's bidding before Joseph could say that the mention of trouble in Washington had been enough to ruin his appetite.

"What news have you, sir?" Joseph leaned forward. He didn't want to miss a word.

"None of it is particularly good, I'm afraid. Lee's troops crossed the Potomac about thirty miles west of Washington on September fourth. They marched north and encamped at Frederick, Maryland, on September the seventh."

The knot in Joseph's stomach eased a bit. "So they didn't attempt an assault on the capital?"

"No. I've learned General McClellan led eighty-five thousand Union troops out of Washington to face Lee. My report states there are still seventy-two thousand men left to defend Washington. I believe Washington will remain safe. From what I've received, it appears Lee seeks a victory farther north. We can only pray that McClellan stops him in time." He downed the remainder of the coffee in his cup. "You'll need to take great care on your return. Travel will be dangerous. You might be safer if you don't wear your uniform, but I'll leave that decision to you."

The news wasn't as bad as Joseph had anticipated. Still, it wasn't good—at least not for the Union. While he was relieved to know that Confederate troops hadn't entered the capital, he still harbored concerns. Before he departed the mess hall, he decided he would request approval to return to Washington the following morning. Even if he hadn't yet inspected the entire facility, the remaining divisions weren't going to answer the question as to why more cartridges were being produced at this Arsenal. His decision was clear: He didn't want to be away from Clara or Washington a moment longer than was necessary.

He returned to his room in the barracks and flipped through the pages of his journal. His attention settled on an entry he'd made last night. *Powder barrels are situated outside the filling room and at both ends of the porches.* Having barrels of gunpowder close at hand was a time-saving method, yet the danger seemed to outweigh the benefits of the practice. Nevertheless, he'd include it in his report. The decision wouldn't be his to make, though he would express his concerns to Colonel Furman upon his return to Washington. After reading through the remainder of his notes, he closed the book with a *snap* and headed to meet the sergeant.

Each day since his arrival, the heat and humidity had proved taxing, and today was no different. Even a brief shower would be a reason to rejoice, but the skies remained crystalline blue. The only clouds in sight were as white as a fresh winter snow. He'd been told the weather hadn't changed for more than six weeks. And, from all appearances, it wasn't difficult to believe. Deep cracks rutted the grassless terrain, making it difficult to keep from twisting an ankle. He'd soon learned to keep one eye focused upon the ground.

He picked up his pace. He didn't want to keep the sergeant waiting. By the time he arrived, his breathing was coming hard and perspiration trickled down the sides of his face. He returned the sergeant's salute as he approached.

"Appears the heat may be getting the best of you, Lieutenant. We'll take it slow."

Joseph wanted to say there was no need to slow down on his account, but it wouldn't have been true. In addition to the heat, painful cramps surged through his right foot and up his leg.

"I thought we'd begin in the freight department." The sergeant motioned toward the arched openings of a one-story brick structure. "The tall, arched doorways situated on both sides of these structures make for easier access for loading and deliveries."

While the sergeant was speaking, a brawny young man approached. "How can I help?" He trained his eyes toward the doors rather than looking at Joseph or the sergeant.

The sergeant made the necessary introductions and then arched his brows. "Are you the supervisor of this division?"

"I am now. Mr. Holiday enlisted last week, so I was assigned to his position." He swiped his palm on his pant leg and extended his hand to Joseph. "Hiram Scott." He pumped Joseph's hand with unusual vigor. "I tried to enlist, but them recruiters wouldn't take me. Hard to be told that a big strappin' fella like me ain't good enough to fight for the Union. The recruiter said I wasn't fit for duty 'cause of these." He rolled back his upper lip and revealed his toothless gums. "I didn't know front teeth was needed to tear open the gunpowder cartridges." He shrugged. "They said I wouldn't be able to load my rifle quick enough."

Joseph gave a nod. "The recruiters were wise to send you home, Hiram. Your work here is important, too. Without men like you, our soldiers wouldn't have the ammunition needed to win the war."

Hiram offered a toothless smile as he moved his arm in

a sweeping gesture. "What interests you most, Lieutenant? We can start wherever you want."

"I'm interested in the entire freight and shipping process. You'd know best where we should begin."

The supervisor squared his shoulders and started toward the far end of the building. "The cartridges being shipped out are loaded on wagons at the warehouse and delivered through these doors. So far we've been able to keep at least one of the warehouses full at all times. Don't know how long that will last. Shipments have increased over the last couple weeks. I hear the Rebs are having success heading north and they ain't too far away."

Joseph drew closer to the young man. "It's true there's lots of rumors flying around, but it's probably best if we quell any unfounded reports. Folks are already gripped with fear. No need to frighten them any further."

"I s'pose you're right." He stopped as they neared the arched doorway at the far end. "That wagonload will be going down to the dock to load onto the boats. The cartridge crates are painted with waterproof material, and each crate is marked, just like the boxes inside."

Joseph inspected the crates, and for the remainder of the morning he and Sergeant Taft accompanied Hiram through-out the freight and shipping department. They agreed to meet again at two o'clock to inspect the warehouses and boat docks.

Thankful for the respite, Joseph decided to forgo the noon-day meal and return to his room. Even though his stomach growled in protest, elevating his foot for the next two hours would do him more good than a meal. He might even revisit the laboratories. At breakfast, the colonel mentioned he had ordered an increase of the cartridge quotas for the lab work-ers. Joseph wondered what methods the supervisors would use to meet the increased quota and how the workers had received the news. While Joseph believed some success in the labs could be attributed to technique and process, he thought the attitude and motivation of workers was of greater import. He'd seen his belief proven on the battlefield when fewer men with determination and grit had won skirmishes against an enemy who was greater in number and better equipped.

Joseph sat down on the bed, removed his boot, placed a pillow over a footrest nearby, and lifted it to the lower portion of the bed. He lay back and gingerly situated his lower leg atop the pillow-draped footrest. Closing his eyes, he sighed. The foot continued to throb, but at least the cramps had subsided. Thoughts of Clara and his upcoming journey marched through his mind. How long would it take him to return, and would he encounter danger along the way? His skin prickled at the idea of encountering Rebel troops. He hadn't feared charging into battle at Bull Run, but he hadn't been alone. He'd relied on the support of his fellow soldiers. There would be no one but himself to rely upon on his return to Washington.

He forced the thoughts from his mind. Worry wouldn't change a thing, but prayer might help. While he silently prayed, his breathing slowed to a deep, restful cadence, and his body melded into the crooks and curves of the lumpy mattress.

Sometime later, he jolted upright in his bed, startled by the drill sergeant's shouts outside his window. How long had he been asleep? He reached for his pocket watch. He was supposed to be at the warehouse in fifteen minutes. Moving with haste, he pulled on his boots and grabbed his hat. There wouldn't be time to stop at the laboratories before his meeting, but perhaps he could stop on his return. He disliked being late, and this was the second time in one day that he'd likely keep Sergeant Taft waiting.

After rounding the building, Joseph turned left. As he prepared to cross the expanse toward the warehouses, the ground beneath him shook in a violent quake, and he dropped facedown in the dirt. His heart pounded in his ears. Were they under attack? How could General Lee and his troops have made it this far without being discovered?

Screams and shouts filled the air. He lifted his head, glanced about, and stood. Smoke curled in the air above the laboratories. He'd taken only a few steps when another explosion erupted. He staggered. The deafening sound rivaled any battlefield. Even at a distance, he could see the flames shooting upward and hear the screams of the women. *No! Not the laboratory!*

If only he could run more quickly. He silently cursed his deformed foot as he attempted to pick up his pace. Less than a minute later, yet another explosion rocked the earth. Thousands of rounds of ammunition exploded. He was now close enough to see fire and wood catapult and fly in all directions. A picture of the gunpowder barrels sitting outside the cartridge room flashed through his mind. No wonder the whole place had gone up.

He scanned the area. The destruction was unfathomable. The carnage and horror were as great as anything he'd experienced on the battlefield. Yet rather than soldiers, women and children were being ravaged by the exploding gunpowder and flames. Heat radiated throughout the area, and girls rolled on the ground, their clothes devoured by flames. Somehow he had to help. Shielding his face from the heat with an upraised arm, he approached one of the rooms. The ceiling crashed to the floor, the impact forcing him backward.

Chaos reigned. Men from Lawrenceville pulled their new fire truck up a hill and began pumping water from a nearby pond. Some of the men formed a bucket brigade while others covered the screaming girls' burning dresses with coats or shirts. Relatives arrived. Panic shone in their eyes as they surveyed the area, each one hoping to find his wife, daughter, or sister alive. Some clambered over the smoldering rubble, seeking a familiar trinket or piece of fabric that might help them identify the bodies that lay before them.

A woman old enough to be his mother grabbed Joseph's arm. "Help me find my daughter! Please!" Tears streamed down her weathered cheeks. "She's all I've got left."

Her agonized plea cut Joseph to the core. How could he refuse her? "Do you know where she worked? The room number?"

"Number four, but I've never been here before. I don't know where it is."

Joseph's heart plummeted. He feared rooms one, three, and four had been the site of the first explosion, and there was little hope this woman's daughter was alive. "I'm sorry, but I believe number four was destroyed in the first blast."

"Please!" She pulled on his arm. "You have to try."

He nodded and held on to the woman as they circled around the debris. When they neared the collapsed building, the woman clasped a hand to her mouth and stifled a scream. In the midst of the ashes lay twisted metal hoops from the girls' crinolines, shoes, pieces of clothing, shattered glass, and charred fragments of wood.

"No!" Her scream pierced the air. The grieving woman turned into Joseph's chest, and he held her tightly.

"Mama! Mama!"

Joseph turned toward the voice. A young woman held her

skirts high as she navigated her way through the ashes and rubble. The mother gasped and ran from Joseph's arms to meet her daughter. They came together in a crushing embrace only a few feet from him.

The mother cradled her daughter's face between her hands. "I thought . . ." Her words ended in a wailing cry.

"I know what you thought, but I'm fine, Mama." The girl took a backward step. "Look at me. I'm not injured. There were several of us who went late to lunch and were still in line to collect our pay. The ground shook beneath us during the explosions, and Lucy was injured by flying glass. Otherwise, we were the fortunate ones." She stepped forward and once again gathered her mother in an embrace.

A fireman passed by with his hands cupped to his mouth. "Only those looking for relatives or helping clear the damage should remain in the area. The rest of you need to go home."

The mother encircled Joseph in an unexpected embrace. "Thank you for your help. I'm more grateful than you can imagine."

The warmth of the woman's embrace lingered as Joseph offered a prayer of thanks for the workers who had been spared. Then he prayed for the grieving families of those who had perished. They would need strength to overcome this tragic day and the losses they'd suffered.

He walked toward one of the buildings that still stood. Dropping onto the steps, he shuddered. So much devastation. So many victims. If this could happen here, couldn't the same happen in Washington? Was this the cost of higher production? What if Clara was injured or killed?

Silently, he vowed to keep her safe—even if it meant they didn't make the higher quotas.

EIGHT

Clara wiped a tear from her cheek as she packed her lunch. All those who supported the Union were mourning the losses suffered at Antietam Creek. No one had been prepared for the horrific casualties of September 17. When the troops assigned to the Washington Arsenal had marched out the front gates to support General McClellan, no one considered there could be losses in excess of two thousand. Truth be told, most of them had been too busy cheering the soldiers onward. To even think that Union soldiers might die or be reported injured or missing seemed unpatriotic.

So many losses. Would this war ever end?

Clara picked up her lunch bundle and kissed her mother on the cheek. "What time are you expected at the Seward residence?"

"Not until four o'clock this afternoon. She apologized for the lateness, but she tells me her schedule has been unusually difficult lately. I believe that means she's been required to entertain a great deal." She sighed. "In any event, I couldn't object. She's pleased with my work and has recommended me to several of her acquaintances. She says I'm the most talented seamstress she's ever employed." Her mother chuck-led. "Of course, I may be the only one she's ever hired."

"I doubt that! She's the wife of the secretary of state. The wives of influential men always employ maids and seam-stresses." Clara reached for her bonnet. "You'll likely be there late. I'll come over after work and walk home with you."

"Mrs. Seward said she'd have her driver bring me home. That means she's going to want numerous changes to the gown, so you're right, it will be late. You need to get your rest. Don't wait up for me." Her mother followed her to the door. "You best hurry or you'll be tardy."

The wind whipped at Clara's bonnet as she hurried toward the corner of O and 4 ½ Streets and merged into the press of harried workers. She wondered if she bore the same dis-concerted expression. Things had changed since Antietam. Although General McClellan had claimed a Union victory when General Lee retreated across the Potomac to Virginia, a mingling sense of foreboding and urgency remained among them.

"Hey, Clara! Wait up!"

Clara glanced over her shoulder and caught sight of Jer-emiah and Beatrice weaving through the throng. She slowed her pace, but she didn't dare stop. Coming to a halt in this crowd could get one knocked to the ground.

An older woman shoved Clara's arm and pushed her for-ward. "Keep movin'! I don't plan to be late 'cause you want to flirt with your beau."

"He's not my beau." Clara took a sideways step to let her pass. The woman didn't respond, but instead pushed and wriggled in front of two other workers.

Moments later, Jeremiah edged alongside her and nod-ded toward the woman. "That one is sure in a hurry to get through the gates. She must enjoy her work more than the rest of us."

Once Beatrice caught up to them, she looped arms with Clara. "Morning, Clara. Did Jeremiah tell you the news?"

Jeremiah's brows slanted in a frown. "I didn't say nothing. I know how you are. You'd get your back up and be mad at me if I told her."

The muscles in Clara's stomach tightened. After learning of the recent losses suffered at Sharpsburg, she wasn't prepared for another dreadful report. "Is it good or bad news?"

Bea gave a broad smile. "It's good news. President Lincoln issued a preliminary Emancipation Proclamation, freeing all slaves in the Confederate states next January. The slaves will be forever free. Isn't that exciting?" Bea smiled and arched her brows.

Clara dipped her head in a faint nod. Though the news sounded encouraging, the president's proclamation wouldn't end the war. The South had seceded to maintain owner-ship of slaves, and the plantation owners weren't going to set their slaves free just because President Lincoln signed a paper. In truth, the document might strengthen the resolve of the Confederate Army and incite their soldiers to dig in even harder. She prayed not, but the South was as dedicated to their beliefs as the North was to theirs.

"I thought you'd be excited." Bea's somber tone revealed her disappointment.

Clara wanted to rejoice, but after hearing how many had died in Sharpsburg, news of a proclamation seemed trifling. "I'm pleased for the slaves, although I have my doubts the slave owners are going to willingly free them when they don't even recognize Mr. Lincoln as their president. I'll be over-joyed, however, when we hear that the war has ended."

Jeremiah snorted. "Well, it's gonna be a long time before that happens. The war's only just begun, and General Lee's gonna be aching to win his next battle. Winning and losing are matters of pride to military officers. I'd wager that right at this minute he's preparing to attack McClellan."

Clara didn't want to discuss military tactics or think about more men dying on the battlefield. She glanced toward Beatrice. "Where did you get your copy of yesterday's newspaper?"

Jeremiah jutted his neck forward. "A fellow who lives in the downstairs apartment left it on the steps, and I snagged it. I'm not sure if he meant to leave it behind, but I wanted to read something besides week-old news, so I grabbed it. Bea and I spent last evening reading." He lightly elbowed his sister. "You should have brought it for Clara."

Bea's forehead creased. "I'm sorry, Clara. I should have thought of that. I'll put the newspaper near my lunch pail this evening so I don't forget it tomorrow. There were some articles about a few small skirmishes in Virginia and Maryland, and a piece that said General Lee had been hoping to blow up the rails leading into Washington. We can all be glad that didn't happen."

Clara was thankful for that bit of news. Without an operational railroad to bring in reinforcements, Washington might have been captured by Lee. Such a thought was frightening. The three of them squeezed among the crowd entering the archway that led into the Arsenal. When Bea and Clara turned toward the laboratory, Jeremiah split off and headed for the freight and shipping department.

Bea followed Clara into the cylinder room, where Major Rourke stood at the end of the worktables with a sullen look on his face. The two girls hurried to the far wall to hang their bonnets and lunch bundles.

Beatrice tipped her head close as she removed her bonnet. "I'll sure be glad when Lieutenant Brady gets back. Major Rourke is always unhappy about something. He's already scowling and the day hasn't even begun. I feel sorry for his wife, if he has one."

Clara stifled a giggle and dared a quick look at Major Rourke as she hastened to take her place at the worktable. He appeared even more annoyed than usual.

"I have an announcement before you begin work today," the major said. "There has been a tragic explosion at the Allegheny Arsenal near Pittsburgh, and many of the workers were either killed or injured."

The room swam before Clara's eyes. She clasped her hands together, anchoring herself to the moment. She needed to hear the rest.

One of the ladies at the far end of the room leaned across the table. "When did it happen?"

The major set his wrinkled face in a scowl. "Please don't interrupt until I've finished. Then if you have questions, you may ask them."

"Yes, sir." She gave him a mock salute before plopping down on the bench.

Bea covered her mouth with her palm. "That was foolish. He'll make her life miserable from now on."

Right now, Clara didn't care about the possible difficulties Major Rourke might cause her fellow worker. She had to know if the lieutenant had been injured.

The major cleared his throat and withdrew a news clipping from his pocket. "This is a very brief article from the Washington *Evening Star*, September eighteenth. The explosion took place on September seventeenth, the same day as the Battle of Antietam near Sharpsburg. The newspapers devoted most of their pages to reports on the war, which is to be expected. However, the news of such an explosion is also of high importance, especially to those who work in a similar facility."

Clara squeezed her hands until her knuckles turned white. If she relaxed her hold for even a moment, she'd lose control and raise her hand. Her breathing had turned shallow, and her heart pounded like the thundering hooves of cavalry horses.

Major Rourke cast a quick glance around the worktables. "The article is captioned 'Explosion at Allegheny Arsenal—Eighty Lives Lost.'" There were gasps around the tables. The major waited until there was silence again. "The article reads as follows: 'A most frightful explosion occurred at the Allegheny Arsenal this afternoon about two o'clock, in the large frame building known as The Laboratory. About one hundred seventy-six boys and girls were employed in the building at the time of the disaster, of which number seventy-five or so were killed. One explosion followed another until the whole building was destroyed. Those who could not escape in time were burnt up.

"'The scene was most appalling. Dead bodies lying in heaps as they had fallen and, in some places where the heat was intense, whitened bones could be seen through the smoke and flames, whilst at other points large masses of blackened flesh was presented to the eye.

"'Up to the present time, sixty-three bodies have been taken from the ruins. The cause of the explosion is not yet known, but admitted by all to have been accidental.'"

The low hum of voices soon accelerated to a fever pitch. Clara raised her hand, but even if Major Rourke acknowledged her, it would be impossible to make herself heard over the din. Beatrice grasped Clara's arm. "What a terrible tragedy." She glanced around the room. "That could happen to us!"

"Lieutenant Brady is there." Clara pushed the words from between her dry lips.

"That's right. I'd almost forgotten. Do you think he survived? He went there to observe their laboratory, didn't he?"

Clara nodded. She couldn't bear to talk about him with Bea.

Without warning, a shrill whistle filled the room. Major Rourke stood before them with two fingers strategically inserted between his lips. The ladies turned toward him and fell silent.

The major lowered his hand to his side. "I hope I won't be required to do that again. I do understand your alarm, but all this chatter among yourselves isn't going to change a thing. However, we can pray for all those who have been touched by this disaster, and I'm sure each of you will do so." He inhaled a deep breath. "Now, I do have a further report."

Clara shifted her attention to the major. She didn't know if she could bear further bad news.

"Colonel Furman has received word from Lieutenant Brady." The major paused.

Not wanting to miss a word, she leaned in, held her breath, and offered a silent prayer. *Please, God. Let him be unharmed.*

The major clasped his hands behind his back. "The lieutenant reports that he was not at the laboratory at the time of the explosion."

Tears pooled in Clara's eyes. Hoping no one would notice, she dipped her head and retrieved a handkerchief from her pocket.

"Lieutenant Brady had planned to leave Pittsburgh on the

eighteenth but delayed his departure due to the explosion. His return to Washington will be determined by whether there is a need for him to remain at the Allegheny Arsenal until their investigation has been completed and by his ability to coordinate travel. With Confederate troops penetrating the North, travel is both difficult and dangerous. That said, we look forward to the lieutenant's safe and speedy return."

A lady at the back of the room raised her hand. "Do they know why the explosion happened?"

The major shook his head. "A full report hasn't been issued. Officers at the Arsenal are conducting a thorough investigation as to the cause. As I said, it was declared an accident, which is why I thought it necessary to read the tragic details printed in the newspaper. Accidents can be avoided if we are vigilant. I know you tire of hearing the ongoing reminders to exercise care, but we don't want further tragedies at any of our arsenals."

Once the ladies had bobbed their heads and hummed agreement, they continued to visit among themselves. Beatrice nudged Clara with her elbow. "Were you crying when the major was talking about Lieutenant Brady?"

Clara shook her head. "I had something in my eye, and I was attempting to get it out."

Beatrice cupped Clara's chin and looked into her eyes. "Hmm. I don't see anything."

Clara pulled away. "That's because it isn't there any longer."

"That's certainly good news." Beatrice tipped her head to the side. "I was sad to hear the lieutenant won't be returning for a while longer, weren't you?"

"Of course. I think we all miss him. He's much nicer than Major Rourke."

"And certainly much better looking, don't you agree?" Bea arched her eyebrows.

"Yes, but even if he weren't handsome, I'd think him a better supervisor. Major Rourke issues commands like we're a group of recruits. His methods seem to create resentment, and he's too aloof. The lieutenant is far more approachable." Clara checked herself. If she continued dithering on, there would be little doubt that she cared for the lieutenant, a matter she didn't care to disclose to Beatrice, or anyone else for that matter—at least not now. "I'm sure we're all thankful he wasn't injured."

Bea's lips slanted in a sly grin. "Some of us more than others, I think."

The ladies startled when a loud crack reverberated at the end of the table. Major Rourke held his riding crop overhead. "I don't want to strike the table again, ladies. Please cease your chattering. There has been ample time to digest today's news. If you wish to visit further, you can do so away from the workroom." He lowered his riding crop to his side. "Please remember what we've discussed here this morning. There is an urgent need to be careful at all times." He pointed to the supplies on the worktable. "Begin work!"

Bea looped her hand through Clara's arm as the two of them departed the laboratory and walked toward their usual spot beneath the large oak. After they'd settled, Bea opened her lunch pail and watched Clara for several moments. Other than the day after his departure, they'd spoken little of Lieutenant Brady. Whenever Bea mentioned his name, Clara managed to redirect their conversation. Truth be told, she'd never explained why the lieutenant had singled her out the evening before his departure. Why had he chosen to tell Clara he had been ordered to the Allegheny Arsenal? While there might be several possibilities, the one that seemed most obvious was a romantic interest between the two. And after seeing Clara's reaction earlier this morning, Bea was determined to find out if her assumption was correct.

Bea lifted an apple from her pail and polished it with the hem of her skirt. "You didn't fool me with that story about having something in your eye, Clara. I know those tears were caused by your concern for the lieutenant. There's more between the two of you than you've told me."

Clara didn't look up. "Perhaps."

Bea frowned. "I thought we were friends. There must be some reason the lieutenant decided to tell only you that he was leaving for Pittsburgh."

"I wasn't the only one who knew he had been ordered to the Allegheny Arsenal. Major Rourke and—"

"I know there were other soldiers aware of his orders. What I'm saying is that you were the only lab worker he chose to tell. I think that's because he cares for you." Bea held the apple in the palm of her hand and twisted the stem until it broke free. "I'm right, aren't I?"

Clara sighed. "I weighed whether I should tell you."

"Why didn't you? We're friends, aren't we?"

"Yes, but I suspicioned you had feelings for him, too. I couldn't decide if it was better to tell you or not. I think I was waiting for the right time."

Bea arched her brows. "This seems to be the right time, don't you agree?" Her stomach churned as Clara recounted the details of the conversation she'd had with the lieutenant—and their agreement to correspond.

Bea clenched her hands. She had been certain she could

win him for herself, but it appeared that wasn't going to happen. She wondered how long the lieutenant had admired Clara from afar. Had orders to leave Washington been necessary before he could gather the courage to speak up? If she'd begun working in the laboratory a week or two earlier, could she have won his affections? There was no way to be sure, yet she did know she couldn't let this ruin her friendship with Clara—it was too important.

Clara reached forward and squeezed Bea's hand. "I should have told you. I hope you haven't lost any eligible suitors because of this."

"You need not worry. There haven't been any men gathered outside the apartment pining for me." Bea forced a smile. "Besides, I only want a suitor who is the perfect man for me. I hope the lieutenant will prove to be the perfect man for you."

"Thank you, Bea. That's most kind. I've been worried this might harm our friendship."

"No, of course not. The lieutenant never gave me any reason to think he would ever be interested in me, so how could I let this come between us? I value your friendship much more than something so insignificant. Besides, I'm always pleased when someone I care for finds true happiness."

Clara returned the remnants of her breakfast into her pail and stood. She extended her hand to Bea and helped her up. "We'd better get back. We can talk more about this at noonday break."

Bea shook her head. "There's nothing more to say. I think you've answered all my questions. Now we must hope the lieutenant makes a quick return so that things return to normal in the laboratory."

Clara pulled her into a quick hug. "Thank you, Bea. I was

afraid this was going to be the end of our friendship, but you've proved me wrong."

Bea wanted to tell her that under different circumstances, this would have been more than enough to end their friendship. But these were different times. Besides, men were frequently known to change their minds. Once the lieutenant returned, who could say what might happen? Bea allowed that thought to salve her wounded spirit as she stepped inside the laboratory.

The days that followed the explosion had resulted in both physical and mental exhaustion. Joseph's nightmares had returned and permeated his sleep with fragmentary horrors, only now the recent explosion mingled with the sounds of cannon blasts and gunfire from battle. Even so, he'd felt compelled to attend the inquest and listen to the witnesses describe the events surrounding the explosion.

Although many had considered it far too soon to begin an inquest, the county coroner set the wheels in motion the morning following the explosion. Joseph had been surprised that the commander agreed to a civilian inquest rather than demanding a military investigation. However, it seemed the commander wanted answers as quickly as possible.

When several families objected, the newspaper carried an article that quoted the coroner as stating he needed access to unsullied memories of the incident. In addition, he pointed out that the Confederate Army was approaching northern borders, and this incident might be an act of war and not a workplace accident. He ended his comments by asserting that the sooner he completed his investigation, the sooner the Arsenal could return to supplying Union troops with much-needed ammunition. The coroner's explanation had the desired effect, and he had proceeded with vigor.

The witnesses had appeared, and one after another they detailed the events leading up to the explosion. Joseph carefully listened to each of the witnesses. The wagon driver who had been delivering barrels of gunpowder testified that immediately before flames engulfed the gunpowder, he'd seen a spark shoot up from his horse's rear shoe when it connected with the wagon wheel directly behind it. When questioned about his injuries, the fellow stated he'd been thrown from the wagon by the force of the explosion and he'd received only a few scrapes and bruises—a fact that amazed Joseph.

The wagon driver's testimony was later confirmed by one of the girls who had been on lunch break at the time. She'd been walking on the porch of Room Number 12 when she saw a spark fly from beneath the horse's hoof and the resulting flame that lit the gunpowder barrels.

There were several quarry workers who stated that the stone road outside the laboratory had been a foolish idea. One by one they testified that the stone used for the road would spark when struck by metal. Another mentioned the dry conditions hadn't helped matters, either.

Testimony of the quarry workers had been followed by several laboratory workers who swore the supervisors were lax in making the boys sweep up and gather the loose gunpowder. Two of the lab workers stated the boys swept loose powder into the roadway, and the supervisors knew of their actions but didn't reprimand the boys.

The days of testimony had been grueling, and the decision of the inquest jury had created considerable upheaval. The decision had been divided, but the majority ruled that primary fault lay with the colonel and two of the lieutenants assigned to the laboratory. The other jurors stated they didn't believe any members of the military were at fault, and they placed blame on two of the civilian supervisors.

Along with many others, Joseph had been stunned by the decision. He'd been certain the civilian supervisors would be held accountable, so he wasn't surprised when the colonel immediately requested a military investigation to replace the civilian decision. Joseph didn't blame him. Although going through another proceeding would be difficult for all concerned, he didn't understand how the colonel and lieutenants could be held responsible. None of them had been present at the time of the explosion, none of them had been present when the roadway was installed, and none of them directly supervised any of the civilian employees.

While Joseph thought another investigation necessary, he hoped he wouldn't be around when it ensued. Listening to the testimony one time had been more than enough. He was ready to return to Washington and see to the safety of his own workers—and Clara.

NINE

Joseph arrived in Washington after midnight. His mind and body were as worn and weary as when he'd been discharged from the hospital following his injuries at Bull Run. But instead of wounded and dying soldiers plaguing his thoughts, his mind was seared with visions of the charred and dismembered bodies of women and children—many so unrecognizable that only the attendance records could be used to acknowledge their presence on that fateful day. A mass grave had been prepared for them, a haunting reminder of the soldiers he'd seen buried in the same manner. He hadn't yet forced the horrors of Bull Run from his mind, so how could he ever forget what he'd witnessed in Lawrenceville?

The explosion in Lawrenceville had been overshadowed by the catastrophic losses at the Battle of Antietam, but some now referred to September 17 as the bloodiest day in the nation's history. For most of the residents of Lawrenceville, the deaths on that ill-fated day hadn't been soldiers, but sisters, daughters, mothers, and wives—meagerly paid government workers who would never again return to their homes.

Nevertheless, life had gone on—at least for some. Two

weeks after the explosion, the commander requisitioned another building to be used as the laboratory, and the newspaper ran ads for open positions at the Arsenal. Girls and women lined up to fill those jobs. If they were frightened, they suppressed their anxiety. Despite the charred ground and absent buildings, the young ladies acted as if nothing had happened. They needed to earn a living, and the Union needed the cartridges they would produce.

After arriving at the Washington Arsenal and settling in his barracks, sleep had eluded Joseph, and morning came far too soon. He longed for more rest, but realizing he'd soon see Clara gave him the incentive to get out of bed and into his uniform. Forgoing breakfast, he walked toward headquarters, doing as much as he could to conceal his limp. Colonel Furman would expect a detailed report before Joseph returned to his regular duties as supervisor in the cartridge lab. While he planned to outline his findings, he wanted to avoid detailing the ugliness he'd observed.

A private announced Joseph's arrival to the colonel, who greeted him at the door to his office. "Good to see you, Lieutenant Brady. I received word from Colonel Simon that you'd departed. I thought it might take you a little longer to get here, what with some of the trains operating on irregular schedules." He patted Joseph on the shoulder and gestured to the chair opposite his desk. "Have a seat. I'm pleased to see you've returned to us unharmed."

Joseph settled into the chair. "It's good to be back, sir." When he'd first received this assignment to the Washington Arsenal, he never thought he'd say that, but he meant every word. It was good to be back where he could resume a somewhat normal existence. He needed hope for brighter days—they all did.

"I've read only a brief newspaper report of the explosion. That account was enough for me to know we must do everything possible to prevent such an event here in Washington." He leaned back in his chair. "I've seen no report giving a cause for the explosion. What can you tell me in that regard?"

Joseph detailed the findings of the coroner's inquest. "I don't know when the military investigation will be completed, but I'm sure Colonel Simon will keep you advised. As far as I know, it hasn't yet begun. As I mentioned earlier, everyone agreed that a spark from the horse's hoof caused the explosion and fire. However, there was disagreement as to who should be held responsible."

"Unofficially, then, what do you think? Do you believe the explosion could have been prevented?"

"Sir, since we are working with gunpowder, it's impossible to say. I do believe there are practices that would make the Arsenal safer."

The colonel tapped his fingers atop his desk. "We need to have a complete examination of our lab. Wherever there are shortcomings, we must immediately see that they are corrected. Any worker who fails to comply with our safety rules must be discharged. We don't want to have more lives lost due to poor preparation or training. I'll expect a written report of your experience there, and I will then call a meeting of all supervisors to discuss any immediate changes needed in our facility."

The colonel stood, a clear indication their meeting was over. Joseph followed suit, pleased to be finished with the interview. Writing a detailed report wouldn't be difficult, since he'd maintained a journal while in Lawrenceville. Still, he wished he could offer more to ensure the safety of the workers here. He exhaled a long sigh as he neared the colonel's office door.

"By the way, Lieutenant, I believe Major Rourke will be pleased to see you've returned. I've heard a few rumblings that he hasn't enjoyed his temporary assignment." The colonel chuckled. "The major is accustomed to commanding soldiers, but he discovered that supervising women requires a different approach. From what I'm told, he's been slow to adjust."

Joseph grinned. "Thank you, Colonel. I was fearful he might want to remain in the lab. It's good to know the major will welcome my return."

Clara winced. "What?" She frowned at Beatrice, whose sharp elbow had jabbed her in the ribs.

"Look!" Beatrice tipped her head toward the door.

Clara inhaled a sharp breath. The lieutenant was back. *Finally.* She'd received only one letter from him, which had been written before the explosion. She couldn't withhold her smile. How she wished she could jump up from the table and welcome him—tell him how much she'd missed him. Would he think her too forward to say such a thing? Perhaps not. His sweet letter to her had voiced his desire to return and spend time with her.

She glanced at the other ladies, and their smiles were as broad as her own. All of them were pleased to see him. The workers couldn't wait to be rid of Major Rourke and his blustering, angry behavior.

Major Rourke's broad smile pushed his beefy cheeks upward until his eyes were no more than slits. He jumped up from the desk and waved the lieutenant forward with enthusiastic abandon. Clara had never seen the major appear so elated. As Lieutenant Brady passed, his arm brushed Clara's back and sent a tingling sensation racing up her spine. She couldn't be certain he'd intended to make physical contact with her, but she certainly hoped so.

The two officers saluted before the major extended his hand to the lieutenant. "I can't tell you how happy I am to see you." He narrowed his eyes and looked him up and down. "Glad to see you didn't suffer any injuries in that explosion. Our reports have been meager." The major stepped closer and lowered his voice.

"The major doesn't want us to hear what he's saying." Beatrice reached across the table, retrieved a precut paper, and ducked her head close to Clara. "He's probably telling the lieutenant about our unruly behavior and how I nearly instigated a walkout."

"The lieutenant has always been fair-minded. I don't think he'll take the major's word without further investigation. I'm sure he'll be reasonable and won't hold it against you." Clara kept her head bowed, barely moving her lips as she spoke. The major liked nothing more than to reprimand the ladies for talking during work. They all knew why the rules were in place, yet it was difficult to sit squashed together for hours on end without saying a word to each other.

The major strode to the end of the table and tapped his riding crop on the edge. "Ladies, as you can see, Lieutenant Brady has returned from his duties at the Allegheny Arsenal. This means I will be returning to my previous assignment, and the lieutenant will take over as your supervisor. I hope you will continue to do your best to produce the necessary ammunition for our brave Union soldiers so they may win the war." The major appeared startled when the ladies burst into applause. "I'm certain you're applauding because I'm leaving, but I truly don't mind. I'm as pleased to leave as you are to have me go." That said, he strode from the building, his heavy footfalls echoing his departure.

Lieutenant Brady stepped into the space recently vacated by the major. "It is good to be back in Washington." He smiled and let his gaze sweep over the ladies, making eye contact with each. "I want to have a meeting with all of you to discuss some important issues. I will want your full attention during the meeting, so I won't want any work conducted during that time. However, I know your pay is dependent upon attaining quotas, so I'm going to let you decide if you want to relinquish a portion of your breakfast or your lunch break so you can continue to meet your quotas. If you would rather have the meeting during work hours, I'm willing to do that, as well. You ladies will decide what will work best."

"We get to vote?" One of the girls hadn't been able to contain her enthusiasm.

He nodded. "Yes, but in order to allow for secret voting, I'm placing a box and slips of paper on my desk. If you want to have the meeting during work hours, mark an X on your paper and drop it in the box. If you want to have the meeting during breakfast or lunch break, mark an O on your paper. In order to be sure no one votes more than once, the box and papers will only be available when I'm at my desk." He arched his brows. "Questions?"

The same girl leaned forward and waved. "Do we still have to work the extra hour each afternoon like Major Rourke ordered?"

Joseph frowned and rubbed his jaw. "The major didn't address that topic with me." He looked at Clara and smiled. "Could you give me the details, Miss McBride?"

His smile had been enough to send her stomach fluttering. "I'll do my best." Being careful to avoid mentioning Beatrice by name, Clara detailed the absent workers and increased quotas. "The major decided an extra hour each day would be required to prevent shoddy work and meet our new quotas. I believe the other ladies will return to work now that you've returned. If so, the extra hour won't be necessary."

"Do you know why they weren't reporting for work?"

Before Clara could respond, Beatrice took control. "They disliked the way the major treated us. He's a tyrant. Before anyone else thinks you should know, I'm the one who confronted the major and threatened a walkout." She beamed at him as if she'd done something wonderful.

"I see." He rubbed his chin. "I'm sure that extra hour each afternoon has created difficulties for some of you ladies. We'll do away with the extra hour. If we need to lower quotas, we'll do so, but if you can influence the absent workers to return, I'd be appreciative. If not, perhaps some of you have acquaintances who are looking for work. We are always willing to train new workers." He pulled the chair back from the desk and sat down. "You may return to your duties. Please adhere to all safety regulations."

The ladies murmured their thanks before the room fell silent and they resumed work. For the remainder of the day, the ladies worked with renewed vigor, a lighter feeling inside the lab now that the major had departed.

When the bell rang to signal the end of the workday, the lieutenant signaled Clara. "If it isn't inconvenient, I'd like to speak with you, Miss McBride."

Beatrice spoke up from behind Clara. "I'm the one who threatened the major with a walkout, so it's probably me you need to talk to instead of Clara."

The lieutenant shook his head. "No, it's Miss McBride I want to speak with."

Beatrice's shoulders drooped like a wilted tulip. She circled around Clara and slowly moved to the row of pegs along the wall to retrieve her lunch pail and bonnet. She glanced over her shoulder when she neared the door. "Jeremiah and I will wait for you near the front entrance so you don't have to walk home alone, Clara."

The lieutenant stood. "No need to wait, Miss Hodson. I'll escort Miss McBride home."

Beatrice shot Clara an inscrutable look. Was it surprise, or had there been a hint of jealousy? It had been clear Bea had hoped to win his attention. She thought him quite handsome. Learning of his plans to court Clara didn't mean Bea would, or could, immediately suppress her feelings for him. While the thought was somewhat disconcerting, Clara trusted Bea, and she couldn't fault her new friend for harboring a bit of jealousy.

Still, that look signaled there would be a lot of questions tomorrow morning. Until recently, Jeremiah and Beatrice had lived a rural existence and were naturally more inquisitive. They hadn't learned that city folks tended to keep their personal lives a bit more private.

Clara pushed away thoughts of Beatrice and Jeremiah as she approached the lieutenant. He settled his gaze on her, and she could feel the heat crawling up her neck and coloring her cheeks. "It's warm for October, don't you think?" Flicking her open hand in front of her face, she pretended to fan herself.

He agreed and smiled. "Did you receive my letter?"

"Yes. I was pleased to hear from you. I read a short article in the newspaper about the explosion." She hesitated. "I was worried about you when I didn't hear from you again."

He sat down on the corner of the desk. "I should have written to let you know I wasn't injured. There was chaos after the explosion, and so many who needed help—"

She held up her hand and stayed him. "You don't need to explain. I know it must have been terrible. I can't imagine."

"And I don't want you to. Those images will never leave me." He offered a wan smile. "My only hope is that we can all learn from the tragedy at Lawrenceville and create a safer workplace for everyone." He inhaled a deep breath. "I've been eager to return so we can talk about the future."

"I'd like that very much." She tucked a strand of hair behind her ear.

"Have you told your mother I'd like to speak to her?"

"I may have mentioned your name on one or two occasions, and she knows I received a letter from you." She smiled while she tied her bonnet ribbons.

He tipped his head back and laughed. "Well, I'm pleased to learn that I deserved a mention. I plan to walk you home, but I'd rather call on her when she's expecting me. When do you think would be best?"

"We live in a boardinghouse, and the keeper doesn't permit visitors anywhere except the parlor. Unfortunately, the parlor is usually occupied by several other residents, so our conversation won't be private." She slipped her hand into the crook of his arm and they went on their way.

"Then what if I called on you and your mother, and the three of us went to the park?"

"That would be wonderful." Clara bobbed her head, her excitement mounting. "What about a picnic on Sunday afternoon? The boardinghouse keeper will permit us use of the kitchen. Mother and I can pack a basket lunch for the three of us."

"I don't want to cause extra work for either of you. Are you certain you want to have a picnic?"

"Absolutely. Mother and I both enjoy being outdoors whenever we can. A picnic will be great fun." She hesitated. "Unless it rains. In that case, we'll have to have our picnic in the parlor." She wrinkled her forehead while picturing the three of them sitting in the middle of the parlor sharing a picnic lunch as the other boarders settled around them for a game of whist. "We need to pray for sunshine on Sunday."

"Or another alternative for our picnic."

They turned at the corner of South O Street. Weedy flowers poked through cracks in the uneven sidewalk, their proliferation yet another layer of unsightliness in the shabby neighborhood. An unexpected wave of embarrassment overcame her. What would the lieutenant think of this place?

She gave a slight tug on his arm and came to a halt. "This is where I live. Mother and I have adjoining rooms on the second floor. It's our home for now."

He extended his hand and cupped her chin. "I missed you, Clara."

She placed a trembling hand on his arm. "I missed you, too, Joseph. I prayed for you every day while you were gone."

"I hope you'll continue to pray for me." He took both her hands in his. "I fear our part in this war is only beginning."

TEN

Clara exhaled a sigh of relief as she arrived at 4 ½ Street the following morning. Neither Beatrice nor her brother was in sight. Ever since getting up this morning, she'd been contemplating how much she should tell Beatrice about her meeting with Joseph. There was no doubt in Clara's mind that the minute she encountered Bea, there would be questions—lots of questions.

Thus far, Clara had been tight-lipped about Joseph's plans to court her. Although she had told Bea the two of them planned to correspond during his absence, she hadn't mentioned the letter she'd received shortly before his return. She wasn't sure why, but a small part of her worried that Bea still might ruin everything. Maybe it was because Bea continued to make comments about the lieutenant's good looks. Or maybe it was because Clara didn't quite believe her new friend had given up all hope of winning Joseph's affections.

Clara was nearing the corner of Q and 4 ½ Streets when a hand grasped her arm. She struggled to maintain her balance as she wheeled around. "Bea! I almost fell."

"I called your name, but you didn't stop."

"I didn't hear you." Clara glanced over her shoulder and

scanned the throng of workers. "Where's Jeremiah this morning?"

"He had to go in early to help load a shipment going out before dawn. I don't want to talk about Jeremiah. Did the lieutenant walk you home? Tell me what you two talked about. The explosion in Lawrenceville? Major Rourke?" She arched her brows. "Did you get a promotion?" Bea's voice rose as she posed the final question.

"No, a promotion was never mentioned. We didn't talk about work at all, but he did walk me home." Clara gathered her courage and smiled. "He's going to request my mother's permission to court me."

"What?" Beatrice's mouth dropped open. "I know you told me you were going to correspond with him, but you never said you received a letter. You barely know each other."

"That's why he's going to court me—so we can become better acquainted. Isn't that what most couples do?"

"Yes, I suppose, but it seems so sudden. I mean, he just returned and the very first thing he's going to do is request permission to court you? It just seems strange to me."

"It's true. He's going to speak to my mother on Sunday afternoon." Clara wasn't certain what to make of Bea's reaction. She had expected Bea to be pleased. Instead, she appeared disturbed and disappointed. Hadn't Bea said she was happy when her friends found true happiness? And wasn't it Bea who had expressed her hope that the lieutenant would prove to be the perfect man for Clara? "I thought you'd be happy for me."

"Your news surprised me, that's all. I'm sure I'll see much less of you now. You'll want to be with the lieutenant in your free time."

As Clara attempted to allay Bea's thoughts, Bea shook

her head. "Say what you will, but I know how such things work. He will come first."

"I value our time together, Bea, and I will always make time for you. Surely you know that."

Clara's words seemed to fall upon deaf ears, and an uncomfortable silence fell between them as they walked beneath the stone archway and entered the Arsenal grounds. Clara wasn't sure what more to say or do. Further attempts to reassure Bea would likely have little effect—at least for now.

When they neared the laboratory, Bea grabbed Clara's hand. "I'm sorry for acting like a spoiled child. It's just that I value our friendship. I'm afraid of losing you. Even so, I'm truly pleased that the lieutenant has chosen to court you. I hope he will make you very happy." She gave a half smile. "I must admit I'm still a little jealous."

"Please don't be jealous. We'll still have time to visit, and there's no need to worry about losing my friendship." Clara gave Bea's hand a quick squeeze as they entered the cylinder room.

Joseph greeted her with a smile when she entered the lab. While they both understood the need to remain detached during the workday, she noticed him looking at her several times throughout the morning. Or maybe it was merely her imagination. A portion of his job was making certain they were performing their work in a safe and orderly manner. He couldn't do that without watching them.

This morning he'd ordered the cleaning boys to sweep the loose gunpowder from the floors every half hour. They were no longer permitted to brush the powder into the streets. Instead, they were given dustpans and buckets, a method that demanded a bit more work. Unhappy with the change, the boys failed to appear on the half hour.

When they finally did arrive, the lieutenant called them over to his desk. His jaw twitched as they gathered in front of him. "I gave an order to appear on the half hour to sweep the floors. None of you appeared at six o'clock or six-thirty." He lowered his voice and leveled a stern look at them. "If you want to keep your jobs, you'll be here every half hour to remove the loose gunpowder as I've ordered or you'll be immediately terminated. This is a matter of safety for everyone working in this laboratory. Do I make myself clear?"

All but one of the boys murmured they understood. The lone exception raised his hand and waited until Joseph nodded at him. "Major Rourke said we needed to sweep only a couple times a day, and we could sweep it onto the porches or out on the street."

Joseph sighed. "Major Rourke is no longer in command, so you'll now follow my orders. Some of our previous practices created a dangerous risk. Didn't you hear about the explosion at the Allegheny Arsenal? We don't want that to happen here. By doing as I've instructed, you will help keep all of us safe, and you'll be earning your wages instead of sitting around most of the day."

Though the boys didn't appear happy, they didn't offer further argument.

Joseph gave a firm nod. "I will not abide any excuses. Begin sweeping and make certain all the loose gunpowder is dumped in the buckets." He straightened his shoulders. "I will expect you back here at seven-thirty and every half hour henceforth until the end of your workday. You have sufficient time to sweep each room and return within the allotted time. I've done so myself to be certain. I'll also speak with the supervisors in the other rooms each day to make certain they remain pleased with your work."

The boys' faces were etched with defeat when they finally set to work. Clara had never heard Joseph speak with such intensity. There had been something different in his voice. She couldn't decide if he simply believed the boys needed a more forceful leader or if the explosion in Lawrenceville had motivated him to make and enforce changes.

With the first clang of the breakfast bell, Beatrice leaned toward Clara. "Please continue to eat breakfast and lunch with me. If you don't, I'm going to think you haven't forgiven me for the way I behaved on the way to work. I'm truly happy for you and the lieutenant."

"Thank you, Bea. Of course we'll continue having our meals together." Clara was certain any change in their daily routine would reinforce Bea's idea that their friendship was in jeopardy, and Clara didn't want to add fuel to that fire.

After donning their capes, they walked to their favorite spot not far from the laboratory. Clara was surprised when she looked up and caught sight of Jeremiah. He plopped down beside his sister. "We got an extra break since we came in early. I'm starving. You got anything for me in that bundle?"

"When did you eat the breakfast I sent with you?"

Jeremiah leaned against the tree trunk. "Weren't you listening? We got an early breakfast break since we started so early. I ate it then."

Bea frowned. "You couldn't have been all that hungry. You had mush before you left the house this morning. You should have waited. There's nothing extra except a piece of bread." She removed a hunk of bread from the bundle.

"That'll do." He leaned forward and extended his hand. "They got us moving at double time today. For a while, I thought they was gonna have us empty the warehouse. I never loaded so many crates of ammunition at one time."

"We've got better things to talk about than the war, Jeremiah." Bea removed a jelly sandwich from her pack.

Jeremiah nudged her. "Like what?" He shoved the bread into his mouth.

"Like the lieutenant is going to ask Clara's mother if he can court Clara."

Jeremiah coughed until tears rolled down his cheeks. Bea patted him on the back until he finally stopped. He wiped his eyes with his shirtsleeve, then looked at Clara. "Sorry. That bit of news took me by surprise. I guess Bea didn't tell you she'd been pining over the lieutenant." He turned his gaze on Bea. "Guess you didn't make as big an impression on him as you thought."

She glared at her brother. "I'm happy for Clara, and you should be, too."

Jeremiah shrugged. "I suppose. In that case, you should request a transfer to the packing room."

"Why would I do that? Mr. Grant is a horrid supervisor. Almost as bad as Major Rourke." Beatrice shuddered and shook her head.

"Mr. Grant isn't the supervisor anymore. One of the sergeants who was a freight supervisor has been transferred to the packing room. He's in charge now. He's good-looking and easy to get along with. You might have more luck with the sergeant than you had with the lieutenant." Jeremiah guffawed and nudged his sister.

Bea shook her head. "I don't know. I didn't much like working in the packing room. Besides, I like having Clara nearby."

"Don't be foolish, Bea. You and Clara can't talk at work, so what difference does it make if she's sitting beside you? The two of you can still visit during breakfast and lunch. I thought you wanted to find a beau so you'd have someone besides me to talk to in the evenings."

"That's true, but I still don't like the idea of the packing room."

Jeremiah stood and brushed the back of his pants. "Try to help and this is what I get from you. I gotta get back to work."

Clara gathered up the remnants of her lunch and waited for Bea. "How come he's so intent upon you finding a beau all of a sudden?"

"He probably thinks I won't be so prickly with him if I'm busy with a beau." Bea picked up her bonnet and lunch bundle. "Instead of worrying about me, maybe he should find a gal to keep him busy. Then he could tell her what to do and leave me alone."

Clara chuckled. "Maybe he should do just that."

Bea stood and brushed off her skirt. "Jeremiah has always liked telling me what I should or shouldn't do. But I don't want to transfer. Instead, I'll convince him that I'm doing just fine where I am."

Clara matched Bea's stride as they walked back toward the cylinder room. "I'm glad. I don't want you to transfer, either."

When Sunday afternoon finally arrived, Clara could barely contain her excitement. She'd hurried her mother home from church to prepare sandwiches. Mrs. Ludwig had given her mother permission to use the kitchen, since the boarding-house offered only breakfast and evening meals. She had even offered slices of leftover ham for their sandwiches. Clara's mother had purchased bread at the bakery on her way home last evening and had also splurged on three Scotch short-bread cookies.

Mrs. McBride picked up their bonnets and led the way downstairs. Clara followed with the bag of supplies. "If Mrs. Ludwig returns before we leave, will you ask if we can borrow canning jars for water?"

"Did I hear my name?" Wearing a calico apron, Mrs. Ludwig stood at one side of the worn oak worktable.

"Good afternoon, Mrs. Ludwig. I didn't know you'd already returned from church. Clara and I were discussing our need for jars so we can enjoy something to drink with our lunch."

"I have some empty ones stored in the pantry you can use. I'm glad to see you have a pretty day for your outing." She crossed the room and pushed aside a thin curtain that substituted as a pantry door. She placed two pint jars on the worktable. "There you are. One for each of you."

Clara smiled. "Could you loan us three, Mrs. Ludwig? There will be three of us at lunch."

The older lady's gray eyebrows arched like twin peaks. "Oh? A friend you've made at the Arsenal?"

Clara glanced at her mother, who nodded before explaining to Mrs. Ludwig. "Yes. A young lieutenant who is requesting my permission to court Clara. I haven't yet met him, but from what she's told me, he's a fine young man."

The keeper's lips drooped into a frown. "A soldier isn't what I'd want for my daughter, if I had one. They're like bees that flit from flower to flower, looking for the sweetest nectar. Why don't you consider someone more stable, Clara? A storekeeper or banker? What about Mr. Markam? He's established and seems kind." She hesitated. "Perhaps a little odd, but kind."

Clara chuckled. "Mr. Markam is far too old for me, Mrs. Ludwig, and there's nothing wrong with soldiers. They're brothers, fathers, and sons, just like the other men living in Washington, and I don't think they flit about any more than any other man without principles. Lieutenant Brady is a fine man."

"Well, time will tell. Of course, it isn't my decision." She pursed her lips and looked at Clara's mother. "Mr. Markam—"

"Is far too old for my daughter," Mrs. McBride cut in. "Perhaps you should consider him as a suitor, Mrs. Ludwig. He does enjoy your cooking, and you've been a widow for many years." Mrs. McBride offered the boardinghouse keeper a sweet smile. "May I use the bread knife? If we don't hurry, the young man will be here before we're ready."

While Mrs. Ludwig didn't withdraw her offer of the leftover ham, she didn't seem as pleased now that she'd learned a soldier would be joining them. Clara was filling the jars, and her mother was wrapping the sandwiches in cloth napkins when a knock sounded at the front door.

Mrs. Ludwig jumped from her chair and rushed forward. "I'll go. You two finish your preparations."

Mrs. McBride gestured for Clara to finish filling the jars.

Clara sighed. "She'll scare him off, Mother."

Her mother smiled. "I doubt a lieutenant in the United States Army will be afraid of Mrs. Ludwig."

Clara wasn't as certain. She envisioned the older woman telling Joseph that he was at the wrong address or he wasn't expected. They finished packing the basket and had donned their bonnets and Mrs. Ludwig still hadn't returned.

"I'm not sure what's keeping her, but I'm not going to wait any longer." Clara picked up the basket and walked down the hallway. She stopped short when she looked in the parlor. Joseph was sitting in a chair opposite Mrs. Ludwig, who was smiling at him. She appeared completely besotted.

Joseph grinned and stood when he saw her in the doorway. "I was telling your boardinghouse keeper that I noticed loose nails in the railing and a board that needs to be replaced at one end of the porch."

Several wisps of gray hair escaped the braided knot balanced atop Mrs. Ludwig's head. "Lieutenant Brady is going to return and repair them for me. Isn't that kind? I was telling him that I was beginning to think chivalry was dead, but this dear boy has restored my belief."

"I'm pleased to hear that, Mrs. Ludwig. And I'm pleased it was a soldier who was able to restore those feelings for you." Clara offered a tight smile before turning to her mother. "Mother, I'd like to introduce you to Lieutenant Joseph Brady."

"I'm most pleased to meet you, Lieutenant Brady, and I'm delighted we're going to spend some time together."

"I'm pleased to meet you, as well, Mrs. McBride."

Clara looked at Joseph. "Shall we?"

He nodded and extended his hand toward the picnic basket. "Let me carry the basket."

Mrs. Ludwig beamed. "You see? He is such a gentleman."

Clara stifled a giggle as they departed. "Although you don't need it, I believe you've won Mrs. Ludwig's approval."

"Perhaps not, but along with her approval came an offer for us to visit in the parlor two evenings a week without any other boarders present. She said she would inform the others that Wednesdays and Fridays were reserved for us." He glanced at Mrs. McBride. "So long as the door to the parlor is open."

Clara's mother nodded. "Well, I'm sure a chivalrous young soldier would never object to such an arrangement."

Clara looped her hand into the crook of Joseph's arm. "I must say that I'm surprised it took no more than a few nails and a hammer to win Mrs. Ludwig's approval, but I'm pleased she's given us permission to use the parlor."

Mrs. McBride nudged her daughter. "The hammer and nails may have helped, yet I think his good looks are what truly won her over."

"Next thing you know, she'll be inviting you to supper," Clara said.

His face reddened. "She already has. Next Sunday evening."

Clara laughed and looked at her mother. "She must have been certain you'd approve of Joseph."

A twinkle flickered in her mother's eyes. "For once, Mrs. Ludwig and I appear to agree on something."

ELEVEN

eatrice placed what was left of yesterday's stale corn bread in a bowl, ladled beans overtop, then handed Jeremiah a cracked plate. She pulled out a chair, sat down at the table, and glowered at him. "I don't want to talk about this anymore. Everything has to be the way you want it. You never trust that I can do what I'm supposed to without your interference."

Jeremiah's lips tightened into a thin line. "We won't be successful unless you quit thinking about yourself and remember why we're here. I expect you to request a transfer to the packing room tomorrow. I know there's at least one opening, and you need to be the one who fills it. Understood?"

Beatrice folded her arms across her chest. "I think I can be just as successful in the cylinder room. Why can't I stay there a while longer and try?"

"Because I said." He slammed his fork on the table. "You told me you'd win over the lieutenant and be able to get information out of him. That sure didn't work. Clara isn't going to be talking to him about the war, so you won't get anything out of her. We need information, and the sergeant is our best bet at this point. He'll be involved in briefings now that he's a supervisor. Besides, you can do more damage in the packing room. I received a message yesterday on what we're expected to do for the cause while we're here. That may change in the weeks to come, but you're going to be the most important part of the plan—at least for now."

"That's not what I wanted to hear," she said with a frown.

He thrust his chest against the table. "As I recall, you said you'd do whatever was necessary to help the Confederacy win the war. I wasn't dreaming, was I?" His question was stilted, and anger hardened each word.

"You know I'm as devoted to the South as you, but I don't like being confined in the laboratory rooms. If I needed to escape, it would be impossible."

"If you're careful, you won't need to escape. Besides, since coming here, you haven't been asked to do anything except gather information about the lab layout and how it works."

She pushed away from the table and picked up her journal. "And I've done so. I've made drawings of each room. I've taken notes of the amounts and kinds of ammunition, how many workers, where the lab is located within the Arsenal, and the required quotas for each worker. My reports are detailed." She arched her brows. "Can you say the same? Where have you recorded when and how the shipments are made? Do you have notes regarding times and dates they were sent? Have you made drawings of the freight and shipping area?"

Tapping his index finger against his temple, he said, "I have it up here, and when it's requested, I'll write it down."

"If you can remember it. As I recall, you never excelled in memorization."

His brows dipped together in an agonized expression. "I know you've formed a friendship with Clara and now you feel like what I'm asking is a betrayal of her. I warned you that could happen. You need to remember what's at stake here, Bea. If the North wins the war, our lives will never be the same."

"I know, but . . ."

He shook his head. "Don't make excuses, Bea. Tomorrow morning you go in and request a transfer to the packing room."

"What am I going to do in there that I can't do in the cylinder room?"

He scooted to the edge of his chair. "Remember when you were in the packing room when we first got here?"

"Of course. I'm not the one with the memory problem. Besides, it wasn't that long ago."

"You told me that you would wrap ten cartridges and a cylinder that held twelve percussion caps in each packet. Right?"

She bobbed her head. "Either your memory is better than I thought or you looked at my notes." She inhaled a sharp breath. "What's important about the packets?"

"We need to get those packets wrapped without percussion caps. The cartridges will be useless without percussion caps." He folded his hands and grinned.

Her mouth dropped open. "Exactly how do you expect me to do that, Jeremiah?"

"You're clever. I know you can manage to avoid putting the caps in your packets. But that won't be enough—we need to devise some way to have all those cartridges going out without caps. After you're in there a few days, you'll discover some way that can be done."

Fear brushed the edges of her mind. "I don't think there's any way that can be done. You're expecting the impossible."

He shook his head. "It's not me who's depending upon your success. It's General Lee and the Confederate troops. We have to find a way, Bea."

"*We?* You're going to be safe and sound out in the freight department, while you want me to remove the percussion caps from wrapped and boxed packets." A tremor ran down her throat and threatened to cut off her breath. This idea was destined for failure. She'd be caught and imprisoned for treason—or worse, shot. She shuddered at the thought.

"I already said you need to get the packets wrapped without the percussion cap cylinders. I understand we can't remove them after the cartridges are wrapped. Are you even listening to me?"

Anger bubbled deep in her stomach. "Oh, I'm listening, but I haven't heard any genuine plan. Instead, I'm hearing the clang of iron bars locking me in a jail cell."

"Don't be dramatic. I'm not asking you to go in there tomorrow and start prying open boxes. I want you to carefully observe how things are done, especially with the percussion caps."

She sighed and picked at a loose thread on her cuff. "The caps are placed in the cylinders in the cap room. That's where those young girls work. Their fingers are small, so they can fill the cylinders with greater ease. The cylinders are brought into the packing room in crates."

He held up a hand. "Things could have changed some. Once you begin work there, I want you to watch how everything is done. You wait and see. We'll find a way to help the Confederacy. It's what's being asked of us. I don't make the orders, Bea. I'm just passing them along."

She'd had enough arguments with him to know she wouldn't win. He'd accuse her of betrayal, and her denials would then be met with a challenge to prove him wrong. She'd walked this well-worn path more times than she cared to remember, and in the end, Jeremiah always got his way.

The following morning, Bea insisted they leave the apartment later than usual. For the first time since she'd met her, Bea didn't want to see or talk to Clara. This morning Bea would do as Jeremiah had instructed. She'd request a transfer. A part of her longed to talk to Clara and explain why she needed to leave the cylinder room. But that was impossible. Clara could never be her true friend. Clara's loyalty was to the North, and Bea's was to the South. And lest Bea try to forget, she always had Jeremiah reminding her.

Those facts aside, Clara would expect to be questioned about the picnic. She'd be suspicious if Bea didn't inquire. After all, that was what Bea did—ask questions. A spark of jealousy burned deep in her heart as she pictured Clara and the lieutenant enjoying their Sunday afternoon outing. Mrs. McBride had likely granted him permission to court Clara before they'd even arrived at the park, and a sweet romance had begun to blossom. She silently chastised herself. There was no reason to be jealous of Clara's relationship with Lieutenant Brady. He might be handsome, but he could never truly be her beau. He was meant to be no more than a pawn. An officer who, under the right circumstances, might divulge information helpful to the South. And since she'd been unable to win the lieutenant as a suitor and possibly gain important information, she was being relegated to the packing room.

Jeremiah nudged Bea as they hurried toward the lab. "Quit

scowling. Anyone looking at you would think you'd been ordered in front of a firing squad. The lieutenant isn't going to believe you want a transfer if you don't smile and appear eager."

She whipped around and glared at him. "Don't tell me how I should look or what I should say, Jeremiah. I can manage the transfer without your advice."

"Fine. I was just trying to help. I'll see you at breakfast." He turned and stalked off toward the freight yard.

Instead of hanging her cloak and bonnet on the pegs at the far wall, Bea walked directly to the lieutenant's desk. She forced a smile and tipped her head to the side so the brim of her bonnet didn't interfere with her view. "Good morning, Lieutenant Brady."

He looked up from his ledger and nodded. "Is there a problem, Miss Hodson?"

"Yes, sir. I'd like to request a transfer to the packing room. One of the ladies mentioned there are openings, and I'd like to be considered."

He leaned back in his chair and studied her. "Are you unhappy working in the cylinder room?"

"No. I'm not unhappy, but I do enjoy change. I've tired of the repetition, and I perform more efficiently when I'm not bored."

The corners of his lips twitched. "There are no jobs in this laboratory that are not repetitious, Miss Hodson. I believe you worked in the packing room for a short time when you first arrived. Am I correct?"

She nodded.

"Then you know that what I'm saying is true."

"Yes, but stacking and wrapping cartridges is change enough for now." She shrugged her shoulders and smiled.

"By the time the war ends, I probably will have asked to be transferred to every room in the laboratory."

"You're a good worker, so I'd prefer to keep you in the cylinder room. Still, I won't object to your transfer. I'll speak to Sergeant Kessler."

He picked up his pen as if to return to his ledger, but Bea didn't move. When he glanced up, she asked, "Could we go and speak to him now?"

He cleared his throat and pushed back from the desk. "If that's what you want. I had planned to speak to the sergeant and have you transfer tomorrow morning, but we can go now."

"Thank you. I would rather begin right away."

After standing and circling around his desk, the lieutenant gestured for Bea to lead the way. She glanced toward the worktable, where she was met by Clara's confused look. Unable to offer anything more, Bea shrugged and strode out of the room.

Jeremiah's assessment had been correct. The sergeant was as handsome as the lieutenant. And, quite frankly, more to Bea's liking. Rather than streaked blond hair and blue eyes, the sergeant's hair shimmered like black satin, and his eyes were as dark as a midnight sky. He jumped to his feet and saluted the lieutenant as soon as they entered the packing room.

The lieutenant returned the salute, nodded toward Beatrice, and made the introductions. "Miss Hodson once worked in the packing room for a short time, and she's decided she would like to return." He glanced at the worktables. "It appears you have several vacancies."

The sergeant nodded. "Yes, there are four openings, and I would be pleased to have Miss Hodson fill one of them. The fact that you've worked here previously is an added advantage for us." He fastened his gaze on the lieutenant. "How soon can she begin?"

"Right now!" Beatrice slapped a palm to her mouth, then pulled it away. "I'm sorry, you weren't speaking to me, were you?"

The lieutenant chuckled. "I think that was directed at me, but Miss Hodson can begin immediately. As you can tell, she's quite eager to make a change."

"Thank you, Lieutenant, for permitting me to transfer. I've enjoyed working for you." Beatrice offered the sergeant a coy smile. "And thank you, Sergeant, for agreeing to the transfer."

After the lieutenant departed, Sergeant Kessler nodded toward the worktables. "You are free to choose whichever empty space you'd like to fill." He pointed at the far wall. "You can place your belongings across the room there and then begin work."

The four vacant seats were located near the end of the benches. If seated near the end, one could go to the necessary without bothering other workers, but everyone had to get up and move for those seated in the middle. When receiving an hourly wage, the end of the bench was best, but when being paid by the piece, the end was the least favorite seat.

Bea would have preferred a middle seat so she didn't have to get up and down so often, but also so she could watch the other workers. On the other hand, being at the end might prove an advantage. The other ladies wouldn't be able to observe her actions quite so easily.

Much was going to depend upon her observations during these first few days. When working here before, she'd been intent upon performing the work as efficiently as possible.

Now she was looking for ways to sabotage the packets, and she was certain it wasn't going to be easy.

Bea had been relieved to learn that the workers in the packing room and cylinder room didn't take their breakfast breaks at the same time. She wasn't prepared to speak to Clara just yet. Clara knew Bea had been opposed to the move, so she needed a convincing story—something more than the repetition of the work. Clara wouldn't be as easily duped as the lieutenant.

While she counted and aligned the cartridges, her thoughts skittered from one idea to the next. A short time later, the girl beside her nudged Bea's arm and pointed to the cylinders of percussion caps. "You forgot the percussion caps."

"Oh, thank you." Bea smiled at the girl and quickly unwrapped the waterproof paper. It appeared leaving out the cylinders of percussion caps wasn't something that would go unnoticed by the other workers.

Jeremiah would expect her to devise a plan within a few days. She glanced at the sergeant and smiled. With a little luck, she might be able to gather some information from him. He might be her only hope.

When the breakfast bell rang, the workers gathered their food bundles and scurried from the room. Bea dallied behind until only the sergeant remained. "Don't you believe in eating breakfast, Sergeant Kessler?"

"We eat at the mess hall before reporting for work. They feed us a big breakfast. I couldn't eat anything more until noon."

"Do you mind if I remain inside and eat at the worktable?" She cast an endearing smile in his direction. "I'd be pleased to have you sit with me, unless you need to attend to your work."

He stood, clasped his hands, and stretched his arms in front of his chest. "Thank you, I could use a short break."

After unwrapping her bread and cheese, she placed them on a cotton square she spread on the table. "Tell me about yourself, Sergeant. Do you hail from Washington?"

He leaned forward and rested his forearms across his thighs. "No. I'm from Vermont. I've been in Washington for six months. Sure is different. I grew up near the Green Mountains. You ever been to Vermont?"

"No, I'm afraid not. I grew up on a farm in Maryland, not far from the Washington border." She took a bite of cheese.

His dark eyes sparkled. "There's nothing quite as pretty as the mountains. Don't matter what season, they're pretty any time of year. After the war, you should come to Vermont and visit."

"If the mountains are as pretty as you say, I'm sure I'd enjoy Vermont." She glanced around the room. "Have you enjoyed working at the Arsenal?"

"Not much. I thought I'd be off fighting, but instead I'm helping make ammunition for other soldiers." He frowned. "I figure they'll get around to sending me to fight. That's what I signed up to do."

She tipped her head to the side. "Well, I'm pleased you're here, even if you aren't."

"Now that I've met you, I'm having a change of heart." His lips slanted in a lopsided grin. "Do you live near the Arsenal, Miss Hodson?"

"Beatrice. Bea to my friends." She tucked a strand of her light brown hair behind her ear and smiled. "I know you can't address me as Bea at work, but . . ."

"But when we're alone, we'll be friends. You'll be Bea and I'll be Andrew."

"Andrew. That's a nice name. I like it." She folded her napkin and placed the remnants of her food in her bundle. She'd finish the rest at lunch break. It was more important to keep the sergeant talking. "What's it like working here and living in the barracks?"

"The truth is it's pretty dull. Living in the barracks with a bunch of soldiers isn't the greatest. Mostly we play cards and talk about home. Being at work isn't much better. I keep count of the crates going out to shipping and make sure there's enough supplies to keep you gals busy."

Bea gave him an understanding nod. "Maybe you could come to dinner some night at our place. I live with my brother, and he enjoys company as much as I do." She touched a finger to her lips. "In fact, you might know him. Jeremiah Hodson. Dark brown hair, broad shoulders. He works in freight and shipping."

"Jeremiah! Sure, I know who he is. He had a different supervisor when I was assigned to freight and shipping, but I remember him. Good worker. So Jeremiah's your brother." He leaned back. "I'd be mighty pleased to have dinner with you and your brother. You talk to him and make sure he won't object to my coming by for a visit."

"He won't mind one little bit, but if it will put you at ease, I'll talk to him and we'll decide on a day."

At the sound of chattering voices outside the door, the sergeant jumped to his feet and hurried across the room while Bea returned her bundle to the space beneath her bonnet and cape on the far wall.

As soon as the ladies were seated, she picked up a piece of wrapping paper and began stacking cartridges. She was pleased with the inroads she'd made with the sergeant. Having him come and visit at their apartment might not have been the best idea, but anything more would have seemed too forward. Then again, the sergeant didn't appear to be the type who stood on formality.

Now she needed to decide what she was going to tell Clara.

TWELVE

Clara returned to the cylinder room a few minutes early. She had planned to ask Joseph about Bea before going on breakfast break, but he'd been busy with a department supervisor. Though it was difficult to think she'd do so, Clara wondered if Bea might have decided to transfer to the packing room. Jeremiah had posed the idea when they were on break last week, but Bea had flatly rejected the suggestion. And Bea wasn't easily swayed.

During her break, Clara had looked everywhere. When Bea hadn't appeared, Clara recalled that the breakfast break for the packing room had been changed, so she began looking for Jeremiah. Yet she couldn't find him, either. After that, her thoughts had run rampant. Had they quit their jobs and moved? Surely not. They seemed as content as most folks living and working at Greenleaf Point. Surely they wouldn't move away without saying good-bye.

Clara sighed with relief when she saw Joseph. He could shed a bit of light on what was going on with Bea.

He looked up and smiled when she drew near. "You look worried. Is something wrong?"

"Where is Bea? Did she and Jeremiah quit their jobs?"

"I can't tell you anything about Jeremiah, but Bea transferred to the packing room. She said she wanted a change and was bored by the repetition."

Clara frowned. "That surprises me. Jeremiah wanted her to transfer, but Bea said she was going to stay in the cylinder room." She detailed the conversation from last week and shook her head. "Bea didn't say she'd agreed to transfer. Besides, she knows the work in the packing room is tedious. Nothing but counting, stacking, and wrapping. She'll be back within a week."

"She's a good worker. I told her I'd rather she remain in the cylinder room, but I didn't think it was fair to deny her request since they had four openings. I know you'll miss having her nearby, but I think the packing room still takes lunch break when we do." He glanced at the door and then took hold of her hand. "Yesterday was wonderful. I look forward to seeing you when I come over to fix Mrs. Ludwig's railing tomorrow evening."

"I'm looking forward to it, too. When we returned after the picnic yesterday, Mrs. Ludwig mentioned she'd asked you for dinner next Sunday and said you were going to fix the railing Tuesday evening. She said I should tell you that she'll have a special dessert for you afterward."

He tipped his head back and laughed. "If I continue helping Mrs. Ludwig with repairs, I may never have to eat in the mess hall again."

Clara hurried to the worktable when the other workers began their return from breakfast. She was relieved to know Bea and Jeremiah hadn't moved away. Even so, there had to be some other reason Bea had decided to transfer. She pondered the possibilities as the remainder of the morning moved onward at a snail's speed. Once the lunch bell rang, she swiftly gathered her belongings and raced outside. She came to an abrupt halt at the bottom of the steps and looked toward the oak trees.

When she spotted Bea, Clara waved and hurried forward. By the time she sat down beneath the tree, she was out of breath. She leaned sideways and gave Bea a quick hug. "I'm so relieved to see you. I looked for you at breakfast break, and when I didn't see you or Jeremiah, I was afraid you'd packed up and moved away without telling me. You were almost late to work this morning."

"We overslept and had to run most of the way." Bea's smile appeared forced. "You should know I'd never leave town without saying good-bye. Besides, where would we go?" She inhaled a quick breath. "I thought the lieutenant would tell you I transferred."

"He was busy when we left for breakfast, so I didn't get to speak to him until afterward. He was sorry you decided to leave. I know he'd let you return to the cylinder room, and I'd be happy if you'd change your mind. I know Jeremiah mentioned you should transfer, but you said you didn't want to. What happened?"

"At first, I thought it was a bad idea, but later he mentioned that if I had a husband, our lives would be a lot better—three incomes instead of two—and maybe I could even stay home. I got to thinking about it and decided he was right. I want to get married and have a few young'uns one day, and with most of the men off fighting in the war, there aren't many fellas to choose from."

Though Clara listened with an open mind, Bea's explanation didn't ring entirely true. Maybe because she'd never before mentioned a desire to wed or have children. While she'd certainly expressed an interest in Joseph, never had the subject of marriage come up. In fact, the one time they'd discussed having children, Bea had shuddered and shaken her head.

She wanted to be supportive of her friend, but she didn't want Bea to make an unwise decision. "If you meet someone who wants to marry you, I hope you'll do so because you love him and not because he can pay the rent."

Bea unwrapped a piece of half-eaten cheese and a thick slice of bread. "I think it will be for love. The sergeant is better looking than I imagined. We talked through the entire breakfast break. He's very nice and is going to come have dinner with me and Jeremiah one evening, so I think it's a good thing I requested the transfer."

Clara still wasn't certain she'd heard the real reason for the transfer, but she worried that part of it was because Bea hadn't won the lieutenant's interest. "That's nice to hear. I just want you to be happy, Bea."

"Enough about me. I want to hear about the picnic. Don't leave out any details."

Bea's tone was too happy and her smile too bright, yet Clara wouldn't push for more. Instead, she did as Bea asked and described her afternoon with Joseph.

"I'm glad both your mother and the boardinghouse keeper like him. If the keeper is willing to let you two use the parlor, that's going to be perfect when the weather turns cold. I was worried about that, but the problem is solved."

Clara nodded. "Joseph's offer to complete a few repairs around the boardinghouse won Mrs. Ludwig's heart. He's coming by tomorrow evening to fix the porch railing."

"Maybe the four of us could get together one evening." She hesitated. "Unless Joseph isn't permitted to socialize with a lowly sergeant like Andrew."

Clara thought she detected a hint of bitterness in Bea's voice, but maybe it had been her imagination. "When Joseph is off duty, I don't think he's required to account for his time or the company he keeps. We'd be pleased to join you and . . ." Clara hesitated.

"Sergeant Andrew Kessler." Bea closed her lunch pail. "Maybe Jeremiah was right. I needed to make a change."

"While it's good for you, I do miss having you next to me in the cylinder room." She looped arms with Bea as the two of them crossed the grassy slope toward the lab. "If things don't work out between you and Andrew, Jeremiah may try to find a job for you in the shipping and freight department." Clara chuckled. "Or maybe *he* should marry one of the girls who works in the lab. That would help with living expenses."

Bea's lopsided smile said it all. Jeremiah expected Bea to do whatever he wanted, but he'd never inconvenience himself. Bea's submissive behavior with Jeremiah had become difficult to understand. She'd shown no fear when she advocated for the women in the cylinder room, but as soon as he ordered her to apologize, she'd given in. And though she hadn't wanted to change positions at the lab, she'd done what he commanded. Why did Jeremiah have such control? Did he abuse his sister? Was she afraid of him? An alarm scissored deep inside her. Clara had heard stories of men who were violent with their wives, sisters, and children, yet she didn't want to believe Jeremiah could be one of them. She'd never seen any telltale evidence, but that didn't prove anything.

Clara gave her friend a sideways glance. "Does Jeremiah always make the final decisions for the two of you?"

Bea's brows pulled together. "He's the man in our house, but sometimes he lets me have my way."

"Still, he's not your father. I love my brother, but if we were living together, I wouldn't let him have the final say on everything. I don't understand why you always give in to Jeremiah."

"I just said he sometimes lets me have my way. Most of the time he knows what's best for us." Bea clamped her lips in a thin line.

There was no doubt her remarks had troubled Bea. Although Clara wanted to pursue the topic, she'd let it rest for now. She'd find another time when she could broach the subject. If Jeremiah was abusive, Clara wanted to help her friend. While it might not be comfortable for Clara or her mother, they would insist Bea share their rooms at the boardinghouse.

Bea glanced toward the freight yard before returning to the packing room. She had expected Jeremiah to appear and request a full report on what had happened this morning. After all, he'd been the one who insisted she request a transfer first thing. Then again, maybe something had gone amiss at the freight yard and he'd had to change his break times. Clara had mentioned she hadn't seen him during breakfast break.

She stepped inside the packing room with Clara's remarks dogging her heels. The unexpected questions about Jeremiah had been unsettling—almost as if Clara thought Jeremiah had too much control over her. Maybe he did, but Clara didn't know that behind closed doors, Bea said her piece. She didn't always win, but she understood that one of them had to be in charge. If their plans were going to be successful, there was no place for ongoing disagreement. That sort of behavior could result in disaster or death for both of them. Even if she didn't always agree, Bea was willing to let

Jeremiah make the hard decisions. He'd been right so far, and with any luck, it would hold.

Throughout the afternoon, Bea carefully watched the activity in the packing room. Nothing had changed except for the supervisor. By the end of the workday, she was certain Jeremiah's suggestion that she withhold the percussion cap cylinders wouldn't work. She might be successful with one or two packets, but much more than that would be impossible. A few missing cylinders per box wasn't going to do much toward winning the war for the South.

She sighed when the workday ended. Jeremiah wasn't going to be pleased with her report. Perhaps, though, they could arrive at another plan. She donned her cape and picked up her lunch pail before departing. As she walked toward the arch, she heard the pounding of footsteps, yet she didn't turn around. When Clara called out to her, Bea finally slowed her pace.

"Why didn't you wait for me?" Clara's cheeks were bright pink, and she was panting when she came alongside Bea.

Bea moved her lunch pail to the other hand to keep from jostling Clara's faded green skirt. "I didn't see you outside when I left the packing room, so I thought you'd already gone. I haven't seen Jeremiah all day, and I wanted to see if he was waiting for me at the arch."

They hadn't walked far when Jeremiah shouted her name and she wheeled around and came to a halt. When Clara stopped beside her, Bea offered a tight smile. "You don't need to wait for us. I know you like to get home on time so you can eat supper and help your mother with her sewing."

"It will be at least an hour before Mrs. Ludwig serves supper, and my mother is working late tonight. She's doing another fitting for Mrs. Seward, so I'm in no hurry."

Bea inwardly groaned. Most of the time, Clara would offer a quick wave and be on her way. But this evening, when Bea wanted to talk to Jeremiah alone, Clara was hanging on like a cat climbing a tree. There was something odd about the way Clara had been acting today. Maybe it was because Bea had requested a transfer, but that didn't account for the curious remarks she'd made about Jeremiah. Maybe she'd heard something they said that had caused her to doubt them. They'd need to be more careful around her in the future.

Jeremiah pushed his way through a crowd of workers and hurried toward them. He arched his brows at her and grinned. "Got any good news for me?"

"I transferred to the packing room this morning and met Sergeant Kessler."

"Good-looking, ain't he?"

Clara wriggled around a couple of girls to keep up with them, obviously hoping to hear every word.

Bea nodded. "He's handsome and he's nice, too. We had a pleasant chat at breakfast break."

"They might go on a picnic with me and Joseph," Clara said.

"That's not for certain just yet, but I did invite the sergeant to have dinner with us at the apartment. He was real pleased by the invite, although he wanted me to make sure it was okay with you first. He remembered you and said you're a good worker."

"Seems Sergeant Kessler's every bit as polite as he is good-looking. You tell him your brother would be proud to have him come and share a meal with us. Best make it on a Sunday so you'll have time to fix something proper. Ain't much time to fix a nice meal after we get home from work. That's the bad thing about you working, Bea, 'cause I do enjoy me some good cooking." He glanced at Clara. "You should be glad you live in a boardinghouse. You and your ma have someone cooking supper for you every night."

A gust of wind caught Clara's bonnet, and she clapped one hand to her head. "That's true enough. You ever think you should find yourself a wife, Jeremiah? There's lots of single girls working in the laboratory, and I'd guess most all of them could cook a fine meal. Or, if you married one of them, she could keep on working at the lab, and Bea could stay home and cook for you."

"I'm not looking for a wife, Clara. Just a few good meals now and again." He tipped his cap. "I thank ya for trying to solve my problems for me, but I think I can handle them on my own."

Bea relaxed her shoulders and sighed when Clara bid them good-bye and turned at South O Street. As soon as she was out of earshot, Bea looked at Jeremiah. "Clara's been acting strange today." While they continued walking home, Bea detailed her concerns. "Don't you think it's odd that she suggested you look for a wife?"

"No. I'm thinking one of those gals in the cylinder room is interested in me and Clara's trying to play matchmaker." He yanked off his cap and slapped it against his leg. "You have to admit I'm one good-lookin' fella."

"Quit, Jeremiah. I'm trying to be serious. We need to be careful around Clara. I think she suspects something. I'm just not sure what."

"You need to stop worrying about Clara and what she's thinking and tell me what we're gonna do about those percussion caps. What did you discover that's gonna help us?"

They walked up the steps and into the apartment as she related the reason why their plan wouldn't work and the fact that she'd been corrected the first time she attempted to leave out the percussion cap. "We need another plan. I've been thinking on it all afternoon, and there may be one way we can succeed, but it will take your help."

Jeremiah sat down on one of the wooden chairs and leaned it back on two legs. "Let's hear the plan and then I'll decide if it's worth a try."

Bea silently seethed at his condescending tone. "Any plan I have is going to be better than your idea. I just told you how well that worked."

"Quit your jawing and tell me what you're thinking. I want to eat supper before midnight."

The tension was thick as day-old gravy, and she wanted to tell him they'd wait and talk later, but that would only make matters worse. She sat down opposite him and inhaled a deep breath. "What if we could switch the cylinders? Replace the full cylinders with empty ones."

He frowned. "How we gonna do that?"

"The cylinders are filled with percussion caps and placed in crates that are then stacked outside the packing room. When we need more cylinders, the sergeant fetches a full crate from outside the door and places it at the end of the table. The cylinders are distributed among the girls at the packing table, and the empty crate is returned to the cylinder room and the cycle continues."

"I understand how it works. So what's the plan?"

"If you could grab the full crates and replace them with crates of empty cylinders, we'd be packing cartridges without percussion caps. It's basically the same idea you had, sending cartridges without percussion caps."

Jeremiah dropped the chair down onto all four legs and grunted. "How am I supposed to manage switching the crates? I'd have to be around the packing room all the time. And I'd need to get my hands on empty cylinders."

"You'd only need to steal enough for the first crate. You could find someplace to dump the percussion caps and reuse the cylinders out of each crate."

Jeremiah scratched his head. "It would take a lot of planning and even more luck. The only way your plan can possibly work is if something happens to that fella who's been delivering the crates of percussion caps, and I manage to get the job." His lips slanted in a conspiratorial grin. "Once I see who's in charge of the deliveries, I can make sure there's an accident that will keep him out of work. But you're gonna need to use your charms on that sergeant to make sure I'm the one who gets the job."

"So you think it's a good plan?"

"It's the best we got for now." He nodded toward the stove. "I'm hungry. You gonna get started on supper?"

She stretched and yawned. "Actually I think I'm going to take a nap while *you* fix supper. After all, I'm going to need my beauty rest if I'm going to win Andrew's heart. Right, Jeremiah?"

THIRTEEN

The ache in Joseph's foot and the crispness in the morning air hinted that winter would soon arrive. He adjusted his hat as he walked toward the mess hall. Each day since he'd turned over his written report to the colonel, Joseph had hoped to hear from him. Though Joseph had been praying for a speedy reply, thus far he'd been disappointed. The colonel had seemed eager to move forward with instituting additional safety measures, but Joseph now wondered if the colonel's priorities had changed.

Earlier in the week, Joseph had considered sending a written inquiry to the colonel, but then he decided such action might be considered insubordinate. He'd wait a while longer, and if he didn't hear anything by the first workday of next week, he'd request an appointment. Joseph had moved forward on his own and instructed the sweepers to change their ways, yet there were other modifications needed if they were going to provide as much safety as possible at the Arsenal.

A familiar-looking young private approached Joseph and

gave him a smart salute. "I have a message for you from the colonel, sir. I was told to wait for your reply." The private reached forward and proffered the folded note.

Joseph returned the salute, then extended his hand and accepted the missive. After reading the note, he folded it and placed it in his pocket. "Please tell the colonel I am sorry to learn he has been ill and that I will be pleased to meet with him in his office at one o'clock."

As the private hurried off, Joseph continued on toward the mess hall with a renewed sense of purpose. As soon as he finished breakfast, he'd go to the cylinder room and begin reviewing his notes. Enough time had passed that, without a review, he might forget something of importance.

He finished his breakfast and walked to the laboratory. Strange how his foot didn't seem to bother him as much now that his meeting with the colonel had been scheduled. He sat down at his desk and removed his journal and a copy of the report he'd sent the colonel shortly after his return. Making the extra copy for himself had been tedious, but he was now pleased he'd had the foresight and patience, for he couldn't recall the exact details of his report.

When the door opened, he looked up and was surprised to see Clara. He smiled as she walked toward him. "Good morning, Clara. You're early."

She took a seat on the chair beside him and untied her bonnet. "Mother had an early meeting with one of her customers, who wanted a fitting completed before breakfast." She shook her head. "I think Mother should occasionally tell her clients that she's unwilling to work late at night or so early in the morning. Mother disagrees because she worries about losing their business." Clara hiked a shoulder. "There isn't a finer seamstress in all of Washington, so I believe her fears are completely unfounded. However, she doesn't listen to me."

Joseph reached for her hand. "I'm sorry your mother had to leave so early this morning, but I'm pleased to have a little time alone with you. I hope she didn't have to walk far. Our mornings are getting colder."

"She was going to the home of Salmon Chase, the secretary of the treasury. Their mansion isn't nearby, so Mrs. Chase sent a carriage to fetch Mother. I'm sure Mrs. Chase believes she's been most kind and hasn't overly inconvenienced Mother. Of course, she doesn't realize that Mother is up until late at night stitching dresses or making alterations."

"I've heard from several officers that Mrs. Chase doesn't miss a party, so your mother's creations will likely be admired by all of Washington society. She won't be lacking for work once Mrs. Chase spreads the word."

"She truly doesn't need more work. Mrs. Cameron and Mrs. Bates have recently become customers, and now Mrs. Seward has recommended Mother to Mrs. Chase, who has ordered several gowns. I help as much as I can, but I would like her to slow down a bit." Clara shifted toward him and smiled. "Mrs. Ludwig has offered another supper invitation for this Sunday."

Joseph tipped his head to the side. "Is it only supper she has in mind, or has she found another repair project for me?"

Clara chuckled. "She mentioned only supper, but she's told me how helpful you are several times lately. Of course, she also said she thought you were an engaging dinner companion. I think you've won her heart."

"It's your heart I want to win, Clara." He lifted her hand to his lips and brushed it with a light kiss. Her cheeks colored at his declaration, and he decided he should change the subject before the other ladies arrived. "I've got some good news. This morning I received a message that the colonel wants to meet with me this afternoon."

She squeezed his hand. "That's wonderful. Even though you haven't said much to me, I know you've been worried about our safety since your return from Lawrenceville."

He nodded. "We'll soon be able to make some changes, if the colonel will agree with my suggestions." Joseph glanced toward the door. "Sounds like the other ladies are arriving."

Clara stood and smiled down at him. "Don't forget Mrs. Ludwig's invitation. I'm sure she'll want to begin planning the meal as soon as she's certain you've accepted."

"Tell her I'm pleased to accept. Mostly because I'll be able to spend time with you." He chuckled. "Perhaps you shouldn't tell her that last part—she may think I don't appreciate her cooking."

"I'm looking forward to it." She hesitated a moment. "I forgot to mention that Bea and Sergeant Kessler would like to join us on an outing in the near future, as well."

He nodded. Clara's last comment surprised him. He hadn't realized that Sergeant Kessler and Miss Hodson were courting. Not that Joseph minded. They seemed a good match, but he'd need to warn the sergeant against showing Miss Hodson favoritism. Any form of partiality would breed disharmony among the ladies, and they didn't want that to occur in any of the workrooms. Sergeant Kessler would need to be clear with Miss Hodson, just as Joseph had been clear with Clara. All workers must be treated equally.

Before the lunch break, Joseph strode to the end of the worktable and cleared his throat. "Major Rourke will be taking over my supervisor duties this—" Several moans and angry murmurs filled the room. Joseph held up his hand to stay them. "Ladies! Please permit me to finish. The major will be here for several hours this afternoon while I am meeting with Colonel Furman to discuss safety issues. Both the colonel and I thought it best to have a supervisor on duty."

In truth, Joseph hadn't had any say about Major Rourke's return. He knew the major's appearance would prove unsettling to the workers. However, he couldn't object to the colonel's decision. He knew the ladies would perform admirably during his absence, but if something out of the ordinary should happen, who would take charge? He had stressed the need for trained supervisors in each room in his report to the colonel, so he dared not leave his workers unsupervised.

Moments later, the bell rang. Without further objection, the ladies donned their cloaks, picked up their lunch bundles, and hurried outdoors. A brisk wind whipped through the room, carrying gray flecks of gunpowder skittering across the wooden floor. Joseph shook his head. Was there truly any way to make these laboratories safe? He sighed. Perhaps not, but he was compelled to do whatever he could to make them as safe as possible. The thought of more lives lost was enough to rally his determination.

The major appeared only moments before Joseph needed to leave. The major's sour expression made it clear he wasn't any happier to be at the lab than the workers were to have him. Joseph saluted Major Rourke and reported that the lab was operating as usual with no anticipated problems. Grabbing his hat, he strode toward the door. Before leaving the room, Joseph glanced over his shoulder. "I'll return as soon as possible," he said.

The major's only response was a grunt.

Joseph was surprised when he neared the Headquarters

Building and the colonel was standing outside. The colonel stepped toward Joseph as they exchanged salutes. "I've read your report, so I thought it would be beneficial if we toured the facility together. That way I'll have a clearer understanding of the problems. Whenever I can visually assess a problem, I find it helps me arrive at a more satisfying solution." He tipped his head. "Where to first?"

"Why don't we walk through the laboratory rooms, and then we can go to the freight and shipping area. If you'd like to tour the warehouses, we can do that, as well." Joseph instinctively glanced at his foot. He hadn't planned on so much walking or he would have added extra padding inside his boot.

"I was pleased by your report, and we can immediately implement some of your suggestions, Lieutenant. I'm only sorry I was ill and couldn't get back to you more quickly."

Joseph quickened his step to keep pace with the colonel. "I did reprimand the sweepers—the young boys hired to sweep up loose gunpowder. They'd become lax in their duties, and I know it was one of the issues mentioned during the trial at Lawrenceville."

"Good, good. I'm pleased you took the initiative. You mentioned in your report that a portion of the investigation at Lawrenceville centered on the possibility of infiltration by Southern sympathizers who might have caused the explosion. While I know that wasn't the ultimate finding, the possibility of such a thing happening here causes me great concern. The Arsenal can be easily accessed both by water and land, and while I don't anticipate a full assault from the Confederate Army, I do believe there are conspirators or spies—or both—who could do harm to the Arsenal and to the war effort."

Joseph frowned. "I agree that's an area of concern, although I'm not certain what you're proposing."

The colonel returned the salute of a corporal who was passing by. "I understand we want to keep producing at full capacity, but we must be vigilant about who we hire. While most of the workers in the laboratory are ladies, there are countless men who have access to the area, as well. I believe it would be beneficial to make certain we don't have any Southern sympathizers among us, and that any new employees are carefully assessed."

"We need to go down this way to freight and shipping." Joseph gestured to the left. "Are you saying we need to investigate every civilian employee working at the Arsenal?"

The colonel nodded his head. "I think it would be wise to look into the backgrounds of the workers."

Joseph inhaled a sharp breath. "Unless you plan to use some of the soldiers working within the Arsenal to conduct the investigation, I'm not certain how it can be done."

"The military supervisors could be assigned to investigate their current employees, although we wouldn't want word of this to get out. The more people involved, the greater the chance of exposure."

"I agree, and there's a possibility the employees will become suspicious if we suddenly begin questioning all of them about their backgrounds." Joseph came to a halt as they neared the freight division. "What if we questioned only the civilians who have been hired within the past six months?"

The colonel nodded. "That makes sense. We can have each supervisor prepare a list. If there aren't too many, I can have them interviewed at headquarters by one of my aides. We can say that since the explosion in Lawrenceville, orders have been received that all employees hired within the past six months are to be interviewed. That way it won't appear as if we're singling out new employees in any particular group."

As the two men walked through the freight and shipping division, Joseph motioned to the supervisor. "The colonel wants a more detailed look at how freight is being loaded and shipped."

The colonel stepped forward. "Only shipments of gunpowder and ammunition. I don't need the particulars regarding anything else."

The supervisor shrugged. "Not much to it. Normally, these crates of cartridges are delivered to one of the warehouses and stored until needed. But since there's an increased need for ammunition, we've eliminated that step so that now we're loading directly onto boats or railroad cars."

The colonel folded his arms across his broad chest. "And the gunpowder. How's it handled when the shipments are received?"

"It arrives by wagonload, ten to twenty barrels at a time, depending on production at the various powder mills that supply us and the orders placed. We've been seeing more orders recently because of the increased production in the lab. When we get an order from the lab, the barrels are put outside the lab door so they're easy to get to. Them barrels are heavy."

The colonel continued to walk through the area alongside Joseph and the supervisor. "We're going to change that practice," the colonel said. "You'll be notified about the delivery changes once they've been decided upon. Any idea how much powder leaks out of those barrels as they're being moved around?"

The supervisor shrugged again. "Not exactly sure, but I'd guess if you rolled one of 'em across the yard, there'd be a fine streak from one end to the other." He turned his head and spat a stream of tobacco juice. "None of the fellas working with gunpowder are allowed to smoke." He pointed to his mouth. "We all chew instead."

"You need to water down this area after the barrels have been received and moved." The colonel paused. "Understood?"

"If that's what ya want, but—"

The colonel shook his head. "That's what I want—no excuses."

Over the next three hours, Joseph and the colonel visited the remainder of the freight and shipping division, as well as each room in the laboratory.

When they came to a halt outside the laboratory, the colonel sighed. "It appears some changes need to take place if we're going to make the lab a safer environment in which to work, but the nature of the work makes it impossible to offer complete protection. And then there's the human factor, as well—I'm sure there are still men smoking around the gunpowder." He glanced at Joseph. "Why don't we go back to headquarters and compile a list of items you can begin to correct? If any of the supervisors, workers, or soldiers argue about the changes, I want them directed to my office. First thing tomorrow, I'll notify all supervisors that I want a list of the employees hired within the past six months."

They'd been walking or standing most of the afternoon, and Joseph longed to sit down and elevate his foot. No matter how hard he tried, the ache made it impossible to hide his limp as they walked back to headquarters.

The colonel gave him a sideways glance. "Ever consider a cane, Lieutenant? Might ease the pain a bit."

Joseph startled at the remark. "No, sir. I'm not a cripple."

"You're right, you're not a cripple. Truth is, you're a hero who's unwilling to let others know he was injured fighting for his country. I'm afraid your pride is going to cause your injury to worsen. I'd hate to see that happen, but it's your choice."

They continued into the building, made the list of changes Joseph would oversee, and composed a notice for the supervisors regarding new employees. Nothing more was said about a cane or Joseph's limp, yet as he returned to the laboratory, the colonel's warning about his foot replayed in his mind. The doctors at the Army hospital had advised him to use a cane, and he'd rejected the idea. To him, a cane was a symbol of defeat—that he'd been unable to perform his duty as a leader of men. Was that pride? He wasn't sure. Now, hearing the colonel's remark, he wondered how many other people had noticed his limp. He'd accepted that he'd never again lead troops into battle, but deep down he hadn't accepted that he would never be the same man who had gone off to war. He hadn't wanted to believe he wasn't whole. A cane would announce that truth to the world.

He'd given thought to telling Clara but hadn't gathered the courage to do so. What would she think of him? Would she be repulsed? Would she discard him as a suitor? He wanted to believe she wouldn't be affected, that she was a woman who would love him in spite of his injured foot. But he couldn't be sure. And what would she think of walking alongside a man who required a cane to aid him? He couldn't be sure of that, either. He did know that having a cane right now would help alleviate the searing pain shooting through his foot and into his ankle.

Perhaps the determination to hide his limp and refusal to use a cane were matters of pride. What was that verse from

Proverbs? He searched his memory until he recalled what he'd learned as a child. *"Pride goeth before destruction, and an haughty spirit before a fall."* Yes, that was it. He smiled at the wording. He might literally fall if he didn't set aside his pride.

Fourteen

At the sound of footfalls outside the apartment, Bea strode to the door and pulled it open. "Where have you been?"

Jeremiah shoved a cloth bag filled with groceries into her arms. "I've been doing what you asked me to—buying food for Sunday dinner. If I didn't get it done quick enough, you can go next time."

"Something's happened. We need to talk. I've been sitting here waiting for you."

"We talked at lunch break. What's so important that you've got yourself all worked up?" He glanced at the stove and frowned. "And how come you haven't started cooking supper?"

She narrowed her eyes. "There's more important things than food. There are problems at the lab that we need to talk about."

"So? That don't stop you from cooking." He reached for a butcher knife and sliced a loaf of bread. "Any of that ham left? If you ain't gonna fix supper, I'll make myself a sandwich."

"You go right ahead and do just that while I tell you that

the sergeant read us a note from the colonel today." She arched a brow. "Any interest in what it said?"

"Not unless it's got something to do with the freight and shipping department."

"Come Monday I think you're going to hear the same notice we heard in the packing room today."

Jeremiah hiked a shoulder. "So, what's the colonel got to say?"

"All workers hired within the last six months will be scheduled to report to the colonel's office for some sort of inquiry." She leaned across the table. "My guess is they think there are spies working at the Arsenal, and they aim to find out who."

"Well, we ain't spies." He took a bite of his sandwich and leaned back in his chair.

"What's wrong with you, Jeremiah? We're worse than spies. If they find out we're trying to sabotage shipments of ammunition, they'll put us in the brig and try us as turncoats."

He chuckled. "We ain't turncoats, neither. We was born and raised in Georgia, so we can't be considered turncoats—our allegiance has always been to the Confederacy."

She slapped her hand on the table. "This isn't a joke, Jeremiah. I'm going to be called in and questioned, and so will you. The notice said anyone hired within the last six months, which includes both of us."

"There's nothing to worry about. They're just gonna make sure anything you put on that paper you filled out when they hired you matches up with your answers when you go in there. You think they got enough extra soldiers with both the time and skill to investigate every worker hired in the last six months?"

"I don't know. Maybe there aren't that many to check on. And we don't know for sure what they're going to be asking.

You're just guessing it's going to be a few simple questions. I'm not certain, and it worries me."

"Worrying won't change a thing. Besides, it's Saturday evening. There's no way they can question you before Monday morning. Tomorrow you show that sergeant just how sweet you can be. Get him to talking. Hard telling if he'll know any more than what was on that notice, but he might. If he does, do whatever's necessary to find out. I'll make sure you have time alone with him."

Bea curled her lip. "You're so generous. He may be good-looking, but he's not one of us."

After church on Sunday, Clara and her mother returned home and joined the other boarders for a light noonday lunch, the only meal served on Sundays—unless Mrs. Ludwig was entertaining personal company. And, on those occasions, boarders were excluded from the dining room. That rule had changed once the lieutenant began calling on Clara. Now, she and her mother were included at the table whenever Lieutenant Brady came calling.

Once the other boarders had finished their sandwiches and retired to their rooms, Clara pushed away from the table and began to clear the plates.

Mrs. Ludwig wagged her finger and shook her head. "You don't need to clear the table, Clara. I'm sure your mother could use help with her sewing. Poor woman. I don't know how she manages on so little sleep."

"Mother amazes me, as well. However, she agrees that I should help, since you've kindly invited Joseph to enjoy a meal with us once again." Clara gathered the cups and saucers and stacked them at the end of the table.

"In that case, I would appreciate your help—and your company. I haven't had much time to visit with you or your mother." The older woman retrieved an apron from a hook on the kitchen door and handed it to Clara. "If you're going to help, you'd better protect that pretty dress."

Clara slipped on the apron and tied the strings behind her back. "Thank you." She shot a quick smile at Mrs. Ludwig. "Would you like me to wash the dishes, or is there something else that will be more helpful?"

"No, washing dishes would be best. I set a pot of water on to heat before we sat down for our meal. It should be hot enough by now." As she carried a plate with a few leftover sandwiches to the kitchen, Clara followed with a stack of dirty dishes. "Tell me, Clara, am I going to have empty rooms in the near future?"

Clara shrugged, and her brows pulled together. "I'm sure I don't know, Mrs. Ludwig. I seldom talk to any of the boarders except during meals. No one has mentioned moving to me."

"I was referring to you and your mother." Mrs. Ludwig grinned. "I thought maybe the lieutenant was discussing marriage and I'd lose two of my favorite boarders."

Mrs. Ludwig was known for her ability to ferret information from her boarders, but she'd lacked much success with Clara and her mother. They usually retired to their rooms immediately after each meal. Still, Clara wasn't certain if Mrs. Ludwig worried more about losing them as boarders or losing Joseph as a free jack-of-all-trades. While this was only his second dinner invitation, Joseph had been to the house and completed repairs on five different occasions thus far. Each time he came to repair one item, Mrs. Ludwig presented him with several others. And though he didn't seem to mind, Clara thought the older woman was taking advantage. On the other hand, she did grant them the use of the parlor to visit, so perhaps it was a fair trade.

"I don't think we know each other well enough to consider marriage just yet. I will say that he's a fine man and I'm quite fond of him." She placed a stack of dishes into the hot sudsy water. "I believe he feels the same about me, but only time will tell if marriage is in the offing."

"If you're smart, and I believe you are, you won't let him slip through your fingers. With most of the men off fighting in the war, there are a lot of pretty young women looking for a suitor." She measured out flour and dumped it in a bowl, then turned back to Clara. "If he does ask for your hand, I hope you'll find a home close by. He's good help."

Clara almost laughed aloud at the woman's boldness. "I'll keep that in mind."

For the next hour, the two of them worked side by side, Clara washing dishes and setting the table for their dinner with Joseph so it wouldn't be a last-minute chore, and Mrs. Ludwig mixing and rolling pie dough. Together, they peeled and sliced apples for the filling.

Once the pie was ready for the oven, Mrs. Ludwig dismissed Clara. "You go on upstairs and help your mother until the lieutenant gets here. I'm sure he's going to arrive any time now so he can visit with you before supper."

Clara removed the apron and handed it to Mrs. Ludwig with a promise to return if the older woman needed any further help. She glanced at the parlor clock before ascending the stairs. She'd told Joseph to come at three o'clock, and she wanted a few minutes to readjust the strands of hair that had escaped while she worked in the kitchen.

Now that she was away from Mrs. Ludwig's questions and her kitchen duties, her excitement and anxiety mingled into an unexpected nervousness. She was eager to have this time alone with Joseph. Yesterday she'd been pleased when he said he'd like to begin walking her home each evening. However, he'd said there was something important he needed to discuss with her. She wasn't sure what it could be, but his tone had been serious. Her mother's suggestion to cease worrying and begin praying was easier said than done. Clara wasn't even certain what or how she should pray. Finally, she'd simply asked God to provide her with His direction during her time with Joseph. Her prayers had been consistent, and yet, as the time for Joseph's arrival approached, her apprehension increased.

As Joseph walked toward Clara's boardinghouse, he silently practiced what he wanted to say. Maybe he shouldn't have warned Clara in advance. Now there was no backing out. He'd have to tell her about his injury—and the nightmares he still suffered. Granted, they hadn't been as frequent lately, yet they still occurred. But mostly it was telling her about his foot that concerned him. Would she want a husband who wasn't whole? He'd considered waiting until he'd been courting her for a while longer, but it wasn't the honest thing to do. She had a right to know, to make her decision before they made a deeper commitment to each other.

He walked to the front door, knocked, and prayed this wasn't a mistake. Mrs. Ludwig opened the door and greeted him with a huge smile.

She lifted her nose in the air and sniffed. "I hope you like apple pie, Lieutenant Brady."

He laughed and gave a firm nod. "It smells wonderful. You can be sure that I'll want a big slice for dessert."

Before Mrs. Ludwig rang the bell to announce there was a downstairs visitor, Clara appeared at the top of the steps, wearing a lace-collared dress that boasted wide vertical stripes of navy blue and burgundy. His breath caught as the sun shone through an upstairs hallway window and circled her in a golden halo. An ache swelled in his heart until he thought it might burst. What would he do if she rejected him?

Clara fixed her gaze on him as she descended the steps. "I thought I heard your voice. Is Mrs. Ludwig keeping you to herself?" She glanced at the boardinghouse keeper and grinned.

"You can be sure if I were a lot of years younger and a lot better-looking, I'd set my cap for him, even though I know I wouldn't win." Mrs. Ludwig waved a dismissive gesture at the two of them. "You best use your time wisely. There's only a couple of hours until supper, and the parlor's free." That said, she bustled down the hallway toward the kitchen.

"Would you like to walk to the park or sit in the parlor? You said you had something you wanted to discuss with me. I wasn't certain where you would be more comfortable." Her voice was higher pitched than usual and bore a hint of wariness.

"Let's sit in the parlor." With the constantly changing fall weather and after walking from the Arsenal, his foot was aching. Going for a walk wouldn't help.

As soon as they were seated, Joseph took her hand. "I've told you I care a great deal for you, but there are some things you need to know about me. I hope they won't change your feelings, but if they do, I'll understand." He drew in a deep breath before detailing his injury and the frequent nightmares he'd suffered ever since Bull Run. "I'll understand if you no longer want me to court you."

Her brows tightened, and she stared at him for several seconds. "It grieves me to think that you believe I would reject you because of a wounded foot—or any other disfigurement. It's your heart that matters to me, Joseph. While I wish you hadn't ever been in harm's way, nothing you've said changes what I think about you."

He knew he couldn't withhold anything. She trusted him. He didn't want to risk losing her, yet the entire truth might prove too much for her. "There's one more thing you should know."

"I doubt there's anything you can tell me that's going to shake my feelings for you."

He glanced at the floor and then looked into her eyes. "You've asked about my family and, until now, I've avoided most of your questions."

"I never meant to pry." She shifted toward him. "From my own experience, I know talking about family can sometimes produce sorrow. Concerns over my brother and the loss of my father aren't matters I wish to dwell upon. Please don't feel you—"

He held up his hand to stay her. "This is something you need to know. My family has lived in Massachusetts since before I was born. My father was a cotton buyer for some of the large mills in Lowell. When my brother Daniel was old enough, my father would sometimes take him along when he'd go into the Southern states to purchase cotton. When I became a little older, my father took me, as well. My brother and I reacted differently to those journeys. I didn't believe humans had a right to own each other, but my brother disagreed. He was captivated with the lives and customs of the Southern plantation owners and viewed slavery as a means to prosperity."

Clara tucked a curl behind her ear. "Did the two of you discuss your differing views?"

"We did, but it didn't change his view. I even told Daniel about the time our father took me along when he went to meet one of the plantation owners at a slave auction." Joseph swallowed hard. "I watched as a little girl was torn away from her mother and sold to the plantation owner. He didn't even want the child. I don't know what happened to that little girl. There are still times when I'm trying to fall asleep that I can see the fear in her eyes and hear the anguished cries of her mother. Hearing about that mother and child didn't trouble my brother in the least." Joseph sighed. "I never went with my father again, but my brother continued to travel south."

She leaned close to him. "Did your parents condone slavery?"

"They didn't discuss it much. My father viewed it as a necessary evil. He was convinced the slaves were needed in order to produce the cotton in the mills. He said indentured servitude wouldn't work, and the plantation owners couldn't afford to pay wages to the slaves. He quit his job with the mills when his health began to fail, but my brother never changed his views." He shrugged. "So now we're fighting a war to return freedom that should never have been taken away in the first place."

"And what about Daniel?"

"My brother married the daughter of a Southern plantation owner and stepped into the life he had envied throughout his youth. Although Daniel embraced the idea of slavery, I didn't know whether he would join the Confederate Army. After recuperating, I received a letter from my father. He wrote that Daniel was fighting with General Lee's Army of Northern Virginia."

"And you feared I would refuse your continued courtship if I learned of your brother's beliefs?" She glanced toward the parlor door as one of the boarders passed by to go outside.

"Nowadays folks are careful who they choose as friends. There's always a fear of being associated with traitors. I wanted to be honest with you. It isn't easy telling you that my brother has taken up arms and is fighting against the North, but I can tell you without any hesitation that I would die before I would commit a traitorous act."

She brushed her fingers along his jaw. "I believe you, Joseph, and you need not worry any longer. I'm sorry that you've had to carry these burdens alone, but nothing you've told me makes me want to reconsider our courtship. We are placing our lives in God's hands, and as long as we maintain our faith in God and hold true to our beliefs and each other, we'll be just fine."

He gathered her into his arms. Her strength, her beauty, her compassion, all of it was overwhelming. After all he'd told her, he couldn't believe she still desired him. What had he done to deserve Clara McBride?

FIFTEEN

The mouthwatering smell of frying chicken wafted through the small apartment. Bea turned the pieces as they reached a crusty golden brown. If there was one thing this Southern girl knew how to do, it was to fry a delicious chicken. She'd been killing, plucking, and cooking chickens for as long as she could remember. Andrew was due to arrive soon, and she wanted the meal to be perfect.

"Grab that potato masher and get busy, Jeremiah. As soon as the chicken's done, I need to start the gravy, and I don't want it getting lumpy." Bea nodded toward the pot of potatoes.

She'd expected Jeremiah to grumble and refuse. Instead, he grabbed the wooden masher and set to work. "What time's he supposed to get here? I'm starving."

"Two o'clock." She removed several pieces of chicken from the iron skillet and placed them on a serving platter.

His forehead creased in a frown. "Why'd you make it for two o'clock? That's too early for supper and too late for dinner."

"He set the time. Said his momma always served their big

Sunday meal after they got home from church, and it would be two or three o'clock before they ate. I think he figured I'd need the same amount of time, and I didn't argue with him."

"You gonna let him think we go to church?"

She shrugged. "I guess so. But if he asks, I can't very well lie. What would I say if he wanted to know what the sermon was about?"

"You're prob'ly right. If he brings it up, maybe just say you don't like to talk about religion 'cause folks can get in quarrels too easy." He continued pushing the masher up and down in the boiled potatoes. "Maybe you shoulda cooked these taters a little longer."

"Maybe you should get some bigger muscles. Those potatoes are cooked just fine. Put a lump of butter in the pan." She dipped her hand into the flour, gathered a small portion in her fingers, and sprinkled it lightly over the hot grease.

"You want me to leave as soon as we're done eating?"

"I thought Andrew and I would go for a walk after the meal. You can clear up and wash the dishes. When we get back, you should leave. Tell him you're meeting some friends or something."

He gasped and slammed the potato masher on the table. "Wash the dishes? Since when is that my job?"

"You're the one who wants me to sweet-talk the sergeant and get information out of him. The least you can do is wash a few dishes. If that's too much for you, then you can sit in the parlor with him while I clean the kitchen. What's it going to be, Jeremiah? Which one of us needs to spend time with Andrew?"

He exhaled a long breath. She didn't miss the tic in his jaw. Jeremiah didn't like it when he lost an argument. He never wanted her to believe she had any control over their lives. But she did—at least over a few things.

She poured milk into the skillet and stirred until the gravy began to thicken. "Keep stirring while I fix my hair." She peeled off her apron and tossed it on the back of the chair. A quick glance at the clock caused her to quicken her step. He would arrive soon.

There hadn't been time to do much to her hair before a knock sounded at the door. While Jeremiah greeted the sergeant, she gave herself one last look in the mirror, pinched her cheeks, then walked down the hallway with a bright smile on her face.

"Welcome, Andrew. Why don't you join us in the kitchen? Dinner is ready, and I wouldn't want to serve you cold food."

Andrew nodded, and a hank of his black hair fell across his forehead, giving him a swarthy appearance. "I could smell the fried chicken as soon as I walked up the steps to the front porch."

Jeremiah pulled out a kitchen chair and sat down. "My sister is one fine cook, that's for sure. I'd say she's one of the finest in all of Washington."

"And one of the prettiest, if you don't mind my saying so." The tips of Andrew's ears turned the shade of ripe tomatoes.

Jeremiah laughed. "I guess she is, but I'm her brother, so I just think of her as my plain ole sister."

Bea momentarily considered throwing a damp dish towel at him. How dare he call her plain! She carried the bowl of potatoes to the table and met the sergeant's gaze. "And I just think of Jeremiah as my homely, annoying brother." She shot Jeremiah a look that said he'd better cease his attempts to be clever.

Although Jeremiah had already seated himself, Andrew

remained standing. He took a step toward Bea. "Is there anything I can do to help? I'm not much of a cook, but I can carry bowls to the table."

"No, you sit down. All I need to do is pour the gravy in a bowl." She glanced over her shoulder. "We're not like the fancy folks. We don't have one of those gravy boats. We just use a bowl and spoon." Bea carried the bowl to the table, then sat down between the two men.

"My family isn't fancy either, so I should feel right at home. Everything looks and smells delicious." Andrew glanced at Jeremiah, who had picked up the platter of chicken. "Would you like me to pray or were you going to, Jeremiah?"

Jeremiah cleared his throat and rested the platter beside his plate. "You go ahead, Andrew, but make it short." He chuckled. "I'm mighty hungry."

Andrew smiled, bowed his head, and gave thanks for the meal while Bea and Jeremiah exchanged glances. The prayer wasn't long, though Bea didn't consider it short, either. She held her breath and hoped Jeremiah wouldn't say anything. The last thing she wanted to discuss was prayer, Scripture, or religion.

"Praying out loud before meals is one of the things I miss most about home. My pa's a preacher, so when we gathered around the table, we always gave thanks before our meals. Eating at the mess hall is a whole different story. Most a fella can do there is offer a quick silent prayer before meals."

"I prefer silent praying myself," Jeremiah said. "Figure what I got to say is just between me and God and ain't nobody else got to hear it."

Bea nudged Jeremiah's knee beneath the table and glared at him. If he didn't shut up about the praying, Andrew would likely veer off and start talking about religion. He'd already said his pa was a preacher. She couldn't believe that Jeremiah had had the nerve to say he prayed. He didn't even believe in God.

"I should have asked if you like chicken when I invited you for dinner, Andrew. I know there may be folks who aren't fond of fried chicken."

"A person would have to be senseless not to like fried chicken." Andrew forked a chicken leg onto his plate. "It's one of my favorites. I didn't eat breakfast this morning so I'd have lots of room for whatever you served." He grinned. "Probably wasn't a good idea since my stomach was rumbling during church."

Bea inwardly sighed. There he went talking about church again. "One of the girls at work told me it snows a lot in Vermont."

"That's true. I love the winters at home. Hunting and trapping, ice fishing, and tapping the maple trees to make syrup—there's a lot to like about winter in Vermont. It was a good place to grow up, and I look forward to going back one day soon." Andrew lifted a forkful of green beans to his mouth.

"I'm not so sure about the hunting and trapping part, but tapping maple trees sounds like something I might enjoy. How's it done?"

Bea half listened while Andrew detailed every aspect of when and how to tap the trees and then described how they used special equipment to boil down the sap and then can the syrup. They finished their dessert as he concluded his account.

"Knowing all of that could come in mighty handy if we was ever to move to Vermont." Jeremiah nudged her arm. "Don't ya think, Bea?"

"Could be. You never know." She tightened her lips into a thin line and gave her brother a hard stare. "I think Andrew and I will go out for a walk. The weather's mighty nice." She pushed away from the table and set her gaze on the sergeant.

"A walk would be nice, but maybe I should help Jeremiah clear up the dishes and you can rest in the parlor."

Jeremiah shook his head. "No. You and Bea go on." His refusal hadn't been particularly convincing, but Bea didn't give Andrew an opportunity to object further. When he stood, she grasped his arm and led him toward the front door.

As they were walking toward the park, Bea squeezed his arm. "I know you said you weren't happy to be working in the packing room, but I hope you won't request a transfer anytime soon." She fluttered her lashes. "I know having you as our supervisor has certainly made me want to be at work every day."

He chuckled. "I'm pleased to hear that you consider me a good supervisor, but I hope the time will arrive when you'll consider me more than a supervisor."

"I already consider you a friend, Andrew. You're so easy to talk to, and even though I'm not from Vermont, I already feel a kinship with you." She smiled. "Hearing about making the maple syrup brought back memories of canning vegetables on our farm. Life has changed so much for all of us. It's sad, isn't it?"

"Yes, but we need to remain strong and maintain our faith in God. Along with everyone else, I'm praying the war will soon be over. Meanwhile, we do whatever we can to win the war and abolish slavery."

"Of course." She forced a smile. "Did you like working in the freight yard? Jeremiah says he's hoping he'll be able to get a transfer out of there. When he was hired, they said they'd be moving him around to different areas where they were short of workers." After she sat down on the nearby bench, he joined her.

Andrew arched his brows. "There are a number of workers they hire and then shift among various positions. I never supervised Jeremiah, but I heard he was a hard worker. I'm sure any of the supervisors would be happy to have him." He tipped his head to the side. "I thought he enjoyed his work. Has something happened in the freight yard, or is he simply wanting a change?"

She silently chided herself. Why hadn't she and Jeremiah anticipated Andrew's question? One misstep and Andrew might become suspicious. "I don't think anything has happened. Jeremiah likes a challenge and soon tires of doing the same thing every day. While my brother enjoys variety and change, I like consistency. I find change quite unsettling. A little is fine, but too much makes me anxious. And there are so many unsettling things happening at the Arsenal—it's difficult to feel secure."

He offered a gentle smile. "There's no need for you to feel anxious about returning to work in the packing room. Your position is secure. We need all the workers we can hire if we're going to increase production, so why all this concern?"

"That letter from the colonel worries me. The one about workers who have been hired within the last six months." She peered across the expanse of dying grass. "Jeremiah and I have been here for less than six months. That means we'll be questioned."

"The interviews are a mere formality to set the colonel's mind at ease." He took hold of her hand, and his mouth fell open. "You're shivering. We need to return to the apartment. I didn't realize you were so cold. Do you feel ill?"

Bea shook her head. "No. The days are becoming shorter, and the sun has disappeared behind that bank of clouds." She moved closer to him as they walked. "I'll be fine as long as I have you close by to keep me warm."

"My pleasure." He smiled down at her.

Bea didn't question Andrew further until they'd neared the rows of ramshackle houses and tenements that lined 4 ½ Street. "Were you only attempting to set my mind at ease when you said I shouldn't worry about the interview, or have you been told something more? Something that would give me greater assurance."

He patted her hand that was resting in the crook of his arm. "The colonel called a meeting of the officers, and the interviews were discussed among all of them. The colonel was the only one who thought the interviews would be beneficial. Most thought it a waste of time, which could be better used on other issues. Whoever conducts the interviews isn't going to take much time with them."

They turned on South M Street. "But you weren't at the meeting. How can you be sure?"

He chuckled. "You're right, I wasn't at the meeting. The lieutenant who gave me the notice told me, and he was at the meeting."

"Lieutenant Brady from the cylinder room?"

"No. A lieutenant assigned to headquarters. He said the colonel wants to make sure the workers are safe and that no Rebs have been hired. Since the explosion at Lawrenceville, I think the officers in charge of all the arsenals are on edge. They don't want to take any chances of having more civilians injured or killed." He bowed his head against a gust of wind that carried dirt and leaves across their path. "I'm pleased the colonel is taking extra precautions. Now that we've found each other, I wouldn't want anything to happen to you."

"Thank you, Andrew. I truly didn't want to transfer from the cylinder room, but I now believe we were destined to find each other."

"My pa always said that when the time was right, God would send me a good woman. Until I met you, I never put much stock in those words." His dark eyes shone with adoration when he looked down at her.

Bea was taken aback by his comment. There was little doubt the sergeant wasn't experienced with women. If so, he wouldn't have revealed his feelings so quickly. Yet she was pleased with her success. Since transferring to the packing room, she'd done everything in her power to win the sergeant's attentions. She hadn't realized he would be such easy prey, or that he would believe God had a hand in her appearance. The idea fascinated her.

She glanced over her shoulder as they climbed the porch steps leading into the apartment. When they stepped inside, Jeremiah met her gaze. "I'm glad to see you two have returned. I was going to go out for a while. You've saved me the need to write a note." He patted his stomach. "I think that late lunch is going to hold me for quite a while, so I won't be back until around eight. I'm going over to Harry's apartment for a visit."

Andrew extended his hand. "I'll be gone before you return, but I do thank you for welcoming me into your home, Jeremiah."

"No need to rush off, Andrew. I'm sure my sister will want you to keep her company a while longer."

"My pass is good only until six o'clock, so I'll need to get back to the Arsenal before then. I wish I could stay until eight o'clock." Longing shone in his eyes as he looked at Bea.

"Don't let my sister make you late. You wouldn't want your commanding officer to think you'd deserted." Jeremiah grinned. "There's still some pie in the kitchen, and you have plenty of time for that. Just be sure you leave me a piece." He shook Andrew's hand, then winked at his sister. "You two have a nice visit."

"We'll do our best, and you enjoy your time with Harry." Bea knew there was no Harry, yet the lie was good enough to get him out of the house so she'd have more time alone with Andrew. "How about a piece of that pie? I'm sure you worked up a bit of an appetite after our walk."

"That sounds good." He followed her into the kitchen and sat down at the table. "Who's Harry?"

"What?" She swirled around.

"Harry. Didn't Jeremiah say he was going to visit someone named Harry? I don't think there's anyone in shipping and freight named Harry." His forehead wrinkled into tight lines. "Maybe he means Henry Allen. Harry's a nickname for Henry, isn't it?"

"I think it is." Her mind raced to develop some believable response. "Jeremiah was referring to a fellow he's met at the park. They play chess on Sunday evenings quite often." She swallowed hard as she placed a slice of pie onto a chipped plate.

"That's good to know. I enjoy playing chess. Maybe I'll bring my set with me sometime, and Jeremiah and I can enjoy a game." He leaned forward to accept the pie from her. "Unless you play. I'd much rather play a game with you."

"No." She shook her head. "I've never learned. I know it takes skill, but I find it boring. There's too much sitting and staring at the chess board for my liking."

"Is there? Perhaps if you exchanged a kiss with your opponent each time he made a move, the game would end more quickly."

"That sounds like a wonderful idea. If you put that rule in place, maybe I should have you teach me."

"I'd like nothing better."

Bea looked up from her mending when Jeremiah returned. "I thought you were going to be gone until eight o'clock."

"I wasn't sure how much time you'd need, but when he said he had to be back to the barracks by six, I waited in that little church near the Arsenal. I saw him when he passed by and I started home." He hung his coat on a peg near the front door, then sat beside her in the parlor. "How did it go?"

Bea shrugged. "Some good and some bad."

"What does that mean?" He folded his arms across his chest and looked down his nose at her.

"The good part is that it sounds as though the interviews won't be anything too involved. From what he said, the colonel was the only officer who thought it should be done. He's worried about Confederate sympathizers who might try to blow up the place."

Jeremiah grinned. "You mean like us? We're not going to try and blow it up." He leaned sideways and chucked her beneath the chin. "A fire or explosion would be too dangerous for you, and I intend to keep my promise. I know you're afeard of fires. Besides, if our plans work, we can create more trouble at the front lines than we would with a fire. They'd do like Lawrenceville and just move the lab to other buildings and keep on like nothing ever happened."

After stitching a button onto one of Jeremiah's shirts, Bea

used her teeth and broke off the thread. "We have to make sure we don't get caught before we can sabotage the place."

He nodded. "So, what's the bad news?"

"I told him you wanted to transfer out of the freight yard." She'd expected Jeremiah to be angry that she'd told Andrew, yet he merely shrugged instead.

"Just don't say anything more about it until I manage to get that fella ousted who's delivering the gunpowder. Anything else?"

"Yes. You need to learn to play chess."

Sixteen

Joseph and Clara bowed their heads against rolling gales of wind as they walked up 4 ½ Street to Bea's apartment, where they were to join Bea, her brother, Jeremiah, and Sergeant Kessler for coffee and dessert. With each gust, vibrant autumn leaves gathered around their shoes, then fluttered onward. Joseph settled his hat a bit lower on his forehead. "If this wind continues much longer, all the trees are going to be bare come morning."

Clara tipped her head and looked at the sky. "Those clouds remind me that winter can't be far off."

Joseph nodded. No doubt the commanders and soldiers in the field were thinking about winter, as well. War was difficult enough in decent weather, but spring storms created a mucky terrain that proved difficult for man and beast, and the frigid cold of winter brought a grueling set of difficulties all its own. While winter camps would be set up to provide some protection from the elements, there would be an increased lack of food, clean drinking water, and sanitation. Disease would run rampant and take as many lives as most battles. When the warmer weather finally arrived, the melting snow would leave a sea of mud that would mire soldiers, animals, and wagons alike. He wouldn't complain about changing weather—not when he slept in a warm barracks and had plenty of hot food to eat.

Clara's tug on his sleeve brought him back to the present. Her brows dipped low over her eyes. "You didn't hear a word I was saying, did you?"

He shot her a quick smile and shook his head. "I'm sorry. I was lost in my own thoughts. What were you telling me?"

"Bea expressed concern that conversation might prove difficult since you don't know Jeremiah and Sergeant Kessler, so I thought we might play charades." She glanced at him. "I thought it might set all of us at ease. What do you think?"

"So long as I'm with you, I'll enjoy myself. But who's going to decide what charades we'll be acting out?"

"Mrs. Ludwig was pleased to lend her assistance. I have the slips of paper in my reticule." He took her elbow as they climbed the steps. "I promise I haven't looked at them."

"Hmm. You may have to let the rest of us win just to prove your honesty." He chuckled. "I'm joking. I know you wouldn't cheat."

"Thank you, kind sir." Clara nodded toward the door. "Here we are." She led the way up the porch steps and knocked.

Before either could say anything further, Jeremiah appeared with his hair still damp and freshly combed. He hung their wraps on the wooden pegs in the hallway and ushered them into the parlor, where Andrew and Bea awaited them. Andrew stood straight as a stick and lifted his hand to salute before quickly dropping it to his side. He was obviously uncertain what protocol he should follow.

Joseph extended his hand and offered the sergeant a sympathetic smile. "No need for formality, Andrew. We're two civilians enjoying a Sunday afternoon visit and a game of charades."

"Charades?" Bea arched her brows and looked at Clara.

"I thought it might be fun." She reached into her reticule and withdrew folded slips of paper. "Mrs. Ludwig was kind enough to prepare these for us." Clara placed the slips into a bowl on the table and turned to the three men. "Who would like to play?"

All three of them raised their hands. Bea shook her head and frowned at Jeremiah. "I thought you were going to play chess with your friend this afternoon."

Jeremiah settled back in his chair. "This sounds like far more fun than chess. I can always go later. Shall I go first?" Without waiting for a response, he plucked a paper from the bowl and opened it.

"You're a terrible host, Jeremiah. You should have let one of our guests go first." Bea crossed the room and sat down beside Andrew.

Jeremiah ignored her and held up six fingers.

"Six words," they shouted in unison. When he held up only one finger, they called out, "First word."

Jeremiah nodded, bent his arms at the elbow, and flapped them up and down.

"Chicken!" Bea said.

Jeremiah shook his head and continued flapping his arms.

"Bird?" Andrew leaned forward when Jeremiah waved encouragement. "Birds?"

Jeremiah hurried to the hallway and returned with a shabby red velvet bonnet. He held up four fingers and pointed to the frayed feather tucked near the brim.

"Feather," Clara said. "So the fourth word is *feather*, and the first word is *birds*."

"Ha! Birds of a feather flock together," Joseph hollered. "Is that it?"

Jeremiah tossed the paper onto the table. "That's it! Since you guessed correctly, I think you should go next, Joseph."

After withdrawing a paper from the bowl, Joseph held up five fingers and then looked toward the kitchen. He strode to the dry sink, picked up a misshapen bar of soap, returned, and held up one finger. While holding the soap near his shirt, he moved it up and down the sleeve and did the same to his trousers.

"Washing clothes," Andrew said. When Joseph shook his head, Andrew said, "Scrubbing your body?" Joseph shook his head again but waved encouragement to the others.

"Cleaning?" Bea asked. Joseph nodded enthusiastically for her to continue. "Cleansing?" He held his fingers together and gestured in a stretching motion. Bea frowned, then shouted, "Cleanliness?"

"Yes!" He held up five fingers and pointed to the ceiling.

They all looked up, and Jeremiah chuckled. "I think he's offering to clean the ceiling, Bea." They all erupted in laughter.

Once the laughter died down, Andrew leaned forward. "Godliness. Cleanliness is next to godliness. Is that it, Joseph?"

"Right you are, Andrew!" Joseph turned to Clara. "Why don't you go next and let us see your acting abilities, Clara."

She smiled at him, stood, reached into the bowl, and read the saying before holding up eight fingers. She waited a moment and held up three fingers.

"Third word," Andrew said.

Clara nodded and rapidly pointed her finger back and forth between Bea and herself.

Andrew scooted to the edge of his chair. "Girls! Women! Ladies!"

Clara shook her head.

"Friends," Bea shouted.

Clara nodded, held up four fingers, and stepped to Bea's side. She pulled her into a tight hug.

"Hug! Embrace! Squeeze!" The fellows continued to shout their guesses, but it was Bea who raised her eyebrows and said, "Close?"

Joseph hesitated only a moment before he nudged Andrew. "Keep your friends close and your enemies closer. Is that it?"

"Yes!" Clara hurried to his side and dropped down beside him.

Andrew shook his head. "You sure got that one in no time, Joseph." He waved to Bea. "Come on, Bea. Take a turn."

She nodded. "I'll do mine and then we'll have cake and coffee." She reached into the bowl, read the paper, and stepped to the middle of the room. A tiny smile played at her lips as she held up six fingers and gestured that she was going to act out the fourth word. Moments later, she shaped her fingers into a heart and then enveloped Andrew in a giant hug.

"Love," Joseph and Clara shouted in unison.

Bea nodded and moved back to the center of the room before holding up six fingers. She pretended she was holding a rifle and shooting. After several incorrect guesses, Jeremiah shouted, "War! Love and war. All's fair in love and war. Is that it?"

"That's it." Bea grinned at her brother, but he didn't return the smile. Instead, his eyes flickered with a mysterious look.

Perhaps he thought Bea had been too familiar with Andrew. In truth, her hug had seemed a bit overzealous. Then again, who could say?

Moments later, Jeremiah pointed to the kitchen. "I'm ready

for that cake and coffee, Bea." Once Bea and Clara disappeared into the kitchen, Jeremiah turned to Joseph. "Terrible thing that happened in Lawrenceville. I bet you wish you hadn't been there during the explosion."

Joseph placed his elbow on the armrest. "I wish nobody had been there. There were so many young women killed or injured. In the aftermath of Antietam, I fear they've already been forgotten."

"Nobody who works at the Arsenal has forgotten." Jeremiah rubbed his jaw. "What with the colonel looking to make changes and insisting on those investigations, it would be hard to forget."

Andrew scooted forward on the sofa. "I hear tell there's going to be some changes made in the filling room and maybe in the packing room too, but nobody's saying much."

Joseph was uncomfortable discussing the agreed-upon changes with either of the men. Granted, not much had been completed yet. It seemed they took one step forward and then the war took precedence over all else. The colonel was attempting to maintain some secrecy about the process, and while Joseph agreed, he doubted confidentiality was truly possible. The colonel continued to worry that Confederate sympathizers might be working among them at the Washington Arsenal and had decided secrecy was paramount. But from the sound of things, many workers either knew or surmised far more than the colonel would like.

Jeremiah raked his fingers through his hair. "We heard all the new workers are going to be interviewed, but that ain't happened. Not that I'm hankering to be questioned, mind you. They read us a letter or something from the colonel. Now, though, I'm thinking it was just a hoax. I even heard tell the colonel has decided to investigate the soldiers assigned here in the past six months, too. Don't that beat all? Sounds like the colonel don't even trust the men fighting for the Union."

Joseph straightened in his chair. "Where did you hear members of the military are going to be questioned?"

"I don't rightly recall. I think it was one of the new sergeants in the warehouse who mentioned it when he came over to freight and shipping." Jeremiah scratched the back of his neck. "Yeah, I think that's who it was. He said he was transferred here a couple weeks ago. When he reported to headquarters, he was told he'd need to come back for another interview. He thought it was strange and wondered if any of us knew anything about it."

"And?" Joseph asked.

Jeremiah furrowed his brow. "And what?"

"What was he told?" Joseph sighed. He was teetering on the edge of exasperation. One minute Jeremiah acted as though he were a fount of knowledge, and the next he behaved like a youngster without a lick of sense.

"Oh! Just that we'd heard new hires were being interviewed, but we didn't know what was going on with the soldiers." Jeremiah shrugged. "Which is the truth. We never hear what's happening with you fellas unless it affects our work."

Jeremiah's knowledge that soldiers would be interviewed was a direct contradiction to what he'd just said. However, Joseph was more concerned about the possibility of being interviewed than Jeremiah's truthfulness. He'd be forced to reveal his brother was fighting for the Confederacy. If he was permitted to remain at the Arsenal, he'd be an easy target if and when any problems arose.

Yet he might not be one of the soldiers questioned. The

colonel had trusted him and sent him to Lawrenceville after reviewing his initial paper work and conducting a brief interview. Perhaps the colonel wouldn't place his name on the list. The thought quieted his mounting anxiety.

"You feeling poorly, Joseph?" Andrew gestured to his face. "You're as pale as a bucket of fresh milk."

Joseph swallowed hard and forced a smile. "I'm fine. Just having a few thoughts about the war—must have affected me more than I thought."

Bea entered the room bearing two slices of cake. She gave one plate to her brother and one to Andrew. "Let's enjoy our cake, and then Jeremiah is going to go and play chess with his friend. The rest of us can continue with charades, if you'd like." Bea directed a tight smile at her brother.

Clara carried a piece of cake to Joseph and glanced over her shoulder. "If you want to be included in our outings, Jeremiah, perhaps you should find a young lady and begin courting."

Andrew chuckled. "Mazie Carmichael might be a good choice. She works with Bea in the packing room. What do you think, Bea? Should the two of us talk to Mazie and see if she might be interested in Jeremiah as a suitor?"

Jeremiah's dark hair matched his dark expression. "Absolutely not. I don't want to court anyone. I don't need another woman in my life telling me what to do."

Clara chuckled and then returned to the kitchen and brought back the coffee, cream, and sugar.

While talk of Jeremiah courting Mazie continued, he wolfed down his cake and coffee, then pushed to his feet. He carried his dishes to the kitchen and grabbed his coat from a peg. "I'm gonna be on my way. If you're kindhearted, you won't say nothing about those courting ideas to Mazie.

I'm not gonna call on her, so there ain't no need for her to get her hopes up."

After Jeremiah departed, Clara stared at the door and shook her head. "I'm trying to decide if that remark means Jeremiah is kind or arrogant."

Bea grinned and patted Clara on the shoulder. "I would say it's a bit of each."

SEVENTEEN

Clara slipped her hand into the crook of Joseph's arm as they descended the steps from Bea and Jeremiah's apartment and began their walk back to her boardinghouse. She squeezed his arm. "You're so quiet. Care to talk about what's concerning you?"

Joseph's brow creased. "I was thinking about how odd Jeremiah seems to me. One minute he seems lighthearted and jovial, and the next he turns sour. He appears to have his nose in everything."

"Bea's a little off too, but I do like her. She's genuine, and she isn't putting a show on for anyone. She is who she is."

Joseph stopped and turned to face Clara. He took her hands in his. "That's one thing I love about you. You see past a person's exterior to what's on the inside."

Clara's cheeks warmed, and her heart swelled. *Love?* Had he really used that word?

"You even see past my war wounds."

She sucked in a breath. This discussion seemed to have taken an unexpected turn. She looked into Joseph's soulful blue eyes. Did she see guilt in them? Did he think she was doing him a favor? Didn't he realize she didn't care if he walked with a limp?

She placed her hand on his cheek. "Joseph, I need you to hear this. There's nothing for me to see past. It's all part of what makes you the man you are—a man I happen to be very fond of."

He covered the hand she had pressed to his cheek with his own. She felt the hard calluses, so different from the soft flesh of her own hand. "Clara, I know we've been courting only a short time, and I don't want you to think me forward, but I want you to know that I have become more than fond of you."

She released a shaky breath. "I don't think you forward at all, Joseph. Truth be told, it reassures me to know your feelings run as deep as my own."

He cupped her cheek in his palm, lowered his head, and captured her lips in a gentle kiss. When their lips parted, he glanced about. "I apologize for kissing you on a public street, but I couldn't resist."

She smiled and shook her head. "No need for an apology. I enjoyed it very much."

Joseph stepped inside the Headquarters Building as the north wind attempted to push the threatening clouds away from the Arsenal. It had been two days since he and Clara had played charades with Jeremiah, Andrew, and Bea. Two long days for worrying until finally this morning he'd been summoned to the colonel's office.

He took a seat in a chair outside the colonel's door and waited. The last thing he needed was more time for his thoughts to run rampant. He bowed his head and wrestled with how he should pray. He didn't want to be forced to leave the Arsenal because of his brother's choices. Yet he understood the colonel would consider retention of a soldier with Confederate connections a significant risk. In truth, Joseph couldn't fault the colonel if he determined the risk too great. If placed in the colonel's position, Joseph didn't know what he would do.

A booming clap of thunder shook the glass in the nearby windows and interrupted his prayer. Joseph gripped the chair arms as bolts of lightning illuminated the sky. Images of Bull Run flashed through his mind. When another boom sounded, he clutched the chair arms until his knuckles turned white and his fingers ached. He squeezed his eyes together. Right now he needed peace, not a thunderstorm.

"Lieutenant, I'm ready for you."

Joseph startled and jerked around. He didn't know how long the colonel had been standing there looking down at him. "Yes, sir."

He pushed to his feet and followed the colonel into his office. He silently prayed for the strength to be honest and accept the outcome, no matter what the colonel decided. God had provided him with strength and courage in the past, and Joseph knew He would be with him now.

"I hope I didn't keep you waiting too long. These interviews have been taking longer than anticipated." He gestured to the chair opposite his desk. "I'm thankful my time with you will provide some diversion."

Joseph nodded in an attempt to hide his confusion. "I'm pleased to be of assistance, sir."

The colonel rustled through a stack of papers. "Now then." He pushed a paper across the desk toward Joseph. "Look at that list and tell me if I've forgotten anything. You can mark off the items you've already corrected."

Joseph picked up and scanned the page that outlined the

corrections to be made within the laboratory, shipping, and warehouse areas of the Arsenal.

The colonel leaned back in his chair. "I'm giving you full authority to make these changes immediately. If you need additional men to carry out your orders, please let me know. Otherwise, you may appropriate help from any of the workers, supervisors, or soldiers in any of those areas to complete the corrections." He handed another paper to Joseph. "If anyone questions your authority, you may show them this."

Joseph glanced at the order. "I appreciate your confidence, sir. I have already made some adjustments to the storage and security of the gunpowder, but I'll begin immediately with the other changes."

"Excellent. Don't hesitate to instruct our supervisors to make changes in work assignments where necessary. We all need to adapt if we're going to provide our workers with the safety they deserve."

Joseph nodded. "Was that all, sir?"

The colonel chuckled. "I think that list provides enough to keep you busy for quite some time, Lieutenant." His brow furrowed. "Did you want to discuss something further with me?"

Joseph shook his head. "No, sir, but I thought I'd been summoned here for an interview."

The colonel removed his reading glasses and rubbed his eyes. "I don't see a need to interview you, Lieutenant. You fought for the Union and were wounded at Bull Run. I sent you to Lawrenceville, where you were placed in harm's way. You returned to Washington and have provided me with valid methods to make the Arsenal safer." He shrugged. "What more do I need to know? If I didn't trust you, I wouldn't have placed you in charge of safety here."

"Thank you, Colonel, but there's something I need to tell you."

The colonel looked up. "What's that?"

Joseph swallowed hard. "My brother married into a Southern family—plantation owners. I've had correspondence from my father that my brother is now fighting for the South. I wanted you to be aware of this connection in my family."

"Your situation isn't particularly unique, Lieutenant. Unfortunately, this war will continue to see brother pitted against brother, father against son, and cousin against cousin. My trust in you isn't swayed by anything you've told me, although I do thank you for your honesty." The colonel backed away from his desk and stood.

"Again, I thank you for your trust in me."

"It's me who should be thanking you, Lieutenant. I've charged you with an enormous mission."

"I won't let you down, sir." He saluted. "If I can prevent the death of one Union soldier or worker, I'll do it."

Clara kept pace with Bea and Jeremiah as they walked toward the Arsenal. Neither of them appeared to be in good spirits, and she wondered if they'd been arguing. Clara was never certain what topic might set one of them off, yet she missed chatting with Bea on the way to and from work. Now that Bea was in the packing room, they seldom shared lunch breaks together. They hadn't had time for a good visit for days. Even their Sunday get-together hadn't provided them with any time for a private conversation.

Hoping to slow Bea down, Clara looped arms with her. "Are you not feeling well?"

Bea gave her a quick glance. "I'm feeling as good as I can, considering I've got an idiot for a brother."

Clara sighed. "I take it you and Jeremiah didn't have a good evening. Has Andrew called on you since last Sunday?"

"No. He's coming over for supper on Friday evening. He's hoping Jeremiah will play a game of chess with him." She wrinkled her nose. "That's not much fun for me, but he and Jeremiah enjoy talking about work and chess. If I object, it leads to a quarrel with Jeremiah."

"I'm sorry. I do wish you'd come back to the cylinder room. I miss our time together."

Bea slowed her pace a bit, and when Jeremiah was out of earshot, she leaned her head close. "Jeremiah and I were both called in for interviews this week. It didn't go so good."

Clara edged closer. "Why? What happened?"

"It seems my brother can't remember where he's from."

"What? That makes no sense." Clara frowned. Surely she'd misunderstood.

"*He* makes no sense. I'd like to box his ears. He told the investigator that we used to live on a farm in Maryland until our pa died."

"That's what you told me, so what was the problem?" Clara was now totally confused.

"There are two towns near the farm. On his original papers he gave the name of one town, and when they questioned him, he gave the name of another. So then they checked my paper work and called me in and started asking me questions. They compared every answer I gave them against his, and a couple others didn't match. He's so stupid he can't remember his own birthday."

"Oh, Bea, I'm sorry. So, what did they do? Call him back in?" She gasped. "They aren't going to terminate you, are they?"

"I don't think so. I explained that Jeremiah had a high fever right before we left the farm and his memory hasn't been quite right since then. I'm not sure how it's going to end up, but the investigator told me not to worry." She sighed. "That's easier said than done. I don't know how we'll afford to live if either of us loses our job. What am I going to do, Clara?"

Clara patted Bea's arm. "Pray. I think that's the only thing you can do right now. The investigator said you shouldn't worry, so we need to pray and trust that God is going to protect you and your job."

"Prayer didn't keep my pa alive, so I don't think God is going to protect my job. What I need is some real help."

"But God—"

"What about Joseph? He could put in a good word for us with the investigators—that's the kind of help me and Jeremiah need." Bea grasped Clara's hand. "Will you talk to him? Please?"

Clara studied her friend, who had withdrawn a handkerchief and was now blotting her eyes. Clara's heart ached for Bea. Although Clara wanted to argue that Joseph was no substitute for God, it was clear Bea needed reassurance Clara would speak to Joseph. She squeezed Bea's hand and nodded. "Of course. I'm sure Joseph will do whatever he can to help. However, I doubt his word will hold much sway. As your friend, I'm telling you it would be best to put your trust in the Lord."

Eighteen

Two days later, Clara stood beside her mother as they waited inside the front door of the boardinghouse. Each carried a small tapestry bag that contained scissors, thread, needles, punches, hooks, and a few scraps of fabric, as well as other sewing necessities.

Her mother kept her nose only inches from the front door glass. The moment the carriage arrived, she reached for the door handle. "Come along, Clara. We don't want to keep the driver waiting."

Clara's shoes clattered on the wooden steps as she hurried behind her mother. No one could ever accuse Leta McBride of being late for an appointment. No matter the circumstances, she prided herself on being punctual. The driver swung down from his perch and opened the door. Within minutes the carriage jerked into motion.

"I am sorry, Clara. I shouldn't have agreed to a six o'clock appointment." She reached inside her bag and withdrew a paper-wrapped jelly sandwich. "It isn't much, but I hope it will help keep your hunger at bay until we get home tonight."

"You mean *if* we get home tonight, don't you?" Clara unwrapped the sandwich and smiled at her mother. "Thank you. I know you have little control over your working hours. Still, I feel as if these ladies take advantage. If they want you as their seamstress, they should be willing to accommodate you instead of insisting you be ready at their beck and call."

"I'm unwilling to take that chance. We need the money my sewing brings in, and I'm sure there are other seamstresses who would be willing to work late at night." Her mother bowed her head. "I shouldn't have asked you to come along and help me. I know you're tired."

Clara sighed. "I'm more than happy to help you, but that doesn't change the fact that your clients should be more considerate of your needs."

Her mother's lips curved in a weak smile. "She sent a carriage."

Clara chuckled. "You're right. I'm delighted we don't have to walk. Forgive me for complaining, but I worry you don't get enough rest."

Her mother patted Clara's hand. "I worry the same about you. I suppose it's the way of things right now, isn't it? One day, when the war is over, things will return to normal."

Clara wanted to believe that was true, but she wondered if the country could ever be the same. Would families be able to reunite, and could the North and South once again coexist? While she knew the war would eventually come to an end, the healing afterward was sure to be a long and arduous process. In truth, she questioned whether the wounds could ever mend.

She finished her sandwich, folded the piece of paper, and tucked it into her reticule. "You haven't yet told me about the gown you've been so feverishly working on over the past week."

"There are three gowns and—"

"Three? Really, Mother? Three?" Clara's mouth gaped.

"Before you chide me, please listen. There is an important ball next week. As you know, I've been creating a gown for Mrs. Seward. And without my knowledge or consent, Mrs. Seward told Mrs. Chase she was certain I'd be delighted to make her a gown, as well." She shrugged and met Clara's eyes. "What was I to do? Mrs. Chase had already purchased the fabric and was depending upon me."

Clara held up two fingers. "That's two. When did number three enter the picture—or should I say, sewing room?"

Her mother grimaced. "Only two days ago. However, her dress is partially completed. Mrs. Seward pleaded with me to help Mrs. Blair. She's the postmaster general's wife, and they had already accepted their invitation to the ball. Apparently, Mrs. Blair's seamstress is very ill and isn't expected to recover." Her mother blew out a breath. "How could I refuse?"

"I do understand, Mother, but there's only so much that can be accomplished in a short period of time. And while I'm willing to help, I can't offer much assistance except in the evenings."

"I know, my dear. I'm pleased to have you with me this evening. I haven't met Mrs. Blair, and Mrs. Seward mentioned she's a bit high-strung. I'm not sure what that might entail, but I thought you might be able to work with her while I continue with Mrs. Seward and Mrs. Chase."

"All three of them are going to be present?"

Her mother nodded while Clara envisioned the melee that would surely follow. Three women vying for the attention of her mother, and each determined to have a gown that would outshine the others. She could think of nothing more disastrous, yet she held her tongue.

When the carriage had come to a halt, the driver soon yanked open the door and assisted them down. He tipped his hat as Clara descended. "Shall I wait, miss?"

Clara chuckled and shook her head. "Not unless you intend upon sleeping in the carriage." That said, she hurried after her mother.

Moments later, a maid opened the door and greeted Clara's mother with a bright smile. "Good evening, Mrs. McBride. It's good to see you again. The ladies are eagerly awaiting your arrival." She glanced at Clara. "And who is this you've brought with you?"

"My daughter, Clara. She's going to assist me this evening. She's an excellent seamstress." Her mother turned. "Clara, this is Mildred, Mrs. Seward's maid."

"I'm pleased to meet you, Mildred."

The spindly woman adjusted her apron and nodded. "If you're half the seamstress your mama is, those ladies are gonna be mighty pleased to see you, Miss Clara." She waved them toward the stairway. "They're upstairs in Mrs. Seward's rooms."

Clara followed behind Mildred and her mother while taking in her surroundings. She had an excellent view of the sitting room as they ascended the stairs. While it appeared to be well appointed, the room wasn't as large as she'd expected. She'd anticipated huge rooms where the Sewards would host large dinners and dances. The rooms she observed wouldn't hold more than ten or twelve guests. Then again, perhaps all the Washington politicians hosted their parties somewhere other than in their homes.

Mildred opened the double doors leading into Mrs. Seward's private rooms with a flourish, then stepped aside to permit them entry. "Your seamstresses have arrived, Mrs. Seward."

Mrs. Seward stood and stepped forward to greet them. She moved with an extended gracefulness that seemed a perfect match for her elongated neck, thin nose, and lofty height. Though far from a beauty, her striking blue eyes and warm smile enhanced her appearance. "Good evening, Leta." She set her gaze on Clara. "This must be your daughter, Clara." She graced Clara with a brilliant smile. "Welcome to my home. I'm grateful you could accompany your mother. She tells me you're an accomplished seamstress."

The other two ladies rose from their seats and approached, obviously eager to hear how they would fare in the assignment of seamstresses. Mrs. Seward made the introductions and then turned her attention to Mrs. Blair. "Clara is going to help with your gown, Mary. I thought the two of you could use the small sitting room off to the right. I'm sure Clara will want to have a fitting."

Mrs. Seward made it clear Leta would work on her gown before beginning any work on Mrs. Chase's frock. "Of course, if Clara finishes with Mary, she can come and assist with your dress, Sarah."

Mrs. Chase appeared less than pleased by the comment. "I'm willing to wait until Leta completes your fitting."

Clara pretended she didn't hear the comment. If they didn't want to accept her help, so be it. However, at least one of them would go without a new gown for the party. There was no way her mother could complete all three in time.

Mrs. Blair drew near and gestured to a chair across the room. "That's what the seamstress completed before falling ill. I covered it with a sheet to protect the fabric." She sighed. "Although she presented several recommendations, I'm not certain her talents were as strong as she professed.

I should have checked the references before hiring her, but I was a bit desperate."

"We'll sort it out once I get a good look at the dress." Clara offered a reassuring smile. "I'll fetch it and meet you in the sitting room in a few moments."

Clara crossed the room, picked up the dress, and sent her mother a worried look before she stepped into the small sitting room. While Mrs. Blair watched, Clara spread the gown across the settee and removed the sheet. She swallowed hard to keep from gasping. Mrs. Blair stepped closer as Clara lifted the dress by the shoulder seams. It appeared the bodice was intended to be slightly pointed in the center, with a bertha cut low off the shoulders and short puffed sleeves with lace falls. Even without a fitting, Clara could see that the point of the bodice was off-center, which would mean reworking the blue crepe and removing the delicate lace that already appeared overworked.

Fortunately, the skirt was merely basted to the bodice, and none of the flouncing or bows had been attached. In truth, it would have been easier to begin anew with the piece of fabric, ribbons, and lace. She turned and caught sight of Mrs. Blair. Pain was grafted on the older woman's pale face.

Mrs. Blair reached for Clara's arm and dropped into a chair upholstered in a yellow silk print. "It's horrid. What am I to do? My husband will never agree to more money for fabric."

Clara's stomach twisted. The despair in Mrs. Blair's voice was painful. While Clara wanted to assure the woman everything would be fine, she wasn't certain she possessed the talent necessary to re-create the gown. But if she didn't say something quickly, she feared Mrs. Blair would swoon. Whatever would this woman do if faced with a genuine disaster?

Thoughts of her mother's strength when she'd learned her husband had died at Bull Run had been a testament to Leta McBride's faith in God and her ability to face hardship. Even now, with the whereabouts of Clara's brother unknown, her mother remained steadfast and continued to place her trust in God.

Mrs. Blair withdrew a lace-edged handkerchief from her waist and blotted her eyes. "This is the worst day of my life."

Clara tightened her lips in a thin line. After hearing the woman's comment, Clara's earlier sympathy waned a bit. She wanted to tell Mrs. Blair that she was most fortunate if a ruined gown was the most difficult dilemma she'd ever faced in life. But Clara knew when to keep her lips sealed. To say anything that might be construed as insensitive or judgmental could mean the end of her mother's employment with the socially elite ladies of Washington. Besides, Clara's mother had previously related a few stories about her clients and their melodramatic behavior over insignificant matters. Clara wanted to believe Mrs. Blair merely had a penchant for histrionics.

"I don't believe the gown is a total loss, Mrs. Blair. If the stitching is carefully removed, I believe the bodice can be repaired. I may need to take one gore out of the skirt and use the fabric for the bodice if the crepe frays when I remove the lace."

"Oh, thank you for that good news." The matron snapped open her fan and waved it back and forth. "I am *so* relieved. I knew—"

Clara held up her palm to stay the woman. "While the gown can be repaired, I fear it's going to take a great deal of time. Time that neither my mother nor I can offer. As you know, my mother must complete the gowns for both Mrs.

Seward and Mrs. Chase before the ball, and I work at the laboratory every day. Sewing each evening wouldn't permit me the necessary time to complete the dress. Perhaps you or one of the other ladies knows of another seamstress?"

Mrs. Blair shook her head. "None that's suitable." She hesitated a moment. "What's this laboratory you spoke of?" The older woman appeared confused as Clara described her work making cartridges. "And they have women working in the Arsenal where the soldiers are being trained?"

Clara nodded. "Yes. The laboratory buildings are in one section of the Arsenal. Since so many men were needed to fight for the Union, women were hired to take their places in the laboratory."

"I see." She tapped her fan on the side table. "Wait here a moment."

Clara sat down and stared at the gown. They were wasting valuable time, but perhaps Mrs. Blair was going to see if she could simply borrow a gown from one of the other ladies. If so, there was no need to begin work on this one.

A short time later, Mrs. Blair returned with her shoulders held high and a look of triumph on her face. "Our problem has been solved by Secretary Seward."

Clara forced a wan smile and stared at the woman. She wasn't certain how Secretary Seward could do anything to help—unless he had hidden talents with a needle and thread. "I don't understand, Mrs. Blair. How is he going to help?"

"Frances went downstairs and interrupted her husband's meeting to have a little chat on my behalf." She arched her neck and patted her hair. "Secretary Seward has agreed to have you released from your duties at the laboratory in the Arsenal."

Clara's mouth dropped open, and she gave a slight shake of her head. "No, that can't be possible. Colonel Furman is in charge of the Arsenal, and Lieutenant Brady oversees the cartridge section. I believe both men will advise Secretary Seward that it's impossible for me to be away from my duties. It is imperative that the laboratory be fully staffed."

"Now, don't you fret, my dear. If there's a need for someone to take your place making those cartridges, I'll have my maid fill in for you until my dress is finished." Mrs. Blair sat and looked up at Clara. "I asked Mrs. Seward's maid to bring us tea. I think we should have a few moments to relax now that our problem has been resolved."

Clara longed to explain that a maid couldn't substitute for her at the laboratory, but Mrs. Blair would only argue or attempt to find another solution. Rather than try to change the woman's mind, Clara would let Colonel Furman or Joseph explain that she was needed at the laboratory. In the meantime, she'd do her best to re-create the gown during her evenings.

When the maid arrived with tea, Clara declined and continued her efforts to remove the embellishments from the bodice. "You go right ahead, Mrs. Blair. I'd prefer to keep working. I'm hopeful that if all goes well, I can adjust the point of the bodice without being required to refashion it. But I can't be sure until I remove this lace."

"As you wish, my dear, but there's no need to hurry now that you'll have your days free." She poured herself a cup of tea and returned to the chair covered in a lemon-yellow print. "Tell me about yourself, Clara. I detest silence. My husband is quite the opposite, which sometimes creates a bit of strife." She giggled. "Do you have a beau? I do hope he isn't off fighting in the war."

"Yes, I have a beau. He's a lieutenant in the Army and he works at the Arsenal."

"You can be thankful for that! I have a dear friend whose husband insisted on enlisting the minute the country went to war. She begged him to stay home. Her father willingly paid for another fellow to take his place, but her husband went anyway." Mrs. Blair shook her head.

Clara carefully picked out several stitches and then looked up at the woman. "Was he killed?"

"No, but he was injured. Nettie's letters are so sad that I almost dread receiving them. Sometimes I wait for days before opening them."

Clara gave a slight nod. "That's too bad." She hoped Mrs. Blair wouldn't continue. Hearing stories of wounded soldiers would remind her of her father and brother—as well as the injury Joseph had suffered.

Undeterred, Mrs. Blair agreed. "Oh, my dear. You have no idea how sad a situation it has become. Nettie's husband was shot in the arm and had to have one of those amputations performed. Clear up to his shoulder." Mrs. Blair lifted her hand and drew her finger along the shoulder seam of her dress. "They tried to remove it at the elbow, but then he got one of those terrible infections and they were sure he was going to die, but lo and behold, he lived." She leaned forward. "Sometimes I wonder if he wishes he would have died."

Clara snapped to attention. "I truly doubt he would wish himself dead. From what you've said, it sounds as if he's had a miraculous healing."

"I suppose some would say so, although poor Nettie has to listen to him almost every night. He suffers from horrifying night terrors, and during one episode he almost killed her."

Clara jerked and pricked her finger. "*What?*" She retrieved her handkerchief and wrapped it tightly around her finger. "Why did he try to hurt his wife?"

"Oh, he didn't mean to hurt her, but he was still asleep and having one of those nightmares. He thought he was out on the battlefield fighting to save himself. He thought Nettie was the enemy." She sighed. "When she finally got him awake, he was full of remorse. Even so, that didn't change the fact that he'd almost strangled her. Poor Nettie hasn't slept well since. I told her she should move to another room at night, but she says he wants her close by."

Clara attempted to recall what Joseph had said about his nightmares. He'd mentioned they weren't as frequent, but Mrs. Blair's story was frightening. What if he became violent, too?

After checking her finger to make certain it had quit bleeding, Clara picked up the needle and pulled out several stitches. "Has your friend's husband spoken to a doctor to see if there's anything that can be done to help him?"

"They've had appointments with a number of doctors. They've all said that there's nothing they can do for him, and his condition could worsen if he isn't in a quiet setting. They aren't certain what they'll do. One doctor suggested a mental asylum, but Nettie would hear nothing of that. I worry the poor thing will have to live in fear the remainder of her life. I simply cannot imagine." Mrs. Blair refilled her teacup. "You just be thankful your young soldier is safe and sound."

Clara freed the last of the lace, but a growing fear held her fast. Joseph might be safe, but was he sound?

Nineteen

While Clara continued stitching, Mrs. Blair's words of warning skittered through her mind like grease in a hot skillet. Joseph had been clear with her—he still suffered from night terrors. The thought that he could ever harm her during one of those episodes had never entered her mind. In truth, she doubted whether it had ever occurred to Joseph.

Knowing Joseph, she was certain he would forgo marriage to her before taking such a chance and potentially putting her life at risk. Still, if he had no idea such a possibility existed, should she mention Mrs. Blair's dire account to him? Telling her mother was out of the question. To relate such details to her mother would create constant worry if and when Clara married Joseph.

When Mrs. Blair clapped her hands, Clara startled to attention. "I'm sorry, did you say something to me?"

The older woman sighed. "Yes. I was telling you about my early years in Massachusetts, but I don't believe you heard a word, did you?"

"Forgive me, Mrs. Blair. My thoughts were elsewhere."

"I know you're concerned about the dress and that's likely

all you can think about, but please set aside your concerns. I'm going to speak to Frances and see how we should proceed with our daily get-togethers."

There was no stopping Mrs. Blair. She was determined Clara would spend her days sewing. She doubted the woman gave any thought to the fact that even if the colonel agreed to release Clara from her duties, he might not rehire her once she'd completed Mrs. Blair's gown. There was little doubt Joseph would do all in his power to save her position, and there was always a need for good workers. However, the supervisors didn't like to make concessions that might create an appearance of favoritism. No matter how well she'd performed her job in the past, nothing was guaranteed when it came to employment at the Arsenal. And Clara needed her job.

She'd be sorry later if she didn't say something to deter Mrs. Blair now. "Perhaps it would be best if I went to work at the Arsenal until I'm assured the colonel is in agreement and my position will be retained for me. Until then, I'll work on your gown either at home or wherever you elect."

"Dear me!" Mrs. Blair released a long sigh and looked heavenward. "I can't imagine your being so determined to keep that job. Sewing alongside your mother seems far more suitable for a lovely young lady such as yourself. And heaven knows we are in need of qualified seamstresses here in Washington."

Clara didn't want to argue with the woman, yet her knowledge of life beyond the circumference of the political world was sorely lacking. Clara's mother was in demand whenever a ball or large party was scheduled, but nowadays, most ladies made do with day dresses from several seasons past. Instead of being hired to create an entire wardrobe, Mrs.

McBride would typically be summoned to add ruffles or lace to give the appearance of something new. Neither the long hours nor the low wages could be regarded as worthwhile employment.

"My work at the Arsenal pays a fixed wage, Mrs. Blair. Mother and I need a steady income so that we are able to pay our rent on time." Clara lifted the bodice and pointed to the lace. "While I'm at the Arsenal tomorrow, you could attempt to remove the lower edge of lace. I don't think it will prove as difficult as what I'm removing this evening."

Mrs. Blair frowned and shook her head. "I wouldn't even attempt such a thing. I have no skill when it comes to sewing. My mother did her best to teach me needlepoint and embroidery, but I was a complete failure. You don't want me near a needle."

At ten o'clock Mrs. Blair announced her carriage driver was due to return for her. "If all goes well, you'll be released from your duties tomorrow, and my driver will meet you at the front of the Arsenal." She offered a quick wave and a bright smile as she swept out of the room with a flourish.

Both Clara and her mother continued with their sewing until nearly midnight, when Clara's mother had completed a fitting for Mrs. Chase. The muslin pattern would permit her mother to cut and begin the gown at home tomorrow. After carefully protecting the gowns, Mrs. Seward's maid and butler carried them downstairs and placed them in the carriage.

Once they were on their way, Clara nudged her mother. "I think we should have brought the maid and butler along to carry the gowns upstairs when we get home."

A weary smile curved her mother's lips. "That would be lovely, wouldn't it? What did you think of Mrs. Blair? I hope her gown isn't going to require you to begin anew. Mrs. Seward mentioned the gown didn't appear salvageable."

Clara detailed her efforts to save the bodice. "If that fails, I'll have to cut fabric from the skirt, which won't be a perfect solution. She states her husband won't give her the funds for new fabric." Clara shrugged. "I'll do my best, but it isn't her dress that has me worried—it's her determination to have me temporarily removed from my position at the laboratory so I can sew for her. Were you there when she spoke to Mrs. Seward about the possibility?"

"No. I saw Mrs. Blair approach Mrs. Seward when I was cutting the muslin for Mrs. Chase's pattern, but I didn't hear the conversation." Her mother frowned. "What was Mrs. Seward's response?"

"It seems she's in agreement with the plan and spoke to her husband. I have no idea if Secretary Seward has the authority to issue such an order to the colonel, but I'm sure I'll find out before long."

For the remainder of the carriage ride, her mother vacillated between apologies and assurances. They both knew, however, that her mother had no more control than Clara did. Tomorrow Clara would learn her fate.

The following morning, Clara could barely pull herself from between the sheets. Though she longed to remain abed, even a few more minutes would make her late for work.

She stumbled out the door while struggling to throw off the wisps of sleep that clouded her mind. As soon as they had arrived home last night, her mother insisted Clara go to bed. But her dreams had been fraught with visions of a man attempting to choke her. She'd awakened with a jolt, her bedsheets damp with perspiration and her heart pounding as though attempting to escape her chest. Mrs. Blair's tale last evening had affected her more than she'd thought.

Both the older woman's account and the nightmare that followed had influenced Clara's decision to speak with someone. She couldn't deny her blossoming love for Joseph, but would marriage to him mean coping with a lifetime of fear? Granted, Joseph would never intentionally harm her. Yet damage could be done, even if unintentional. She pondered the idea of being afraid to close her eyes at night and the havoc it would create. She badly wanted to believe such a thing wouldn't happen with Joseph.

As she neared the arched entrance to the Arsenal, Bea called her name, edged through the crowd of workers, and grasped Clara's arm. "I looked for you on the way to work and home yesterday. Did you talk to Joseph? What did he say? Can he help us? Did he say if he'd heard anything?"

The frantic look in Bea's eyes caused Clara's stomach to clench. She'd had a few moments with Joseph during her lunch break yesterday, and she'd considered mentioning Bea's dilemma, but Joseph had been absorbed with the necessary changes at the warehouses and shipping departments. He'd barely heard a word she'd said to him. Even when she mentioned going to Mrs. Seward's with her mother, he hadn't seemed to hear. The timing simply hadn't been good, especially to discuss something so significant. Speaking to the colonel on Jeremiah and Bea's behalf was no small matter. She would need uninterrupted time and Joseph's full attention before she broached the subject.

"Well?" Bea reached for her hand. "Did you ask him?"

"I haven't had an opportunity to talk to him in private. I'm sure you'd agree that it's unwise to speak about this when anyone else might overhear." Clara withdrew her hand and continued walking at a steady pace. She hoped Bea would accept her response, but Clara knew that Bea wasn't one to give up easily.

Bea hurried to match Clara's pace. "Didn't he come over last night? I thought he was doing repair work for your landlady." She clutched Clara's arm and pulled her to a stop. "Please, Clara! Talk to me."

Clara shook her head. "No, he didn't."

Bea leaned close as they continued toward the laboratory. "Please talk to him tonight."

"That won't be possible. I'm going to be helping my mother at the Sewards' every evening until the ball. Even with my help, I don't think the gowns will be completed in time for the gala, so I doubt I'll be seeing much of Joseph, except at work."

"What about Sunday? You and your mother won't be working on Sunday, will you?"

"I don't know what Mother will decide about Sunday. I know we'll go to church, and then I'll do whatever she asks the remainder of the day. She's exhausted and worried. I want to do all I can to help her." Clara planned to keep her promise, but the well-being of her mother had to come first. Bea needed to offer some patience and understanding.

"I need your help too, and you said you would talk to Joseph. Surely you can manage a short visit with him on Sunday." Instead of turning toward the packing room, Beatrice continued alongside Clara. "Explain to your mother that it's urgent you see Joseph. And when you talk to Joseph, tell him that if the colonel raises any concerns about Jeremiah, he could offer to have Jeremiah work closer to the laboratory. If Joseph says he'll keep an eye on Jeremiah, that might take care of everything without a problem."

"I'll speak to Joseph, although I can't promise when it will be." She hesitated. "He did say that one of the fellows who delivers gunpowder and loads the cartridge crates onto shipping pallets was being transferred. Maybe Jeremiah could take that job. In the meantime, maybe Andrew could offer some advice."

Bea blew an exasperated sigh. "Andrew is only a sergeant. The colonel isn't going to listen to him. In fact, he probably wouldn't give him the time of day. Besides, Andrew has nothing to do with any of this investigation and the changes being made at the Arsenal. Joseph is the only one who can help—which means I need you to talk to him." Bea immediately softened her tone. "I'm sorry to be so forceful, but I'm so afraid we're going to lose our jobs. I'm sure you can understand my fear. I don't know what we'd do or where we could go." Using the back of her hand, Bea swiped her eyes.

"There's no need for tears, Bea. I do understand your fears. I remember how worried Joseph was when he thought he'd face problems because of his brother. I'll do what I can, but you may need to be patient."

"Why would Joseph's brother be a problem?"

"He married a Southern woman and is living in the South."

Bea's eyes sparked at the revelation. "Truly? Is his brother fighting for the Rebs?"

Too late, Clara wanted to snatch back her words. In her attempt to make Bea feel better, she'd betrayed Joseph's confidence. Or had she? She couldn't recall if he'd asked her to keep the information to herself. Yet she understood such knowledge wasn't something he'd want bandied about.

Bea tugged on her sleeve. "Well, is he?"

"I shouldn't have told you any of this." Clara grasped Bea's hand. "Promise me you won't repeat a word of what I just told you. I had hoped to find a way to relieve your fears and I spoke without thinking. I shouldn't have shared Joseph's personal—"

"Quit fretting, Clara. I won't say anything. I'm just glad you understand how worrisome this is for Jeremiah and me—and Joseph should understand, too."

Clara silently chided herself for her slipup as she turned and strode toward the door to the laboratory. She'd considered telling Bea she might not be working in the cylinder room until after the gala, but that would likely have made matters worse. Besides, she hoped Mrs. Blair's plan would be rejected.

Joseph smiled when she stepped inside. Just seeing his face eased some of her mounting burdens. If a sergeant and corporal hadn't been standing near his desk, she would have approached him. She longed to warn him that there might be an order to release her from her duties at the laboratory, that they needed to have further discussion regarding his night terrors, that she would be working every evening and there would be little time to spend together, and that Jeremiah and Bea needed his help. Yet when was she going to have an opportunity to visit with him?

She walked to the far wall, hung her cloak, and placed her lunch pail on the floor before returning to the worktable. Along with the other ladies, Clara slid onto the long bench. Once the bell rang, she set to work.

Clara and the other ladies had just returned from breakfast when Joseph pushed away from his desk and gestured. "Miss McBride, may I speak to you for a moment, please?"

She circled around the other ladies and drew near his desk. From the look on his face, it was evident he was unhappy.

"I've been given orders to release you from your duties in the cylinder room. It is my understanding that you'll be working as a seamstress for Mrs. Blair until her gown is completed for a gala." He sighed. "I'm sure her dress is far more important than ammunition for our soldiers."

"I'm sorry, Joseph. I was against her making the request. I know I'm needed here, but she was determined, and Mrs. Seward concurred."

He nodded. "I know you aren't to blame. Still, it's difficult to honor such a request when we're falling behind in our output and I'm trying to make changes to ensure the safety of all our workers." He shrugged. "I voiced my displeasure to the colonel."

"What did he say?"

"His exact words were, '*Who am I to argue with the secretary of state or postmaster general? Tell Miss McBride she's to report to the residence of Mrs. Seward. I've agreed to secure her position upon completion of her seamstress duties.*'"

Relief washed over Clara. At least she'd been guaranteed that a job awaited her return. "Before I leave, could we speak privately about a matter of great importance? I'll be working every night, so I doubt we'll have time together."

He tipped his head toward the far wall. "Gather your belongings, and I'll meet you near the giant oak tree in a few minutes."

She did as he'd instructed, and within fifteen minutes Joseph appeared. She'd rehearsed her speech so she wouldn't forget anything. Joseph couldn't be away from his desk for long, so she needed to remember everything Bea had mentioned. There wouldn't be time to discuss her concerns about his nightmares, but that could wait until he was able to call on her again.

His brow was creased in concern as he rushed toward her. He reached forward and gathered her chilly hands in his own. "What's happened?"

"It's Jeremiah and Bea."

His features immediately relaxed. "Oh. Well, that's a relief. I thought you might have received word regarding your brother."

She shook her head. "No, nothing so serious as that, although Bea might disagree." She quickly detailed the difficulties the two had encountered during their interviews and Bea's fear that both might be terminated. "Have you heard anything about them?"

Joseph shook his head. "No, but I haven't heard about any of the interviews. They both need to quit worrying. If Bea explained that Jeremiah had been ill, I'm sure there won't be any problem. He's always received good reports from his supervisors. I'm willing to request his transfer to the laboratory if his supervisor in shipping is willing to release him to me. I could use someone like Jeremiah, who doesn't require a lot of supervision—someone I can trust."

"Thank you, Joseph. It will mean so much to Bea, and to me too, if she doesn't have to worry about Jeremiah losing his job." She squeezed his hand. "And if anything should arise regarding the interview, you'll vouch for both of them."

He hesitated. "I couldn't go so far as to vouch for him, but, if asked, I'm willing to state that I've met Jeremiah and believe him to be a good worker. However, the officers who are conducting the interviews will decide who is to be terminated. From what you've told me, I don't think there's reason for great concern. Enough talk of Bea and Jeremiah." He glanced over his shoulder, then leaned forward and brushed a kiss on her cheek. "I'm going to miss seeing you every day. I think about our future far too much."

His words seared her heart. She had been thinking about the future too, yet she was certain his thoughts hadn't been the same as hers. If only they had time now to discuss her concerns.

She pushed those thoughts aside. There would be ample time after the ball to talk, and stolen moments like this would be few and far between until then.

She looked up and met his velvety blue eyes. How could this loyal, kind man ever hurt her?

He leaned close, and she felt his warm breath on her ear. "While we're apart, remember, I love you."

With a final kiss to her cheek, he pulled away. She watched him walk back toward the Arsenal. The concerns about her friends, her job, the horrible dress, and even the nightmares all fell away like autumn leaves drifting to the ground around her.

Joseph loved her.

TWENTY

Inside the carriage, Clara rested her head against her mother's shoulder. Their long days usually didn't end until evening, and sometimes it was well after ten o'clock when they returned home. Tonight, they'd been even later than usual. Her mother had insisted all the seed pearls be sewn onto the bodice of Mrs. Chase's gown. While Clara was thankful Mrs. Seward had insisted the dresses and fittings take place at her home, she'd learned her mother's patience with a needle was far greater than her own. The hours of stitching delicate lace embellishments and bead-work left her with pricked fingers, a stiff neck, and an aching back.

"Who would believe that sitting in a chair stitching all day long could be so tiresome?" Clara yawned. "I feel as though I haven't slept in a week."

Her mother patted her hand. "Except for seamstresses, I'm sure there are few who would agree that sewing is a te-dious profession. Thankfully, Mrs. Seward doesn't want us to arrive before ten tomorrow morning, so if Mrs. Ludwig isn't too noisy, you can sleep longer than usual."

Clara chuckled. "You know she'll send one of the boarders

upstairs to knock on the door the minute she's ready to serve breakfast."

"In that case, you can eat breakfast and then return to your room and rest until it is time to depart."

A short time later, the Seward carriage stopped in front of their boardinghouse. The driver jumped down, opened the door, and waited until they had entered the house. Clara glanced at the bow-fronted mahogany table in the hallway, where Mrs. Ludwig placed the newspaper and any mail or messages for residents.

Since moving into the boardinghouse, neither Clara nor her mother had received any mail, yet they always checked. They continued to hope there would be a letter from Clara's brother saying he'd been unable to write but that he was fine and would soon be home. Clara thumbed through the meager stack. Her breath caught at the sight of her name. It appeared the missive had been hand-delivered.

Clara waved the envelope at her mother. "I think it must be from Joseph." She ripped open the envelope, withdrew the sheet of paper, and immediately looked at the signature. "It is." She grinned at her mother and pressed the letter to her heart.

"You don't appear as weary as you did only a few moments ago."

Clara smiled. "I know. It's amazing, isn't it?" She could barely wait to get upstairs, where she could sit down and enjoy every word. Once Clara had reached the upstairs landing, she waited until her mother arrived with the key to their rooms.

As soon as she stepped inside, Clara hurried into the small sitting room and quickly perused the letter. She looked up at her mother. "Joseph's letter says Jeremiah has been transferred. He's delivering the gunpowder to the laboratory and loading cartridge crates onto shipping pallets. There haven't been any further inquiries about Bea or Jeremiah since their last interviews. I'm so relieved." She clasped a palm to her bodice. "Isn't that wonderful news?"

"Indeed, it is. I know that you and Bea have become dear friends and you've been worried about her and Jeremiah." She gestured to the letter. "What else does Joseph have to say? Is he doing well?"

She could feel the heat rising in her cheeks. "He says he misses me and would like to accompany us to church on Sunday." She continued reading and then looked up at her mother. "He's had duty the past two Sundays. That's why he hasn't asked before now."

"I think that would be very nice. And you can plan on visiting with him the remainder of the day. I'll ask Mrs. Ludwig if he can join us for supper on Sunday evening. You'll need to send word to him."

Clara nodded. "I'll ask Mr. Gryska if he'll deliver a message for me."

"Excellent idea. I'd forgotten Mr. Gryska works at the Arsenal. A blacksmith, isn't he?"

"Yes. It won't be too far out of his way to stop by the laboratory before work. If Joseph isn't there, he'd be able to leave my letter with any of the workers." She stood, crossed the room, and withdrew a sheet of paper from the writing desk. "I'd better write my note tonight if I want Mr. Gryska to deliver it tomorrow."

"You go ahead with your letter. I'm going to bed." Her mother leaned forward and placed a kiss on Clara's cheek. "If you're not awake in the morning, I'll take your letter to Mr. Gryska. Sleep well, my dear."

"Good night." She glanced over her shoulder. "And thank you, Mother."

Mrs. Seward greeted Clara and her mother with a bright smile when they arrived shortly before ten o'clock the next morning. "I have exciting news."

Clara arched her brows. "For us?" She worried Mrs. Seward's exciting news might entail more work for them.

"Yes, of course. Sit down." She waved them toward the silk-upholstered divan. "I spoke with my husband, and he is in agreement that you ladies have proved yourselves to be two of the most diligent workers we've ever employed. So—" she held her breath for a moment—"you are both invited to the gala as our guests. Of course, your spouse may escort you, Mrs. McBride, and your beau, Clara."

Mrs. McBride cleared her throat. "That's very kind of you, Mrs. Seward, but—"

"I won't take no for an answer. I've gone through my gowns and I found one for each of you. They may need a little freshening, but there are more than sufficient remnants you can use."

The kind woman was so excited, Clara thought she might begin clapping her hands. Clara glanced at her mother, who now appeared dumbstruck. "Mrs. Seward, my father is deceased. He died at Bull Run."

Mrs. Seward clapped her hand over her mouth. "Dear me! I am so sorry. Please forgive my indiscretion. I had no idea." She glanced back and forth between the women, then brightened. "I'm sure you have a beau, Clara. Your mother could accompany the two of you. I want to reward you for your hard work. I insist."

Clara longed to tell Mrs. Seward that attending a gala would be more punishment than reward. Mingling with the wealthy and prestigious members of society wasn't something either Clara or her mother considered recompense for their many hours of work. In truth, what they needed more than anything was additional money. Yet she dare not say so.

Her mother leaned forward. "I hope you will accept my regrets, Mrs. Seward. While I appreciate your kind offer, I must decline. However, I'm sure Clara and her beau would be pleased to attend."

"Then it's settled. Come along with me, Clara, and I'll show you the gown." Clara longed to voice her own objection to the offer, but it was obvious that one of them had to accept. "Tell me about your beau, Clara."

"He's a lieutenant and is stationed at the Arsenal. I'll need to make certain he's going to be off duty the evening of the gala. If not, we wouldn't be able to attend."

"Pshaw! Don't you let that worry you in the least. William will make certain he's released from his duties." She led Clara into her bedroom, where an evening dress of lilac taffeta with lace flounce had been placed on display. "You're slimmer than me, so it may need a few tucks, but I think the lilac color will be lovely with your creamy complexion. Would you like to try it on for your mother?"

"Thank you, but we need to complete the finishing work on your dress. If it's acceptable, I'll take it home and Mother can do a fitting there."

"Of course. And you tell your beau that his uniform is completely acceptable for our affair. He need not worry about formal attire."

"That's most kind, Mrs. Seward. I'll be sure to tell him."

Clara had difficulty concentrating throughout the day. Although her sewing technique didn't suffer, she heard little of what the ladies were discussing. She kept trying to recall what she'd learned about social occasions like galas. What kind of manners were expected? What dances did they do? What food would be served? Several times her mother had to repeat questions that had been directed to her.

As they prepared to depart that evening, Mrs. Seward instructed her maid to pack the gown and deliver it to the carriage. She accompanied Clara and her mother downstairs, and before they departed, she turned to Clara. "I believe my invitation to the gala has caused your mind to wander, Clara. You've been particularly distracted today, but I completely understand. I remember when I was your age. The galas I've attended are some of my fondest memories."

"I'm sure they are." Clara fastened her cloak and took her mother's arm as they departed. She doubted whether attending the gala would be one of her fondest memories. Instead, she was sure it would stand out as one of the most challenging. How did a girl who lived in a boardinghouse and worked in a cylinder room meld into a crowd of aristocrats? She didn't know how to dance, and she wasn't certain Joseph could dance with his injury. If only she'd been able to decline the invitation.

Once inside the carriage, she put voice to her fears. "I understand one of us has to appear appreciative of her invitation, but I truly want to decline."

Her mother shook her head. "I'm sorry, my dear, but we can't affront Mrs. Seward and her friends. A portion of our livelihood depends upon them."

"I know, but this certainly puts a damper on my upcoming visit with Joseph. I'm sure he's going to be unhappy."

Her mother smiled and patted her hand. "Relax, dear. I believe he'll be pleased for any opportunity to be with you."

Sunday's unexpected sunshine and warmth caught Clara by surprise. The past week had been fraught with cool, overcast days that warned of the coming winter weather. After breakfast, she returned upstairs to retrieve a lightweight cape for herself and one for her mother. A knock sounded at the front door, and before she arrived downstairs, Mrs. Ludwig was in the hallway speaking to Joseph.

He looked up as she descended the stairs. His smile radiated a warmth that momentarily erased all the fears she'd harbored since listening to Mrs. Blair's daunting tale. Joseph moved around Mrs. Ludwig and held out his hand as she neared the bottom step.

"You look lovely. It seems so long since I've seen you."

Before Clara could reply, Mrs. Ludwig stepped between them. "I was telling Joseph that since the weather is so nice, the two of you should enjoy a picnic in the park. I'll prepare something before I leave for church, and you can pick up the basket upon your return."

"That's most kind of you, Mrs. Ludwig." Clara reached around the boardinghouse keeper and handed a cape to her mother. "But I don't want you going to so much bother on our account."

The boardinghouse keeper grasped Joseph's arm and gave a slight tug. "This dear boy has offered to return for supper tomorrow and complete a few chores for me, haven't you?"

"I have, but it may be seven o'clock before I arrive."

"That will be fine. Don't concern yourself if you're late—I'll keep a plate warm for you." She patted his arm before releasing him and looked at Clara. "And I want the three of you to join me for supper this evening, as well. You two can have the parlor to yourselves after supper, if you'd like." She immediately turned to Mrs. McBride. "With the parlor doors open, of course."

"How very kind of you to offer supper, Mrs. Ludwig." Mrs. McBride started toward the door. "We best leave if we want to arrive before the services begin."

"Yes, and I need to return to the kitchen and prepare a picnic basket." That said, she waved and hurried toward the kitchen—a woman on a mission.

Mrs. McBride grinned at Joseph as he took her arm. "I do believe Mrs. Ludwig has missed you almost as much as Clara has."

Joseph tipped his head back and laughed. "Perhaps, but I'd like to hope it's for different reasons. I don't think Mrs. Ludwig's interest in me goes beyond replacing rotting wood around the dormers or repairing a bit of plaster. I'm pleased to lend a hand, especially since it means I can have more time with Clara." He patted his stomach. "And a good meal doesn't hurt, either."

A short time later, they entered the church and made their way to one of the few empty pews. Even though many of the men were off fighting the war, the church was crowded. Clara found strength on Sunday mornings at church. A strength that continued to fortify her through the long months of missing her brother, of hearing worrisome news from the battlefields, and of seeing the tears of women lamenting the death of loved ones. A strength she might have to call upon today when she told Joseph about the upcoming gala.

When they arrived home from church, Joseph saw a cloth-covered wicker basket sitting on the kitchen worktable as promised.

Mrs. McBride excused herself and turned to go upstairs.

"Why don't you come with us, Mrs. McBride?" Joseph said. "You shouldn't remain indoors on such a lovely day."

"No, thank you. I'll have a sandwich later. I brought home some sewing, and we've been working such long hours that I have a great deal to keep me busy today. I'll open the windows and enjoy the fresh air in our rooms. You two go ahead. You need a bit of time to yourselves. Besides, I know Clara has a great deal to discuss with you."

He arched his brows. "That sounds intriguing." He picked up the basket and offered her his arm. "Shall we be on our way, then?"

The beautiful weather resulted in many visitors to the park, so locating a spot for their picnic proved more difficult than anticipated. When they had finally found a place beneath one of the towering oaks, Clara spread the faded patchwork quilt she'd brought with her.

Mrs. McBride's comment before they departed had piqued Joseph's interest, but he decided to wait until they were settled before inquiring about Clara's news. She reached inside the basket and retrieved a ham sandwich for him before unwrapping one for herself. Although she'd appeared happy to see him when he arrived, she'd been unusually quiet on their way to and from church. And she'd been just as quiet on their way to the park. Granted, she'd made small talk about the weather and the children playing ball, yet she'd said nothing of substance. Now he wondered if the news her mother had mentioned was something he wouldn't want to hear.

He was almost prepared to inquire when she leaned toward him. "There's something I need to tell you."

Due to her downcast appearance, he steeled himself, prepared to hear that she no longer wanted him to call on her. He reached for her hand and was pleased when she didn't withdraw it. "What is it? You can tell me anything, Clara."

Over the next several minutes, he listened while she conveyed the invitation to the gala. "I'm so sorry, Joseph, but Mrs. Seward was insistent. Mother feared she would lose Mrs. Seward and the other ladies as clients if I refused." She inhaled a long breath. "While I tried to explain that your duties might require you to be at the Arsenal, she said Mr. Seward would make certain you could attend. I doubt your superior officers will be pleased to have a political figure telling them to release you from duty."

Joseph chuckled, relieved that the matter hadn't been what he'd suspected. "I would be pleased to escort you, Clara. I agree that attending the gala could prove somewhat uncomfortable, but if we're together, I think we can manage quite well."

"But I don't know the fancy dance steps and—"

"You'll be fine. When we arrive, you'll receive a dance card. I'll place my name on every line, so that if some fellow asks you to dance, you can say your card is full. Problem solved." He smiled. "However, if you decide you'd like to learn a dance or two, I think I could teach you." He glanced at his foot. "I'm not as surefooted nowadays, but my mother made certain my brother and I learned all the popular dance steps during my early years. We attended dances and holiday parties where dancing was one of the favorite pastimes. Mother wanted to be certain we were educated in the social graces so we would marry into society.

My brother fulfilled that dream when he married, though I don't think Mother had planned on him marrying a Southern belle." He sighed. "That's enough talk about my past, but please don't worry any longer. You'll be the belle of the ball."

Twenty-One

eatrice sat down on the grass beside Jeremiah and opened their lunch pail. She handed him a thick slice of bread and two hard-boiled eggs. Lifting another egg from the pail, she cracked it on her knee and carefully removed the shell before taking a bite.

She glanced up at him. "Any progress?"

A muffled groan escaped his lips. "I get tired of that same question morning, noon, and night. Can't we talk about something else?"

"You're the one who was nagging me when I started work in the packing room. Damaging those cartridge shipments isn't as easy as you thought it was going to be, is it?" She popped the remainder of the egg into her mouth.

"You need to shut your trap. You're mighty big on badgering, but you're short on ideas." He pointed his index finger to his head. "You need to use that brain of yours and come up with some other ways we can get things done."

"Since when do you need my help with ideas? You're always telling me you know how to take care of things." She removed a piece of bread and broke off a bite. "Now that nothing is working out, you expect me to find a way. Instead of pretending you had two or three schemes that would succeed, why didn't you admit you weren't sure of your plans?"

He glared at her. "Those plans have worked in other places, but there's just too many folks around here all the time." When she frowned, he relented. "Well, maybe they hadn't been tried before, but it don't matter anymore. Right now we gotta decide on something that will work." His voice rose in intensity as he continued to speak. "You know the Gray Ghost expects to hear from all the Rangers every two weeks." He raked his fingers through his hair. "I've got nothing good to report."

"Don't raise your voice at me, Jeremiah." She stared off in the distance. "What about the gunpowder? Clara got Joseph to transfer you so you'd have access to the barrels. What was your idea with that?"

"I thought about mixing it with something else, but I don't think that will work. Those barrels are already full, and it wouldn't be possible to mix much into them. If I could get my hands on some saltpeter, I could try that. I think having too much in the mix could ruin the powder. I'm not sure, though."

"Or the whole thing could blow up in your face." She sighed and shook her head. "Anyway, where would you get enough saltpeter to put in all those barrels?"

"I know. I'm just thinking out loud."

She wanted to say his thoughts weren't worth the breath it took to speak them, yet that would only cause a fight. They needed a solution, not an argument. "What about getting it wet? Once it dries out, will it still fire?"

Jeremiah jerked to attention. "Water must damage the

cartridges since they wrap the crates in that waterproof paper. Water! That's our answer." He leaned against the tree trunk. "I could start pouring water into the barrels as soon as they come from the warehouse. By the time they'd rotate for delivery to the laboratory, the powder would be dry."

Bea shook her head. "That won't work. The water will cause some of the powder to clump. The girls will notice right away because the powder won't flow through the funnels. If you're going to use water, it's going to have to be after the cartridges are crated, but before they get wrapped in the waterproof paper."

Jeremiah rested his chin on his bent knees. "That's going to mean another transfer. I need to figure out how to make that happen."

"You were hired to fill in whenever and wherever needed." She hiked a shoulder and smirked. "Maybe one of the fellas working at the warehouse will have an accident." Bea packed up the remnants of their food and stood. "Before you try to get transferred, you need to see if there's any way you'll be able to get the crates wet before they're wrapped." She looked down at her brother. "The only other solution is to make sure every boat carrying those cartridges sinks in the river."

When he brightened at the remark, Bea frowned. "I was only joking, Jeremiah." She extended her hand. "Get up. We need to get back to work."

Two days later, Bea was sitting at their regular spot beneath the oak tree and pulled her cloak tight around her neck. They were going to need to find another place to eat their meals. Soon it would be too cold to sit outdoors. Many of the workers already remained inside during their breaks, but Jeremiah and Bea hadn't yet given in to the changing weather.

Bea fastened her gaze on the grassy slope until Jeremiah appeared. Only then did she begin to unpack their lunch. He plopped down beside her and grinned. "Good news."

"What's that? Has General Lee given us another victory?"

Jeremiah quickly glanced around and touched his finger to his lips. "Keep your voice down, Bea. Do you realize what would happen to us if someone heard you say that?"

"I've been waiting here for five minutes and there's no one else around, so don't get yourself all worked up over nothing." She slapped a sandwich into his hand. "So, what's the good news?"

"I managed to get things figured out." He leaned sideways and tipped his head close to hers. "The boxes of packed cartridges are dated and taken from the lab over to the warehouse. They get stacked there and moved forward by date. About a week before it's time to ship them, they get moved to the wrapping area, where that paper is put around them and they're marked with the name of the Arsenal and date of shipment—that kind of thing." He gave her a satisfied grin.

"So? What's your plan?"

"As soon as those crates arrive in the warehouse, they can be wetted down and no one will notice. They sit at the back, and no one even goes back there until they start moving them forward. By the time they're ready to move, the crates will be dry, but the cartridges should be ruined—at least most of them."

"How are you going to get them wet without being seen?"

"There's one fellow who works the night shift—just keeps

an eye on things so they don't have to use any of the soldiers. He hates being away from his family."

Bea gave him a sideways glance. "How do you know that?"

"I have my ways."

She nudged him in the side. "Tell me. I don't want you doing anything foolish that's going to get us both in trouble before we ever accomplish our goal."

"You have no faith in me, do you?" He didn't wait for an answer. "Joseph asked if I'd mind going over and helping at the warehouse. He said there was a shortage of men there, and he'd divide my duties among the other fellows in the freight yard if I'd go and help out. Of course, I agreed." He shoved his napkin back in the pail. "Turns out the fella who works the night shift had to stay because they didn't have enough help. We got to talking, and he told me how the place works. I told him I wouldn't mind working the night shift. If this all works out, I'd say you could break off your friendship with the sergeant. As far as I can tell, he's been useless."

"I wouldn't go that far. I've rather enjoyed his company." Jeremiah scowled so deeply, she giggled. "And don't forget that if it weren't for Andrew, you wouldn't have met that friend in the park who taught you to play chess. Besides, we can't be certain he won't be useful at some point in the future. It's better to keep him on the string."

Jeremiah frowned and stood. "You best be keeping your head on straight. He may be a nice enough fella, but Andrew's a sergeant in the Union Army. I think you should end things with him now."

"And I said no. Andrew thinks of me as more than a friend. He's been a perfect gentleman and hasn't done anything improper. If I tell him I no longer want him to call on me, he's not going to understand and it could create problems.

His attempts to set things aright between us will mean he'll be around even more." She walked alongside him as they neared the laboratory. "You need to listen to me about this. I know more about how he'll behave than you do. Trust me, he won't give up easily."

"Fine! I'm not going to argue about it, but you need to let him know that I'm going to be working nights so he can't be coming around all the time. That's excuse enough to keep him away most of the time."

She nodded. "If you get the position working nights, I'll be sure to tell him."

As they parted ways, she knew Jeremiah wasn't happy with her, but she truly didn't care. What he'd said was correct. Her relationship with Andrew hadn't proven valuable to their cause. However, it had been nice for her. It had been far too long since she'd been courted, and she wasn't yet willing to give it up. Not for Jeremiah, and not for the cause. Such a sacrifice simply wasn't necessary—at least not yet.

Clara stood in front of the cheval mirror in Mrs. Ludwig's bedroom and slowly turned. The boardinghouse keeper had insisted Clara come downstairs and see herself in the free-standing dressing mirror. Clara's mother, scissors in hand, lowered to her knees and snipped several loose threads along the hem and one of the flounces.

Mrs. Ludwig clasped a hand to her bosom and sighed. "You are absolutely beautiful, my dear. And to think Mrs. Seward gave you that lovely gown. I don't think I've ever seen anyone as stunning as you." She encircled Mrs. Mc-Bride's waist and drew near. "You must be very proud of your daughter."

Her mother nodded. "Yes, but more so because of who she is inside rather than her outward appearance. Although I must agree that she looks beautiful." She captured her daughter's gaze in the mirror. "The lilac shade brings out the green in your hazel eyes." She stepped to Clara's side and smiled. "Come along. Before I departed this afternoon, Mrs. Seward gave me a band of lilac velvet for your hair. I believe we have enough time for me to weave it into your curls."

Clara glanced over her shoulder as she lifted her skirts to climb the stairs. "I do hope this party won't be as awkward as I anticipate. While I appreciate Mrs. Seward's gesture, it has given me no pleasure. My stomach has been churning all day. The mere thought of walking into their home and being announced has my nerves on edge. I fear I'll embarrass myself and Joseph."

They entered the bedroom, and her mother gestured for her to sit in the chair. "I know you don't want to go, Clara, and I'm sorry I forced this upon you."

A tear shone in the corner of her mother's eye, and Clara immediately gathered her in an embrace. "Oh, Mother, forgive me. I am so sorry that I've continued grumbling. I know how important it is to keep your clients happy. And I understand that Mrs. Seward believes she's given us a lovely gift." Clara lowered onto the chair. "Most young ladies would be delighted to have such an offer. Who knows what will happen? We may have a wonderful time." She chuckled. "And I may discover fancy parties hold far more excitement than I could ever anticipate, though I'm doubtful that will occur."

Her mother bent forward and brushed a kiss on Clara's cheek. "I'd better hurry or Joseph will arrive before I've finished with your hair." She positioned the ribbon across Clara's forehead. "Hold it in place while I lace the ends through your curls. Mrs. Seward gave me detailed instructions on how to fashion the ribbon through your hair, so I hope this is correct." Her mother handed her a small mirror. "You can watch to make certain you like what I'm doing."

Clara held the mirror with one hand and pressed the lilac ribbon to her forehead with the other while her mother carefully laced the velvet trim through her chestnut-brown curls. She hadn't before noticed that her mother's fingers, once long and straight, no longer stretched to their full length and revealed knobby protrusions at some of the joints. Why hadn't she noticed before this? No wonder her mother would take a few minutes to massage her hands throughout the day.

Glancing over her shoulder, Clara held her mother's gaze. "Do they hurt?"

"What? My fingers?"

Clara nodded. "I wish you didn't have to sew all the time."

"They ache when the weather changes or when I've been sewing for a long time, but it happens with age. Take a look at Mrs. Ludwig's hands and you'll see hers are the same." Her mother smiled. "And she doesn't sew." She stood back and gave Clara's hair an admiring look and squeezed her shoulder. "Don't you fret about my hands. Just go to the gala and try to have a good time. If need be, you and Joseph find a quiet place and enjoy your time with each other."

Clara stood and embraced her mother. "Thank you. I'll remember what you've said, and I'd like you to rest for the remainder of the evening. None of your other orders are pressing. Promise me you won't work tonight."

"I promise. Now, gather your cloak and reticule. I believe I hear Mrs. Ludwig talking to Joseph."

After kissing her mother on the cheek, Clara collected her belongings and walked to the top of the stairs. Joseph stood in the entry beside Mrs. Ludwig. He looked up as she descended the stairs. With each step she took, his smile grew wider.

A glow of appreciation shone in his eyes, and he extended his hand to her when she approached the bottom step. "You look beautiful." He took her cloak from her arm. "Let me help you into your cloak. Our carriage is waiting."

She turned as he draped the cloak across her shoulders and then led her down the front steps while Mrs. Ludwig continued to cluck her good wishes. Once inside the carriage, Clara giggled. "With all the good wishes Mrs. Ludwig was sending our way, you'd think we just got married."

Joseph smiled. "I can only wish that were true."

The heat rose in Clara's cheeks. Did he think she was attempting to be coy and put ideas in his head? She struggled to think of a response that would negate such an impression, but nothing came to mind. After all, she too had spent a great deal of time thinking about what it would be like to be Joseph's wife. She considered attempting an apology but decided that might make matters worse. She needed a change of topic.

"You look quite handsome in your uniform. Did any of the other officers ask where you were off to?"

"Several of them. I think they were jealous and wanted to know how a fellow like me managed an invite to a fancy party." He chuckled. "I said I wasn't giving away any of my secrets, but I did tell them I was escorting the most beautiful woman in all of Washington. That was as much as they learned from me. I'm not about to give them an opportunity to steal you away from me. There are a few of them who are far more handsome than me."

She clasped a hand over her heart and laughed. "I don't believe that is possible, Lieutenant Brady."

"Take my word for it—there are any number of fellows who wear a uniform and could easily turn a lady's head."

Clara's smile faded. "Even if that's true—and I'm not certain it is—I'm sure there isn't another soldier at the Arsenal who is as kind and thoughtful as you. Those virtues are far more important to me than one's appearance."

"Thank you, Clara." He covered her gloved hand with his own. "You're shaking. Is something wrong?"

She forced a smile. "I'm nervous about the gala. I think I'll be fine once we're inside and we can disappear into the crowd."

"Clara! You're far too pretty to disappear in any crowd. Please don't be anxious. I promise I'll be right beside you, and I'm not going to let anything, or anyone, create a problem. Do you believe I can protect you?"

"Of course." She longed to add that although she was sure he could protect her from physical harm, she wasn't so sure he could protect her from unseemly remarks that would likely be whispered as they mingled with the other guests. Instead, she offered a weak smile and attempted to still her hands.

When the carriage stopped in front of the three-story brick edifice, Clara glanced out the window before stepping down. Fancy carriages lined the driveway leading to the Seward house. Most were owned by the attendees and would remain in place until after the party. Their own rented carriage would depart and return for them after the late dinner that would begin at midnight.

She held Joseph's arm in a viselike grip as they arrived at

the front of the receiving line. Once the butler announced them, they were greeted by Mr. and Mrs. Seward.

Secretary Seward appeared momentarily confused about their identity, until his wife mentioned Colonel Furman. At the mention of the colonel, a spark of recognition gleamed in the secretary's eyes. "Ah, yes. I do remember who you are, Lieutenant. As I recall, the colonel mentioned you were injured at Bull Run. Am I correct?"

The color heightened in Joseph's cheeks, and he bowed his head. "Yes, sir." His answer was no more than a whisper.

Before Secretary Seward could say anything more, the butler announced another couple, and Clara walked alongside Joseph to the other side of the room. The gaslights flickered and cast eerie shadows along the walls. And though the night air was cool, the crush of guests warmed the room. The draped windows were ajar to cool the room, yet the chilly breeze prevented guests from lingering along the room's outer circumference—the place where Clara had hoped to hide from view.

She need not have worried overly much, as the other guests walked by Joseph and her as though they were invisible. They'd been there only a short time when the music began and the Grand March was announced.

Joseph took her hand. "There's no way to avoid the March. Just follow the ladies when we separate and then we'll come back together. It's really walking gracefully rather than dancing. You'll do fine."

Her heart beat like a drum as they lined up with the other guests. Clara was thankful they were near the end of the line so she had time to observe what those in front of her were doing. Each time she was forced to move away from Joseph, she was careful to keep him in sight. His movements were surprisingly graceful and his limp barely perceptible. In truth, she doubted a casual observer would notice it.

Once the Grand March ended, a quadrille was announced. Joseph nodded to the side of the room. "We won't do that. Perhaps you'll agree to a waltz a little later." He tipped his head close. "It appears the secretary doesn't enjoy the quadrille, either. He's walking in our direction."

Clara groaned inwardly. She hoped he wouldn't want to discuss Bull Run. Surely he was aware that reminders of the battle would be difficult for any soldier, especially one who had been wounded. Clara was deep in her thoughts when a woman across the room screamed.

Joseph whirled, pushed Clara to the side, and bounded toward Secretary Seward. A shot rang out as both men fell to the floor.

TWENTY-TWO

The sounds of shouting men and shrieking women electrified the room. The butler and several other men gave chase. A lady standing near Clara swooned and dropped to the floor. A mountain of pale-green taffeta and lace covered the woman's shoulders and face when she landed at Clara's feet. But Clara didn't offer to help the woman. She had to get to Joseph.

She fought her way through the crowd that surrounded Joseph and Secretary Seward. She had nearly reached them when one of the men kneeling at Joseph's side waved his arms in a wild gesture. "Get back. All of you! We need some air. I can't care for them with all of you hovering over us."

Care for them? Clara's heart pounded with fear. She was surrounded by the throng of onlookers, unable to see a thing. She turned sideways and pushed against the crowd, but her voluminous skirts deterred her movement. With each forward step, the retreating crush of guests pushed her farther away. She couldn't see around the broad shoulders or much taller guests, who paid no heed to her begging requests to let her get through to Joseph. Instead, she was carried on a sea of taffeta, crinolines, and morning coats to the far side of the room.

Was he injured when he fell? Had he been shot? Was he even alive? From this distance, she couldn't determine a thing.

Anger and fear mounting, she once again attempted to push aside the gathered guests. "I need to get through! That soldier is my escort!" She prayed that her shouts would garner the attention of someone in the crowd, someone who would clear a path and lead her to Joseph. But only a few guests turned her way, and even they didn't seem to understand her need to be at Joseph's side.

She continued her attempts to elbow through the crowd when there was a shout from the physician. "I need Clara McBride. Move aside and let her through."

"I'm right here!" Clara waved and shouted until the surrounding guests finally cleared a path. She caught sight of Joseph's dark blue uniform and his black shoes. One foot appeared to be twisted at an odd angle, and she gasped at the sight. Had he reinjured his foot when he fell?

Once she'd jostled past two remaining onlookers, Joseph's motionless body came into full view. His eyes were closed, and a pool of blood had formed beneath his head. He was as white as fresh-fallen snow. A scream lodged in her throat. She lifted a gloved hand to her lips and fought to keep her wits about her. Taking another step closer, she watched his chest for signs of movement. Was he breathing?

The doctor glanced up at her. "Miss McBride?" Without waiting for a response, he continued, "He asked for you before he slipped into unconsciousness."

"He's been shot?" She attempted to quell her rising panic. Had Joseph lived through the battle of Bull Run only to return and be shot at a gala? This was her fault. She should have refused the invitation from the outset.

"It doesn't appear that he has." The doctor gestured toward Secretary Seward, who remained sitting on the floor. "I believe the lieutenant saved the secretary's life."

Mrs. Seward gasped as she neared the two men on the floor. The secretary appeared somewhat dazed, but with the aid of his wife and a servant, he slowly rose to his feet. Once standing, he riveted his eyes on Joseph. "How is he, Dr. Billings? Do tell me this young soldier isn't going to suffer any permanent injury because of me."

Dr. Billings looked up at the secretary. "I can't say for sure just yet, but I believe his prospects for a complete recovery appear good. I need to perform a complete examination."

Mrs. Seward, still holding to her husband's arm, gave a firm nod.

"With your permission, sir, we're going to move him upstairs to one of the bedrooms for a full examination. I believe the blood is from a cut on his scalp. He seems to have hit his head when he fell." He turned to Clara. "You can come and wait outside the room, if you'd like. Once I've finished tending to him, you can sit near his bedside."

The doctor's words eased Clara's fears, until they lifted Joseph and his right foot turned at an odd angle. Her worries over another injury to his foot immediately returned.

She grasped the doctor's arm. "Joseph was injured at Bull Run." She nodded toward him. "His foot appears to be turned in an awkward manner. Did he suffer an injury to his leg or ankle?" She hesitated. "Or perhaps reinjure the foot?"

The doctor turned toward the staircase. His brows dipped into a frown, and he tweaked the end of his mustache. "I hadn't noticed his leg, but I promise I will check him from top to bottom and advise you if there are any injuries other than to his scalp." He placed his hand beneath Clara's elbow and led her through a group of guests who had moved to the foyer.

Secretary Seward, who now seemed to have overcome his earlier confusion, directed the guests to step aside. "Until we know if the scoundrel has been captured, I would suggest we all remain inside the house. I don't want to think he may be lurking about outside, but there's no way to be sure."

A man near the back of the group waved. "I sent my coach and driver to the police station to request help. A policeman should be here soon."

"I think we should go in groups of three and see if we can find him," another man called out.

"That's not wise. He has a weapon. We're better off in here," another yelled.

"He got inside once, so he can do it again."

Clara cringed at the retort. She didn't want to think the villain would return. Yet, if he knew his aim had been off and he truly wanted to kill the secretary, he might come back to finish the job. A thread of fear crept up her spine.

Once she'd taken her place outside the bedroom door, the sounds of muffled arguing continued below stairs, then finally ceased. A short time later, a patrolman wearing a double-breasted navy-blue uniform and helmet appeared at the top of the steps. The silver insignia on his helmet identified him as a member of the Washington, D.C., police.

He strode toward her and touched the brim of his helmet. "Good evening, miss. Secretary Seward tells me that you accompanied the injured lieutenant to the party this evening. Is that correct?"

"Yes."

The patrolman glanced down the hall. "I'll be right back. My feet are aching. I'm going to get that chair so I can sit down while we talk." He used his thumb to point to a chair sitting outside one of the bedroom doors.

Had the policeman waited a moment, Clara would have told him that he wouldn't need a chair. After all, there wasn't much for them to talk about. She didn't know anything about the intruder, and the doctor hadn't reappeared with news of Joseph's condition. Instead, she folded her hands in her lap and watched him drag the chair along the carpet runner. Rather than placing it beside her, he positioned the chair directly opposite hers.

When he sat down, their knees were almost touching. Annoyed, she scooted back in her chair and frowned.

He smiled in return. "I like to observe folks when I question them. I can't do that if I'm sitting beside you."

"That makes perfect sense when you're interrogating a possible suspect. However, I'm a guest whose escort was injured during the melee, so I don't believe you need to question me as though I'm a criminal, Patrolman"—she squinted at his nametag—"Hanstover."

"Hanover. It's Patrolman Hanover. And you are?" His lips curled in an indulgent smile.

"Clara McBride. Miss Clara McBride."

He removed a pencil and pad from inside his jacket. "Well, Miss Clara McBride, where do you live?"

She watched his brow furrow when she answered. "I know you're wondering how a young lady who lives on South O Street would be invited to a gala at the Seward residence, so let me explain."

He leaned back in the chair and listened as she detailed the circumstances surrounding her presence at the gala. "The invitation included my escort, Lieutenant Brady. He's the one who was injured while protecting Secretary Seward."

Hanover nodded. "The secretary told me the lieutenant saved his life." He made a notation on his pad and then looked up. "So you support yourself as a seamstress, Miss McBride?"

"No, I work at the laboratory in the Arsenal. My mother is a seamstress, and I was assisting her with gowns for several of her clients."

"I see. How long have you worked at the Arsenal, Miss McBride?" The patrolman placed the end of his pencil between his teeth and stared at her.

"Almost a year. I was among the first women hired after the war began." She tipped her head to the side. "What does any of this have to do with what happened tonight?"

He jotted something in his notepad. "We like to have background information on all parties involved in a crime. Sometimes we find that the tiniest bit of information can prove helpful, and I know you want us to capture the culprit who injured your beau."

"Of course, but—"

"We'll be done soon. What about friends who work at the laboratory, Miss McBride?"

Discomfort enveloped her like a thick morning fog. "Why does that matter? I'm worried about Joseph, not friends who work at the laboratory."

He shrugged. "As I said, you never know when some jot of information will help us solve a crime." He leaned forward and rested his arms across his thighs, further diminishing the narrow distance between their knees. He raised his eyes to meet hers. "I believe I was inquiring about friends who work at the Arsenal."

She frowned. "I know every lady who works in the cartridge lab, and many of the other ladies who work in the other rooms. The supervisors are known to everyone who works there. I also know some of the men who work in the freight and shipping department."

"Those would be acquaintances. Do you consider any of those workers friends? In other words, Miss McBride, do you socialize with any of the other employees at the Arsenal?" He nodded toward the closed bedroom door. "Other than the lieutenant."

"Not many, but a few."

"And do they live in the same general area as you?"

She nodded. "They do."

He blew out a long sigh. "And their names?"

"I'll tell you their names when you tell me what this is about. I believe there's more to your questions than some hope of a morsel that might help you in the future." She folded her arms across her waist and met his steady stare.

"Do you have something to hide, Miss McBride?"

"No, I don't, Patrolman Hanover." She tightened her lips into a thin line and waited.

"One of the police officers chased after a person who ran near the Seward residence in a southerly direction. We figure he's likely a civilian worker at the Arsenal."

"And was he apprehended?"

"No. Many of the fellows who live near the Arsenal know how to conceal themselves in an alleyway or stairwell. They're like the rats that inhabit the area—always aware of a hole in which to hide." He stroked his jaw with his palm. "And now, Miss McBride. The names of your friends?"

"I still don't know why the names of my acquaintances are of importance."

"As I said, the assailant ran in the direction of the Arsenal. You're the only one at this party who lives in that area, Miss McBride. It stands to reason that we would want to know the names and addresses of your friends—those who knew you would be attending this gala."

A spiral of filmy cigar smoke floated up the steps like a translucent ghost seeking shelter. Clara watched it twist and turn until it reached the plasterwork ceiling and disappeared. She wished she could do the same. Why didn't the doctor return and save her from this incessant questioning? Was Joseph in need of more medical care than the doctor had predicted?

"Miss McBride!" The patrolman's exasperated tone brought her back to the present. "The names?"

"There are only three whom the lieutenant and I have met with socially. Sergeant Andrew Kessler, Beatrice Hodson, and her brother, Jeremiah Hodson. Beatrice and Jeremiah live together in an apartment on South M Street. Sergeant Kessler is Miss Hodson's beau, and he lives at the Arsenal. You'll find this information completely useless, but I hope you'll now leave me to wait in peace."

He stood and returned his chair to its place down the hallway, but before descending the stairs, he returned to her side. "It was not my intention to cause you further discomfort, Miss McBride. Please know that I'm merely doing my job. I want to find the man responsible for the lieutenant's injuries. If the assailant is a determined assassin, there's no telling who he might attempt to kill next. Like me, I'm sure you don't want to see anyone else injured." He turned and walked toward the steps. When he had neared the top of the stairway, he glanced over his shoulder. "I'll be back to speak with the lieutenant once the doctor gives me permission."

She nodded. There was no doubt he would return. Patrolman Hanover was determined to glean every possible detail from the Sewards' guests, or at least from her—and Joseph. If the patrolman hadn't accomplished anything else, he'd successfully imposed a mounting sense of apprehension. But she wasn't certain why.

Clara paced the hallway runner until she was convinced it would soon be threadbare. She was certain she could bear to wait no longer when the bedroom door finally creaked open and Dr. Billings appeared.

"I'm sorry you've had to wait so long. Patients who suffer a blow to the head can sometimes develop inflammation of the brain. I wanted to watch the lieutenant and make certain he wasn't showing any such signs."

"So, he's fine?"

The doctor smiled. "For a man who fell and hit his head while trying to protect his host, I'd say the lieutenant is doing quite well." He took a deep breath. "You asked about his prior injury and if there had been any further damage to his right leg or foot."

Clara nodded. "Or his ankle. It appeared some part of his right limb had twisted."

"Yes. I did notice the leg was turned somewhat as they carried him out, but after a full examination, I can assure you there is no injury to his leg or ankle, and his foot was well protected. His only injury was to his head." Chattering voices floated upward, and the doctor glanced toward the stairway and shook his head. "I thought all the guests would be gone by now."

"I'm sure a few have left, but the police seem to be intent upon questioning everyone."

"Any word if they caught the scoundrel?"

"Not that I've heard, but after the policeman who questioned me returned downstairs, I haven't seen or heard from anyone."

"I'll go downstairs and see what I can find out. Give me a few minutes and I'll be back." The doctor nodded toward the bedroom door. "You can go in now and sit with the lieutenant. He's likely still asleep. I gave him a small dose of laudanum."

"Thank you, Dr. Billings. I know Joseph is grateful you were here to care for him."

"My honor, Miss McBride." He gave a little wave as he made his way to the stairs. "I'll be back shortly to give you a report and to check on my patient."

Clara opened the bedroom door and tiptoed to Joseph's bedside. At the sight of him, a tear slipped down her cheek. She sat down and gently lifted his hand into her own. Though his eyes remained closed, the steady rise and fall of his chest allayed her distress. The fear that he'd suffered further injury or died had given her pause.

While she had waited, her thoughts remained upon Joseph and a possible future with him, and whether she could set aside the horrible pictures that had been painted by Mrs. Blair. She'd weighed both the advantages and the consequences of marrying Joseph, and the advantages had been the winner. She would gain far more with a husband who displayed love for God and for others than without him.

At the sound of footsteps in the hall, Clara turned toward the door. "How's our patient doing?" The doctor approached the bedside.

"Still sleeping. He's been quite peaceful."

"Good. I wanted to let you know the police have been

unsuccessful thus far in their attempts to capture the intruder. They chased him as far as South K Street before losing sight of him." He glanced down at Joseph. "I believe one of the policemen still wants to speak with Joseph. You might come down and let me know when he awakens."

Clara nodded. "I'll do that."

Once the doctor left the room, Clara lowered her head and kissed the back of Joseph's hand. "I know you can't hear me, but I want to tell you how frightened I was that I might lose you. I thought my heart would break when I saw you lying on the floor. I love you, Joseph, and I want to spend the remainder of my life with you." She longed to kiss his cheek but worried he might awaken. "Of course, I could never say any of these things if you were awake, but perhaps they've somehow seeped through and you'll know the depth of my love without hearing me speak the words."

His eyes fluttered open, and a smile played on his lips. "I've heard everything you said, and your words are far better medicine than anything the doctor can order for me." He offered a weak smile and touched a finger to his cheek. "I do believe a kiss might help me even more."

She glanced over her shoulder at the door before leaning forward and placing a lingering kiss on his cheek.

TWENTY-THREE

lara returned to the Seward mansion the following morning and once again took up residence outside Joseph's bedroom door while Dr. Billings conducted his examination. She'd been waiting only a few minutes when she heard a knock at the front door, followed by footsteps scurrying up the stairs.

Mrs. Seward's maid motioned to the bedroom door. "The patrolman has returned and wants to speak with the lieutenant. I told him the doctor was here, but he said he'd wait."

Clara nodded. "Thank you. I'll advise the lieutenant as soon as possible."

If nothing else, the patrolman was persistent. Although he'd wanted to speak to Joseph last night, Mrs. Seward had declared the hour late and bid him return in the morning. Clara had hoped he wouldn't arrive, but his appearance made one thing clear—they hadn't yet captured the assailant.

A short time later, the bedroom door opened and the doctor greeted her with a broad smile. "The lieutenant is doing quite well. I've tested his memory, and it appears to be fine. The sutures will heal nicely, though he may suffer from headaches for a period of time. The patient is already dressed, if you'd like to go in. I believe he's eager to depart."

"Again, thank you for all you've done, Dr. Billings. You've been most kind."

He tipped his head in a slight nod. "You take care of him and make certain he comes to my office in a week to ten days so that I can see how he's progressing."

"I'll do that." She waited only a moment before entering the bedroom.

As she was stepping inside, Joseph turned and picked up his hat. "Good morning. You're a wonderful sight." Seeing they were alone, he leaned forward and kissed her on the cheek. "I'm ready to thank the Sewards and be on our way."

"I'm afraid you're going to have to stay a bit longer," Clara said. "The patrolman has returned and wants to question you."

Joseph sighed. "I don't think there's a lot I can tell him that he hasn't already heard, so it shouldn't take long. Let's go downstairs and get this over with."

Mrs. Seward appeared in the foyer as they descended the stairway. "The doctor says you're doing quite well, Lieutenant. I'm pleased for the good news." She gestured toward a room off the foyer. "The officer is waiting to speak with you. The two of you can join him in the sitting room. I'll have coffee brought in for you."

Joseph attempted to decline the coffee, but Mrs. Seward brushed aside his objection. If they were going to have coffee, this was going to take longer than either of them wished. The patrolman stood when the two of them entered the room. He nodded to Clara, then introduced himself to Joseph.

"I had hoped to speak with you last night, Lieutenant, but the hour was late and I believe the doctor had given you some medication, as well. I'm sure you'll be better able to answer my questions this morning."

Joseph hiked a shoulder. "I'll do my best, but I didn't see much. I don't think there's much I can tell you that you wouldn't have already heard from some of the other guests."

"The mind is a strange thing, Lieutenant. On many occasions, folks believe they haven't seen anything of importance, but after going over the facts, they recall some little thing that jars their memory. The next thing you know, they remember something of great importance. Let's hope that occurs with you this morning." The patrolman removed his notepad and stub of a pencil from his inside jacket pocket. "Unless you observed something odd when you first arrived at the party, why don't you begin telling me what happened shortly before you heard the gunfire?"

Joseph rubbed his temples. "Nothing strange happened early on. Miss McBride and I had joined in the Grand March. After that, the musicians began playing a quadrille, and we made our way to the far side of the room." He lowered his hands.

The patrolman stopped writing and looked up. "Any particular reason you didn't continue dancing?"

Joseph glanced at Clara. She scooted to the edge of the settee. "Because I'm not an accomplished dancer. I don't know the steps to a quadrille and didn't want to embarrass the lieutenant."

The patrolman gave her a sympathetic smile. "Not much of a dancer myself." He glanced down at the notepad. "So you walked to the far side of the room. Exactly where would that have been?"

Joseph hesitated only a moment. "The east side. We were near the tall windows that look out onto the street."

"And were the windows open?" He arched his brows. "If you recall."

"They were. The evening was quite chilly, but with so many people in the room, the fresh air was necessary. I remember feeling a light breeze while we stood there." Joseph's brow tightened. "So, you believe the gunman may have climbed to one of the balconies and entered through a window?"

"I can't be sure, but it does make sense. The butler was at the front door, so I don't think he entered there. And the shot was fired from the direction of the window."

Clara perked to attention. "How do you know that?"

"Several guests caught a glimpse of him. He was standing near the open window when he shot, and he retreated the same way. There's a tree near the balcony of the ballroom windows. He likely climbed it and from there gained access to the ballroom."

Clara wondered why he was asking Joseph when he already knew the answers, yet she refrained from saying anything. The patrolman had seemed annoyed by her earlier interruption.

"Let's get back to what you saw, Lieutenant. You were standing by the window. . . ."

Joseph nodded. "Yes. I'm not sure why, but I think I glanced over my shoulder. I saw a flash and—"

"The gun firing?" the patrolman asked.

Joseph shook his head. "No. The gun didn't fire until I lunged toward the secretary. I believe the flash was caused by a reflection of some sort. Perhaps the metal trim on the weapon reflected in the gaslight or in a mirror. I can't be sure."

The patrolman leaned forward. "Think back. There is a mirror in that room. Perhaps you saw more than you initially thought. Close your eyes and take a minute. Attempt to re-create the scene in your mind."

Clara watched the patrolman, who kept his eyes fixed upon Joseph until he finally opened his eyes. "I vaguely recall he might have been wearing a canvas jacket and a flat cap." He glanced at Clara. "The kind Jeremiah sometimes wears."

"The hat or the jacket?" The patrolman looked at Joseph. "Both."

The maid arrived with the coffee, and as the lieutenant flipped through his notepad, Clara poured them each a cup. "Almost every civilian man working at the Arsenal wears a canvas coat and flat cap now that the weather has turned cooler."

The patrolman seemed not to hear, or was he intentionally ignoring her? He tapped a page with his pencil. "This would be the same Jeremiah Hodson you mentioned as one of your friends who works at the Arsenal and lives on South M Street? And he also knew that you and the lieutenant would be guests at the party? Is that correct?"

"Yes, he's the same person. But he wasn't aware we were attending the party."

Joseph shook his head. "He probably did know we were at the party. Bea stopped by one day after you'd received the invitation. She wanted to know when you'd be returning to work. I mentioned the gala to her." He glanced at the patrolman. "Bea pretty much shares everything with her brother."

Clara grimaced and folded her arms across her chest. "But since he is our friend, he wouldn't attempt to shoot Joseph."

"The assailant was attempting to shoot the secretary, not Joseph. We assume he's a Southern sympathizer or a revolutionary attached to the Confederate Army who has crossed the border." The patrolman met Clara's hard stare.

"He could even be a spy of some sort who is now living in Washington—we can't be sure—but it only makes sense that the assailant is a Southern supporter."

Clara frowned. It sounded as though the patrolman had already made up his mind that Jeremiah was the assailant. She'd heard stories about how the police could become single-minded when attempting to solve crimes—especially when they suspected some downtrodden individual. Was that what Patrolman Hanover was doing? She hoped not.

Joseph turned back to the patrolman. "If there isn't anything else you need from me, Miss McBride and I would like to be on our way."

"I believe I have everything I need, Lieutenant. Thank you both for your cooperation." He stood and extended his hand to Joseph. While they were shaking hands, the patrolman glanced at Clara. "One more thing, Miss McBride."

Clara inwardly groaned. More than anything, she wanted to leave. "Yes?"

"Do the Hodsons normally attend church services on Sundays? If not, I thought I could pay them a visit when I leave here."

"I can't say for certain, but I think you'd have a better opportunity to find them at home this afternoon." She forced a smile and walked to the foyer, where the butler stood at the ready.

Before leaving, Joseph refused Secretary Seward's offer to send them home in his carriage. "It's a beautiful day, and I believe we'd enjoy the walk."

Once they'd departed the house, Clara took his arm. "You're certain the walk isn't going to create more pain in your foot?"

He looked down at her and smiled. "My foot is just fine,

Clara. It isn't that far. Besides, the fresh air will help clear my head and give us time to visit." He patted her gloved hand resting in the crook of his arm.

She lifted her skirt as they circled around a puddle of muddy water. "That patrolman was like a dog after a bone once you mentioned the hat and jacket were like the ones Jeremiah wears. I do wish you had simply said the hat and jacket were similar to the ones worn by many workers at the Arsenal."

He shrugged. "I wasn't pointing a finger at Jeremiah. The explanation was merely an attempt to describe what the intruder was wearing—nothing more."

"I know, but I had already been asked the names of friends who worked at the Arsenal and where they lived, so when the patrolman heard Jeremiah's name, it seemed to raise even more suspicion." She arched her brows. "Don't you think?"

"If the patrolman goes to talk to them, they have nothing to fear. He'll likely ask where they were during the time of the shooting. Once they account for their time, he can remove them from his list of suspects."

"Perhaps, but the fact that they live on South M Street and the assailant ran in that direction didn't help, either." She sighed. "I can't imagine how many people live in this area. Just because the shooter ran in that direction doesn't mean he lives down here."

"I'm sure the police realize that's true."

Church bells pealed in the distance, and Clara shook her head. "And he didn't even apologize for keeping us so long that we missed church services."

"I'm sure the Lord understands."

"Even if I don't?" She glanced up at him and giggled. "You're right. I'm being peevish, but I know Bea and Jeremiah will be unhappy with me when the police come calling and they discover it's because I mentioned their names."

"Once you explain, I'm sure they'll understand." Joseph patted her hand. "You need to quit fretting."

They turned south on 4 ½ Street when Clara shaded her eyes. "Isn't that Bea up ahead, walking in our direction?"

Joseph peered at the figure in the distance and nodded. "I believe it is. Appears she didn't make it to church this morning, either."

As they drew closer, Clara waved. She wanted to call out, but she dared not exhibit such unladylike behavior. She waited only a moment or two before once again waving as she tugged on Joseph's arm. "Let's hurry. She didn't wave in return. I don't think she recognizes us. I want to tell her she'll likely receive a visit from the police."

Joseph gently pulled back. "I don't think that's wise, Clara."

She came to a sudden halt and looked up at him. "Why?"

"If you tell her, and the police get wind of it, they may become even more suspicious and wonder why you thought it necessary to warn them. I think it's better to simply let things progress spontaneously."

She certainly didn't want to give the police further reason to suspect Bea and Jeremiah of any wrongdoing. She tipped her head in a firm nod. "You're right—again." When they neared South G Street, Clara noticed that Bea had disappeared. She tightened her hold on Joseph's arm. "Where did Bea go? Did you see her turn off?"

Joseph shook his head. "No, but she must not have seen us. Maybe she's off trying to locate Jeremiah and cut through the back way to the park." He grinned. "I'm pleased she turned off. I think we have far better things to discuss than the possible police visit, don't you?"

Her cheeks warmed. "Yes, I was so frightened last night."

"You should know by now that my head is too hard to be broken with a little fall." He chuckled. "Besides, you'd have killed me if I died."

She playfully slapped his arm. "That is not funny. I'm being serious." She inhaled a deep breath and gathered her courage. "And while I'm being serious, there's a matter of importance I need to mention." Rather than waiting for Joseph to respond, she immediately related Mrs. Blair's disturbing account from the previous week. When Clara had completed the tale, she looked into Joseph's eyes. "I must be honest with you. Her story frightened me."

Joseph led her to a bench in the adjacent park and gathered her hands in his. "If I'd ever suffered a nightmare serious enough to injure anyone, I would have told you. Truth be told, if I even thought the possibility existed that I might harm you in any way, I wouldn't have asked for permission to court you. I can tell you that my nightmares have diminished, although I can't promise I won't suffer from them some time in the future. Still, I don't want you to marry me and live in fear. If that possibility exists—"

She placed her finger against his lips. "Your honesty is all that I needed. I know that you can't see into the future, but your words have eased my concerns. With God's help, I'm certain we can face whatever may come our way."

"I couldn't agree more." He brushed a kiss on her cheek. "And that reminds me—I have something for you. I had it with me and planned to give it to you after the gala." He fished a folded paper from his pocket and held it out to her.

"What is it?" She took the paper and waited for his response.

His eyes twinkled. "Open it."

She unfolded the paper and noticed his familiar script. Her heart melted when she realized he'd copied for her the words of Robert Burns's poem "A Red, Red Rose." She mouthed the words as she read.

When she neared the end of the first stanza, Joseph cupped her cheek. "'As fair art thou, my bonnie lass, so deep in love am I; and I will love thee still, my dear, till all the seas go dry.'"

Tears filled Clara's eyes. "You have it memorized?"

"Thanks to my mother, yes, every word." He traced her lips with the pad of his thumb. "But they meant nothing until I met you."

She started to speak, but he silenced her with the tender press of his lips. Waves of joy washed over her. God had blessed her with the love of this wonderful man. Joseph loved her, and she'd love him forever.

The following morning, Bea and Jeremiah were waiting when Clara arrived at the corner. There was little doubt they'd had a visit from the police. Bea's forehead was creased in thin folds, and Jeremiah's lips pulled into a sour grimace as she drew near.

Clara forced a tight smile. "Good morning! It's been so long since we've walked to work together. How are you?" Had they noticed the joyfulness in her tone had been strained?

"Not so good. Seems we have you and your lieutenant to thank for sending the police our way yesterday afternoon." Jeremiah scowled and moved to one side while Bea remained on the other. She was sandwiched between them like ham on rye.

"Why'd you do that, Clara? I thought we were friends." Bea nudged her arm.

Clara frowned. "We are friends, and I didn't send them. They asked for the names of any friends who worked at the Arsenal. I gave the patrolman your names and said you lived on M Street. That's as much as I told him."

Jeremiah shook his head. "Maybe that's all you said, but that patrolman said there was a shooting at that fancy party you attended, and Joseph described me as the shooter."

"That's an absolute falsehood. Joseph never described you. He mentioned the intruder's clothing was similar to what you wear. Nothing more."

"There had to be more to it than that or they wouldn't have come knocking on our door and all but accused me of entering that mansion through an open window and shooting at the secretary and wounding Joseph."

"If you'll give me a chance, I'll tell you exactly what happened."

As they drew near the arched entrance to the Arsenal, Jeremiah clasped her elbow and nodded to the left. The three of them came to a halt at the far side of the stone archway.

Jeremiah folded his arms across his chest. "I'm waiting. Go ahead and see if you can convince me you're not to blame."

Clara glanced toward the laboratory. She might be late for work, but if she didn't defend herself right now, Jeremiah was going to think she was guilty. She recounted the evening's events, beginning with the Grand March and ending with the final interrogation on Sunday morning.

Once finished, she looked back and forth between the two of them. "If you don't believe me, that's your choice. But I didn't do anything but answer the policeman's questions."

"And Joseph? Does he believe I'm innocent?" Jeremiah tugged at his cap and pointed to his canvas coat.

"Joseph was merely attempting to describe the intruder's

clothing and used yours as an example. He said once the police were certain of your whereabouts during the incident, you'd be removed as a suspect, so there was nothing to worry about."

When the work bell sounded, all three of them took off at a sprint. While Clara wasn't sure if she'd convinced Jeremiah, she'd seen the acceptance in Bea's eyes. She was sure of it.

Twenty-Four

Late November 1862

Beatrice poured boiling water into the teapot and sat down at the scarred kitchen table. She pointed to the chair opposite her, and Jeremiah dropped onto the chair with a thud.

He glowered at her. "I already know what you're going to say. I don't need to hear it."

"Do you? Then tell me, what is it I'm going to say?" Bea folded her hands atop the table and stared at him.

"You're gonna tell me how stupid it was to try to shoot Seward. We're never gonna agree, so quit harping at me. Every time one of those policemen come knocking, you start in on me. I'm sick of it. We don't agree. You think you're right and I know I am. I needed something substantial to report—something that would let the Ghost know we're doing all we can for the cause. So there ya have it. Besides, if I would have been successful, the bluecoats might not be advancing on Fredericksburg."

Bea sighed. "You don't even know that's true. You get one missive saying Seward was attempting to convince Lincoln to advance on Fredericksburg, and you sneak into that party and start shooting. You think that's going to impress the Gray Ghost or any of the Rangers?" She leaned forward. "Now we have the police knocking on our door every few days, and you tell me you're sick of hearing me nag you?" She shook her head and glared at him. "They've got more evidence than we know about or they wouldn't keep coming back."

His face tightened into a scowl. "If they knew anything, they'd quit snooping around and arrest me. If it weren't for Joseph and his blabbering, the police would have never shown up on our doorstep. If I would've just killed Seward, we wouldn't have these worries."

"Well, you didn't. You messed up, and now you're not willing to admit it. Think about it, Jeremiah. Your foolishness could ruin the whole plan. How do you think that's going to sit with the Ghost?"

"Quit making a mountain out of a molehill. Ever since I changed to the night shift, things have been moving along. Any ammunition leaving here has been soaked with water, and even if some of it fires, those soldiers will discover their gunpowder is gonna misfire or, more likely, be too damp to load." He leaned back and balanced on the rear legs of the chair. "Instead of giving me a hard time, you should be patting me on the back for my success."

Bea curled her lip in a sneer. "If you thought you were having such great success, why didn't you report what you've accomplished and forget about trying to kill Seward? You put us in a bad spot, Jeremiah. What happens if the police arrest you? Have you even considered that? We need to decide on how I might proceed without you. I sure can't replace you on the night shift at the warehouse."

"You're always borrowing trouble, Bea. Even when things

are going smooth, you find some reason to make life miserable."

"Is that right? I think your actions have more to do with making life miserable than anything I say or do." She sighed. "Arguing isn't going to help us. We need a plan." She lifted the teapot and filled her cup with the amber liquid. "Any suggestions?"

"I told you, my suggestion is that we cross that bridge when we come to it."

"Well, I'm not willing to do that." She took a sip of her tea, then clanked the cup on the chipped saucer. "Here's what I'm thinking we need to do. If the police show up and want to arrest you, I'll say that I was the intruder."

He laughed. "That's downright foolish. Who do you think is going to believe that piece of nonsense?"

"Don't worry about that. I can be very convincing when needed. I'm not afraid of weapons. I know how to load and shoot a rifle. I brought home more rabbits and squirrels for dinner than you ever did."

"Because I was out plowing and planting, not because you're a better shot than me. And you ain't never shot a Colt."

She nodded. "That's right. So, we need to find someplace outside the city where you can teach me how to use the Colt—enough that if they question me, I'm able to give proper answers. It won't matter if I'm a good shot. After all, you didn't hit your target." She tipped her head to the side and grinned.

He stared at her for a moment. "I'm not gonna let you step in and take the blame, Bea. First off, I couldn't live with myself if I did that. And second, they'd never believe it."

"Why not? We're about the same height, and if I was wearing that bulky canvas coat and cap, no one could tell if it was you or me. If one of the guests had gotten a good look at your face, the police would already have a drawing that resembled you, and you'd be in jail right now."

He rubbed his jaw. "I guess that much is true. They're just poking around to see if either of us changes our story."

Bea nodded. "And the fact that you were supposed to be working at the warehouse makes you less of a suspect than me."

"Except nobody can vouch for me being there." He shrugged. "After all, I was able to leave without anyone being the wiser, which was good that night, but it does damage my alibi."

"Maybe a little. Still, your alibi is better than mine. I was at home alone. Nobody can assure the police of my whereabouts, so my plan to confess is what's needed. Your work at the warehouse has to continue. We need the Union troops to receive as much defective ammunition as possible."

"I'll think on what you're saying. The truth is, I don't know how long it will take before one of those field officers realizes the malfunctioning ammunition is from the Washington Arsenal. Once they put it together, there will be an all-out investigation, and our names will soon be at the top of their list."

Bea considered his words. Maybe she was worrying about the wrong thing, but she didn't want to take any chances. Even so, Jeremiah's warning was a good reminder to keep her eyes and ears open. Even though he disagreed with her, maintaining her relationship with Andrew remained necessary. The sergeant could prove to be a good resource when trouble started to brew at the Arsenal headquarters, and there was no doubt it would. The only question was how soon.

Jeremiah glanced out the window and pushed away from the table. "I gotta get to work." He shrugged into his coat and pulled the flat wool cap low on his head.

Bea crossed the room and picked up the lunch pail. "I still want you to teach me how to load and shoot the Colt. Just in case." She extended the lunch pail but held it tight.

Jeremiah grasped the handle, and when she didn't release it, he gave a nod. "I'll teach ya, but I still think I'm right and you're wrong."

She smirked. "That's what you always think."

He tugged the pail from her hand with a grunt, and she watched as he strode out into the night.

Bea hoped he was right, yet in her heart she already knew the police had Jeremiah pegged. She was his only hope.

Joseph tossed about on his thin mattress, unable to find a comfortable position. Sleep hadn't come easily since the shooting at Secretary Seward's mansion. Although his nightmares hadn't returned, sleep usually eluded him until near time to rise. He sat up and dropped his legs over the side of the bunk. Moonlight shone through the barren tree limbs and cast dancing shadows across the parade field outside his window. Nowadays, nighttime shadows were the only activity seen at the training fields of the Arsenal. Drills had diminished, and recruits were no longer trained. Instead, they were sent to the front as soon as they signed up. The generals and colonels at the front wanted more men—trained or not. The Union's lack of success was proving an embarrassment to the North and to President Lincoln.

Joseph rested his forearms across his thighs. There was

no sense lying down. He was wide awake now. Maybe if he took a walk, it would help. He donned his uniform and boots, grabbed his hat, and walked out the door. He inhaled a deep and cleansing breath. The crisp, cold air filled his lungs and awakened his senses to the stillness of the night. Standing here, it was difficult to believe that only fifty miles away, battles raged and men were dying.

He walked to the end of the barracks and turned toward the river, heading in a southerly direction. The night unfurled in deepening shades as Joseph continued onward. When he neared the river, he glanced toward the warehouses and noticed a flickering light. Jeremiah would be on duty. If nothing else, Joseph's insomnia would permit him an opportunity to observe warehouse duties during the nighttime hours.

Jeremiah's request for a transfer to the night shift had come as a complete surprise to Joseph. Granted, it paid a little more because they had so much difficulty filling the position, but working at night meant he was alone on the job, and he was sleeping whenever there were any social activities. Then again, since Jeremiah wasn't interested in courting, maybe he didn't mind the odd hours. No matter the pay, Joseph was certain the hours weren't ones he would want to work, but he was glad someone was willing. Having a guard stationed at the warehouse was a necessity, and they needed civilians rather than soldiers doing the job.

He adjusted his approach toward the far side of the building, where the watchman's desk was situated. Windows had been placed on all sides to permit the guard a view in all directions. If a trespasser approached by land or water, an observant watchman should have no problem spotting the interloper.

Drawing closer, Joseph listened and watched for Jeremiah to exit the doors, order him to halt, and demand identification. Instead, the only sounds breaking the silence were the rhythmic slapping of water along the shoreline and the hoot of a distant owl. The hairs on the back of Joseph's neck prickled. Something wasn't right. He stopped, leaned against a big pine tree, and peered toward the windows. He hoped to catch a glimpse of Jeremiah, but he couldn't see any sign of movement inside the warehouse. What if Jeremiah was lying on the floor ill or wounded? Had an intruder broken in? From this distance, there didn't appear to be any damage to the doors or windows.

Joseph's breathing thickened. A battle drum pounded inside his chest and pumped a rush of blood through his veins. His senses alert, he remained by the tree and considered his options. He lowered his hand to his waist. How he longed to feel the cold metal of a revolver or saber, but he had no weapon. With the moon as his only source of illumination, he studied the immediate area until he spotted a thick tree limb under a nearby elm. He closed the short distance, picked up the limb, and rushed from tree to tree, hoping to hide his presence from anyone who might be watching. The only defense he would have against an intruder would be the tree limb and the element of surprise.

He lunged toward the tree closest to the doors, his breathing heavy. After a moment to calm his nerves, he picked his way forward.

"Who goes there?"

The shout sent a chill of fear through his entire body. "Lieutenant Joseph Brady! Is that you, Jeremiah?"

"You scared me outta my wits, Joseph! What are you doing tramping around at one o'clock in the morning?"

Joseph walked toward Jeremiah, who was holding a leather bucket in each hand. "I couldn't sleep and decided to take a walk. I thought you'd be inside the warehouse."

Moving both the hand-pump fire truck as well as an abundance of buckets close to the warehouses had been among Joseph's suggestions for improving safety at the Arsenal. Colonel Furman had agreed to requisition enough buckets to form a bucket brigade that would stretch from the warehouses down to the river—and he'd done so. But the colonel had objected to moving the fire truck. He believed it should remain in a more central location.

Joseph hadn't argued. The explosion and fires in Lawrenceville had occurred at the laboratory and not at the warehouses, yet the pure volume of ammunition stored in those few buildings was enough to make him shudder. He didn't want to think of the havoc that would be wreaked upon the Arsenal if one of those crates ignited.

Tonight, some of the buckets were full of water and aligned in a row outside the door, while others were empty and scattered about. Joseph glanced around and attempted to make sense of the situation. When he could think of no logical explanation, he frowned.

"What are you doing with the buckets?" Joseph gestured to the array of buckets. "Why are you filling them with water?"

Jeremiah set the two full buckets by his feet and cleared his throat. "When I started working down here, we'd had a good bit of rain, and I didn't worry too much about fire. But it's been mighty dry this fall, and I keep fretting that there's a strong chance of fire." He pointed toward the surrounding vegetation. "What with all these trees and such, I thought it would be best to be prepared. When I get here at night, I fill the buckets so if a fire breaks out, I'll be prepared until help arrives."

"I see." Joseph paused. "But who's keeping watch for possible intruders who might set a fire while you're running back and forth to the river?"

Jeremiah shoved his hands into his pockets and shrugged. "I make it back and forth in no time at all. If anyone was approaching, I'd see 'em." He grinned. "I saw you, didn't I?"

"I could have set fire to this place and been gone before you ever knew I was around. I was worried that you'd been attacked and might be lying on the floor needing help. My approach would have been quite different if I'd wanted to set fire to the warehouse."

Jeremiah propped his muscular frame against the warehouse door. "I was just trying to protect the place."

"I think your idea is very resourceful and it could prove beneficial in the event of a fire. The thing is, Jeremiah, before you begin taking matters into your own hands, you need to gain the approval of your supervisor, who would, in turn, seek approval from the colonel. I know you've never served in the Army, but even when you're working for the military, you have to follow procedure."

"I s'pose you're right. I should have gotten consent first." He pushed his cap back on his head. "I just thought I'd do something useful, and it would help make the time go by quicker if I was busy."

Water trickled down Joseph's arm when he picked up one of the empty buckets. He stared at his damp sleeve, then picked up another empty bucket and felt inside. It too was wet. He attempted to gather his thoughts. If the buckets were filled one time and left outside the building, why would they need to be filled every night? The water wouldn't evaporate much at this time of year. And why were some of the empty buckets wet? What had happened with the water that was in them?

He looked from the empty buckets to Jeremiah and posed his questions, then waited for Jeremiah's response.

Jeremiah didn't hesitate with his answer. "I been wetting down the ground around the building in the hopes of keeping it better protected. I was planning to begin digging a trench and filling it." He chuckled. "Sure am glad I didn't do that without permission—the colonel might have me strung from the gallows."

Joseph relaxed his shoulders and shook his head. "I don't think that would have happened, but you shouldn't proceed without approval. Why don't I speak to Colonel Furman? I think he'll be impressed with your ideas, and if we can find someone else willing to work the night shift, he might approve a helper, so the two of you could take turns carrying the water and keeping watch."

Jeremiah shook his head with such force his cap fell to the ground. "No. I don't want any help, Joseph. I like working by myself. I'd rather quit filling the buckets if it means I've gotta put up with some fella yammering at me all night. I get enough of that from Bea."

The forceful response surprised Joseph. With all Jeremiah's talk of wanting to avoid a fire, Joseph had expected just the opposite. While he could understand Jeremiah's desire for peace and quiet, his adamant refusal of help seemed odd. Like it or not, Joseph would speak to the colonel about a worker or two to assist with the trenches. Although he was assigned to protect the warehouses, Jeremiah needed to understand he wasn't in charge.

On his return to the barracks, Joseph replayed his conversation with Jeremiah. While Joseph couldn't put his finger on any one thing, Jeremiah's behavior had been out of kilter and strange—even for Jeremiah.

Twenty-Five

Bea untied her bonnet as she stepped through the front door of the apartment, her thoughts fixed upon what she would prepare for supper. As she hung her bonnet on a peg inside the door, she caught sight of Jeremiah sitting at the kitchen table and startled.

"What's caused you to get up at this time of day?" she asked.

Jeremiah was never awake when she returned home from work. When he had switched to working the night shift, he'd set a new schedule for himself. He remained awake until early afternoon, then went to bed and didn't get up until after Bea had arrived home and prepared dinner. Thus far, the arrangement had worked well. This was the first time he'd been awake to greet her since he'd begun working nights.

His eyebrows slanted together in a frown, and he spread his hands flat on the table. "I had a bit of trouble at the warehouse last night and wasn't able to sleep."

She removed her woolen cape and hung it beside her bonnet before sitting down at the table. "What kind of trouble?"

Jeremiah related Joseph's unexpected appearance and

their lengthy exchange before he leaned back in his chair. "It was hard to tell if he believed me or not. I'm never sure what he's thinking."

"Don't overthink it. His concerns were valid, and you gave him answers that made sense. He has no reason to doubt your word. He's had lots of worries about safety, so he should be pleased with what you told him you're doing. I'm sure he thinks it's important to protect the warehouses. He may be a little jealous he didn't think of the idea himself." She smiled. "You're just lucky he didn't go into the warehouse and see the water all over those crates. I truly don't know what you would have done if that had happened. You need to consider yourself fortunate."

"Well, I haven't told you the worst part yet."

She scooted to the edge of her chair and rested her forearms on the table. "What else?"

"Joseph liked the idea so much he's going to talk to the colonel about hiring another night watchman so there's always someone keeping a lookout. If that happens, I can't continue wetting down the crates." He shook his head. "Instead, I'll be out there digging a trench around the warehouse by moonlight and lantern. That idea doesn't give me much pleasure."

"They'll have trouble finding anyone who wants to work nights. If they do manage to hire someone, you'll have to see that he meets with an accident of some sort—one that will keep him away from the warehouses."

Jeremiah nodded. "I'm not sure I like that plan." He cast a dark look in her direction. "I'd be taking a heap of risk if things went sideways."

She pushed away from the table and walked to the cupboard. "True enough, but you're the one who's always telling me we agreed to the danger when we signed up for this. Besides, neither of us can be at any greater risk than we are right now. We can be hung for treason, the same as we can be hung for killing someone."

"You mean the same as *I* can be hung for killing a workman. You wouldn't be involved in that part."

Bea sighed. "I think your lack of sleep is affecting your attitude. You need to keep your wits about you. Be careful what you say and do."

"Easy enough for you to say." He shifted in his chair and folded his arms across his chest.

She moved to his side and placed a hand on his shoulder. "I'm not used to you sounding desperate. We're fine. Nothing has changed. Maybe you should lay low for the next few nights and see if Joseph returns. What do you think?" She gave his shoulder a squeeze. "And don't forget that you promised another lesson with the Colt. I need to be able to protect myself when you're not around, especially now that there's more trouble brewing."

He snorted. "I know, I know. I'll get to it when I get to it." Before she could answer, he gestured to the stove. "You gonna get started cooking supper? My stomach's rumbling."

"I'm sorry you weren't able to sleep, but at least you haven't lost your appetite. Of course, that would make life a lot easier for me."

"Maybe, but you wouldn't know what to do with yourself if you didn't have me to take care of."

She crossed the short distance to the stove. "Won't be much tonight. I'm saving on grocery money so I can fix a nice meal when Andrew comes over tomorrow evening."

Jeremiah's chair scraped on the wood floor as he pushed away from the table and stood. "I told you it was best to tell him you'd lost interest in seeing him. He ain't been any help to us, and we don't need to keep feeding him." He walked toward the kitchen door. "I'm gonna change into my work clothes, since it'll probably be time to leave before you ever get me some supper on the table."

She nodded at him over her shoulder, determined to avoid further talk of Andrew. "I think Sunday afternoon would be the best time for us to spend some time practicing with the Colt."

Her words had been enough to silence him. She didn't want to hear his churlish remarks about supper, and she didn't want to argue about Andrew, or Joseph's visit to the warehouse, or the possibility they could both be hanged. Instead, they needed to turn their thoughts to forming a plan of escape—something foolproof they could rely upon when they needed to get out of Washington.

Even though Jeremiah understood they needed an escape plan, he always disliked taking the time to discuss strategy. He preferred to make decisions on the fly, while Bea favored a clear-cut arrangement before moving forward. In this instance, they needed to have everything prepared in advance. She could depend upon Jeremiah to locate and secure any required supplies, yet it was imperative they develop and carry through on an agreed-upon plan. In truth, Jeremiah usually relied upon her ideas, but she depended upon him to make certain her ideas were tactically feasible. Their complementary strengths and weaknesses were the primary reason the Ghost had assigned them to work together.

Neither Bea nor the Ghost could have predicted Jeremiah would go off on his own without a plan—and without Bea's knowledge. The failed shooting at the Seward mansion had been proof enough Jeremiah wasn't a strategist. Now Bea could only hope he wouldn't strike out on his own again. He could be far too irrational when caught off guard, and she didn't want him doing or saying something foolish the next time someone unexpectedly appeared at the warehouses.

Bea pressed her fingers down the front of her dress and made a fleeting stop in front of the hall mirror. After patting her hair one final time, she pasted on her brightest smile and swung open the apartment door.

Andrew grinned as he thrust a small bouquet of asters and goldenrod in front of her. "I hope you have a jar or vase you can put them in."

"Of course. Thank you, Andrew. How thoughtful." She didn't fail to notice the dirt still clinging to a few of the stems. "You didn't by chance pick these from some nice lady's garden, did you?"

He chuckled. "I don't think she saw me."

"If she had, I think she would have come after you with a broom."

Andrew shrugged. "They wouldn't have lasted much longer, what with the cold weather. Last time I walked by, I noticed she had them covered with some rags to keep off the frost." He sat down on one of the kitchen chairs. "I decided I would save her a bit of work if I removed some of the blooms."

"Hmm. I'm not sure she'd agree, but I do thank you. Hope you don't mind eating supper a little later than usual. I thought we could wait until Jeremiah wakes up, and he can eat with us before he leaves for work."

"That's fine with me. I'd even be glad to help, if you want. I'm pretty good at peeling potatoes and frying bacon, if either of those is on the menu."

Bea reached into the bottom of a rickety wooden cabinet and removed four potatoes and placed them on the table in front of him. "Bacon isn't being served this evening, but I'd be happy to have you peel the potatoes in a little while." She sat in the chair opposite him. "Tell me what's been happening with you at the Arsenal. It seems like a long time since we've had time alone to visit."

His attention remained fastened on the potatoes for a moment. When he finally looked up at her, his eyes had lost their earlier glimmer. "I was going to wait to tell you this, but since you asked about the Arsenal, I guess I'll go ahead with the bad news." He jiggled his leg in a rapid up-and-down motion.

Bea leaned toward him. "What is it?"

He sighed and reached for her hand. "I got orders this morning."

"Orders? You mean . . . ?"

He nodded. "Yes." He glanced around like there might be someone else nearby, then turned back to her. "I'm being sent to the front. The war is escalating, and General Burnside has requested all available troops at the Washington Arsenal be ordered to join him and be placed under his command." Andrew squeezed her hand. "I don't want to leave you, Bea. I care for you and had hoped we could have a future together."

She wanted to ignore his loving remarks about a possible future and ask the important questions but stopped herself. Right now, she must play the part of a distraught young lady who feared for the life of her suitor. "Oh, Andrew. This is dreadful news." She pushed away from the table. "Let's go and sit in the parlor, where we can be more comfortable while you tell me more."

Bea's thoughts were a jumble as she sat beside him on the sofa. She needed to be careful how she posed her questions, or Andrew might become suspicious. Still, she needed to discover as much as possible. She might never see him again, and lately he'd been her only source of information. If Clara knew anything beyond new quota numbers being set in the cylinder room, she wasn't sharing the details with Bea. In truth, her friendship with Clara had waned ever since the incident at the Seward mansion. She wasn't certain if it was intentional, but she was beginning to believe that Clara was avoiding her. Then again, perhaps she felt a sliver of guilt, for it was Joseph's comments that had caused the police to come calling at their home.

Andrew's sigh pulled her from her thoughts, and she gently patted his arm. "You're going to be fine, Andrew. You'll come back to Washington, and we'll be able to resume our courtship just like you were never gone. You know I'll wait for you, don't you?" She batted her lashes and leaned closer.

He brushed a kiss on her cheek, then lifted his hand to her face and turned her head. His eyes shone with love and sadness. Without a word, he dipped his head and captured her lips in a passionate kiss while drawing her into a tight embrace.

She struggled to place her hands against his chest and pushed away. "Andrew! I care for you, but"—she shook her head and scooted away—"I can't permit you to take advantage of me. I'm distressed that you'll soon be leaving. Even so, we can't allow our emotions to get away from us. I have my reputation to protect." She nodded toward the bedroom door. "Besides, Jeremiah could walk out here at any moment. Knowing my brother, he'd yank you off the sofa and punch you in the nose, and I would never want that to happen."

"I'm sorry, Bea. I was overcome by my fear of the war and leaving you behind. I would never want you to think I would take advantage of you." He gently lifted her hand to his lips. "I value you far too much ever to do anything that would offend you."

"I know you wouldn't. You're frightened, and you have no control over your future, but you need to remember you'll be coming back to me. If they don't send you too far off, perhaps you'll return in only a few months. After all, you're needed at the Arsenal, too." She stroked his arm with her fingers. "Did your orders say where you're being sent?"

"Yes, but you can't tell anyone." He waited until she nodded her head in agreement. "General Burnside is encamped at Warrenton, Virginia, and has requested additional troops."

Bea clapped her hands together and feigned delight. "You see! You're not going to be sent far away. There will be a small skirmish, and then you'll be back to me in no time at all."

"I hope that's true, yet things don't seem to work out that way. Seems like once you're sent to the front, they keep you there."

She offered a bright smile. "Do you know when you're leaving?" How she wished she could fire all her questions at him at once. Avoiding all this sweet talk would save her a lot of time and anxiety. Choosing how much or how little to ask was like tiptoeing around a nest of rattlers. One misstep could end it all.

"I'm not sure. All I know is I can't leave the Arsenal again after tonight." He touched a lock of her hair. "I'd be forever grateful if you'd snip off a piece of your hair so I could carry it with me."

She sighed and cupped his chin in her hand. "Of course. I would be honored." She lifted her sewing basket from beside the divan and removed a small pair of scissors. She handed them to Andrew, then held a lock of hair between her fingers. "Why don't you snip it off right below my thumb and forefinger?"

After he snipped off the piece of hair, she took it from him and moved to the writing desk across the room. She placed the lock of hair in the center of a small piece of paper and folded it inside, then handed the packet to Andrew.

He put the keepsake in his pocket. "Thank you, Bea. I'll keep this with me always."

"You must write to me as soon as you can. And I promise I'll write back if I know where to send my letters."

He sighed. "I'm hoping my orders will change. There are problems at the Arsenal right now, and I believe I would be more help to the Union if I remained here."

His response struck a chord, and Bea alerted to full attention. If Andrew thought something at the Arsenal was more important than General Burnside's campaign, it had to be significant. Before he left this apartment tonight, she would make certain he revealed every detail.

When his stomach rumbled, Bea glanced at the clock and jumped to her feet. "If I don't get supper started, it won't be ready before Jeremiah has to leave for work."

Andrew followed her to the kitchen, and while she fried pork chops, he peeled and quartered the potatoes. Dinner was almost ready when the bedroom door opened and Jeremiah appeared. He rubbed his eyes and frowned as he stepped into the kitchen.

Before he could make a disparaging remark, Bea stepped to his side. "Andrew has just told me he's going to be sent to the front soon. I'm so glad I invited him to supper tonight. Otherwise, I wouldn't have gotten to see him before he departed." She directed a hard look at her brother.

"I'm sorry to hear that, Andrew. I'm going to miss seeing you. I sure hope you're able to shoot a few of those Rebs." Jeremiah sat down at the table.

Andrew gave a slight shake of his head. "I'm not big on the idea of shooting anyone. The thought of killing someone who has a family or a sweetheart waiting at home isn't something I find appealing." He let his gaze linger on Bea. "I know I'm hoping to come back to Bea."

Jeremiah grimaced. "If Bea's all you got to look forward to, you might as well stay out there till the war's over."

Bea slapped him with the dish towel. "That's not kind, Jeremiah. Maybe I should feed your pork chop to the stray dog that's always outside the door."

Although Jeremiah asked about Andrew's assignment, the sergeant didn't reveal anything except that he'd likely be leaving within a couple of days. When Jeremiah attempted to gain more information, Bea nudged his knee under the table. If need be, she'd stomp on his foot to keep him quiet. By now Jeremiah should know that she was the one Andrew trusted. For the remainder of the meal, she did her best to keep the conversation light.

Once they'd finished the meal, Jeremiah leaned back in his chair. "Guess I'll go back to the bedroom and let you two have a little more time to visit. I thought maybe we could walk back to the Arsenal together, Andrew."

Andrew nodded. "Sure thing."

"Let's go back to the parlor. I can do the dishes after you're gone. I don't want to wash dishes on our last evening together." They settled side by side on the divan, and she didn't attempt to discourage him when he put his arm around her shoulder.

She carefully prefaced the conversation with comments about how much she would miss him and how much she cared for him before moving on to securing the information she really wanted. Her timing had to be just right.

"I'm going to miss you far more than you know, Andrew. I hope that you're right and they change your orders and keep you at the Arsenal." She looked up at him and smiled. "Do you think they might?"

He hiked a shoulder. "I talked to Joseph, and he agreed with me. He said he was going to speak with Colonel Furman and see if he could get my orders changed. Joseph said he could use another pair of eyes at the Arsenal."

"What's happening that he needs someone else watching after things?"

"There's been word sent back from the front." He lowered his voice to a hoarse whisper. "There have been crates of defective ammunition delivered to the soldiers, and they're trying to trace where they came from. They don't think it's from our Arsenal, but they can't be sure just yet."

Bea's breath caught. "Oh, that's terrible. Do they think someone is doing something to the cartridges before they leave the Arsenal?"

"That's one idea, but there's other things they need to examine. The colonel doesn't believe the cartridges are coming from the Washington Arsenal. Still, there's going to be a complete investigation. I want to remain here and assist in that effort. I'd be more useful with the investigation than fighting at the front." He took a deep breath. "And it would allow us to be together."

She turned to face him. "Oh, I do hope that happens, Andrew. I can't think of anything that would please me more than a change in your orders."

Bea's thoughts raced as she considered the opportunity of having Andrew remain and help with the investigation. Nothing could be more advantageous than having her smitten beau report the investigation findings to her as they happened.

And if the finger-pointing was eventually directed at Jeremiah, they'd need to have an exit plan in place—and she was just the woman to do the planning.

Twenty-Six

When the lunch bell rang, Clara and the other ladies gathered around a table that was used for dining during the winter months. As soon as she'd eaten, Clara excused herself and donned her cape, bonnet, and gloves. She walked outside, inhaled a deep, stinging breath, and filled her lungs with the crisp air. A quick walk around the grounds would be a welcome relief for her aching back and cramped legs.

The late-November sun shone through the tree branches and cast spidery shadows across the path. Clara smiled down at the imaginary web and stepped through the maze like a child playing hopscotch. A light wind fluttered through the trees, and she pulled her cloak tight around her neck as she strode toward the massive stone arch at the Arsenal entrance. She wouldn't go as far as the arch or she'd be late returning to work. Then again, perhaps if she quit picking her way through the shadows, she could make it.

"Clara!"

At the sound of her name, Clara glanced over her shoulder toward the laboratory. Bea was clutching her cloak with one hand and holding her hat in place with the other as she ran toward her. Clara came to a halt and waved, surprised that Bea was seeking her out. She and Bea hadn't talked since the morning she'd attempted to clarify the comments that she and Joseph had made to the police. Clara wasn't sure if Bea was still angry about the police visit or if she had changed her schedule. Clara had hoped that after her explanation, Bea and Jeremiah understood the comments to the police had been innocent, though she remained uncertain.

Bea was panting when she came to a stop beside Clara. "Give me a minute. I'm out of breath." She patted her chest while she took several quick breaths. "I've been watching for you every day on my way to work." She gulped another breath. "I haven't seen you. How have you been? I miss you."

Clara tipped her head and looked at Bea. "I still leave home at the same time and walk the same route each day. Perhaps you're leaving home earlier or later than you used to?"

Bea shrugged. "Maybe that is it. I can sleep a little later in the morning now that I don't have to nag Jeremiah to get dressed and out the door. It's rather nice having him work nights." She slipped her hand into the crook of Clara's arm and pulled her close. "We need to have a nice long visit, just the two of us. I was hoping you'd agree to come over this evening. Jeremiah will be at work, so he won't be around to bother us."

Although she should remain at home and help her mother with some sewing, Clara wanted to mend their friendship. Perhaps she'd ask her mother if there was some smaller article she could take and stitch at Bea's apartment.

When she didn't immediately answer, Bea pinned her with a pleading look. "Please say yes."

"I'll do my best. I need to help my mother with some sewing. Maybe there's some handwork I can bring along to complete while we visit."

Bea squeezed her arm. "I can hardly wait. You could even come for supper."

Clara shook her head. "I can't do that, but I'll try to be there by seven-thirty." The bell rang in the distance, and they both took off at a run. When they neared the laboratory, Clara turned toward the cylinder room and waved. "I'll see you this evening."

Throughout the remainder of the day, Clara thought about the upcoming visit with Bea. Why had she been so determined to see her this evening after more than a week had passed without a word from her? She'd seemed almost frantic when Clara hadn't given her an immediate answer. Her behavior had been so odd. Bea was usually in control and self-assured. The one who could either solve all the problems or find someone else who could do so for her. Was that what this was about? Did Bea have a problem? If so, was she hoping Clara would be the one to help?

She walked up the steps of the boardinghouse and tried to push the thought aside. Bea was probably lonely with Jeremiah working nights, and if Clara could help fill that void, she should do so—at least occasionally.

Her mother looked up from her sewing when Clara entered their rooms. She leaned down and kissed her mother's cheek. "I think I smelled cabbage downstairs."

"Mrs. Ludwig's famous cabbage rolls."

Clara wrinkled her nose. "I should have accepted Bea's invitation to supper."

"Bea invited you for supper? I thought she hadn't been meeting you to walk to and from work."

"We haven't been, but she stopped me at lunch and invited me to come over. I told her I had promised to help you. But if there's something I could take with me, I'd like to go and visit with her after supper."

Her mother leaned to one side and reached into her sewing bag. She withdrew a linen infant gown centered with a panel of pin tucks edged in lace. "I made this for Mrs. Seward."

"Mrs. Seward? Surely she's not having a baby."

"No." Her mother shook her head. "The gown is a gift for her niece's new baby. You need only embroider on the tiny bodice and along the lace that edges the pin tucks." She hesitated a moment. "And if you have time, perhaps along the hemline, as well. I don't think it will take long, and you can visit while you sew."

Clara carefully folded the tiny gown and wrapped it in a piece of cloth before placing the garment in her sewing bag. "Let's go downstairs and enjoy our cabbage rolls." She opened the door, glanced over her shoulder, and grinned. "I don't think it will take me long to eat my supper."

During supper, Clara managed to eat most of her cabbage roll by making certain she accompanied each bite with a small piece of bread. As soon as she'd finished, she excused herself, hurried back upstairs, and donned her cloak, bonnet, and gloves.

She picked up her sewing bag and stopped in the dining room only long enough to bid her mother good-bye. "I'll be home by ten o'clock."

Mrs. Ludwig reached for the bowl of potatoes and smiled

at Clara. "See that you are. I wouldn't want to lock you out. You'd be frozen by morning."

"Don't let her scare ya, Miss Clara." Mr. Gryska, who rented a single room upstairs, waved his napkin in the air. "If she locks ya out, just throw a pebble at my window and I'll come downstairs and unlatch the door."

The laughter of the boarders followed her down the hallway, and she smiled at the thought of throwing pebbles at Mr. Gryska's window. Once outside, she quickened her pace. The temperature had fallen at least five more degrees, and the wind cut through her cloak with surprising ease. Though the apartment wasn't far away, the bone-chilling wind made the walk far more uncomfortable than Clara had expected. No doubt it would be even colder on her return. She pushed the thought aside as she knocked on the apartment door a short time later.

Bea opened the door and frowned. "I didn't realize it was so cold." She rubbed her hands up and down her arms, then rushed to close the door. "Is it the wind? It didn't seem this cold earlier."

Clara nodded as Bea took her cloak and hung it on a peg. She lifted her sewing bag and followed Bea into the parlor. "Mother did ask me to do a bit of embroidery while I'm here. I hope you don't mind. I'm used to visiting while I sew, and I promise I'll hear every word you say." When Bea shook her head, Clara removed the infant gown from her bag and unwrapped the cloth.

Bea leaned forward to gain a better look. "Oh, hold it up so I can see."

Clara lifted the gown and pointed to the lace edging along the bottom. "Isn't it lovely? It's a gift for one of Mrs. Seward's nieces who recently gave birth."

Too late, Clara realized she shouldn't have mentioned the Seward name, for Bea immediately glowered. "Speaking of the Sewards, that policeman seems to have a fondness for this apartment house. He's out there almost every evening." She motioned to the front of the house. "He moves behind that huge oak when either Jeremiah or I draw near. Guess he thinks we can't see him."

"Patrolman Hanover?" Clara arched her brows.

"Right. The one who thinks Jeremiah is responsible for the shooting at the Sewards' mansion." She cleared her throat. "Thanks to Joseph."

"So, you're still angry with him?"

Bea shrugged. "A little. It's hard to get over what happened when there's a patrolman loitering outside our door all the time. At least he can't bother either of us when we're at work. I thought maybe he'd be coming to the Arsenal every day, but Andrew told me the police have no authority at the Arsenal—only the military do—so Patrolman Hanover can't bother us there. In some ways, it makes me want to stay on the other side of those arches all the time."

"Don't be silly, Bea. Even the soldiers don't want to live at the Arsenal. You would hate having to be there all the time. Besides, I didn't see anyone outside the house when I arrived." Clara reached in her bag and withdrew a needle from her sewing kit. "I do wish you wouldn't continue to hold a grudge against Joseph."

"So you've said."

Clara wanted to get off this unpleasant merry-go-round and visit about something else. She'd come here to mend their friendship, not argue. Clara threaded the needle with a piece of pink embroidery thread and pushed the needle into the thin fabric. "How is Andrew? He seems to be quite smitten with you."

Bea smiled and nodded. "We're very fond of each other. But the chances of us ever having a future together are unlikely now that he's received orders and is being sent to the front." She pushed her lips into a disgusted grin. "I'm sure Joseph already told you about his orders."

Clara sucked in a breath. "No, I didn't know. Honest, Bea. So, when does he leave?"

"He was told they'd probably be leaving in a few days, maybe even tomorrow—he wasn't given an exact date. He was here last evening, but he can't leave the Arsenal anymore. I'll probably never see him again. He'll go to the front and be killed."

"You mustn't think like that, Bea. We both need to pray for his safe return."

"That's your answer to everything. I already told you that prayer didn't keep my pa alive, and I don't believe it's going to help Andrew. I'm sure there's been somebody back home praying for all those soldiers who have already died in the war. Didn't do them much good, either, did it?"

Clara frowned. "I'm going to pray for Andrew whether you do or not. God hears our prayers. They aren't always answered the way we'd like, but He hears and knows our hearts. If you want to place blame, you need to condemn man, not God."

"That doesn't help me or Andrew. I need a plan that will keep Andrew here." Bea edged closer. "If I thought there was some way to do that, would you help?"

Clara continued embroidering the gown's hemline with pink feather stitches. "Andrew can't disobey his orders, and there's nothing I can do that would help him remain here."

"But if you could?" Bea arched her brows.

There had been a hint of aggression in Bea's voice. An edge that caused Clara's heart to race. Bea was up to something, and she obviously hoped to draw Clara into the midst of her plan. That thought gave Clara pause.

"If it isn't anything illegal or immoral, I would be willing to help, but it's difficult to answer when I don't know exactly what you want me to do."

Bea's shoulders drooped. "You should know I wouldn't ask you to do anything illegal or immoral. I'm hurt that you would even think such a thing."

Clara silently chided herself. Rather than making things better between the two of them, she was only making matters worse. "What is it I can do, Bea?"

"When Andrew told me about his orders last night, he mentioned he'd talked to Joseph about possibly getting them changed so he can stay here and help Joseph with an investigation." She hiked a shoulder. "I'm sure Joseph has told you all about that."

"No, he hasn't said a word."

So, this was why Bea had been so eager to have Clara come for a visit. She hoped to gain some sort of favor. Clara had arrived anticipating restoration of their friendship—a return to the companionship they'd once shared. However, it appeared their reestablished friendship wasn't Bea's primary objective—she wanted something more. Clara braced herself. There was little doubt the request involved Andrew and his recent orders. That also meant Joseph would somehow be involved. Clara winced at the possibility. She wanted to mend her friendship with Bea, yet she doubted there was any way she or Joseph could help. She also worried Bea wouldn't accept a negative response.

Bea's tight smile signaled a lack of belief. "You're telling me Joseph hasn't mentioned that most of the troops at the Arsenal are leaving—that they've been ordered to join General Burnside at Warrenton, Virginia?"

Clara gasped and shook her head. "How do you know that?"

She was certain Andrew shouldn't be sharing information about where the troops were being sent. While he could freely divulge that he'd received orders, exposing the fact that he was joining troops fighting with General Burnside and that they were encamped at Warrenton shouldn't be disclosed to anyone.

Bea shrugged. "Andrew told me. He said I couldn't tell anyone, but I was certain you already knew."

Clara's stomach tightened in a knot. "But I didn't. You betrayed his confidence, and he betrayed his military training. If anyone discovers he's been telling you military secrets, he could be punished as a traitor."

"I think your comments are a bit extreme, Clara—especially in this instance. You're not going to tell anyone, Joseph and Andrew already know, and I'm not going to make further mention of the information."

Clara placed the tiny gown in her lap. "What about Jeremiah? I would venture a guess that you've already told him."

Bea shook her head. "Only that Andrew received orders and will be leaving—nothing more." She lifted her hand as if taking an oath. "I promise."

A stab of doubt pierced her. But Clara wanted to believe her friend, so she offered a fleeting smile. She hoped Bea understood the seriousness of the matter. On occasion, Bea seemed to place little concern on matters that were of great importance—at least that was how it appeared to Clara.

While she didn't want to think that her friend wasn't loyal to the cause, the fact that Bea would share confidential military information worried her. Even worse was the fact that Andrew would tell Bea. How had she coaxed the information from him? Clara pushed the question from her mind. In truth, she didn't want to know the answer.

Bea reached for Clara's hand. "Here's where I need your help, Clara." When Clara attempted to withdraw her hand, Bea held fast. "I don't want Andrew going to the front. There's little doubt that he'll die, and I'll never see him again."

"You don't know that, Bea. I've already said we need to—"

"I know. Pray." Bea shook her head. "Just listen to me for a minute. He wants to remain here and help Joseph with the investigation."

Clara frowned. This wasn't making any sense. "How can Andrew help Joseph investigate the shooting at the Sewards' mansion? Joseph isn't involved in the investigation."

Bea exhaled a long sigh. "You know I'm not talking about the Seward investigation. Andrew wants to help with the investigation into the fouled ammunition that's been received by troops fighting on the front lines."

Clara's mouth dropped open. "I know nothing about this. Is it ammunition from our Arsenal? When did this happen, and how much of it was damaged?" She narrowed her eyes. "Is this information from Andrew, as well?"

"Yes, but don't judge us, Clara. We're in love, and I want him near me. Besides, he truly believes he can help Joseph discover how this has happened. There isn't any word as to how the ammunition was damaged or which arsenal made the ammunition, but that's why he wants to remain here—so he can help determine who is responsible." Bea touched a handkerchief to the corner of her eye, although Clara hadn't noticed any tears. "I hope you'll be willing to speak to Joseph and see if he can influence the colonel to change Andrew's orders."

"I admire Andrew's wish to help, but I don't think his noble desires will be enough to keep him here. I'm sure there are soldiers who are especially proficient in these inquiries. Unless Andrew has some unique knowledge or ability, I don't believe anything Joseph says will affect Andrew's orders."

Bea tucked her chin and scowled. "What you think doesn't matter. You need to ask Joseph."

Clara was rendered momentarily speechless by Bea's forceful demand. The silence stretched and thinned like morning fog. Clara waited, but Bea didn't retract her request. Instead, she continued to look into Clara's eyes with an air of determination and expectancy.

Finally, Clara mustered her courage. "I can't possibly do what you're asking, Bea. I'm positive Joseph doesn't have enough influence to gain a change of orders for Andrew. I doubt that even the colonel could supersede an order requiring his troops be sent to the front. You're asking for the impossible."

"You don't know it's impossible since you won't even ask. If you were a true friend, you'd be willing to plead Andrew's case to Joseph." She curled her lip. "Of course, you don't have to give the matter much thought because you know Joseph won't be sent along with the other soldiers. It isn't fair that Joseph gets to stay while Andrew and the others must go."

Clara's head snapped back as though she'd been slapped. Did Bea really believe what she'd just said? How could she believe Clara cared so little about the soldiers marching off to war? Her father had died at Bull Run, Joseph had been injured in that same battle, and she had no idea of her brother's whereabouts. She cared deeply about the men fighting for the Union. If Bea was a true friend, would she even question Clara's compassion? The thoughts tumbled on top of each other like a ball rolling downhill and gaining speed.

After picking up her sewing kit, Clara shoved the needle and thread inside, folded the tiny gown and tucked it into her sewing bag, and stood. "I think I should go now. Nothing I say is going to please you, Bea, but I have always attempted to be a true friend."

Bea tugged at her hand. "Don't go, Clara. I'm sorry. You're right. I was selfish to ask you to interfere. Since the first day we met, you've been a faithful friend. You have to believe that if I weren't so frightened for Andrew, I would never have asked you to speak with Joseph." She stood and embraced Clara. "You're the very best friend I have ever had. Please forgive me. I don't want you to leave until I know you're not angry."

Clara sighed. "I forgive you, Bea." She returned Bea's hug, then strode to the door and gathered her cloak. "I really must get home."

Bea followed her to the door. "You promise you're not angry?"

Clara tied her bonnet and pulled on her gloves. "I promise. I'm hurt, but not angry. Wait at the corner, and we can walk to the Arsenal together in the morning."

Clara turned the knob and pushed open the front door of the boardinghouse. She wouldn't need to throw pebbles at Mr. Gryska's window tonight. She'd returned home far earlier than Mrs. Ludwig's ten o'clock curfew. She removed her gloves as she walked up the flight of stairs to the rooms she shared with her mother.

Her mother greeted her with a look of surprise when she stepped inside the apartment. "You're early. I thought you and Bea would need hours and hours to catch up on all your visiting." She glanced at the clock. "And here it's not even nine o'clock. I hope you didn't have to return home because you weren't feeling well."

Clara set her sewing bag on the floor and then removed her cloak and bonnet. "Our visit didn't go well." She picked up her sewing bag and crossed the room. "I'm afraid I didn't complete the fancy work on the infant gown, but I promise I'll complete it tomorrow evening."

Her mother patted the settee cushion. "Don't worry about the handwork. Sit down and tell me what happened between you and Bea."

Still chilled from the frigid wind, Clara rubbed her hands together and settled beside her mother. She leaned close and rested her head on her mother's shoulder. "There are parts of our conversation that are sensitive, and I can't repeat them, but I'm terribly disappointed in Bea. I feel as though the only reason she asked me to come for a visit is because she wanted a favor. When I said I didn't think I could be of any help, she became angry and made unkind remarks about Joseph and me."

Her mother shifted and set aside the garment she was stitching. "As I recall, this isn't the first time Bea has asked you for a favor. You two were barely acquainted when she asked you to have her moved from one room to another in the laboratory? Isn't that right?"

Clara nodded. "Yes, but that wasn't anything I wouldn't have done for others."

Her mother nodded. "I know, my dear. You always want to help. But Bea seems to depend on you for favors. I recall she also requested your help when there was a question about Jeremiah giving incorrect answers about his birthplace during an investigation, and then again when he wanted to change duties at the Arsenal. Didn't Bea ask you to request Joseph's help with those problems?"

"Yes." Clara bobbed her head. "But then she became angry over the incident at the Sewards' gala, and I've been attempting to make amends."

"She may think you'll be willing to do whatever she asks in order to restore your friendship, but you can't always rely upon your own understanding. You need to weigh the seriousness of what she is asking of you. Would a true friend ask such favors? There's a verse in Proverbs, chapter eighteen, which says a man who has friends must show himself to be friendly and then he will become closer than a brother. I know you want to be loyal to Bea, but you need to balance that loyalty with wisdom. Is she showing herself to be a good friend to you?" She laid her hand on Clara's arm. "Good friends stick around long enough to know when you're sad or frustrated. They also know and care if you're happy. They're supportive and rejoice with us. Do you believe Bea's actions are intended to deepen your friendship or to serve her own selfish desires?"

Tears pricked Clara's eyes. She didn't want to answer her mother's question, but deep inside she knew the truth. All Bea had ever done was *ask* from their friendship. She wanted only to receive, and never to give. Had Bea ever truly cared about her?

Clara blinked back more hot tears. Bea had heard and shared military secrets, and if Clara told Joseph, what would happen to Andrew?

Fear hovered over Clara like a threatening rain cloud. If Bea could betray their friendship in this way, what more might she expect? Could Bea even be trusted?

TWENTY-SEVEN

oseph, along with two other officers, sat in Colonel Furman's office. They'd all three been summoned for a meeting, which could mean only one thing—they would be hearing news of a serious nature. Together with Colonel Furman, the three of them were the only officers currently stationed at the Arsenal. Over the past year, all other officers had been ordered to lead troops and support the Union at the front.

The colonel tapped his index finger against the edge of his desk and focused upon the two officers sitting to Joseph's right. "I don't know if you men will view this as exciting or frightening news, but you've both been ordered to command a company of the Arsenal troops and lead them into battle."

One of the officers leaned forward. "We'll each lead a company?" he asked, his voice brimming with excitement.

The colonel nodded. "Yes. Those are the orders I've received. Make certain the men remain prepared for deployment at a moment's notice. While the final orders haven't yet been received, I'm of the opinion that the Arsenal troops will be direct support for General Burnside and his men, who are already in Virginia. Each of you is appointed to your new command effective immediately." He shoved a paper across the desk to each of them. "I've divided the men, and they are listed by name and rank. When you leave here, they will be under your command."

Joseph gave the two officers a sideways glance. An intermingling of pity and envy churned in his belly. He wasn't certain why the colonel had included him in this meeting, but it was painful to know he'd be left behind. He knew what these men would experience once the battle commenced. He could still smell the gunpowder, hear the shrieks of pain, and smell the rot and decay of war. And yet the soldier in him longed to return and fight for the justice and equality of all.

The colonel shifted his attention to Joseph. "Since it's impossible for you to return to the front, Lieutenant, you may be wondering why I called you to this meeting."

Joseph nodded. "Yes, sir, I am."

"I wanted you to be aware of the imminent changes taking place, since the departure of these two officers will place a great burden on your shoulders. I was given advance notice of this change and have used the opportunity to hire civilians who will fill some of the vacancies caused by the deployment of our troops." He glanced at the other two officers. "You gentlemen may be excused to take command of your troops while Lieutenant Brady and I go over his new assignments."

The two men stood, saluted the colonel, and departed. Once they'd exited the office, the colonel opened one of his desk drawers. "I have a list of duties for you, Lieutenant. I thought we would go over them, and if you have questions or objections, please feel free to speak up."

Joseph had been in the Army long enough to know that even though he had been given permission to speak, he was expected to withhold any opinions or questions until the colonel had presented his plan.

The colonel glanced at the sheet of paper in front of him. "Rather than only the cylinder room, you will now be in command of the entire laboratory. The supervisors of the warehouses, loading docks, and stables will report to you, as well, and I would request you make daily visits to ensure all is operating smoothly. You will need to hire additional civilian employees, but if they are hired for sensitive positions, I will need to interview them, too. I trust you to promote any employees you believe capable of fulfilling the duties of any vacated position. You should strive to maintain the loyalty of our trained workers so they don't quit. This is a critical time, and our employees need to understand that their efforts are of vital importance to the Union."

"I'll be certain to emphasize that fact, sir." Joseph had placed his palms on the desk and prepared to stand when the colonel waved for him to remain seated.

"I wanted to hear a report on your investigation into the faulty ammunition. Have you heard anything regarding the markings? Do we know if they were shipped from our docks?"

Joseph shook his head. "I expected to hear yesterday, yet there's been nothing so far. While I don't want to believe they were shipped from the Arsenal, there's always the possibility. As soon as I receive word, I'll send a messenger to notify you."

The colonel shook his head. "No messengers. I had a visit from a newspaper reporter, who said someone attempted to sell him information about an investigation into faulty ammunition going to the front. The reporter wanted me to verify the assertion."

"What?" Joseph's mouth dropped open. "But there are so few of us who were aware that this had happened."

The colonel's lips tightened. "I know, but there are always folks who are willing to sell their soul for fame or money. It's a sad state of affairs, so we must be exceedingly careful with any further news."

"As soon as I hear, I'll personally bring word to you." Joseph pushed to a stand, saluted, and left the colonel's office.

On his return to the laboratory, Joseph silently recounted the events since he'd learned of the defective ammunition. The only person he'd spoken to was Andrew. Because they'd formed a friendship, Joseph believed the sergeant would prove a good partner in the investigation. Andrew was well versed in military procedures and knew the importance of classified information. Surely he wouldn't have told anyone.

While Joseph didn't want to accuse Andrew, he needed to know the truth. Andrew was among the soldiers departing for the front. Once he departed the Arsenal, there wouldn't be further opportunity to speak to him.

Despite the biting cold, Joseph's palms perspired as he approached the barracks. He didn't want to believe Andrew had betrayed him, yet the colonel had expressed continuing trust in the few men he'd briefed. When Joseph stepped inside, the soldiers immediately came to attention and saluted him.

"At ease, men." Joseph glanced around the room. "Is Sergeant Kessler here? I need to speak to him."

"He said he was going to meet his gal over by the cannons for a farewell kiss." Several of the men chortled.

Joseph thanked the men before he departed for the arched entrance. The fact that Andrew had left the barracks after the soldiers had been ordered to remain prepared for a rapid departure gave Joseph pause. He hadn't expected Andrew to be a soldier who would disobey orders. Then again, Andrew was a young man in love who wanted a final kiss before marching off to war. While Joseph understood those feelings, he couldn't condone them. Disobeying orders was a serious matter, especially in a time of war.

Bea waited by one of the cannons near the Arsenal's entrance. On their walk to the laboratory this morning, Clara had adamantly refused Bea's appeals. In truth, Bea understood that Clara wanted no part in a plan to keep Andrew at the Arsenal. While she could have accused Clara of disloyalty, she understood that such an accusation would only create a deeper divide between them. Bea might have need of her in the future, so she'd simply smiled and said she understood Clara's decision.

Clara's position hadn't caught Bea by surprise. She'd both expected and prepared for such a refusal. Before Jeremiah departed for his night shift, she'd given him a message that he could deliver to Andrew.

Pushing to her tiptoes, Bea strained to gain a better view of the path leading from the barracks. If Jeremiah had failed to deliver the message, she'd rake him over the coals the next time she saw him. She pulled her cloak tight around her neck and used the cannon to shield her body from the wind. Her teeth chattered. Why hadn't she thought to wear her heavy sweater underneath her cloak today? If there was no sign of Andrew in the next few minutes, she'd have to turn toward home.

The bitter wind penetrated her boots and gloves, and the next time she ventured a peek down the path, her fingers were numb. She'd taken only a few steps when she heard Andrew call her name, and she turned. He was running toward her. She rubbed her gloved hands together and danced from foot to foot to help warm her limbs.

"Where have you been? I'm nearly frozen. I was preparing to leave when I heard you in the distance."

"Come over here and I'll warm you." He took her hand and led her back to one of the cannons. "Scoot down here where we can't be easily seen." When she hunched down, he pulled her onto his lap and vigorously rubbed her hands and arms before enfolding her in an embrace. "I'm sorry I was late, but it isn't easy getting out of the barracks. If the commander finds out I'm gone, I may be considered a deserter."

"That's ridiculous. You're right here on the Arsenal grounds. How is that deserting?"

"You may be right, but I'm disobeying orders all the same."

She grinned. "Maybe they'll throw you in the brig and keep you at the Arsenal." She brushed a kiss on his cheek. "I don't want you to go, Andrew."

"I know, and I don't want to go, either, but I have to follow orders."

She grasped his hand. "Don't be angry with me, but I've done something that I hope will keep you in Washington."

Andrew tipped his head back and pinned her with a suspicious look. "What is it you've done?"

For the next several minutes, Bea recounted her conversation with Clara, carefully detailing everything she'd said before gracing him with a tentative smile. "I'm hopeful Joseph will have enough sway to keep you at the Arsenal."

He stared at her, his eyes narrowed and clouded. "Please tell me this is merely your attempt to be amusing." When she slowly shook her head, he grimaced. "I was abundantly clear with you, Bea. I said you couldn't repeat anything I'd told you. Not about the faulty ammunition, not about troops being sent as reinforcements, and not about where General Burnside is encamped. Instead of keeping your promise, you've told Clara everything." He covered his face with his hand. "How could you do this to me?"

Bea wanted to laugh and tell him he was a fool who had been easily duped, but she couldn't—not yet. For now, she needed to maintain the role of a love-sick damsel who couldn't survive without her man. The thought nearly made her retch.

"I'm so sorry, Andrew. My intentions were good. I wanted to keep you here with me. Is that so wrong?" She swiped an imaginary tear with her gloved hand. "I know you could provide Joseph with the help he needs to resolve whatever has gone awry with those cartridge shipments. I thought I was helping all three of us."

"Sergeant Kessler!"

At the sound of Joseph's commanding voice, Andrew pushed Bea from his lap and jumped to his feet. "Yes, sir!" Andrew lifted his hand in a smart salute.

Bea waited behind the cannon. She would need to come to his defense, even though he could be of no further use to her. Now that he'd divulged confidential information, Joseph would never again trust him. And even if Andrew should learn something of importance, he would never tell her—better for both of them if he marched off to war. If he was imprisoned, both Andrew and Joseph would expect her to visit the brig, and that wasn't something she wanted to do.

Joseph frowned at them. "Why are you here, Sergeant Kessler? You have disobeyed a direct order to remain on alert in the barracks."

Before he could answer, Bea stepped from behind the cannon. "None of this is Andrew's fault, Joseph. I'm the one who is to blame. I betrayed his confidence and sent a note begging him to meet me here. I said I would drink a bottle of laudanum, then lie down and die if he didn't meet me."

"Your fellow soldiers said you'd come to meet Bea for a farewell kiss. Which story is it, Andrew?"

"Both." Andrew scraped the toe of his boot along the frozen ground. "I was afraid of what she'd do if I didn't show up, but I wanted to kiss her one more time, too."

Joseph exhaled a long breath and watched the vapor rise toward the barren tree branches. "Did you consider showing the note to your commanding officer and asking permission to meet with Bea? Given the contents of her message, he would likely have allowed you a brief visit with her."

Andrew shrugged. "I was afraid he'd deny my request, and then I wouldn't be able to slip out." He bowed his head and kept his eyes fastened to the ground. "I'm guessing that coming out here is the least of my problems." He finally looked up. "Have you spoken to Clara?"

"Clara?" His brows dipped, and he shook his head. "I haven't talked to Clara, but I have talked with Colonel Furman. I can't tell you how disappointed I am."

"You can blame it all on me," Bea said. "I should never have nagged Andrew to confide in me."

Joseph shook his head. "There's blame enough for everyone, Bea, but it's Andrew who will suffer the consequences."

"Not if you keep everything to yourself. There's no reason to report any of this, Joseph. I haven't told anyone but Clara."

There was a hollow ring to Joseph's laugh. "Truly? You expect me to believe you haven't said a word to your brother? You tell Jeremiah everything. And who can say how much he's shared with the other workers? I can't just forget what's been said and done, Bea. I took an oath when I joined the Army. And, above that duty, I have an obligation to live according to God's Word. I could never do what you've asked." He pulled his hat low as a brisk wind threatened to lift it from his head. "In truth, Bea, I'm surprised that you would ask me to remain silent."

Bea inwardly groaned. Now he was going to berate her for a lack of Christian morality. He was as bad as Clara. They truly deserved each other.

Andrew reached for her hand. "Bea is only trying to save me, Joseph. Please don't judge her."

"I'm not judging her; I'm merely stating I was taken aback by her request and telling her why I couldn't comply with her wishes."

Although she was sure it wouldn't work, she didn't want to quit without attempting to persuade Joseph one final time. "Even if Andrew could provide the help you need to investigate the faulty ammunition? He's quite clever, and the enlisted men talk to him more freely than they will to the officers. If the soldiers know anything, they'll confide in him."

"There aren't going to be many soldiers left at the Arsenal, and I doubt any of them have information that would be helpful." He gestured to Andrew. "You best kiss her good-bye, and then we'll stop at headquarters and see if the colonel is working late."

Bea tipped her head to receive Andrew's kiss. He appeared embarrassed by Joseph's presence, and his kiss was fleeting. For that she was thankful. He would make some Northern woman a good husband if he lived long enough.

She forced a smile. "If they send you with your company, be sure to write me. I promise I'll do the same."

Andrew nodded and moved to Joseph's side.

"If Andrew's sent to the brig, I'll tell Clara to let you know, because I'm certain you'll want to visit."

Once the two men turned, Bea hurried toward the arched entrance and shrugged. She cared little that Andrew might find himself behind bars. What she did care about was getting home so she could start a fire and warm herself.

TWENTY-EIGHT

oseph and Andrew walked in silence as they crossed the Arsenal grounds. Joseph was taking no pleasure in escorting his friend and fellow soldier to the colonel's office. He longed for something he could say that might ease Andrew's fears, but nothing he could offer would matter right now. Joseph had no say in Andrew's fate.

Side by side, they walked up the front steps and inside the cavernous building. Joseph could see a flicker of light in the colonel's office. A part of him had hoped the commander had left for the night. He gestured to the private standing outside the colonel's door.

When the young man approached and saluted, Joseph nodded toward the door. "Any chance we could have a few minutes of the colonel's time? It shouldn't take long."

The private pointed to the empty chairs nearby. "I'm not sure, Lieutenant, but I'll ask. Please have a seat. I may be a few minutes."

Joseph sat down while Andrew paced the short distance between the colonel's door and the end of the hall, until the private had returned and they were ushered into the colonel's office.

After saluting, the colonel motioned the men toward the chairs, then looked at Joseph. "What can I do for you, Lieutenant?"

As Joseph related the happenings, the colonel's usually ruddy face paled. He leaned back in his chair and sighed. "With the men departing at any time, we don't have adequate time or officers to convene court-martial proceedings." He turned a stern eye on Andrew. "You should be thankful for that fact, Sergeant. I don't believe you'd evoke a great deal of sympathy."

Andrew folded his hands in his lap. "I know what I did was wrong, but I'm not a traitor, Colonel. I love the Union, and I want to go with my company and fight."

The colonel cleared his throat. "These are difficult times that require tough and immediate decisions. Rather than place you in the brig, I'm going to strip you of your rank and have you escorted back to your barracks, where you'll remain until you receive further orders from your company commander." He continued to talk while penning a note. "You will be sent to the front as a private, not a sergeant, and I hope you will prove yourself a valuable soldier who will follow orders. If so, when and if you return, your future will depend upon how you conduct yourself from this moment forward."

"Thank you, sir." Andrew bowed his head.

"Don't thank me, Sergeant—show me I've made a wise decision."

He folded the note and stood. "Lieutenant, please remain here. I need to discuss something with you privately." The colonel walked to the door and gestured to the private standing guard by the door. "Escort this soldier to his barracks and give this note directly to his commanding officer." The colonel stood by the doorway until Andrew had departed, then closed the door and returned to his desk. He dropped into the chair and shook his head. "I hope I haven't made a mistake."

Joseph offered a weak smile. "I believe Andrew is a good man—a good soldier—who let his feelings for a woman alter his conduct. The young man is truly smitten with Miss Hodson. Still, I think he will be far more help to the Union serving with his company rather than sitting idle in the brig."

"Thank you, Lieutenant. I needed that vote of confidence. Decision-making can be a lonely and crushing business." He took in a deep breath. "Now, let's move on to this matter of defective ammunition that's plaguing our troops. Still no further word regarding the crate markings?"

Joseph shook his head. "I wish I could tell you I'd heard something more, but I haven't."

"Tell me, Lieutenant, do you believe Sergeant Kessler's lady friend might have spoken to that news reporter who called on me?"

Joseph hesitated. He didn't want to believe that Bea would do anything so despicable. "Perhaps, sir, but my best guess is that a returning wounded soldier mentioned there were problems with faulty ammunition and then word of it spread from there. When I was in the hospital after my injury, there was a news reporter who came and talked to the wounded soldiers. We also had a news reporter and an artist who traveled with our regiment. Most of the time they remained at our encampment and questioned us when we returned, but I recall a few times they came with us. It's a wonder they didn't get killed."

"I suppose that could be how word traveled back here. I know some of those newsmen will even pay for a story, and if a person is hard up for money . . ." His voice trailed off before he looked up at Joseph. "I just don't want to think that Sergeant Kessler or his young lady would do such a thing."

"Nor would I," Joseph said.

The colonel nodded toward the door. "Unless you have something more, you can go now. Please keep me informed as soon as you have further news regarding the ammunition."

The moment he stepped outdoors, a blast of freezing air awakened Joseph's senses, and thoughts of his earlier conversations replayed in his mind. He attempted to recall his first meetings with Bea and Jeremiah. There had always been something a bit odd about them. Nothing he'd ever been able to put his finger on, but merely a feeling they weren't exactly who or what they represented to others.

Joseph prayed his remarks to the colonel had been accurate. He'd initially judged Andrew as a man who could be trusted to maintain confidential information, and he'd been wrong. And though he wanted to believe Bea hadn't repeated any of the information to Jeremiah, his gut was telling him otherwise.

A part of him wanted to march down to the warehouse and talk to Jeremiah—see if he could learn anything from him. He could unexpectedly appear at the warehouse and use the incident with Andrew as a pretext for his visit.

He pulled his collar high around his neck, then changed directions. He could go to the warehouse later. Jeremiah would be there all night. Right now he'd rather spend time with Clara. He needed to be with someone he trusted and cared for—someone who could set the world aright—even if only for a brief time.

Perhaps Clara's sweet smile would wipe away his sadness. A sorrow that had swept over him after his recent meeting with Bea and Andrew. He plunged his hands into his pockets as he replayed the incident in his mind. It seemed as if Bea could manipulate almost anyone to perform her bidding. She was a woman who had no scruples and expected favors from everyone she met. Andrew had been a fool to put his trust in Bea. Joseph kicked a pebble along the hard dirt path. He stopped short and watched the stone tumble toward the gutter as he recalled something Andrew had said. When Joseph first confronted Andrew, he'd asked if Joseph had spoken to Clara. Joseph pondered the thought. What did Clara know that worried Andrew? Was she keeping secrets, too?

His earlier thoughts of needing to be with the one person he could trust, the woman who could set the world aright, gave him pause. Was Clara that woman, or was she yet another enigma? His apprehensions remained as he trudged up the steps of the boardinghouse. He certainly didn't want to be like Andrew—a fool in love with a deceitful woman.

Clara sat in the chair near her mother and threaded her needle with a strand of pale-green thread. "Did you deliver the infant gown to Mrs. Seward?"

Her mother smiled and gave a nod. "I did, and she was very pleased, especially with your fancywork. She plans to deliver the gift tomorrow. What about your day? Did you and Bea walk home together?"

Clara pulled the thread taut and knotted the end. "No. I waited a short time, but when she didn't appear, I continued home. It's far too cold to stand outside waiting for her. We walked together this morning, but there seems to be an air of discomfort between us. I believe it's going to take time to restore our friendship to what it once was."

Her mother sighed. "I think you first must decide if Beatrice is someone worthy of your friendship. I don't want to see her hurt you again, and I worry she'll come around only when she wants another favor." Her mother turned toward their apartment door. "Did you hear a knock downstairs?"

Clara hiked a shoulder. "I'm not expecting Joseph, and I doubt it's Bea. Perhaps one of the other boarders has a visitor."

Moments later, Mrs. Ludwig called up the stairs, "Clara! You have a visitor."

Clara set her sewing aside and glanced at her mother. "I guess I was wrong." As she reached for the doorknob, she glanced over her shoulder and lowered her voice to a whisper. "I do hope it isn't Bea." She walked into the hallway and peered down the stairs.

Joseph stood in the foyer and looked up at her. "Are you accepting uninvited guests this evening?"

"Only you." She graced him with a broad smile.

Mrs. Ludwig stepped around Joseph. "I know your parlor is very small, so if the two of you would like to use the downstairs parlor, I'll make certain you have time alone." She grinned up at Joseph. "And I'll even bring you two some tea and leftover dessert."

Joseph gave a quick nod. "I appreciate your thoughtfulness. Thank you, Mrs. Ludwig."

After telling her mother she and Joseph would be in Mrs. Ludwig's parlor, Clara hurried downstairs to meet him. By the time she arrived, he'd already removed his coat and hung it in the foyer. He gestured to the parlor door. "Shall we?"

Clara nodded and led the way. "I'm surprised to see you.

On the way home, I overheard some of the workers say that the soldiers were confined to their barracks and there were a lot of changes about to take place at the Arsenal. I thought maybe you'd been confined to the Arsenal, as well."

He appeared surprised by how quickly word had spread among the workers, then shook his head. "No, I wasn't included in those orders."

"You appear unhappy. Is it because most of the men are departing to join General Burnside at Warrenton while you'll need to remain here?"

He reared back as though he'd been slapped. "How did you know that, Clara?"

She arched her brows. "About General Burnside?" When he nodded, she looked away. "You already knew about his location before I mentioned he's at Warrenton."

"I did know, but how did you learn the information? That was my question. Was it from Andrew or from Bea? Which one of them talked to you?"

She sighed. "Andrew told Bea that the Arsenal troops were going to be ordered to Warrenton to reinforce General Burnside's men. She didn't want Andrew to go with them. Instead, she wanted you to convince the colonel to keep Andrew here so he could help you with the ammunition investigation."

"And Bea told you all of this so that . . ."

"So that I would ask you to speak to the colonel on Andrew's behalf."

He frowned. "But you didn't."

"No, I didn't." She shook her head. "Bea was unhappy when I refused her request. Our friendship hadn't completely healed after the incident at the gala. Unfortunately, I think my refusal to help with Andrew may prove to be a more difficult issue to mend."

Joseph gathered her hands in his and looked into her eyes. "Listen to me, Clara. Bea isn't worthy of your friendship. She's a conniving woman who will do anything she can to serve her own desires."

"Although I now believe Bea isn't the most upright person I've ever met, I still want to think she's been motivated by a wish to help those she loves. I think that's why she became angry when I wouldn't do as she asked."

"But don't you see? That's exactly what I'm telling you. She's completely self-serving. She's willing to lure anyone into her schemes, no matter the ill effect it may have on them. She didn't care about the consequences any of her so-called friends might suffer. Not Andrew, not me, and not you, either."

Clara's thoughts swirled as she considered his words. She didn't want to write off her friendship with Bea as though it wasn't worthy of more reflection.

Before she could further consider Joseph's comments, he tipped her chin and met her gaze. "Did she tell you she was going to entice Andrew to leave the barracks after he was on strict orders to remain in the barracks with his company?"

Clara swallowed. "No. She wasn't waiting for me after work, but I assumed she'd gone home without me. Is that when she met him?"

"A short time later—after there were only a few people on the Arsenal grounds. They hid over by one of the cannons near the entrance." At the sound of footsteps in the hallway, he lowered his voice. "Did Bea ever mention having an acquaintance who worked at the newspaper or meeting with a news reporter?"

"No, never. What's going on, Joseph?"

"I can't tell you all the details. I'm worried about Bea's

loyalties, both to you and to the Union. Surely you can see why." He pushed to his feet and walked toward the mantel. For long moments, he seemed transfixed by the fire. Finally he turned to face her. "It isn't my place to tell you what to do, Clara, but I think you should at least begin to distance yourself from her."

Clara blinked at him. First her mother and now Joseph. Neither of them believed Bea was a true friend.

Joseph's eyes shone with unyielding urgency. "Associating with Bea could put you, your mother, and your reputation at risk."

"And it could affect your reputation, as well. Correct?"

"There is that possibility, yes, although that has nothing to do with what I'm saying." He retrieved his cap and coat. "You want to see only good in Bea, yet she truly isn't deserving of your unwavering loyalty."

Tears threatened to fall, but Clara willed them away. "The Bible says a friend loves at all times. We don't get to pick and choose when that is convenient."

"But we do get to choose the company we keep." He donned his coat and stepped into the foyer.

"You're right, we do." Clara offered him a faltering smile. "I've listened carefully, Joseph, but before I heed your advice, I need time to think—and pray."

TWENTY-NINE

a bright morning sunshine filtered through shifting tree branches and cast reedy shadows along the dirt path as Joseph walked toward the laboratory the following day. The sun's brightness belied the freezing temperature, and Joseph tucked his chin tight against his wool military coat.

Thoughts of his conversation with Clara had left him with a restless night. He'd gone over and over the words they'd exchanged. Her reaction hadn't come as a complete surprise. Clara was one of the most loyal people he'd ever encountered. Although he had hoped she would immediately cut ties with Bea, he understood her need to give thought and prayer to such a decision.

A courier approached with a sealed missive. "Lieutenant Brady?"

Joseph nodded and glanced at the soldier's hand.

"I was ordered to deliver this directly to you and wait to see if there was a response."

Joseph gestured toward the mess hall. "Let's go sit down. You can have a cup of coffee while I read this and decide if a response is needed."

The young man rubbed his gloved hands together. "Coffee and the warmth of a mess hall sound good to me, sir."

They walked the short distance with the thud of their boots on the hard-packed dirt the only sound between them. Their breath created plumes of white vapor that mingled and rose overhead—a silent reminder that it was too cold for idle conversation.

Once inside, Joseph pointed to the far end of the room. "If you'd like something to eat with your coffee, there should be some eggs and biscuits left over from breakfast. Ask one of those boys back there to give you a hand."

"Thank you, sir."

Joseph nodded, then pulled out a chair and sat down at one of the marred plank tables. A shiver of excitement mingled with a sense of foreboding as he broke the seal. This was the message both Joseph and the colonel had been waiting for, the missive that should offer further details about the defective ammunition.

He scanned the contents, his eyes darting back and forth across the lines of information. He clenched the paper between his hands and shuddered. The crates of flawed ammunition had come from the Washington Arsenal. The letter revealed that the ammunition had been intentionally damaged. This was clearly sabotage, and the commander of the Army demanded that a full investigation of the Arsenal move forward until the saboteurs were arrested and imprisoned for treason.

Joseph needed to meet immediately with the colonel and go over the letter's contents. As soon as the messenger sat down at the table, Joseph folded the letter, placed it in his pocket, and stood. "I need to go to headquarters. Why don't you eat your breakfast and then meet me at the colonel's office, where I'll have a response waiting for you to deliver."

The soldier had already forked a bite of biscuit and gravy into his mouth. He bobbed his head. "Meet you there."

While the words were spoken around a mouthful of food, Joseph nodded his understanding before hurrying out the door and crossing the expanse to the Headquarters Building. He saluted the private, told him he had urgent news for the colonel, and was quickly ushered into the interior office.

The colonel looked up and returned a fleeting salute when Joseph entered. He waved at a chair. "Sit down." He leaned forward, his chest touching the desk. "I hope you're bringing me good news, Lieutenant."

Joseph shook his head. "I'm afraid not. This message is definitive—the crates came from the Washington Arsenal."

The colonel's brow furrowed. "Yet the first word we received regarding this incident said they couldn't determine where they'd come from. How are they now certain they're from our Arsenal?"

"The numbering system we use on the crates had been smudged to make it impossible to read our Arsenal markings on the crates. At first, the fact that the numbering was blurred and unreadable went unnoticed. Later, when the soldiers were experiencing problems with the ammunition, they began checking crates to determine if there was a connection of some sort." Joseph set the letter on the colonel's desk. "You'll want to read the entire letter, but from the investigation conducted in the field, it appears the ammunition got wet before it was delivered."

"Wet." The colonel tweaked his mustache. "Any reports of storms where our boats took on water while delivering ammunition?"

Joseph shook his head. "The letter rules out any such issues, though it does say we should consider whether there were any problems at our loading docks before the crates were wrapped with the waterproof paper."

"I suppose that's a possibility," the colonel said, "although I have my doubts. How often have you visited the docks since we first received word there was a problem?"

"Several times. My visits were always unannounced, and I never observed anything that caused me concern. The men, both soldiers and civilians, were attentive to their work, and the crates I inspected were in good condition." Joseph hesitated a moment. "I have to admit, however, that the crates I inspected were already wrapped and being loaded."

The colonel shook his head. "I'll go over the details of the letter. Why don't you return around five o'clock? I have meetings scheduled with the company commanders the rest of the day."

"The messenger who delivered the letter was told to wait for a response. I left him in the mess hall with orders to come to your office after he finished his breakfast."

"You need not wait. I'll prepare a written response for him. We can visit later."

Joseph saluted the colonel and walked back outside. He had hoped to remain with the colonel and develop a plan to move forward with the investigation. Instead, he'd have to wait. Self-condemnation began to take hold as he crossed the Arsenal grounds toward the laboratory. Why hadn't he been able to see what had been happening right beneath their noses? He retraced the steps he'd taken and his investigation of the Arsenal throughout each step of the cartridge-making process. Nothing had been amiss—at least nothing he'd been able to discover. His rising uneasiness soon gave way to anger—at himself for his inability to locate the culprits, and at the offenders for their cunning stealth that had continued to mystify him and cause the deaths of so many Union soldiers.

Perhaps if he made a list of everything he'd done and considered what he'd actually seen and examined, it would help. Besides, it would benefit him as he prepared for his meeting with the colonel later today. The colonel was a meticulous man, and once he'd reviewed the letter, he'd want more than the general overview Joseph had given him in the past. He'd want the minute details of Joseph's investigation.

First, he wanted to consider the possibility that there could be offenders working in more than one area of the Arsenal. They'd likely need to know each other and coordinate their activities. Perhaps he should check the records to see if several civilians had been hired near the same time and if they shared any connection. He returned to headquarters and, after requesting and reviewing the personnel records for civilians hired within the past six months, discovered that only a few employees met his criteria.

There were two young men from the same town in Pennsylvania. They'd been hired a day apart, and both worked at the docks. He wrote down their names. Only a few others had been hired on the same day, and they worked either at the forge, bakery, paint shop, or carpentry shop, so he dismissed them as possible offenders. And, given the information in the latest letter, there was no reason to consider anyone working in the laboratory. If the gunpowder had been wet before it was distributed to the women in the filling rooms, it would contain lumps. The damage would have been evident, and the powder would have clogged the funnels. None of the women or supervisors had reported problems with any of the gunpowder.

Jeremiah and Beatrice had been hired within a week of each other. Although Jeremiah now worked at the warehouse, he'd been initially hired to work at the freight yard. While the crates of ammunition filled at the laboratory were loaded onto wagons at the freight yard, they were then moved to the warehouse. There was little chance anyone could damage the crates without being seen, but he wanted to be certain. He donned his coat and walked along the laboratory's porch to the far end, where he could observe workers in the freight and shipping department. Even with the decreased number of soldiers, there were too many workers for anyone to smudge or scrape numbers from the boxes unnoticed.

Joseph was about to go inside when the wagon driver slapped the reins and the horses moved forward and pulled the wagon out of the freight yard with a full load of crates. Joseph continued to stare at the departing wagon. Could the driver stop along the way and cause damage to the crates? Was that even a possibility? He walked down the two porch steps and waved at the supervisor.

The bewhiskered supervisor approached. "What can I do for ya, Lieutenant?"

Being careful to pose his question in a cordial manner, he quizzed the supervisor regarding the wagon's route and amount of time allocated for delivery. "Do the drivers sometimes take longer than you'd anticipate?"

The older man chuckled. "They'd better not or they won't have a job. I've got things timed out to work real smooth so everyone stays on schedule." He tucked his fingers behind his suspenders and pumped out his chest as he described the procedure.

After listening to the details, Joseph was sure there would be no opportunity for foul play between the freight yard and the warehouse. Although he longed to go indoors and warm himself, he decided another visit to the warehouse was in order.

His visit with the warehouse supervisor proved as unproductive as his visit with the supervisor of the freight department. As Joseph prepared to leave, he glanced over his shoulder at the supervisor. "Any luck hiring another night watchman?"

The supervisor shook his head. "No one yet. We hired one fella right after we began looking, but he lasted only for a couple of nights."

"What happened? Decide he didn't like working nights?"

The older man shrugged. "Not sure. He just never showed up after that second night—didn't even come to collect the pay that was owed him. I figure he decided to enlist."

"I see. Thanks for answering my questions." As he walked out the door, Joseph was pleased to see there'd been no work on the trench. Until they hired another guard for the night shift, Jeremiah needed to remain inside near the windows where he could keep watch.

It wasn't until he'd neared the laboratory that Joseph recalled the numerous buckets that had been outside the warehouse—some empty, some filled with water—for protection in case of fire, Jeremiah had told him. Yet there had been no water buckets outside the warehouse this morning. His stomach knotted tight as he returned to the warehouse. He had a few additional questions for the supervisor.

The colonel leaned over his desk and studied Joseph's notes. When he'd finished, he settled back in his chair. "You've been very busy since you left my office earlier today." He tapped his finger on the final paragraphs. "Your conclusion may be correct. Thus far, it's the only plausible explanation, and the only way to find out if you're correct is to surreptitiously visit the warehouse tonight. We need to formulate a plan so there's no chance of error."

"I agree." Joseph folded his hands atop the desk. "Since Mr. Hodson is a civilian, do you think it would be wise to include the local police?"

"That's likely a good idea. If we discover Mr. Hodson is the one responsible, the police can take him into custody. I do want the offender captured and the illicit activities brought to a halt. I'm only sorry that you and Mr. Hodson are acquaintances. I know that must make this even more difficult. If you'd prefer, I could release you from further involvement."

"Please don't, sir. Acquaintance or not, I want the offender placed behind bars. I don't like to think it's Jeremiah, yet everything points in his direction. We'll know tonight if we can erase his name as a possible suspect or if our investigation has concluded. Meanwhile, I'll pay a visit to the police station."

By the time he arrived at the police station, Joseph's thoughts were running rampant. While he didn't want to wrongfully accuse anybody, he couldn't help but believe Jeremiah was the chief culprit. If so, he feared Bea was deeply entrenched in the treachery, as well. And if the two of them were sabotaging the ammunition, there was a likelihood Jeremiah was the shooter who had attempted to assassinate Secretary Seward.

As he neared the station, Joseph attempted to rein in his accusatory thoughts. He didn't want to believe Jeremiah and Beatrice were spies or saboteurs, though such a belief would explain a great deal—their odd behavior, their requests to change duty assignments, Bea's appeals to Clara and Joseph for favors, and Bea's willingness to jeopardize Andrew's military career.

"Lieutenant! I didn't expect to see you today." Patrolman Hanover extended his hand. "How can we be of assistance?"

"I need to speak with your captain, if he's in."

The patrolman nodded. "He is. I'll take you to his office." As they proceeded down a narrow hallway, he glanced over his shoulder. "You here to see how we're progressing with the investigation over at the Seward residence?"

Joseph smiled and gave a slight nod. He did want to know if further progress had been made, but for now he didn't want to discuss matters with anyone other than the captain.

"I've been staying on the investigation pretty close—been watching that Jeremiah Hodson's apartment to see if there's been any comings and goings. Ain't seen nothing of importance as yet. Captain said he's got an investigator working on it, but they don't tell me much." He curled his lip. "You learn anything more about Hodson being involved in the shooting?"

Joseph shook his head. "Like you, I have my suspicions, but the military doesn't have any jurisdiction to investigate. The shooting took place in the city, and all those involved are civilians, so our hands are tied."

The patrolman ushered Joseph into the captain's office and waited to see if he'd be invited to remain. When the captain asked Hanover to close the door on his way out, Joseph didn't miss the patrolman's look of disappointment.

He understood and yet he was thankful. The fewer who knew of this plan, the better.

Immediately after supper, Clara prepared to walk toward town. Her mother had forgotten to purchase the lavender thread she needed to complete a dress for one of her clients. Clara bundled into a thick sweater and her warmest cloak. After donning her bonnet, she worked her fingers into a pair of warm gloves and descended the boardinghouse steps.

"Clara, wait!" Her mother came to the top of the stairs, carrying her velvet muff. "I know you have gloves, but the muff will provide added protection against the weather. I do feel terrible having you go out in the cold."

"It's fine, Mother. I walk to and from work in the cold every day. Besides, I've had a hot meal and time to warm up since my return home."

Her mother waved the muff. "Please, Clara."

Rather than argue any further, she ran up the stairs, grabbed the muff, and raced back down. "I may stop and look at the new fabrics while I'm at the store, so I could be gone for a while." That said, she hurried out the door before her mother could attempt to wrap her in another layer of clothing.

She was nearing South M Street when Bea rounded the corner. Her head was bowed against the frigid air, and she walked at a rapid pace. Clara opened her mouth to call out but stopped herself.

Joseph's words echoed in her ears. *"I'm worried about Bea's loyalties—to you and to the Union."* Still, he didn't know Bea as she did. Bea had a good heart, didn't she? But what if Joseph was correct and Bea was using those around her for her own selfish aims?

Bea hadn't been waiting at the corner this morning and hadn't appeared after work, either. Perhaps she was embarrassed and didn't want to talk about what she'd done. Yet wouldn't Bea want to know what had happened to Andrew? Was she so ashamed that she believed Clara wouldn't speak to her? Or had she cared less for Andrew than what had appeared to others?

What if Joseph was right?

Please, Lord, give me wisdom. Guilt washed over her. She should have been praying that all along. She'd been leaning on her own understanding and not on the Lord. She'd prided herself in being a loyal friend. Would that pride now cost her Joseph? *Lord, make my path straight.*

Her gaze locked on Bea, who continued walking toward town. Clara was seized by an unexpected internal nudge to follow Bea. After drawing in a deep breath, Clara set out behind her friend. Her heart racing, she followed at a distance, and when Bea came to a halt in front of the newspaper office, Clara flattened herself against a storefront. She watched as Bea tapped on the office window. Moments later, a man appeared. They talked for only a short time before Bea extended her gloved hand. Clara inhaled a sharp breath as the man counted out a sum of money and placed it in Bea's hand.

Before Bea could turn and see her, Clara stepped inside the millinery shop. From her vantage point, she could see if Bea walked by but still remain out of Bea's view.

The owner approached, and Clara shook her head. "I'm just looking, thank you."

The woman frowned and went back to stitching fur along

a bonnet edge. Clara held her breath and waited while attempting to sort out what she'd just observed. When they'd talked earlier, Joseph had told her about a possible disclosure to the newspaper regarding the troop encampment at Warrenton. Was Bea responsible? Clara didn't want to believe her friend would divulge confidential information that could result in the defeat of Union troops, yet why else was she taking money from that man?

Before she could further evaluate the situation, Bea strode by the window. Clara waited only a short time before she returned outdoors and stood in front of the store, watching Bea retrace her steps. She was likely returning home. But what if she wasn't? What if she had some other clandestine meeting tonight? Rather than stop and purchase the thread, Clara continued to follow her friend. When Bea walked past South M Street, Clara's heart quickened. So Bea wasn't going home!

Maintaining a safe distance, Clara followed her past South O Street. She continued onward until she had passed through the arch and onto the Arsenal grounds. If she was going to the brig in the hopes of seeing Andrew, she'd be sorely disappointed. Thankful for a full moon, Clara secreted herself behind a large oak and continued to watch. She'd been certain Bea was heading for the brig, but then she turned and quickened her pace.

Clara stepped out from her position behind the tree. A branch cracked beneath her foot, and she froze in place. Bea glanced over her shoulder but then continued without stopping. Clara's heart pounded in her ears while she waited a few moments longer. Rather than keeping to the path, Bea zigzagged through the trees and toward the river. Suddenly it became clear—Bea was going to the warehouse to see

Jeremiah. But why hadn't she gone directly down the path? Was she fearful someone might see her? But why would it matter if she was seen? Did she fear the newspaper reporter had followed her?

Clara's thoughts swirled. What if Bea was a traitor after all?

THIRTY

Keeping away from the main path, Joseph, along with Captain Finley of the Washington Police and Colonel Furman, neared the warehouse. They'd carefully planned their approach. The police captain would circle around near the rear door while the colonel went to the opposite end of the building, where he could observe that area. Depending upon where they located Jeremiah, Joseph would approach him as the others watched and waited.

Although Captain Finley carried a gun, it wouldn't be loaded this evening. However, he had declared his billy club would remain close at hand. Neither Colonel Furman nor Joseph would carry a pistol. As Joseph had pointed out, a single spark in a warehouse full of ammunition could get them all killed.

They stopped in a thicket opposite the warehouse and watched for any sign of Jeremiah. A lantern glowed on the desk beneath the windows, but Jeremiah wasn't there. Joseph looked at the two men. "There aren't any buckets along the side of the warehouse. I don't see him sitting near the window. Can either of you see him?"

Captain Finley shook his head. "I don't see any movement. Maybe I should go ahead and circle around the building. I'll stay there and keep watch. If I see him down at the river, I'll signal."

All three of them had agreed to imitate an owl's hoot to signal each other. Joseph wasn't sure whether any of them could deliver a good imitation, but they didn't have time to practice bird calls now. If everything went as planned, Jeremiah would either willingly surrender or prove himself innocent, and they wouldn't need any signals—at least that was their hope.

Once Captain Finley and Colonel Furman were in place, Joseph kept low and crept toward the doors nearest to the watchman's desk. He pressed close to the door and listened. He waited only a moment before cautiously pushing down on the latch, hoping it wouldn't clank as it lifted off the metal latch. A sigh of relief escaped his lips.

Then, crouched low, he gently pushed against the wooden door. The hinges creaked. He held his breath and waited. Certain he hadn't been heard, Joseph peeked through the narrow opening. Still no sign of Jeremiah. He pushed the door only far enough to squeeze through the opening, then flattened himself against the wall. His heart drummed as he stilled himself and listened. Was that the sound of sloshing water? A moment later, he heard something metal hit the floor. He waited. The sounds repeated. A *swoosh* of water, followed by the *clang* of metal.

He edged farther into the cavernous warehouse and finally caught sight of Jeremiah. A crowbar leaned against one of the opened crates. The wooden lids hung askew. A knot tightened in Joseph's stomach as he watched Jeremiah pick up a bucketful of water and pour it into one of the open crates.

Joseph leaped forward, completely forgetting to hoot for the other men. "Stop! What are you doing, Jeremiah?"

Jeremiah wheeled around, his eyes shifting from place to place. In one swift movement, he took a sideways step, grabbed the crowbar, and brandished it in a semicircle. "Don't do anything foolish, Joseph. If need be, I'll use this."

Taking in the sight, realization struck Joseph like a bolt of lightning. "So you're the cause of the defective ammunition. You're a Reb." Joseph shook his head. "I don't understand your thinking, Jeremiah. If you wanted to destroy our ammunition, why go to all this trouble? Why not set fire to the warehouse?"

Jeremiah curled his lips. "I coulda done that—we even thought about it, but we liked this better. See, if I set fire to this place, I ruin the ammunition, but none of the Union soldiers die. We wanted to be sure whatever we were doing would mean Yankee deaths. Our leader decided this was the best way to ensure success on the battlefield. And it's working, too. All those defective cartridges that have already been shipped out are going to continue to help us when Burnside tries to move into Fredericksburg." He tightened his grip on the crowbar. "Each night when I'm pouring water into these crates, I think about Yankee soldiers and the fear that crawls up their spines when they fire their weapons and nothin' happens." He shrugged. "It gives me great pleasure."

"You're a coldhearted, vicious human being, Jeremiah."

He laughed. "Am I? War is war. What's the difference between sticking a bayonet in a fella's gut and watering down cartridges?"

"There's a big difference between meeting your enemy on a battlefield and hiding out in a warehouse watering down ammunition. If you can't understand that distinction, there's little hope for you." Joseph took a step forward.

Jeremiah lifted the crowbar higher. "You gonna come at me without a weapon? You think you're stronger than this crowbar?"

Joseph shook his head. "No, I don't, but I am going to be sure you're punished for your treasonous actions."

"Oh, are you? Well, you go ahead and see what you can do, but you better be prepared to stand trial for treason yourself." Jeremiah lowered the crowbar to the ground and leaned on it. "If you go to the police or the military, I'll share your little secret and say you were involved in this scheme with me."

Joseph tipped his head to the side. "What secret is that?"

"That your brother is fighting with the Rebs. I think they'd find it real interesting to know he lives on a plantation down South. I'd wager he even owns his share of slaves. Little wonder he's on our side."

At the sound of footsteps, both men startled and turned toward the door. Bea came to an abrupt halt and waved in Joseph's direction. "What's he doing here?" She stepped closer to the men. "Out for another walk, Joseph, or were you looking for something in particular?"

"You could say that. I was in search of the traitor who's been damaging our cartridges. Fortunately, I've found him." His brows dipped low. "I'm disappointed to discover that you're a part of this deceit, Bea. I'd like to say I'm surprised, but unfortunately I'm not. The two of you are quite a team; neither of you is smart enough to be working on your own. Who's sending you orders? Is it Norris or someone else in the Confederate Signal Corps?" He saw a flicker of surprise in Jeremiah's eyes. "You look surprised. We know far more than you think, Jeremiah."

Jeremiah sneered. "You don't know who we're working for, and we're not about to tell you, are we, Bea?" His words carried a note of warning.

She shook her head and drew closer. "Of course not."

Jeremiah thunked the crowbar against one of the crates, too near the metal clasp for Joseph's comfort. "The lieutenant and I were discussing his Southern relatives before you walked in and interrupted us."

"We weren't discussing my relatives, Jeremiah. You were threatening to tell the colonel I have a brother fighting in the Confederate Army."

Jeremiah's features tightened into a scowl. "It wasn't a threat, Joseph. That was a promise. I may end up in jail, but unless you turn around and pretend you never saw me here tonight, you'll be sitting in the brig yourself."

Joseph looked from Jeremiah to the crowbar to Bea. How disappointed Clara would be to find out that her friends were traitors.

As soon as Bea entered the warehouse, Clara crept after her and pressed close to the open door. She'd expected to hear Bea say something to Jeremiah about her encounter with the newsman. Instead, she listened to Jeremiah threatening to ruin Joseph's future. A threat made possible because she had told Bea about Joseph's brother. A wave of nausea washed over her, and she leaned against the brick building. She was having difficulty hearing but recognized the timbre of the men's voices. What was going on in there?

Why were they yelling? Perhaps she could sneak inside without being seen. Then again, Bea might be standing near the door and spot her the second she entered. When Clara could no longer bear the tension, she took a deep breath and edged through the narrow opening. A lantern hung from a support beam and cast yellowish shadows across the room.

"Clara!" Bea grabbed Clara's arm and jerked her hard toward the group.

"Let her go," Joseph ordered.

Bea gave her a shove toward Joseph. Clara stumbled, and Joseph caught her. He clasped her hand in his. "Clara, what are you doing here?"

"I'll tell you what she's doing here." Jeremiah whirled toward his sister. "She followed you here, Bea. You messed up again. How many times have I told you to be careful?" His eyes shone with fury. "Did she follow you from town?"

Bea shot an angry look at Clara. "I don't know. If I had known she was behind me, I would have gone home instead of coming here."

"Care to tell us why you're following Bea?" Jeremiah swung the crowbar in an arc and let it come to rest on his shoulder.

Joseph squeezed her hand, and Clara took it as a sign it was all right for her to share. She forced a weak smile. "I wanted to know where she was going."

"This isn't the time to be clever. Why were you following her and where did she go?"

After Joseph had given Clara a slight nod, she recounted how she'd followed Bea to the newspaper office and had watched Bea talk to the newsman and take money from him. "How much did he pay you, Bea?"

Bea smirked. "Not nearly enough. He was able to write quite a story from the information I gave him about General Burnside and Warrenton."

Clara's anger mounted. Bea was enjoying the fact that

she'd made a fool of her. "I didn't want to believe you were a Southern sympathizer, but so many things have now become clear. You were never my friend."

"I did like you a bit, Clara, but it was difficult for me to truly relate to someone so naïve. Fooling you wasn't much of a challenge, but please know that you provided me with some excellent assistance." She pinned Clara with a wicked smile. "As usual, y'all have underestimated us. You see, Jeremiah and I are more than Southern sympathizers. We were both born and raised south of the Mason-Dixon Line, and we're Southerners through and through. That's why we were more than willing to become attached to one of the most elusive spy networks—"

"Shut up, Bea. You've already said too much." Jeremiah's eyes glistened with anger.

Clara shook her head in disbelief. How could she have allowed this vile woman into her life? She had taught Bea how to make cartridges, had welcomed her into their rooms at the boardinghouse, and had confided in her. She recalled the times they'd eaten meals together with Joseph and Andrew. *Andrew!* He would be devastated by the news of Bea and Jeremiah's betrayal.

"What about Andrew? This news will be his undoing. He planned to return and marry you. How could you be so callous?"

A short distance away, Jeremiah snorted. "Marry her? You think Bea was going to marry Andrew? Even if we weren't Southerners, that would have never happened." He smirked and looked at his sister. "Tell 'em why, Bea."

A gleam flickered in her eyes. She was seemingly enjoying this. "Because I'm already married."

Clara's mouth fell open. "Married? I don't believe you. If

you're married, where's your husband?" Realization struck her, and she didn't wait for an answer. "Oh, I know. He's fighting with the Rebs, so you were free to come north and do your part. Is that it?"

"You're wrong again, Clara. Like I said, you're so easily deceived." She tilted her head toward Jeremiah. "Meet my husband, Clara. Mr. Jeremiah Hodson."

Clara's mind reeled as she attempted to comprehend what had been said. Bea couldn't possibly be married to Jeremiah. No, it couldn't be true. "Jeremiah is your husband? But you loved Andrew. I saw the way you looked at him."

Bea struck a seductive pose and batted her lashes.

Clara glared at her. "And I even saw you kiss him. What kind of woman—a married woman at that—would act in such a manner if she didn't have feelings for the man?"

"A woman like Bea. One who has no scruples about using her feminine wiles to gain information from a soldier—in this case, Andrew." Joseph spat the words at Bea.

"Right you are, Joseph." Bea smirked. "See there, Clara? Your soldier boy has it all figured out."

Joseph shook his head. "The two of you have been weaving a cobweb of lies since the first day you stepped foot in Washington, but it's time for the deceit to end."

Jeremiah swung the crowbar from his shoulder and held it out in expectation of a fight. "Ready when you are."

Joseph pushed Clara behind him, but instead of advancing, he turned his head toward the door at the far end of the building and hooted three times.

Jeremiah scowled. "That some kind of battle cry to throw me off?"

Before Joseph could answer, Captain Finley and Colonel Furman rushed into the building. When Jeremiah swiveled toward the police captain and raised the claw hammer, Joseph tackled him from behind, throwing him to the hard dirt floor. Jeremiah landed facedown, and Joseph fell on top of him.

Captain Finley tapped his billy club on Jeremiah's shoulder. "If you're smart, you'll quit struggling and stand up. Otherwise, you're going to feel the pain of this billy club when I put it to use on your hard head. I would truly hate to waste my energy on such a sorry excuse for a man, but I will if you make one wrong move."

Clara blocked Bea when she attempted to run toward the side door, and Colonel Furman stepped in to take Bea in hand. He held her by the arm and walked her back toward Jeremiah and Captain Finley. "You two are finished with your traitorous acts. You'll both be going to jail and then be tried for treason. There won't be any difficulty convicting the two of you."

Jeremiah spat on the floor. "I'd count myself proud to die for the South, but don't count me out just yet, Captain. Unless those policemen you have working as jailers are smarter than the ones who were investigating the shooting at the Seward mansion, they'll never keep me in your jail." His shrill laugh echoed in the cavernous warehouse before he narrowed his eyes at Clara. "I do want to thank you for defending my honor, Clara. When these buffoons were trying to pin that shooting on me, you were my staunch defender."

While Clara didn't want his thanks, hearing that Jeremiah hadn't been the shooter helped to restore a modicum of her dignity. "Thank you. I'm pleased to know I was correct and that you weren't involved in the horrid event at the Seward home."

Bea chortled, and soon Jeremiah joined in her laughter. "I

didn't say you were correct, Clara. I thanked you for defending me. Joseph and the police were right, of course, but your arguments on my behalf helped keep them at bay. In truth, I wouldn't admit to it now, but I wanted to humiliate you a bit more. Maybe then you won't trust so easily. In fact, maybe you and the colonel should both rethink whether you trust the lieutenant. Just like us, he's hiding secrets about his past and his family."

THIRTY-ONE

ven though Captain Finley had hauled Bea and Jeremiah away, Clara could still hear Bea's final remark echoing in her mind. She'd stood back and watched as her former friends were handcuffed and marched away. But Clara's faith in others wasn't going to be destroyed—not by Bea and not by Jeremiah. Although she was angry they had used her trust to advance their own traitorous activities, she felt pity for what lay in store for them.

Clara was deep in thought when Joseph and the colonel joined her. The colonel gestured to the door. "Why don't you take this young lady to my office? I'll join you after I've secured the building and arranged for one of the soldiers to come over and stand guard. We can finish our discussion there."

After Joseph had taken Clara's arm, they walked outside. The cold of the night seeped through Clara's cloak. Even the muff did little to warm her hands, and she began to shiver. Joseph wrapped his arm around Clara's shoulders, pulled her close, and led her from the warehouse. Neither of them spoke during the long walk to the colonel's office, yet Joseph's heavy breathing told her he was trying to regain control of his emotions.

Icy fear fisted around Clara's heart, only making her teeth chatter more. What would happen now that the colonel knew about Joseph's brother? Would Joseph end up in the brig?

Joseph opened the door to the colonel's office and helped Clara into a chair. He struck a match and lit a lamp on the desk. He frowned when he spotted Clara's chattering teeth. "You're freezing. I'm going to get a fire going to get you warmed up." He opened the door to the little potbelly stove, added a log, and fanned the embers to a flame.

The door opened, and Colonel Furman entered. "Ah, thank you for lighting the stove, Lieutenant. Sorry it took me so long. I received word that John Mosby and his raiders have been attempting to disrupt federal communications and supply lines between Fredericksburg and Washington over the past few weeks. I think further investigation is going to reveal that Mr. and Mrs. Hodson are connected to Mosby and his raiders. If so, it would explain a great deal. The Gray Ghost, as he's known to his fellow raiders, never has had any scruples about how many civilians he might endanger with his tactics." The colonel took a seat behind the desk and motioned Joseph to a chair beside Clara. "Thank you both for your very capable assistance tonight."

Clara held her breath. The man's demeanor had turned serious. The moment of reckoning was upon them.

The colonel reached for his pipe. "I'm sure glad you told me months ago about your brother being a Reb."

Clara turned to Joseph. "You did?"

"He didn't need to, but he told me when we started making the inquiries." The colonel leaned forward. "There are a lot of men who have family fighting on the other side, but

Lieutenant Brady's loyalties were never in question in my book. He's an exemplary soldier, and although you probably don't need to hear this, he has wisdom beyond his years. I see a great future for him." He pushed to stand. "I should probably write the report about this tonight, but I'm going to head home. Lieutenant, bank the fire and lock the door when you two leave."

As soon as the colonel had departed, Joseph knelt in front of Clara and took her hands in his. "When you walked into the warehouse tonight, I was never more afraid in my life. Even Bull Run didn't scare me like the possibility of your getting hurt. Are you all right?"

The tender love in his piercing blue eyes made her heart swell. Tears pricked her eyes.

"Clara, what is it? Did Bea hurt you?"

She cupped his cheek, now stubbled by a day's growth of beard. "I'm fine, Joseph. I was just so worried about you. I didn't think the colonel knew about your brother, and I was afraid you'd end up in the brig. I should have known you wouldn't hide your past, and I should have trusted you about Bea. I've been such a fool."

He smiled against the palm of her hand. "You were never a fool. Those two played a game that someone like you—someone who lives to serve others and believes in them unerringly—cannot possibly comprehend." He stood and pulled her to her feet, then slipped his hands around her waist. "But I must say, we make quite a team."

"We do." She rested her hands on his upper arms. She could feel the muscles bunched beneath his coat, and she marveled not only at Joseph's physical strength but also at the strength of his character and faith. Honest. True. Unwavering.

"I love you, Clara, and I hope your mother is still awake, because there's something I'd like to ask her."

Then, before she could respond, he captured her lips in a tender kiss. As the kiss deepened, her heart flamed. Their love was a friendship that had caught on fire. Like the heat generated in the potbelly stove, their home would be filled with warmth. It would spread to their children and their children's children. And someday she'd be able to tell them that it all began with a single spark.

Author's Note

Many years ago, my husband and I visited the Springfield Armory National Historic Site in Springfield, Massachusetts. For my husband, a career soldier and a military history enthusiast, this was a bucket-list visit. And while I enjoy all things of a historical nature, this particular site wasn't on my radar, much less my bucket list. Still, I learned a great deal on this visit, and somewhere deep inside it remained with me. And now, some twenty-one years later, I've written a book that is set in an arsenal—not in Springfield, but in our nation's capital during the early years of the Civil War.

During those tumultuous war-torn years when the men went off to fight for either the North or the South, women were needed to fill positions in the arsenal laboratories where ammunition was produced. Although little has been written about these women, they worked long shifts performing important and dangerous work. There were explosions and lives lost at almost all of the arsenals.

The explosion depicted at the Allegheny Arsenal in Lawrenceville, Pennsylvania, is a true event. The lives of seventy-eight civilians were lost in that explosion, the greatest civilian disaster of the war.

The attempted shooting of Secretary Seward depicted in the book is not a true event. However, Secretary Seward was the victim of an assassination attempt on the same night President Lincoln was assassinated. Seward survived the multiple stab wounds inflicted upon him and continued to serve as secretary of state under Andrew Johnson.

The "Gray Ghost," John S. Mosby, was a Confederate Army cavalry battalion commander who led Mosby's Rangers in many successful raids and acts of sabotage. However, he was never involved in sabotage against any of the Union arsenals.

Although fiction, I hope this story has provided you with some new and interesting information regarding our nation's history and the men and women who gave their lives to protect our freedom and rights. It is my prayer that our country will remain strong and free, and that we will once again become a nation that worships, loves, and trusts in God.

Special thanks to . . .

My editors and the entire staff at Bethany House, for their devotion to publishing the best product possible. It is a privilege to work with all of you.

Wendy Lawton of Books & Such Literary Agency, for her guidance, dedication, and spirit of encouragement.

Mary Greb-Hall, for her ongoing encouragement, expertise, and sharp eye.

Lorna Seilstad, dear friend, remarkable traveling companion, and critique partner.

Mary Kay Woodford, my sister, prayer warrior, and friend.

Tom McCoy, my brother, supporter, and friend.

And always to Justin, Jenna, and Jessa, for their support and the joy they bring me during the writing process and the rest of my life.

Above all, thanks and praise to our Lord Jesus Christ, for the opportunity to live my dream and share the wonder of His love through story.

Judith Miller is an award-winning author whose avid research and love for history are reflected in her bestselling novels. Judy makes her home in Overland Park, Kansas. To learn more, visit www.judithmccoymiller.com.

Sign Up for Judith's Newsletter!

Keep up to date with Judith's news on book releases and events by signing up for her email list at judithmccoymiller.com.

More from Judith Miller

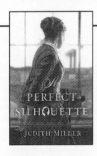

To help support her family and make use of her artistic skill, Mellie finds employment at a daguerreotype shop, where she creates silhouette portraits. When romance begins to blossom with one of her charming customers, her life seems to have fallen perfectly into place—but when the unexpected happens, will she find happiness despite her hidden secrets?

A Perfect Silhouette

You May Also Like . . .

Gray Delacroix has dedicated his life to building a successful global spice empire, but it has come at a cost. Tasked with gaining access to the private Delacroix plant collection, Smithsonian botanist Annabelle Larkin unwittingly steps into a web of dangerous political intrigue and will be forced to choose between her heart and her loyalty to her country.

The Spice King by Elizabeth Camden
HOPE AND GLORY #1
elizabethcamden.com

Determined to uphold her father's legacy, newly graduated Nora Shipley joins an entomology research expedition to India to prove herself in the field. In this spellbinding new land, Nora is faced with impossible choices—between saving a young Indian girl and saving her career, and between what she's always thought she wanted and the man she's come to love.

A Mosaic of Wings by Kimberly Duffy
kimberlyduffy.com

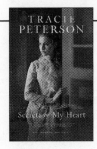

Reunited with childhood friend and lawyer Seth Carpenter, recently widowed Nancy Pritchard must search through the pieces of her loveless marriage for the truth behind her husband's death after his schemes come to light. But as they pursue answers, their attraction to each other creates complications, and dark secrets reveal themselves.

Secrets of My Heart by Tracie Peterson
WILLAMETTE BRIDES #1
traciepeterson.com

◆ BETHANYHOUSE

More from Bethany House

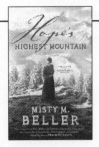

On her way to deliver vaccines to a mining town in the Montana Territory, Ingrid Chastain never anticipated a terrible accident would leave her alone and badly injured in the wilderness. When rescue comes in the form of a mysterious mountain man, she's hesitant to trust him, but the journey ahead will change their lives more than they could have known.

Hope's Highest Mountain by Misty M. Beller
HEARTS OF MONTANA #1
mistymbeller.com

Years of hard work enabled Douglas Shaw to escape a life of desperate poverty—and now he's determined to marry into high society to prevent reliving his old circumstances. But when Alice McNeil, an unconventional telegrapher at his firm, raises the ire of a vindictive co-worker, he must choose between rescuing her reputation and the future he's always planned.

Line by Line by Jennifer Delamere
LOVE ALONG THE WIRES #1
jenniferdelamere.com

When Beatrix Waterbury's train is disrupted by a heist, scientist Norman Nesbit comes to her aid. After another encounter, he is swept up in the havoc she always seems to attract—including the attention of the men trying to steal his research—and they'll soon discover the curious way feelings can grow between two very different people in the midst of chaos.

Storing Up Trouble by Jen Turano
AMERICAN HEIRESSES #3
jenturano.com

◊ BETHANYHOUSE